LOVING NETTA WILDE

LOVING NETTA WILDE

THE NETTA WILDE SERIES
BOOK 6

HAZEL WARD

ACKROYD
PUBLISHING

Hazel Ward

www.hazelwardauthor.com

Ackroyd Publishing

ackroydpublishing.com

1

THIS WAS A BAD IDEA

Five minutes ago, it had been a normal Friday morning. Five minutes ago, Netta had been poised to walk through the door, get into her car and go about her usual Friday business. She'd even got as far as picking up her keys and opening her mouth to say goodbye to Liza who was on her way downstairs in her pyjamas. But the look on her daughter's face signalled something cataclysmic had happened and, in that instant, it stopped being a normal Friday morning.

'Dad's been thrown out.'

Netta's mouth formed a perfect O. Then, her entire face screwed up into a squiggly question mark. 'He's been... What?'

'Arianne's locked him out and she won't let him back in.'

'But it's his house. How can she lock him out of it?'

'Dunno, but she has.'

'Oh.' With nothing left to say on the matter, Netta closed her mouth. Her ex-husband had been thrown out by his partner, the awful Arianne. Comeuppance had taken its time, but it had been worth the wait.

She was so engrossed in the delicious irony of his predicament that Liza's question passed her by.

'I'd completely understand if you said no. I mean, it's not like he deserves any sympathy. Only he's homeless. He's got nowhere else to go, except a hotel.'

'A hotel? Yes, I suppose.' Netta still wasn't fully concentrating. She was thinking about a morning some years earlier, when Colin had forced her out of the family home. He'd suggested a hotel then. Rather smugly, as she recalled.

'Okay, a hotel then. I'll have to go with him though.'

All at once her own rather smug thoughts came to a halt and she realised exactly what Liza was asking. Could Colin Grey, the man she loathed more than any other person in the world, come and live with them? The answer to that was easy. No. Absolutely not. But what she hadn't yet grasped was why he needed a minder. 'Why will you have to go with him?'

'I'm worried he might do something stupid. He's been a bit weird lately.'

'A bit weird?'

'Yeah. Like, really down about everything. And now this.'

'Can't he go to his mum and dad? I'm sure they'll take him in.'

'He won't go to them. You know what they're like.' Still caught halfway between upstairs and down, Liza turned to go back up. 'Can I use your little case for my things?'

'No, wait. It's silly when we've got the room. He can stay here. For a while anyway. Until Will comes back.'

This was a bad idea. The worst of ideas. Netta chewed on her thumbnail. It was an unappealing habit that she wasn't normally guilty of, but all of sudden she'd become a nail biter. Bad ideas so often bring bad consequences and if assaulting her nails was the worst of it, she'd consider herself lucky. But she wasn't that naïve. There was absolutely no way she was going to get off that lightly.

What had she been thinking? What kind of insane, foolish do-good sentiment had driven her to agree to it? The last thing she wanted in her life right now was her ex-husband. Correction. The last thing she wanted in her life at any time, ever, was her ex-husband. And yet. And yet here she was, about to let him stay under the same roof. Not only that, she was going to collect him and bring him over here because, apparently, Arianne had also locked him out of his car. Yes, this was definitely a bad idea.

Now fully dressed, Liza sat down on the sofa and pulled on her trainers. 'Are you sure about this, Mum? It's not too late to back out.'

If only that were true. Sadly, it had been too late the minute Liza had brought up Colin's situation, and that was before she'd even floated the idea of him staying with them. In theory, Netta could have said no. But the thought of Liza living out of a hotel room with the man who could twist and turn anything and anyone to his advantage was too much to contemplate. She'd agreed because she'd had no alternative. And because she'd been trying to prove to her daughter that, as a grown woman, she was above all the things she should be above. Even if she wasn't. So that was it. Fate sealed. She added a bad feeling to a bad idea and bad consequences. Bad things were ganging up on her in droves.

'Mum?'

'Hmm?'

'I said, are you sure?'

'Yes, I'm sure.'

Through the lounge window she saw Frank on his way back from a morning run. She hadn't had a chance to tell him yet, and it was only right that he was told, seeing as how he was the main man in her life, even if they lived next door to each other rather than together in the same house. 'I'll just let Frank know what's happening and then we'll go.'

She caught him while he was still on the street, clutching his side and stretching. He'd only started running a few months ago and it still looked like it was killing him.

'Is this really something you want to do?' he said, once she'd spilled the details.

'No it isn't, but I feel like I'd be letting Liza down if I said no. It'll only be for a few days. A week at the most, I expect. I might have to spend more time over yours though. Sorry.'

'There are some benefits to him being here then?' He kissed her cheek, his clammy skin leaving a damp patch.

Netta wiped the side of her face. 'Eww, sweaty. Right, I'd better go and fetch him.'

'Just think of the good all this sweating's doing me,' he said, his eyes all sparkly and smiley. 'Do you want me to come over when you get back?'

'Yes please. He'll be slightly less unpleasant if you're around.' She noticed Liza waiting on the front step. Hopefully she hadn't heard anything. Liza knew what Colin was like, so there was no need to worry on that count, but Netta didn't want her to hear she'd only agreed to this for her sake. Mind you, her daughter wasn't stupid, she'd probably already worked that out.

They were in the car and on their way before Liza said: 'I know this is going to be really hard for you, Mum. I don't suppose it helps but I'm like, really dreading it.' Maybe she had heard then.

'It does help. Thank you, darling. We'll get through it if we stick together.'

'Is that code for, if we don't let him manipulate us?'

'And we've got Frank next door. We can always escape to his if it gets too much,' she said, ignoring Liza's question.

'Frank's so sweet.'

Sweet? Netta could think of many positive words to describe him but sweet wasn't one of them. Anyway, surely there was an age limit for that? Frank was sixty-one. He must have crossed the threshold by now. Although, in Liza's eyes, he'd be in the old man category which probably meant he was back in the requalification zone when it came to sweetness.

Liza pulled out her phone and started swiping and tapping. 'Just letting Dad know we're nearly there. Do you think you and Frank will get married sometime?'

Netta shot her a glance and almost missed the changing lights. She slammed her foot on the brake and they both jerked backwards in the sudden stop. 'I have no idea. It's not something we talk about. Or even think about.' Well, she didn't. She couldn't speak for Frank.

'Really? We talk about it sometimes.'

'We? Who's we?'

'Me and Will. We think Frank would be a good step-dad. I mean he kind of is already, anyway. Kelly thinks so too.'

'You've talked to Kelly about it?'

'It comes up.'

Kelly, Netta's self-proclaimed daughter-from-another-mother and one-time housemate was off travelling the world at the moment. It would appear that didn't stop her from registering her views on Netta and Frank's relationship status.

'I'd have thought you'd have more interesting things to talk about.'

'We do but, you know, there's a lull occasionally.'

'I see. Well, thanks for that. Nice to know we're here for you whenever there's a lull.'

The traffic was fairly quiet, and they reached Moseley in

reasonable time. 'Almost at the scene of the crime. Brace yourself,' said Netta in an attempt to keep their spirits up. But it was in vain: the good humour was already draining from them as they turned into Colin's road. By the time they reached his house, it was completely gone.

'Oh my God!' If Liza had looked shocked earlier on, it was nothing to the way she looked now. Not that Netta could blame her. Because, in the middle of his drive, Colin Grey was sitting on top of an upturned suitcase, surrounded by an assortment of bags and boxes, looking very, very sorry for himself.

2

AN UNWELCOME RESCUE

If this wasn't the worst day of Colin's life, he didn't know what was. Actually, there had been a worse day, but it was a long time ago and he hardly thought about it these days. Not unless he was in the mood for thinking about what ifs and what might have been. Right now, the only what ifs he was interested in was what if he hadn't complained about Arianne's cooking last night, what if he hadn't decided to avoid speaking to her this morning, and what if he hadn't walked into the village for a decent breakfast rather than that bloody gruel she insisted they punish themselves with? Because if he hadn't done all or even one of those things, he might not be finding himself locked out of his own house. His own house mind you, not her house, because when did she ever contribute anything except her increasingly lacklustre charm? Similarly, he might not be finding himself sitting on a suitcase, like some fucking vagrant, for all the world to see. Thank Christ Adam and Jude, next door, were on holiday because Colin did not know how he was going to explain this one away. Of all Arianne's deranged outbursts, this had to be the maddest.

And now, as if things couldn't get any more horrendous, his ex-wife was here. The woman who, he knew for a fact, despised him and the ground he walked on, was taking him in. That was an extremely bitter pill to swallow. Not just for him but for her too. She must have agreed to it for Liza's sake. She certainly wouldn't have done it for his. He hadn't exactly been turning cartwheels himself at the proposition, but Liza had pushed him into it, and he was too tired to do anything other than sit on this suitcase and wait for someone to rescue him. He just wished it wasn't Netta Wilde coming to the rescue.

Netta's car pulled up in front of him. She stayed behind the wheel, but Liza was straight out, looking every inch her mother's daughter. 'Is she inside?'

Colin assumed she was referring to Arianne and nodded.

'Right.' Liza made for the house like she was about to storm it. She tried the lock with her key and failed. Obviously. In the last year, Arianne had installed more bolts and double locks than Fort Knox. If Colin had been a cynical man, he'd have said she'd been planning this for a while. Actually, he was a cynical man, but he was also fully aware that Arianne wasn't that smart. The woman could barely plan out a shopping list. Considering theirs consisted mostly of green mush, brown mush and yellow mush, it was hardly rocket science but such was the extent of her mental capability.

Ignoring the bell, Liza pounded her fist on the door. 'Open up, Arianne.'

The door remained shut, as he knew it would. She banged even harder. 'I said open up.'

The letter box flap lifted. Perhaps there was a chance. Colin stepped closer, just as a piece of paper slipped out and landed on the step. Liza picked it up, read it and tutted loudly.

He peered over her shoulder. 'What does it say?'

'*Go away or I'll call the police.*' She bent down and shouted through the letterbox: 'You've like, stolen my dad's house, so I don't think so somehow.'

'I'll have him for domestic abuse,' Arianne shouted back from the other side.

Liza stood up and looked at Colin, her eyes wide with disbelief. Unfortunately for him, it was the wrong kind of disbelief.

'Darling, that's rubbish. If anything it's the other way round.' He tried to laugh it off but he knew he was only making things worse.

'Shall we go?' Netta was at his side. He'd been too busy with Liza to notice her sneaking up on him.

He turned to her. 'It's not true.'

There was a flash in her eyes, a flash that said, *maybe not this time.* He immediately resented it. The way things had turned out with them, it had never been abuse. Never. Not on his part anyway.

'She's not going to let you in. We might as well put your things in the car.' She pulled Liza away. 'Come on. We'll work out what to do when we're home.'

They filled the boot and one half of the back seat with his possessions. Liza opened the front passenger door. 'You okay in the back, Dad?' She narrowed her eyes, daring him to say no.

Colin decided to take the hint, mumbled an agreement and slid onto the back seat. It wasn't as if he wanted to sit next to the ex anyway. As they drove away, he took a last look at his home. Someone was in the front bay window. Someone who was not Arianne.

They took the corner a lot faster than he would have taken it. Too fast for the baggage on the other half of the seat. A rolled-up pair of socks fell out of a loosely tied plastic bag and landed in his lap. He noted with displeasure they were an old pair that had at least one hole. He tossed the socks back into the bag and looked inside to see what else was in there. A short but frantic sort through confirmed his fears. Arianne hadn't even bothered to pack the decent stuff. In fact, he wasn't entirely sure that this wasn't a bag he'd recently sorted for a charity collection. Colin let out a long drawn-out sigh that nobody else acknowledged. In terms of awfulness, this day was the gift that kept on giving.

No one spoke on the way to Netta's house. Not that there was anything to say really, except thank you, but he hadn't built himself up enough to do that yet. Instead, he tried to remember the last time he'd been in a car with Netta and Liza. It would have been before Netta left. Will would prob-ably have been there too. No. He couldn't remember when it was. So he cast his mind back to the early days when the kids were small. When they'd been happy. Trips to the wildlife park because Will had been obsessed with lions. Coming back home, the children dozing in the back, him and Netta laughing about Liza's reaction to the monkeys, always a mixture of horror and awe. But he was getting his dates mixed up. The wildlife park trips would have been after things began to fall apart. There wouldn't have been laughter then.

'We're here,' said Liza, stating the obvious.

'I'll take you up to your room,' said Netta. 'Lize, can you go and tell Frank we're back?'

She took him up to a decent size bedroom at the back of the house. Judging by its contents, he guessed it was Will's. 'Nice room.'

'It's Will's.'

'I thought I recognised the trademark tat.' The joke had been an attempt to pretend he knew more about his son than he actually did. Netta said nothing. He shoved his hands in his pockets. 'By the way, thank you. This must be difficult. If it's any consolation, it's bloody awful for me. The whole thing I mean, not just being here with you.'

She nodded. 'He'll be back from uni soon, Will. You'll have to go then.'

'I'm sure it won't be long. Arianne will come round.'

'And if she doesn't?'

'She will.' He thought of the person in the window of his house. It wasn't someone he recognised but one thing he could see, it was a man. A big man, by the look of it. Colin wondered what the big man's shoe size was and whether he was about to become the recipient of a drawer full of decent socks.

They heard voices downstairs. 'That'll be Liza and Frank,' said Netta.

'Come to keep an eye on me, has he?' Yet another joke that flatlined.

'Something like that, yes. I'll leave you to unpack.'

'What she said. It really isn't true.' It sounded a bit desperate. He knew it would, but he couldn't stop himself saying it.

Her expression was impassive, making it difficult for him to read her. But then, when could he ever do that? 'If you say so, Colin.'

Okay then. It seemed there was no need to worry about the expression. The words told him all he needed to know about what she was thinking.

3

THE MOST CIVILISED CONVERSATION

The sound of a creak on the landing woke Netta up. Not that she'd been properly asleep. How could she be? Frank had suggested they spent the night at his. She'd been tempted, but the thought of Colin in her house, poking his nose in her things made her say no. Silly really, because she'd be at work tomorrow morning and then he'd be able to poke around as much as he wanted to. But it felt like she was making a stand by staying, like she was making it clear to him that she knew his game and she was not going to let him play it.

Today had been awkward. Arianne shouting that word through the letterbox had hit her like a slap in the face. She was no fan of Arianne. Couldn't stand the woman, if she was honest. But it didn't mean she deserved that kind of treatment. Abuse. Such a strong word. Such an unkind word. Colin had denied it. Naturally. But then he would, wouldn't he? When did he ever think he'd done anything wrong?

She closed her eyes, willing herself to go back to sleep but another creak forced them open. Lying next to her, Frank let out a little sigh. She looked him over. It was a sleep-sigh, nothing more. He was dead to the world, a sign of his new-found interest in all things healthy. Earlier in the year, he'd gone on a road trip with his brother and cousin. Since then, his cousin who was a sort of personal trainer and health guru had taken him in hand. Frank was on the way to becoming leaner, fitter, and generally more glowy. In the meantime, all this exercise was making him drop off as soon as he climbed into bed. It was a killer on the romance front. Not that she was looking for any action when her ex-husband was across the way.

There were movements on the stairs. She doubted it was Liza. Her daughter was another heavy sleeper and besides, she knew how to avoid the creaky parts of this old house. They all did. Except Colin. Her first thought was the dogs. Her youngest dog, Betty, would be in Liza's room, but the oldest, Maud, always slept on her favourite chair in the lounge. For some reason, Netta was overcome with concern for her, which was illogical because as far as she knew, Colin had no history of animal cruelty. But illogical as it was, she was up and reaching for her dressing gown.

Skipping over the noisy parts of the staircase, she made her way silently down and poked her head around the study door. It was empty. On the other side of the hall was the lounge. There was a bluish light in there coming from the sofa. Maud was sitting upright in her chair. She glanced up at Netta, let out a grumbly little growl and then looked back at the sofa where Colin was hunched over his phone.

'Colin.'

He jolted and dropped the phone. 'Shit. Sorry, you startled me. Did I wake you? I was trying to be quiet.'

Netta moved over to the armchair and put a protective hand on Maud. 'I'm a light sleeper and it's an old house. Creaks and groans everywhere.'

'Cosy though. Homely.'

'That's how I prefer it.' She thought of Colin's house, their old home. It was nearly as old as this one but the inside was all very modern and sleek. She'd had no hand in its decoration when she lived there. He'd made sure of that.

He pointed to Maud. 'I don't think she likes me.'

'She's very discerning. Did you come down for anything in particular?'

'I couldn't sleep. Mind's racing.'

'I have some herbal tea if you want it. Some sort of night-time concoction my friend Neil swears by. Smells a bit like old socks but it tastes okay. I drink it when I'm desperate.'

One corner of his mouth turned up into a half smile. 'That would be very nice. Thank you.'

Netta flicked on the light in the kitchen. Colin shuffled in after her like a weary old man. She noticed how thin he looked in his baggy sweatpants and T-shirt. It had struck her earlier that his cheekbones and jawline were more prominent than the last time she'd seen him. Liza had mentioned something about him and Arianne being on a natural foods diet and she'd put it down to that. But those sorts of diets were supposed to be healthy, weren't they? Colin didn't look healthy.

She gestured towards the breakfast room. 'I usually drink it in there. Take a seat. I'll bring it in.'

He was looking out into the moonlit garden when she took the teas in. 'I thought I saw something out there. Probably a fox.'

'I expect so. We have at least one that visits regularly. Have you decided what you're going to do?' They'd talked briefly about options earlier. Mostly it was Netta and Frank doing the talking with some input from Liza. Colin had said very little. He'd seemed a bit shell-shocked.

'Not exactly. I suppose I should talk to a solicitor but … I don't know. I've tried calling her. She won't answer. I've messaged.'

'Any reply?'

He shook his head. 'I could always stake the house out, I suppose. Wait till she goes out and let myself in with Liza's key. She can't stay in there forever.'

'Well, it's a plan. Sort of.'

'Sort of? I thought it was pretty good.' He smiled at her, the way he used to when she first met him, shy and a little bit lost. That smile had helped to heal her heart once after it had been ripped apart by someone else. Colin had nursed it and put it back together. Pity he then crushed it and tossed it onto the scrap heap.

'If you have Liza's key, can't you just let yourself in anytime?'

'No. She keeps the doors bolted when she's in. She's very security conscious. I just wish she'd talk to me so we could sort things out.' He looked out into the night. 'I've got some commissions I'm working on. I need to get back to them.' It was strange that work was his main concern and not getting back with Arianne.

'Frank has a studio set up in his breakfast room. If you ask him nicely, he might let you have some space in it. Assuming you don't get back in, that is. Is it over then, you and Arianne?'

'I don't know. I'm still hopeful but things haven't been great for a while. She can be quite difficult to live with.'

'So can you,' said Netta, remembering that he'd often said the same thing about her.

'So I've heard. I'll think about asking Frank. Just in case.' He gave her another shy smile. 'Do you know, I think this might be the most civilised conversation we've had in years.'

'I was just thinking the same thing myself.' Netta wrapped her hands around her cup and loosened the tension she was carrying in her shoulders. But before she had a chance to get too relaxed, a twenty-year-old memory flashed up. A hospital bed. A lost baby. Colin standing over her: 'Whose was it?' And then that word popped back into her head. That short, nasty, unkind word. Abuse.

4

GERALDINE IS SORT OF SPEECHLESS

Despite the lack of sleep, Netta was up early. It was Saturday, a market day, and she didn't have much choice. Everyone else in the house did have a choice, so it was a surprise to find Liza sitting in the kitchen with a bowl of cereal. 'Morning. I've made some tea.'

Netta poured a cup from the pot. She'd been a tea bag in a mug kind of person before Liza had become something of an eco-warrior. Now it was a teapot and leaves or risk a lecture. Not that she minded really. It was all for the right reasons and she was proud of her daughter for making a stand. She'd even been on a few marches with Liza and her friends, along with her mum. One family, three generations marching for the future. How about that?

Her mum was coming to give them a hand on the market stall this morning. Just for a few hours when it was busiest. There used to be three of them running their little jam and pickles business, Netta, Kelly, and Neil, but since Kelly had gone travelling it was just the two of them. They'd found someone to replace her on the production side because most of their produce was sold through retailers these days. But the Saturday artisanal markets were a good sideline, so Neil and Netta had kept them going on their own with occasional help from family and friends.

'Are you seeing Nan this morning?' asked Liza.

'Yes. Have you said anything to her?'

'About Dad? No, not yet. I can call her if you want me to.'

'It's okay. I'll speak to her today.'

Liza bit down on her bottom lip. 'Do you think she'll take it really badly?'

Netta looked across the table at her. Should she tell Liza how her nan was likely to take it? Best not. 'I'm sure she'll understand.'

'She hates him doesn't she? I know she tries to make out she doesn't, but she's not exactly the best liar in the world.'

'I think it's true to say she's not keen.'

Liza laughed. 'Mum, you're an even worse liar than Nan. That thing Arianne said about domestic abuse, do you believe her?'

'I honestly don't know. What about you?'

'Same here. I don't want to take his side just because he's my dad and also, because I know how he can be, but I can't say I've noticed it when I've been with them. She's usually the one going apeshit over the slightest thing. Last time I was there, she went mad because I'd put a cup on the wrong dish-washer shelf. Completely blew up. That's why I hardly ever stay now.'

'It's not always obvious though.'

Liza reached for Netta's hand. 'I know.'

With no grandchildren in the vicinity to curtail her reaction,

Geraldine Wilde wasn't holding back. 'If this is some kind of joke, it's a very poor one.'

'It's not a joke.' Netta had taken her aside as soon as she'd arrived and told her the news.

'Well then, I don't know what to say. I'm speechless. Absolutely speechless. That you would think it was okay to let that man stay under your roof, after all he's done to you. Have you lost your mind? Because that's the only reason I can think of why you'd do such a thing.'

Netta took a breath and wished that her mum was actually speechless. 'I did it for Liza. She was worried about him. I didn't want to, but I was backed into a corner.'

'Silly girl, she's too soft.'

'She knows what he's like, but he's her dad.'

'Yes, I am fully aware of that, Netta. I need to phone your father. God knows what he'll say. I just hope he contains his fury, for Liza's sake.'

Netta put a hand over her mouth to hide the smile that was forming at the thought of her dad, the mild-mannered Arthur Wilde, containing his fury. Her mum's expression made it clear she hadn't hidden it well enough.

She was saved by a well-timed interruption from Neil. 'Excuse me butting in, ladies, but it's getting a bit busy. I could do with some help.'

Her mum shot him a withering look. 'We're rather busy here too, if you don't mind, Neil.'

Something very close to pain and bewilderment flashed across Neil's face. Under normal circumstances, he could do no wrong, as far as her mum was concerned. But these were not normal circumstances and he'd been well and truly told off. 'Sorry, Geraldine.'

She gave him a cursory glance. 'I'll be with you shortly. I need to call Arthur.'

Netta took Neil by the arm. 'Come on, we've got customers waiting.'

'She didn't take it well, then?' he whispered.

'She did not.' She cast her eyes over to her mum who was shaking her head, waving an arm and talking, all at the same time. 'Poor old Dad.'

By the time her mum returned she'd calmed down enough to prove that she was by far the best sales person out of all of them. The customers loved her. Especially the older men. Not that long ago, she'd had been taken in hand by her style savvy sister-in-law and had blossomed into a chic septuagenarian who could easily pass for ten years younger. It got her a lot of interest from men of a certain age. They were wasting their time. She only had eyes for one man. But that didn't stop her exploiting their attentiveness when it came to increasing profits.

Today's market was in Moseley village which wasn't really a village, just a suburb in the south of Birmingham, but it had a sort of bohemian, urban-village feel about it. There were a lot of arty types who lived here, including Colin when he wasn't being locked out of his own home. Colin liked to give the impression he was a bohemian arty type who cared deeply about the world. Providing you didn't scratch too deeply under the surface, he got away with it.

Her dad turned up just a little before two, when they'd pretty much packed up for the day. 'Colin's moved in then, has he?' He was talking to Netta, but his eyes were on her mum, or rather the man talking to her mum – mid-sixties, tight jeans, loose shirt, red bandana around his neck.

'Just temporary, Dad. Very temporary.'

'Don't let him get under your skin, Nettie.'

'I won't. Frank and Liza are keeping an eye on him.'

'Good. Do you still want us to come over tomorrow?'

'Of course. Life goes on as normal. Unless you really don't want to see him.'

He turned to look at her for the first time. 'No, we don't want to see him, but we want him to see us. We want him to know we've got his number. We'll be there. Now, I've come to pick your mum up before she gets whisked away by yet another admirer. Can't keep them away.'

'I don't think you need worry, Dad. You're well ahead of the competition.' She glanced in her mum's direction but got distracted by a familiar peroxide blonde head walking through the stalls further up. 'I'll be back in a minute,' she said, as she ran off in pursuit of Arianne.

Arianne crossed over the main road. Netta tried to follow, but the traffic lights changed before she got there, and the road was too busy with cars, so she had to wait. By the time she was able to get over, Arianne was disappearing into a middle eastern café. Netta got to the window in time to see her taking a table that was already occupied by a man. She sent a message to Colin:

Now's a good time to get back in your house. Just spotted Arianne in a café in Moseley village. Go there straight away.

She noted that he'd picked the message up. With any luck he'd be in the area already and he'd be back home and out of her hair within hours.

Before she had a chance to congratulate herself on a job well done, a message came back:

No point. She's changed the locks.

5

FILTHY LOOKS AND DEATH STARES

Colin lay in the bed that was his son's. Naturally, his son wasn't there. If he had been, Colin wouldn't be in this bed, or even in this room. He wouldn't even be in this house, his son disapproved of him that much. Five years. That's how long it was since they'd last spoken properly. Five years since Will had found out Colin was lying to Netta about his earnings. A silly mistake on his part. He shouldn't have left his accounts out where anyone could see them. He and Netta were already divorced by then, but she was still paying for everything and he was still officially a stay-at-home dad with no real income. If she'd bothered to take any interest in his work when they were together, she'd have known it was starting to sell. But she didn't, so who could blame him for not letting on? When it all eventually came out, she'd made a scene and insisted on selling the house. Those secret earnings of his had been enough to help buy her out, so it worked out for the best really. Except that Will refused to have anything to do with him. Arianne blamed Netta for that, but Colin knew his son was a man of principle. Principles were great, providing they didn't get in your way.

There was a throng of visitors downstairs that he had no inclination to join. He'd been expecting them. Liza had warned him about their Sunday-morning ritual, a gathering of all the people who'd adopted the little dog Maud's puppies. Apparently, a walk in the park was involved, followed by brunch in Netta's kitchen. It all sounded very pleasant, if you liked that sort of thing. He'd never been a dog lover. He wasn't a dog hater either, he just didn't see the point of them. Or cats for that matter. Mind you, he didn't see the point of anything at the moment. Not since that message from Arianne. He was still having trouble taking it in. Changed the locks, she'd said. Changed the locks to his doors! *How dare she? I mean really, how dare she?*

There was a tap on the bedroom door. 'Dad, we're heading off now. Will you be okay?' Dear, sweet Liza. She was the only one that cared.

'Yes thanks, darling. Have fun.' He'd added an upbeat lift to that last bit. It was important to sound positive, even if you felt like slitting your wrists.

He heard the front door close and waited until the sound of chatter and laughter drifted away before getting out and sitting on the edge of the bed. God, he ached. He'd had a fall on Thursday evening and the stiffness was really kicking in He moved slowly towards the dresser and let his fingers linger over the handle of the bottom drawer. Netta had cleared the other drawers out for him, but the bottom one held Will's things. He pulled it open. There wasn't much in there, some tatty pants, a few socks, and a sweatshirt. He picked up the sweatshirt and breathed in. It smelled slightly unpleasant. Body odour. Young person's sweat. Will's sweat. He wondered if he should put it in the wash. Would anyone thank him for it? Probably not. They'd say he'd been snooping. Technically, they'd be right, but that wasn't the reason he'd looked. He filled his lungs with the mildly disgusting smell of youth, folded the sweatshirt up, and put it away.

The kitchen was gloriously quiet and still. Sometimes, all Colin wanted was a few moments of stillness. You'd have thought a little thing like that would be a simple enough ask, wouldn't you? Apparently not. Apparently, such a request was an act of heinous selfishness, punishable by death of a thousand nags. In Arianne's books anyway. Here, he had stillness coming at him in spades. Especially if he shut himself away in Will's room.

He made himself an espresso. Netta's coffee maker was quite decent. Not as top of the range as his own but it was more than adequate. According to Liza, it was Frank's. Netta had bought it for him. Frank seemed to spend a lot of time round here, which was perhaps why the machine wasn't in his kitchen. He seemed a nice enough bloke. From Belfast originally but he'd lived here for years, on all accounts. Under normal circumstances they would probably have got on, but Frank was screwing Netta. It shouldn't bother Colin, but it did.

A whining noise sent him swivelling round a hundred and eighty degrees. He cast his eyes downward and saw the little dog, Maud, sitting by his feet. 'Oh, it's you. I thought you'd be out gallivanting with the others.' He tutted at himself. Talking to animals? Surely he wasn't that desperate for conversation?

Maud cocked her head to one side, then whined again. She was a cute little thing. If you liked dogs.

The dog went with him into the breakfast room, keeping an eye on him just like the others when they were here. The sun was streaming in through the French windows and the room was bathed in a bright white hue. It was no wonder Frank used his breakfast room as a studio. The light was perfect. It was pretty good in Colin's own studio at home, but not like this. His studio had been a garage when they'd first moved into the house. The conversion was paid for with one of Netta's annual performance bonuses. At the time, she'd been Annette Grey, a rising star in the corporate world. He'd been proud of her, but by then, it was already too late to tell her that.

He took the same chair he'd taken on Friday night when he and Netta had sat here and talked. In spite of everything she'd done to him, it had been nice to be with her again, basking in her radiance. Even in the dark, she was radiant. She was never anything but radiant.

The warm and solid body of the little dog pressed against his leg. Huh! How about that? Maybe he had a friend after all. He patted its back and closed his eyes. The sun cloaked his skin and he could feel its stark brightness without the need to open them again. Yes, it would be good to paint in here. If the mere thought of painting again didn't make you want to run away and hide. He remembered the commissions he had waiting for him at home, some half-finished, some not even started. He should get in touch with his clients and explain there were complications. They'd already been waiting longer than usual due to the other complication. Yesterday, Frank had offered to make room for him next door, so he could start them again. But it was so much effort, and he was tired. Really tired. And anyway, picking up a brush again required more than mere energy.

Something wet and sloppy landed on Colin's face and woke him up. When he opened his eyes, he saw it was a hairy dog-

shaped mammoth slapping a big pink tongue all over his flesh.
It wasn't the other dog that lived in this house, or even Frank's
dog. This was a new one.

'Buster, behave. Come here. Sorry, mate. It's Colin, isn't
it?' A tall, black man with a strong Brummie accent grabbed
the dog's collar. 'I'm Chris. Neil's husband. We're just about to
eat. Come and join us.'

The kitchen was full of people, dogs and the smell of
something delicious cooking. Sausage and bacon if he wasn't
mistaken. Colin's stomach did a double somersault. How long
had it been since he'd eaten proper sausage and bacon? It felt
like a hundred years. He searched the room for a welcoming
face other than Chris's. A fit-looking white guy with tattoos
and a shaved head gave him a friendly nod. This, he
presumed, was Neil. Colin recognised him from the few times
he'd been to Netta's market stall. He knew everyone else.
Unfortunately.

Liza was sitting next to Frank. She broke off from their
conversation long enough to cast her eye over Colin's shabby
appearance. 'Hey, Dad. We didn't realise you were in there.'

He eased himself onto an empty chair. 'I must have
dropped off.'

Arthur Wilde, his one-time father-in-law, gave him a curt
nod. 'Colin.'

Colin tried a smile, but it wouldn't come. 'Hello, Arthur.'
He glanced over to the worktop where his former mother-in-
law was making sandwiches side by side with Neil. Colin
managed a nod that matched Arthur's. 'Geraldine.'

Geraldine returned his greeting with a blank stare. 'Bacon
or sausage?'

'Or you can have both if you're really hungry. I'm having
both,' said Chris.

'Both would be lovely. Thank you.'

'Tea or coffee?' said Netta.

'Er, tea please.' With the exception of the ex-in-laws everyone was being nice to him. It was a bit disconcerting. Luckily, Geraldine was on hand to add a dose of reality. She smacked a plate down in front of him and threw him a glare that suggested he better not ask for sauce. Colin immediately thought of Arianne and mumbled a thank you. You'd have thought that might have pleased her but no, not Geraldine. The old cow hit him with another filthy look and flounced off to sit by Arthur who was giving him the hard stare. They'd changed since he'd last seen them. Geraldine had always been very dowdy but she must have had one of those make-overs you used to see on TV. She was looking pretty amazing now, especially for her age. Arthur appeared to have upped his game too. Necessity, Colin supposed. He'd tried it himself once when he and Netta were still a couple. Not that she'd noticed. She was too busy shagging the man who never needed to worry about upping his game. Doogie Chambers, Netta's first, second and probably only love. Poor Frank, he had no idea.

Eventually the ex-in-laws gave up on trying to wear him down with their death stares and joined in the conversation around the table. Colin didn't say anything. Naturally. He had nothing to add and anyway, they didn't want him here. They were only putting up with him because they had to. They carried on regardless, as if he was invisible. He ate his sausage and bacon sandwich, drank tea and listened to the banter that flowed easily from one side of the table to the other. Liza was teasing Frank about something, poking fun at him. Anyone would think he was the one who was her dad.

Colin finished the sandwich. He could have happily eaten a second one and possibly a third, but he knew better than to ask. Besides, all this chumminess was making it hard to swallow.

The chair scraped along the floor as he stood up and all heads turned to him. 'I'd better get properly dressed,' he said, feeling suddenly exposed. He left the room, before it all got too much.

6

THINGS THAT WEREN'T RIGHT

Frank was sitting opposite the doorway, so he had a good view of the hall. He watched Colin limping towards the stairs and concluded that something wasn't right. Obviously, there were many things about Colin Grey that weren't right. The man was a snake who'd made Netta's life a misery, even after he'd thrown her out. But aside from that, there was something odd about the way he was carrying himself. Colin was in his fifties, but he was walking like an old fella. Then there was this whole thing with Arianne. There seemed to be no sensible reason why he shouldn't call the police, or consider talking to a solicitor but so far, he'd been reluctant to do either.

Geraldine stood beside Frank, her eyes also following Colin until he disappeared upstairs. 'What's wrong with him? He looks as if he's in pain.'

'I noticed that too,' said Frank. There were more nods and mutterings around the table to confirm that he and Geraldine weren't the only ones.

'He thinks it's flu,' said Liza. 'He told me yesterday he was feeling really stiff. That's why he's been in bed so much.'

Geraldine picked up the empty plates and stacked them by the drainer. 'It's a possibility, I suppose. But if you ask me, it looks like he's had a damn good hiding.'

'Surely not, love,' said Arthur. 'I can't see Colin getting into a fight.'

Geraldine rolled her eyes. 'I didn't say he'd been in a fight, Arthur.'

For some reason, everyone looked at Frank. Did they think…? Ah come on. Surely not. 'Nothing to do with me. I haven't touched the man.'

Everyone assured him that nobody was thinking such a thing, a bit too emphatically for Frank's liking.

It was left to Geraldine to dispel his theory that he was getting a label pinned on him that was completely unwarranted. She put her hand on his shoulder. 'Of course you haven't, Frank. Don't be silly. It probably is just the flu.'

'I'm sure that's all it is,' he said, even though he didn't believe it for a minute. He'd received a few batterings in his life. Mostly from his da as a kid, but there had been one time when a so-called friend had set about him with a baseball bat. It took weeks for him to heal, weeks before he stopped hobbling along like a man more than twice his age. So he knew a thing or two about batterings. The way Colin was holding himself, it looked like he did too. Unless he was genuinely ill. But not with the flu. You didn't get that kind of weight loss with the flu. Geraldine caught his eye, and Frank knew she was thinking exactly the same thing.

Everyone had gone home and Frank and Netta were in the garden. Netta was reading the Sunday papers. He was prepping for tomorrow's classes. It was almost the end of term which meant it was almost the end of his teaching career. A few months ago, he'd handed in his notice. He was leaving when his college closed for summer. The end of an era and the beginning of a new one. He was about to become a full-time artist. It was a scary but exciting prospect, and he couldn't wait. But in the meantime, he had lessons and pupils to think about.

Liza came out to see them. 'I'm going to a campaign meeting. I've checked up on Dad. He's asleep again. Do you think it is the flu?'

Netta's smile was the reassuring sort. 'I expect so. It can be quite horrible sometimes. We'll look in on him again later. You go to your meeting. And please don't get arrested. I don't want to have to visit you in prison.'

Liza giggled. 'Don't worry, it's just a meeting about reducing our carbon footprint. See you later.'

'I look forward to hearing what the next thing is that we've got to give up,' said Netta, after Liza had gone.

'Well if it's coffee, beer or wine, I for one will be totally gutted. Which reminds me. I'll buy some more coffee tomorrow. We're getting through it a lot faster now Colin's here.'

'What are we going to do with him? I don't know if there is anything physically wrong with him, but he's definitely not his normal self.'

Frank looked up from his notes. 'I guess that's understandable. His ego's been bruised.'

'If that's all it is, he'd be even more superior than he normally is. It's more than that. He seems to have given up. He's hardly been out of bed since yesterday morning. When he arrived here on Friday he was embarrassed and a bit quiet, but nothing like this. And why won't he confront Arianne? She has no claim on that house. Why won't he talk to the police or something? If it was me, I'd be doing something.'

'If it was you now, you would. But what about the you

before you came to live here? Would she have been so keen to fight?'

'What are you saying?'

He put down his pen. 'I guess I'm just saying things may not be as straightforward as we think they are.'

'You think what Arianne was saying about domestic abuse was the truth? That could be why he's so reluctant to go to the police.'

'I don't know what I think. All I know is he looks worn out and pitiful.'

Her eyes narrowed slightly as she took him in. Then, she picked up her paper again. 'Don't let him fool you. Before you know it, you'll be feeling sorry for him and then we'll all be in trouble.'

He watched her for a few minutes hoping her face would soften, or perhaps she'd throw him a smile to signal that all was okay. But she kept her eyes on the newspaper and her mouth firmly set. He gave up and went back to his notes. She was upset. He'd upset her. It had never happened before, and he didn't like it. Frank looked up at Will's bedroom window. It was shut. The curtains were closed. Behind them lurked an unwelcome presence. He needed to find a way to get rid of it because the sooner Colin Grey was out of here, the better.

7

ALL A MAN NEEDS

Netta chewed on her wholesome granola. She preferred jam on toast for breakfast really, her own jam, naturally, but she was trying to support Frank's new healthy lifestyle. Apparently, oats were very good for you, for all sorts of reasons that she couldn't remember. Frank was over in his house this morning, presumably eating his own healthy breakfast. It was Thursday. Colin had been here almost a week, most of which he'd spent in bed. She'd hardly seen him and it no longer seemed necessary for Frank to be here all the time. Although she wouldn't admit it to anyone, Netta was glad of the breather. She'd been a bit tetchy with him on Sunday afternoon and he'd been tiptoeing around her ever since. It was a tad irritating.

Above her head, the sound of Liza venting her anger leaked through the floorboards and into every empty space in the otherwise quiet house. Aside from an occasional low grunt, it appeared to be a one-sided conversation. A door slammed. Probably the one to Will's bedroom. There was a definite stomp in the footsteps thundering down the stairs and along the hall. Liza stopped at the kitchen table and plonked herself on a chair.

Netta poured a of cup of tea and pushed it over to her. 'Everything all right?'

'Not really. He's just lying up there doing nothing. I don't know when he last washed. He's just useless. Totally useless. And he stinks. He seriously needs to take a shower and stop bumming around.' She threw her arms in the air. 'I just don't know what to do with him. I'm terrified of leaving him.'

Netta moved over to sit next to her. 'I don't think you have anything to fear. Your dad's not the sort to do anything silly. He's more of a brooder. And he wouldn't want you bunking off on his account. Getting your degree's important to him. Didn't you say how happy he was that you were taking art? He regretted not doing it himself. He hated accountancy.'

'I just, I just…' Liza's eyes started to brim.

Guilt pricked at Netta's conscience. Yes, she'd agreed to let Colin stay here until things were fixed but what else had she done to support her daughter? Nothing. She'd let Liza carry the burden all on her own. 'Listen, I have to go to work now but I'll talk to him when I get back. I'm not sure he'll listen to me but I'll try.'

'Would you?'

'Only if you promise to go to classes today.'

Liza sniffed and nodded. 'I promise. Thanks, Mum.'

Netta closed the van door. They'd just finished loading it up for the weekly delivery. 'Can you manage without me for an extra hour? There's something I need to do after I've dropped these off.'

'Sure,' said Neil. 'Nothing to worry about is it?'

'I'm going to talk to Colin. He's gone downhill since last week. It's upsetting Liza, otherwise I'd just leave him to stew.'

'Do you think he might be depressed?'

She shrugged. 'I don't know. It's a possibility. Then again, he might just be playing us. You can't tell with Colin.'

'You know who you should ask? Geraldine. She understands that stuff.'

'She went to a therapist, Neil. That doesn't make her a psychiatrist. Anyway, she hates Colin. She'll probably be glad he's wallowing in his own filth.'

Neil held out his hands. 'Just saying. Might be worth asking her advice.'

Netta pulled up outside her house and let herself in. Maud and Betty came down from the landing to greet her, then followed her back up after she'd checked downstairs for signs of Colin.

The bathroom door was closed, and she could hear the shower running. Liza must have got through to him after all. The door to Will's bedroom was ajar. She stepped in and breathed in the sour air, body odour, stale food, and dog, if she wasn't mistaken. Given that he'd shut himself in here for the last six days, she'd been expecting the body odour. Even the stale food. Less so the dog smells. She didn't remember Colin being a fan of dogs. More to the point, she hadn't realised the dogs were fans of Colin.

She opened the curtains and windows and proceeded to strip the bed. Fresh air was needed, along with clean bed linen. It might not cure Colin of whatever was wrong with him, but it was a start. Next, she bundled up the sheet, quilt cover and pillowcases into her arms, keeping them as far away from her nose as possible. Straight into the washing machine with them, before they contaminated her and the rest of the house. Like some school matron on a dorm cleaning mission, she marched back onto the landing with her arms full and bumped straight into him.

Colin pulled the towel that was wrapped around his lower half a little tighter but Netta was still shocked by his appearance. The last time she'd seen him semi-naked in a towel was when she'd surprised him by wrecking his studio after finding out he'd been shafting her. This recent sight of him confirmed what she'd suspected since seeing him in his baggy night-clothes. He'd lost weight. A lot of it. There was a new scar just below his left collarbone. New to her anyway. Presumably, he still had that tattoo on his back though. *London Calling*, the Clash album cover. God only knows who he was trying to impress with that.

'What are you doing?' he said, interrupting her thoughts.

'The bed needs changing. You took Liza's suggestion on board, I see.'

He looked at his feet. He used to do that a lot when he was younger if he was embarrassed. It was something he had in common with Will. Possibly the only thing they had in common. 'I wasn't expecting you back yet.'

'I came back to talk to you. Liza's worried about you.'

'She doesn't need to be.'

'I told her that, but it seems my reassurance isn't enough to stop her caring about you. So here I am.'

'I don't deserve her.' He looked at his feet again. She remembered how she used to find the habit quite endearing.

'No, you don't.'

He swallowed. She noticed his Adam's apple moving up and down and again realised how much sharper his jawline had become. Not in the smooth sharpness of youth sort of way. More like someone who'd been on a drastic diet. For the first time, she considered that there might actually be something physically wrong with him.

'Can I at least get dressed?'

'Yes please.' She'd meant it to come out as sarcastically as it did, but she hadn't been prepared for his reaction. He blinked several times over and she thought for a minute he was going to cry. The frailty of him was shocking and had been so unexpected that she felt a sharp stab of remorse.

He kept his back to the wall and his eyes on the ground as he edged along. The only thing between them was the bundle of dirty bed linen. When he was past her, she took a step towards the stairs, but something made her look at him as he turned to go through the bedroom door. Perhaps it was to check if he still had that tattoo on his back. She didn't know if that was why she looked but whatever it was, she looked. Yes, it was still there, but it was more difficult to see than before because it was covered in bruises of all shapes, sizes, and colours. Netta gasped.

He spun round. 'I had a fall. Not here. Last Thursday night. I'll be down in a minute.'

It was ten minutes before he came down. He looked better. Not just because he was cleaner but because he looked more like the old Colin, fully dressed. No bruises, scars or skinny ribs to feel sorry for. It was easier for her that way.

She handed him a cup of tea and a sandwich. 'You look like you could do with some food inside you. Let's go and sit in the lounge.'

'Could we go in the breakfast room instead? I like it in there.'

'I thought the sofa would be more comfortable for you. With the bruises. Don't they hurt?'

'Not so much now. They were at their worst over the weekend.'

So her mum had been right on Sunday. She'd noticed something was wrong. Frank had too. 'It must have been quite a fall.'

'I tripped on the stairs.'

'Did you go to the hospital?'

'No need. I was fine.'

He didn't look fine. He didn't look fine at all. And how could Arianne have thrown him out after a fall like that? She noticed Maud was leaning against his leg, reminding her of the doggy smell upstairs. 'Have the dogs been keeping you company while we've been out?'

'If I don't let them in they won't stop scratching the door.' Colin's hand dropped down to Maud's side and gave it a pat. Maud looked up at her with a decidedly sorry expression. Even Maud was guilt tripping her now.

'I couldn't help noticing you've lost weight. Have you seen a doctor about it?'

'It's the natural foods diet, nothing to worry about. Or rather it was until I came here. I'm sure I'll soon put it all back on now that I'm not following Arianne's strict regime.'

'So you've checked with a doctor then?'

'Yeah, yeah. All fine.'

It was obvious he was fobbing her off but short of calling him a liar, there wasn't much she could do about it. 'Have you given any more thought to what you're going to do? Will you go to a solicitor?'

'I don't know. I'm sorry. I know you want me out of here, but I need more time. I'll find somewhere else soon. I'm just not ready yet.'

Ready for what, she wondered. 'Is there anywhere else? Do you have any friends?'

'Not as such, no.'

'I'm not asking you to leave just yet.'

'But when Will comes back from uni.'

She nodded.

'Have you told him yet?'

'Not yet.' She'd been hoping she didn't have to. When she'd agreed to this, she'd expected it to be over and done with by now and there'd have been no need to say anything to Will. But that was looking increasingly unlikely.

'Just say when you want me to go and I'll go.'

'Okay. In the meantime, we need to get you back on your feet.'

He stroked Maud's wiry back. 'If you leave the clean sheets and stuff out, I'll tidy the room up and make the bed. And I'll do my best not to worry Liza anymore.'

'Good. I have to get back to work. You'll be all right?'

'Yeah. Please don't mention the fall to Liza. It was just a silly accident, but it will definitely worry her.'

'Okay.' She got up to leave. It didn't feel like she'd done enough but it was as much as she could do for now.

'You've made a good life for yourself here, Net. I'm glad.'

It stopped her in her tracks for a heartbeat. She hadn't anticipated a statement like that. Not from him.

Colin had been on Netta's mind all afternoon. For once, it was nothing to do with something he'd said to upset her. It was him, the sorry state of him, his lack of … everything. And that thing he'd said to her earlier on about being glad she had a good life. It really sounded like he meant it. It just wasn't Colin. In the end, she'd decided to take Neil's advice, which was why she was standing on her parents' doorstep.

Her mum let her in. 'I suppose it's that bloody Colin.'

'You suppose correctly.'

'Kettle's on and I've just baked a fruit cake. Come in and sit down.'

'Well, that wasn't quite what I was expecting,' said her mum, half an hour, one cup of tea and a slice of cake later. 'I thought you were going to say he's been stirring it up again.'

'I don't think he's got it in him, Mum.'

'You're not feeling sorry for him, are you?'

'Of course not, but I can't just leave him to shuffle about the house like some ghost. For one thing, it's not fair on Liza and for another, Will's coming home next week.'

'He's still not talking to Colin then?'

Netta shook her head. 'Apart from the odd awkward moment when they've bumped into each other, it's been about five years.'

'Well, in that case, we'd better do something. It's not doing Colin any good skulking around on his own all day. He needs something to take his mind off things. Something positive that will help to sort him out.'

'Painting might do that, but he's not doing any. All of his equipment's locked away in his house. Frank's offered the use of his studio but he seems to have lost all interest.'

'Something else then.' Her mum glanced out the window. 'Your dad's here. Let him in will you, love? He'll have his hands full.'

Netta opened the front door and was nearly knocked over by Minnie, the youngest of Maud's offspring, excitedly greeting her. Behind Minnie, Netta's dad was carrying a box full of vegetables from his allotment. 'Hello, sweetheart. If I'd known you'd be here I'd have brought more veg back. I've got more than we can manage at the moment.'

Her mum was already in the kitchen, refilling the kettle.

'She's come to talk about Colin, Arthur. He's gone very downhill.'

Her dad put the veg box on the worktop and started to sort through its contents. 'He needs to get out of the house. Get the sun on his face. That'll cheer him up.'

'Simple and straightforward as ever, my love,' said her mum.

'Well sometimes, all a man needs is a spade and a sense of purpose to stop him feeling sorry for himself.'

'And sometimes it's a bit more complicated than that. Although, this time you might have a point.' Her mum gave him a sweet smile. 'Didn't you say you and Clyde were about to start on a new project?'

He looked up at her with an onion in one hand, a bunch of carrots in the other, and an uneasy expression on his face. 'I have a feeling I'm not going to like this.'

She gave him a kiss. 'Think of it as doing your bit, love. Greater love hath no man and all that. Oh and by the way, Nettie, don't worry about Will coming back. Worse comes to the worse, Colin can live here.'

8

TAKEN IN HAND BY THE EX-IN-LAWS

'Did I mention Nan and Grandad are coming over this morning?' Netta was talking to Liza, but Colin was all too aware the announcement was meant for him.

'Oh cool.' Liza was buttering toast. She had that look on her face that people used when they were trying to fake surprise and weren't doing a very good job of it.

'Yes, Grandad's looking for some help at the allotment. Some kind of expansion project.'

Colin looked up from his breakfast. He hoped, he really hoped they weren't suggesting... He saw their sneaky sideways glances towards his end of the table and realised that, yes, they actually were suggesting that very thing. He stood up abruptly before their next move ensnared him. 'Well, I've got a few phone calls to make. Have a good day, both of you.'

'I'm at the foodbank today, so I'll be back earlier than usual.' Netta threw him a more obvious, "*I dare you to say some-thing derogatory*" stare. He pretended he hadn't noticed. She'd started volunteering at the foodbank soon after she'd lost her high-flying, highly paid job. It had bugged him when he'd found out about it. Not, as she probably thought, because he didn't agree with charitable works. He did. He just hadn't agreed that she should have been doing charitable work rather than provide for her family. Obviously, that soon became academic when she discovered his belt and braces approach to their household finances, so he was long past the point of caring how she spent her time.

'And I'm not at uni, I'm working from home. Frank's home actually. He lets me use his studio,' said Liza.

'That's very good of him. Is it one of his teaching days today then?' said Colin.

'No, he'll be there too.'

'Okay, might see you later then.' He made it sound cheery. It was important to sound cheery. Like life was a breeze. Like all the shit in the world wasn't landing on his head at the exact same time.

He shut the bedroom door and took up his usual position on the edge of the bed. She painted in Frank's studio? She'd never, not once, ever asked to paint in his studio. She hadn't even joined his classes when he'd invited her to the art retreats he taught in Italy. Colin cradled his head in his hands. Being cheery was a fucking nightmare when everything you ever cared about was in freefall. And now the ex-in-laws were coming round to apparently drag him to an allotment. Well, absolutely not. Absolutely fucking not.

He tried Arianne's number for the umpteenth time. Amazingly, she picked up. 'I'm only answering this to tell you I'm blocking your number, Colin.'

'Arianne, please my darling, I'm sorry. Whatever it is I've done, I'm sorry. Please talk to me. Tell me how I can put things right.'

'I'll tell you what you've done. You've abused me, with your insults and looking down your nose at me.'

'Darling, I said I wasn't keen on dinner. That's hardly abuse.'

'See! You're at it again, looking down your nose at me like I'm some kind of trailer trash. Enough is enough, Colin. You've crossed a line. And I've moved on.'

'Arianne, you're still in my house. You haven't moved anywhere.'

'And I'm not going to. I'm just as entitled to live here as you. I have rights.'

'I don't think you do, love.'

'We'll see what my solicitor says about that.'

'If you're talking about that cousin of yours, she dropped out before she finished her degree.'

'She didn't drop out. She took a gap year that got extended. And no, I wasn't talking about her actually. I have an appointment next week. In the meantime, if you try to approach me or the house, you'll have Byron to deal with.'

'Who?'

'Byron. As I said, I've moved on. Goodbye Colin. Consider yourself blocked.'

Blocked! Fucking blocked? Fucking Byron? And all because he said he was sick of fucking lentil dahl. Hadn't she made him suffer enough? He slid off the bed onto his knees and crouched up into a ball. This might just be the third worst day of his life.

The bedroom door opened. Colin heard the pad of paws on the carpet. A wet nose stained his right ear with something that was probably gross and unpleasant. It belonged to Betty, the big dog. He stayed in his crouching position in the hope she might get bored. She did not get bored. In fact she tried to hump him. He rolled over and saw another dog, very like

Betty, observing the whole disgusting scene. Oh no! It was Geraldine and Arthur's dog.

'I've never known Betty do that.' Balls. Arthur was in the room, too. He thought it was a bit odd that dogs could turn doorknobs.

Colin sat up. 'It must be my irresistible charm.'

'I doubt that very much.' Arthur puffed out his cheeks. 'Right, do you want to come with me to the allotment?'

'No.'

Arthur put his hands on his hips. 'You're not making this easy.'

'Still, no.'

'Okay, last chance. Colin, would you like to come and help out at the allotment? It would do you good to get out in the fresh air.'

'Again, no.'

The ex-father-in-law tutted. 'Don't say I didn't warn you.' He went out onto the landing. 'I tried, Gee.'

Before Colin could say piss off, Arthur and take these dogs with you, Geraldine was standing over him. He really wished he'd used those few seconds to stand up because at this very moment, as he sat on the floor, Colin felt very small. Although, even if he'd been at full height, he had the feeling he'd still feel small. Geraldine had that kind of effect on him.

'Listen to me, you ' Her finger was inches from his eyeball. 'If I had my way, you'd be on the streets or left in some dark hole to rot away until you disappeared from our lives completely. But there are more important things at stake than my feelings. You're the father of my granddaughter and I can't see her unhappy. And much as I think you're a despicable toad, I do believe you love Liza, and you want what's best for her. So Colin, you will get off your backside and you will go to the allotment with Arthur. And when you come back, you will tell Liza you loved every minute of it, even if you hated it. Do I make myself clear?'

The finger was still pointing dangerously close. Colin looked to Arthur. Arthur exhaled loudly. 'Best you say yes, Colin. She's only just warming up.'

Thankfully, Geraldine folded her arms. At least his eyesight was safe for now. He was sure she wasn't this bad before. It must have been since she went bonkers and had to see a therapist. She unfolded her arms and looked very much as if she might be considering a resumption of finger pointing. Or possibly worse. 'I'm waiting.'

'Yes, all right. I'll go.' Better that than have his eye gouged out.

Geraldine gave him a smile that was pure evil. 'Well done. Right, I've made you both a packed lunch. I don't expect you back until mid-afternoon at the earliest. Off you trot.'

9

A REPUTATION SHOT TO PIECES

'I don't like it any more than you do, Colin, but we don't have a choice.' Arthur pulled up in the allotment car park which turned out to be not too far from Netta's house.

Colin was still not convinced that his choices were that limited. 'We could just say I came with you. I could make myself scarce for the day.'

'I don't tell lies. Especially to my wife. That would be disrespectful. And anyway, she'd see right through me. And through you too for that matter. She's no fool. You'd do well to remember that.'

'Why, what's she going to do to me?' If Arthur thought he was frightened of a little old woman like Geraldine, he was very wrong. The only reason he was here was because he wanted Liza to think he was doing something positive.

'Hopefully we'll never find out.' Arthur got out of the car and let his dog out of the back.

Colin remained in his seat. This was all very stupid. He was a grown man who could make his own decisions. And he was definitely not scared of Geraldine Wilde.

Arthur opened the passenger door. 'Stop acting like a pranny and just accept we're stuck with each other. Come on, I'll show you around.'

Colin huffed the loudest possible huff, just to let the ex-father-in-law know that he was not happy, either about being here, or about being called a pranny. His huff had no impact whatsoever on Arthur who remained in the same spot, his arm resting on top of the door. For fear that his resistance was now beginning to make him look like an actual pranny, Colin exited the car and followed Arthur along a path that circled all around the site.

As they walked along, Arthur pointed out the highlights. There weren't many. The place wasn't exactly bustling which was lucky because the old sod insisted on stopping to talk to every person they passed, each conversation as tedious as the next. After what seemed like an interminable time, they stopped at an allotment that was full of green stuff. Vegetables presumably. 'This is my pride and joy. We hardly ever buy veg in the shops now.'

His pride and joy? What a small world Arthur lived in. If he'd painted something good, or even made something with his hands, Colin could understand the pride. But this? This was just a few rows of stuff you could pick up for a couple of quid in the supermarket. Where was the pride and joy in that? Arthur was looking at him, obviously waiting for him to say something. Colin felt obliged to respond but didn't want to encourage the old man too much. You never knew where that could lead to. 'Very nice. What do you want me to do?'

'Nothing here. We're only stopping off to pick up some tools. There's another patch we're helping to tidy up. You're all right with some digging, are you? Won't be too much for your delicate hands?'

'I'm an artist, Arthur, not a pianist. I can manage a bit of digging.'

'That's all right then. Only I heard you employed a gardener these days.'

Colin didn't like the way the old git made it sound like he was in some way less of a man, just because he didn't do his own gardening. 'I have more important things to do with my time. I've got a living to earn.'

'I see. I suppose it's a lot harder for you since Netta put an end to your sponging.'

'I wasn't sponging.'

'Well I was going to say embezzling, but I was trying to be polite.'

'I wasn't embezzling either. I was just...' No, the words wouldn't come. Anyway, what was the point? 'Shall we just get on?'

Armed with an assortment of gardening tools, they went back on the main path towards the far end of the site. A narrower track veered off to the left, just before the path began to curve round. They followed it through an overgrown thicket with just enough space for them to get through without being scratched.

'That needs cutting right back,' said Arthur. 'I don't believe anyone's bothered with it in years.'

When they squeezed through the bush, it quickly became obvious there was more needed doing than a bit of digging, but it was impossible to tell exactly how much because the entire area was overgrown and thick with weeds and bushes.

'This way.' Arthur went ahead along another makeshift trail that had been beaten out of the mass of tall greenery surrounding them.

It wasn't too long before the dense forest of weeds came to a sudden end and Colin was able to see a small piece of land that had been chopped down to stubble. 'Wouldn't it have been better to start from the hedge?'

'Probably, but the others wanted to begin with that one. It has sentimental value. It used to belong to a chap they were friends with. He died a few years back, I think. When he went, the council decided they were going to turn this part into a car park for the leisure centre on the other side. That's why it's been left. The council changed their mind, and we got the allotments back, but they need an overhaul before they can be offered out.' Arthur gestured to a rickety shed in front of an eight-foot wall. 'It's a good sun trap. Nice and quiet too. Right. You start digging out the cleared patch. Take out anything that's not dirt and stick it in that wheelbarrow. When the barrow's full, take it to the composting area.'

Many years ago, when Colin was at school, his history teacher had been inordinately fond of the Victorians. There was nothing about that era he didn't relish lecturing them on endlessly. But there was one particular aspect of Victorian society that he delighted in more than any: the penal system. It occurred to Colin that this allotment would have had the Victorians, with their fondness for pointless hard labour, rubbing their thighs with glee. It also occurred to him that he was being punished for the way things had turned out with him and Netta, and that when Arthur relayed the story of their day to Geraldine later, the two of them would also be rubbing their thighs with glee.

'Can you manage that?' Arthur's face was straight, but Colin was in no doubt that in his head, he was turning cart-wheels of joy.

'Yes. What will you be doing?'

Arthur pointed in the direction of the jungle of over-growth. 'I'm going to start on that. Minnie, lie down and stay. I don't want to be slicing your head off.'

The dog lay down in front of the shed with her head on her paws. She was a big thing, although not as big as the other three of Maud's puppies. Aside from colouring and a wiry coat, none of them looked like little Maud. The father must have been a size.

Colin began digging, determined to prove to Arthur that he would not be broken. One hour in and his resolve was beginning to fade. He'd spent most of that time removing weeds and the odd root vegetable. The wheelbarrow was full but there was very little earth that was weed free. All the same, it was a good enough excuse to give his sore hands a rest.

The dog, Minnie, got up and followed him, giving Arthur a mournful look as they reached him. He stopped scything and wiped his brow. 'Okay, you can go, but don't wander off. Keep an eye on her, Colin.'

So his enforced labour had been extended to babysitting dogs now? Colin tutted and set off with Minnie at his side. With some effort he shoved the wheelbarrow through the gap in the thicket and kept it upright enough not to lose its contents. A year or two ago, when he'd had a bit more about him, this kind of thing wouldn't have been quite so hard. Bloody Arianne. This was all her fault.

Halfway along the main path, he realised he didn't know where the composting area was. Arthur must have pointed it out to him on the highlights tour, but he hadn't been listening. He stopped and looked around. Where the hell was it?

'You lost?' An elderly man appeared from behind a row of tall, leafy canes. He wore overalls and a straw trilby.

'I'm looking for the composting area.'

'It's over there.' He nodded at Minnie. 'She not with you then?' His accent sounded Caribbean.

'Sort of. I'm helping her owner out.'

'Okay. I thought you'd come to see your daddy.'

'I beg your pardon?'

The man ignored him. 'Colonel, your girl's here. Colonel.' A big hairy black and grey monster of a dog came out from behind a shed and ambled towards Minnie. 'That's her daddy, yer know. Where's Arthur?'

'Other side of that hedge.'

'He started without me? I'll get my tools.'

'Over there you said?' Colin pointed in the direction the man had vaguely indicated but he didn't get an answer. The man was already disappearing into his shed. Colin walked on, then remembered Minnie. He turned back in time to see her forcing a new hole through the thicket, aided and abetted by the monster dog. Well, it was one way of getting it down, he supposed.

When he returned, he found the man and Arthur standing over the patch he'd dug so far. He heard Arthur say: 'He's not much of a gardener.'

The man pushed back his trilby and scanned Colin. 'I can see that. Clyde Wilson.'

'Colin Grey,' he said, rising above the insult.

'Colin is Netta's ex-husband,' said Arthur.

Clyde Wilson looked Colin up and down extremely slowly and whistled through his teeth. It would seem his reputation had gone before him and had already been shot to pieces.

10

TWO AMBUSHES AND A CAPPUCCINO

.

When Frank's own daughter, Robyn, had been living at home they'd sometimes sit down together and paint. They were some of the happiest times of his life, him and his darling girl sharing something they both loved. Now that she was making her life in Edinburgh, Robyn didn't have much time for painting. It was a pity, but kids grow up. One minute you're changing their nappies and the next, you're helping them with their first mortgage. That was life.

In some ways, Liza plugged the gaping hole that Robyn had left when she moved away from home. He still missed his daughter but moments like these, him and Liza painting together, helped to remind him that life was also about swings and roundabouts, losses and gains. He didn't get to paint with Robyn anymore, but he really enjoyed the times when he and Liza worked, easels side by side. She was a lot chattier than Robyn. Frank normally worked alone, and it had been a bit off-putting at first, but he'd got used to it and soon found he liked the noisy Liza times as much as the quiet ones on his own. Besides, it wouldn't last forever. Liza was almost twenty-one. Sooner or later she'd move out of Netta's and make her own way in the world, just like Robyn.

That road trip he'd been on over the Easter holidays had been life changing. He'd come back a new man. New-man Frank was a fitter, healthier, more passionate version of himself. New-man Frank made the most of precious moments and embraced life's ups and downs. New-man Frank was going to enjoy this time with Liza for as long as it lasted.

He was painting a landscape from a sketch he'd made on that road trip in readiness for an exhibition he had coming up in the autumn. Liza was painting a portrait. She'd started it last week and it was beginning to take shape. The subject's character was already beginning to emerge. Strikingly so. Frank stopped for a minute to admire it. She was talented. No doubt about it. 'I love the way you've used tones and textures to capture the essence of him.'

She seemed pleased with his observation. 'Thanks. I'm trying to be bolder and freer.'

'Well, you're getting there, for sure. Has your dad said anything about getting back to his painting? Your mum said he had some commissions waiting.'

'No. He hasn't said much about anything since Arianne messaged to say she'd changed the locks. I kind of want to go and kick the door in or something but when I told him, he asked me to stay away. I just don't get it. When we were kids and all living in that house, he was horrible to Mum. Like, he really controlled her. And now he lets Arianne treat him like a doormat. I'm not saying I want him to be back to the way he was with Mum, but I wish he'd stand up for himself.'

'We'll have to get him back to doing some painting. That might revive him. If you get a chance, tell him he can use this place. I've offered already, but I'm not sure he thinks I'm serious.'

Liza frowned. 'You're kinda nice, aren't you?'

'I have an ulterior motive. We need to help him get his house back before Will comes home.' It wasn't exactly lying. They did need to get Colin away before Will came back from uni. But the real reason was that Frank wanted him gone. He and Netta hadn't had words last Sunday, but she'd been pissed off with him over that remark he'd made. He wasn't used to it and he didn't like it. Nor did he like having Colin lurking about the place like some malevolent spirit. So no, he wasn't being nice. He was doing whatever he could to get that sneaky shite as far away as possible.

'Boring. I thought you'd have a much more exciting ulterior motive,' said Liza.

'Such as?'

'Oh I don't know. Maybe something like you wanted to ask Mum to marry you.'

What the feck? Frank almost fell off his seat. 'Well that came from nowhere. Why would you be saying something like that?'

'Dunno. I suppose because you're great together.'

'That's very nice of you to say so, but your mum and me haven't talked about marriage. We're happy as we are.'

'So you don't want to get married then?'

'I didn't say that. It's just never occurred to me, to us.' Well, it hadn't occurred to him, and he was pretty certain it hadn't occurred to Netta either. Had it?

'We all think you should go for it.'

'Do you now? And who might "we" be?'

'Me, obviously. Robyn.'

'Oh, so you've discussed it with Robyn?'

'Yeah. She thinks it's a great idea. So do Kelly and Will.'

Bamboozled. Frank was feeling bamboozled. He was having a lovely day painting and suddenly he was in the middle of an ambush. Could he be ambushed by one person? He could if she had back up allegedly provided by all of the younger members of their hybrid family. He needed an escape route. Think, think. 'Talking of Will, have you spoken to him since your dad got here?'

'No, I'm avoiding him in case I let it out. Mum said she'll tell him when she picks him up from York, if Dad's still here. Nan's said Dad will have to go and live at theirs if he hasn't got his shit together by then. Oh my life, can you imagine that?'

No, Frank could not imagine that, but seeing as Geraldine was now walking through the gate between his garden and Netta's he decided to take the opportunity to find out if it was correct. 'Is that right, Geraldine? Have you offered to put Colin up?'

Geraldine stepped in through the French windows. 'Hopefully it won't come to that, but yes I have. Although I'm not sure Arthur's too keen, but we all have to make sacrifices, don't we?'

Liza giggled. 'Nan, you know Dad would hate that?'

'Yes. And excuse me for being blunt, sweetheart, but there's not much your dad doesn't hate. He'll just have to live with it, unless we can find an alternative. Like I said, sacrifices. Isn't that right, Frank?'

'Er, yes indeed.' Geraldine was giving him a look that probably meant something. Unfortunately, Frank had no idea what it was.

'Anyway, I was about to go and meet a friend for coffee, but she's had to cancel, which is a shame because I just fancied a cappuccino.' Geraldine was giving him another of those looks. This time, however, Frank knew exactly what it meant.

'Will I make you one here, Geraldine?'

'Oh that would be lovely, Frank. Thank you. Liza, why don't you pop back over to yours? I've made some muffins this morning. Bring three back with you. They're blueberry and oat, Frank. Almost healthy.'

It was no use arguing with Geraldine and actually, her blueberry and oat muffins were delicious. Frank set about making three coffees on his machine which was exactly the same as the one that lived in Netta's house but somewhat older and tattier.

He set down a cappuccino in front of Geraldine on the breakfast table. She grabbed his hand as soon as he let go of the cup. 'Quickly, Frank, while Liza's not here. I do have a Colin Plan B, but you might not like it.'

'I see.' Frank was beginning to get an inkling about that look she'd given him earlier and he was almost certain she was right. Whatever Plan B was, he was not going to like it.

'You know how much Arthur and I detest Colin?'

'I think I do, yes.'

'We're willing to do our bit and take him in, but I'm fearful of what Arthur may do to him. He's not as easy going as you might think. He can be quite uncontrollable when he's riled.'

'Arthur?' Surely not Arthur Wilde? The man was a saint.

'And to be perfectly honest, if it happened, I'm not sure I'd be able to stop myself egging Arthur on. So, I was wondering if it might be better all round if Colin moved in here until we can get rid of him. What do you think?'

'I er, I er…' Shit and double shit. Colin Grey in his house, under his feet, day and night, night and day. No, no, no, no, no!

'Obviously, we'd all support you. I think every one of us wants to see the back of him as quickly as possible. Don't you agree?'

'I guess so.'

'So you'll take him then, if necessary?'

Frank screwed his eyes up. Ambushed again. 'I suppose.'

'Good. We've got to work together on this, Frank. It's the only way to get shot of him.' She raised a hand to wave at Liza who was coming back, then let it fall. 'Oh.'

Frank followed her gaze. Liza was nearly with them. A few yards behind her was Will.

'What a lovely surprise.' Geraldine plastered a smile across her face and held out her arms. As she got up to wrap them around her grandson, she whispered: 'Plan B, Frank.'

Plan B it was then. Bollocks.

11

SAVED BY COLIN PLAN B

Netta's expression must have given her away, because her friends at the foodbank were eyeing her as if she'd just received the most terrible news. 'It's Will,' she began, still holding the phone against her ear despite Frank having cut the call some moments earlier. 'He's come home early,' she added after registering the alarm on their faces.

Her audience ran through a range of visible emotions and finally settled on bewildered. Only Neil understood the implications. 'What about Colin?'

'He's at Dad's allotment. I need to go.'

Neil walked out with her. 'If Colin needs somewhere to stay, he can come to ours. Things will work out, don't worry.'

She nodded, wishing she had his optimism. 'Thank you. I might need to hold you to that. Mum and Dad have offered, but he won't want to go there. I thought we'd have more time to work it all out.'

The drive home was spent composing her speech. In her head, she tried this way and that to explain to Will why she'd taken his father in. None of them seemed good enough to make up for her son's sacrifice. He'd walked away from Colin because of her, or more precisely because of what Colin had done to her. When Will found out that he was bleeding her dry while earning plenty of money with his paintings, he chose a side and moved in with Netta. That was his sacrifice. Although in truth, he didn't behave as if it was one. He seemed happy not seeing Colin. She suspected that was because he was afraid that he'd inherited some of Colin's traits. As far as she could see, he hadn't, but try telling him that.

Her hand shook as she unlocked the front door. She should have been braver and warned him while he was still in York instead of putting it off. But it was too late now. He was home and she was going to have to deal with the consequences of her inaction. Was it only a week ago she was telling herself that bad ideas and bad consequences so often went hand in hand? If this wasn't the proof she needed, she didn't know what was.

Will was in the lounge, petting the dogs. The look he gave her said it all. He'd been betrayed. Guilt's bullet shot straight through her heart. Liza came in from the kitchen and Netta realised that no matter which path she'd taken, guilt would have got her one way or the other. She too had chosen a side, and it hadn't been Will's.

'I thought you were staying another week.' Shit. What a stupid thing to say. It had definitely not been in any of the speeches she'd rehearsed.

'I got a lift from one of my housemates. I didn't have that much to bring back.' He looked down at his feet and she was suddenly reminded there was that one trait Will and Colin had in common. But only that one. Biologically speaking, Will was Colin's son but that was as far as it went. He was her son, her dear sweet boy, and he was hurting.

She threw her arms around him. 'I'm sorry, darling. I'm so sorry.'

He squeezed her tight. 'It's okay, Mum. Liza and Nan explained. We've got a plan.'

Her eyes shot to Liza. 'We have?'

Liza nodded. 'Yep. Plan B.'

'Plan B?'

Before Liza could answer, Netta's mum appeared in the doorway. 'Colin's moving in with Frank. He'll be close enough for us to help him but he won't be staying here. Not ideal from Will's perspective but he's agreed to try and make it work.'

Netta turned to Will. 'Are you sure? Even if he stayed at Frank's and didn't eat with us, you might bump into him outside.'

'I'll try to make sure that doesn't happen. It won't be for long anyway. Me and Belle are going away with her family in a few weeks. I'm gonna stay at hers tonight.'

'Good idea, love. That'll give us a chance to get Colin moved over and lay down a few ground rules,' said her mum.

'I'll drop you over there,' said Netta.

Will gave her a weak smile. 'You don't have to.'

'I know. I want to.'

'I understand why you said he could stay. It was Liza, wasn't it? You didn't want to let her down,' said Will, as they drove away.

'Yes. But in doing so, I've let you down.'

'No you haven't. Don't feel bad. It'll work out.'

That was the second time she'd been told that today. Netta hoped it was true. 'Are things okay with you and Belle now?'

He smiled properly for the first time. 'Yeah, we're good.

We're going to try to get jobs in the same town. We want to get our own place.'

'Oh Will, that's wonderful news. I'm so happy for you.' She genuinely was. For a while last year, it looked like he'd made a silly mistake that had all but finished their relationship, but they'd agreed to give it another try.

'Do you think Frank will be all right having him there?' said Will.

God, yes, Frank. She hadn't thought about him in all of this. She wondered whatever happened to Plan A. Perhaps her dad had put his foot down about having Colin in his house as well as on his allotment. If so, who had come up with Plan B? Probably not Frank. Come to think of it, there'd been no sign of Frank when she got home. So where was he?

12

WEREN'T THERE ALWAYS CONDITIONS?

Colin stopped digging and stretched his back. It was aching but the strange thing was, he didn't care, because he'd just realised something. He hadn't given any real thought to Arianne since he'd left Netta's that morning. She'd popped up in his mind every now and then, but he'd been too busy breaking soil and banishing weeds to stop and think about her. He hated to admit it but the Victorians might have been on to something with their hard labour theories. He hadn't enjoyed a single minute of it. That went without saying. But, and it was a tiny but, there was something very, very slightly satisfying about tidying up a plot of land. Obviously, it was nowhere near on a par with painting. At least it wouldn't have been, once upon a time.

He reminded himself again to get in touch with the clients who were waiting for him to finish their commissions. Maybe if he asked Arianne nicely, she'd let him have the ones he'd already started, along with his brushes and paints. Now that she'd blocked him, he'd have to go to the house. He could do that. He could face her. Absolutely he could. But why put himself through all that torture when he already knew what the answer would be? She was punishing him, and she couldn't do that by giving him the only thing he poured his heart and soul into. Not quite the only thing he loved, but definitely the only thing he loved doing. Once, anyway. He'd lost it. He couldn't say when exactly. One thing was certain though. It had already started long before Arianne had tricked him out of his home. So even if he did pluck up the courage to ask her and in a rare moment of common decency she said yes, he doubted very much if he'd actually be able to lay paint down on the canvas.

'Brew's up.' Arthur called him over and handed him a cup of tea. He'd brought a camping stove and kettle down from his allotment shed along with some fold up chairs when they'd stopped for lunch. Geraldine seemed to have made enough sandwiches for everyone on the allotments. Clearly, she knew Clyde would be helping to eat them. Although it had to be said, it had been so long since Colin had eaten proper food, he'd made quite a pig of himself. In fact, since he'd moved in with Netta, his stomach had come out of hibernation and become something of a bottomless barrel.

He took a sip of tea and winced. It was so full-bodied you could stand a spoon up in it.

Clyde laughed. 'Arthur does like his tea strong. I'm more of an Earl Grey man myself. I like it delicate. I would say just like my women but there was nothing delicate about my wife, except her heart.'

'Clyde's wife died of a heart attack,' said Arthur.

'Yes, I got that Arthur, thank you.' For Christ's sake, there was no need to spell it out. Did the man think he was an idiot?

Arthur snapped open a plastic container. 'Geraldine's made us some cake. Fruit.'

Clyde rubbed his hands together. 'You're a lucky man,

Arthur. Married to a beautiful woman who can cook like an angel. Isn't that right, Colin?'

Colin forced a smile, aware that it would look as forced as it truly was. He had never thought of Geraldine as anything other than an awkward old bitch and he was loathe to change that opinion. Although he had to admit, she did make good cakes.

'Here's Ursula.' Clyde waved to a tall, slender woman with long grey hair and a golden tan who was picking through the roughly hewn path. In a loose bright blue dress, she looked out of place, unless you looked downwards and saw the sturdy walking boots on her feet.

'You're just in time for tea and cake,' said Arthur.

'Oh I can't stop, I just popped over to tell you there's someone at the gate asking for you, Arthur. Frank?'

Arthur jumped up. 'Ah yes. I'll be right back.'

Colin watched Arthur and the woman, Ursula, shoot off through the hedge. What was Frank doing here? It seemed he couldn't get away from the man.

'You're getting the hang of the digging now. Getting into your rhythm,' said Clyde.

'I guess I was out of practice.'

'It used to belong to a friend, this patch. Samuel Sweeting. He was a good man. Much loved. Much loved. Died right on this spot.' He pointed to Colin's feet.

'What, this spot here, where I'm sitting?' Colin shifted his chair further back.

'That's right. It was very peaceful. He was sitting right there, listening to the cricket on the radio, and he just nodded off. Shame he didn't stick around to the end. West Indies hammered the English. He'd have been happy about that. He loved his cricket and his allotment. He died in the place he loved best. Doing the things he loved best. Yer can't say fairer than that.'

'Didn't he have any family?'

'Yes. Ah, here's Frank. Right, I'm done for the day. I'm going home for a decent cup of tea and a shower, then I'm away to my club. It's dominoes night tonight. Come on, Colonel.'

The big dog hauled himself up and took his place at the old man's side. It was hard to believe this was the father of little Maud's pups, although the evidence couldn't be denied.

Frank sat down in Clyde's vacant seat. 'Colin.'

'Frank.'

'There's been a development. Will's home.'

'I thought he wasn't due back until next week.' Colin's insides took a giant leap. This could be his chance to talk to Will. Maybe they'd be able to find some common ground. But then reality hit and he remembered the condition of his stay. When Will got home, he was out the door. Crap. He was homeless again.

'He surprised us and came back early.'

He didn't like the way Frank included himself in the surprise, as if Will was his family. 'Can I see him?'

'No, he's gone to his girlfriend's for the night. The thing is, Colin, you're going to have to move out of Netta's. You can move into mine. For now. But there are conditions.'

Colin screwed up his eyes. Of course there were conditions. Weren't there always conditions? What was it with these people and their fucking conditions? 'What conditions?'

'You can't go over to Netta's, and you mustn't try to interact with Will. He doesn't want to engage with you. I'm sorry.'

But was he though? Was Frank genuinely sorry, or was he

enjoying Colin's humiliation as much as the rest of them? 'I'm not sure I like those conditions.'

'I'm not sure I like having you in my house, to be honest, but we are where we are. If I were you, I'd take the offer before I change my mind. The alternative is either a hotel, your own family, or Geraldine and Arthur's.'

Geraldine and Arthur's? Colin shuddered. Somehow, living with his parents or his sanctimonious sister didn't have a ring to it either. And hotels were expensive, unless you went to one of those really seedy ones. He might have given up accountancy long ago but he still knew a poor financial decision when he saw one.

'Or you could try to get back into your own house,' said Frank.

Colin gritted his teeth. 'I'm not ready for that yet. I accept your offer.'

'And you'll stick to the conditions?'

'Yes, I'll stick to the conditions,' he said, much as he wanted to tell Frank O'Hare where to shove his bastard conditions.

13

___

POUTY SCOWLS AND A FROZEN SMILE

It was Tuesday afternoon and Netta was back home early because it was a foodbank day. The morning had started out cool and she'd gone out in jeans and a T-shirt but by the time she was on her way home, the sun had woken up and she was so warm she'd had to change into shorts and a strappy top as soon as she got in. The shorts were new, and she was still nervous about them, but Liza had assured her she had the legs to carry them off. She stood in front of the mirror chewing on her lip. She supposed they didn't look too bad.

She did a bit of a prance around and practised a look she'd spend hours perfecting when she was a girl. It was a cross between a pout and a scowl. The result made her laugh out loud. How could she ever have thought that was sexy?

She stopped prancing and took herself in. She wasn't normally the sort of person who spent too long studying her appearance. She had been when she was younger and more in love with herself, but Colin had put paid to that when he found out about her affair. Netta sometimes wondered if it had been anyone other than Doogie whether he'd have been so relentless in making her pay for it. But from the moment she met Colin, he seemed to know everything about her and Doogie and he'd always had this thing about being her second choice. As soon as they'd finished university, he couldn't get them far enough away from anything to do with Doogie. That included her best friend, Claire. And Manchester. Actually, maybe he had a point about Manchester, because as soon as Netta went back there, she took up with Doogie again and look what happened then.

Even now the thought of Colin standing over her in that hospital room, her womb emptied of its precious cargo, made her shiver. And afterwards, his conditions. The way he insisted she toned down everything about her brash, vulgar, disgusting self. It marked her. It had been a long time before she could look at herself in the mirror with anything less than loathing.

She did the pouty scowl again. 'Fuck you, Colin. I'm wearing these shorts whether you like it or not.'

She flipped the finger at an imaginary Colin, gave her tush a little shake and went down to the study to do some work. Pouty scowls and prancing around were all very well but she had invoices to send off.

When the house was originally built, the study had been a dining room, but the previous owners had changed its function long ago and that was how it had remained. Although now, it was more of an office come hideout when things got too noisy. Not that it occurred too often these days. When Will, Kelly and Liza were all here, it could be quite riotous. But Kelly wasn't here anymore. Will and his girlfriend were about to take their relationship to the next level, and it was quite possible that Liza would be gone too at some point. She'd be on her own again. Except, this time she'd have Frank next door, her friends close by, and the dogs. She'd be all right. Probably.

Betty came in from the hall and growled at Maud who was curled up on the sofa. She was normally very soft and easy going. Although, on all accounts she'd been a bit snappy with Minnie too recently. She growled again.

'Betty, behave. What's up with you?'

Betty left Maud and stuck her head on Netta's lap. Netta scratched the dog's ears. 'What's the matter, darling? Are you feeling a bit out of sorts? Do we need to take you to the vet?'

Naturally, Betty didn't answer, but a knock at the front door set both dogs barking.

Netta peeked through the window to see who it was, and her jaw dropped. Of all the people she might have expected to see on her doorstep, Doogie Chambers was not one of them. And just when she'd been thinking of him too. Sort of thinking of him anyway, in a roundabout way. They were friends now rather than lovers, but he'd never been to her house before, and he lived a long way off. Although his mum lived on the north side of Birmingham these days, so perhaps he was visiting her.

Doogie saw her and flashed a broad grin. A single butterfly made a long winding trip from her stomach to her chest. He still had that effect on her.

'You gonna let me in then?' he said when she opened the door.

She folded her arms but couldn't stop a smile sneaking out. 'Not sure. I'm a bit stunned, to be honest. What are you doing here? I didn't think you even knew my address.'

'I've got Spike in the car.'

His dog? He'd brought his dog with him? 'I thought he never left Scotland.'

Doogie shrugged. 'Don't know how long I'm gonna be away. It didn't seem fair on Grace.'

'Uh huh. Go on then, go and get him. I'll get the coffee on.'

Spike, the long, lean lurcher slinked through each room of the house, closely followed by Betty and Maud. At least Betty wasn't snapping at him.

'How come you don't know how long you'll be away? Has something happened?' she said.

'Nope. I just fancied a bit of time in the city.'

'And you didn't think to let me know you were coming?'

He gave her another of those grins she could never resist. 'Sorry. It was a bit last minute. So much so, I forgot my mum and stepdad are on holiday.'

'So where are you staying?'

'Haven't worked that out yet.' Yes, he had. He absolutely had.

'I suppose you're expecting to stay here?'

'If that's not going to rock the boat with your man next door.'

He meant Frank but, of course, there was more than one man next door. Actually, now that she thought about it, having Doogie here could be the one thing that might trigger Colin into action. 'Yeah, about that. Colin's moved in with Frank. Temporarily.'

'The accountant? You're kidding me, right?'

'I wish I was.' Was it her imagination or did he not look that surprised?

'I don't get it. If this Arianne doesn't have any claim to the house, why doesn't he do something about it?' said Doogie.

They'd moved into the garden now. Spike was wandering around, marking everything with his scent. Frank's dog, Fred, was watching through the French windows next door. Frank was out with friends from work, celebrating his last week in teaching. Colin was on another enforced allotment visit. Netta had a feeling neither would be happy when they got back. Well, she knew for a fact Colin would be extremely unhappy. Frank, she wasn't so sure about. Officially, he and Doogie had never met. But that wasn't really the case and because of that, she couldn't work out his feelings towards Doogie. Before that road trip, she'd have said they were largely positive, but then she found out he'd stayed at the farm belonging to Doogie's partner, Grace. The thing was, Frank had never mentioned being there. Neither had he mentioned that he and Doogie had crossed paths during the stay. Netta had worked it out and had confirmed it with Doogie, although she'd been a bit sneaky with her questions because Doogie had no idea who the man he'd been chatting with was. So Frank was keeping it secret, Doogie was in the dark, and she'd got to the point where she was becoming too embarrassed to mention it to either of them. But it didn't really matter anymore because very soon, her ex-lover and her current lover were about to meet, and it was going to be very interesting watching their reactions.

Will and Belle appeared in the kitchen, then Liza was there too. There was some discussion and then Will and Belle came outside. Netta guessed the discussion was about her visitor. She stood up as they approached, feeling slightly apprehensive, and introduced everyone.

Will was all smiles. 'Hi. I thought you looked familiar. I've seen you in some of Mum's old photos.'

'You've just finished at York, yeah?' said Doogie.

'Yeah. Just got to look for a job now.' Will put his arm around Belle. 'Belle was at Leeds. We're trying to get jobs in the same town this time so we can live together.'

Doogie nodded. 'Living apart from the people you love is hard.'

Netta wasn't quite sure what he meant by that, since it was coming from the man who'd lived apart from the people he loved by choice, but she wasn't going to go there. 'Well, you're both welcome to live here for as long as you want. Speaking of which, Doogie's staying for a while. And so is Spike.'

'Is that Spike in Frank's garden?' said Belle. 'He's beautiful.'

Will laughed. 'Another dog. The way things are going we'll have more dogs than people around here.'

His laughter was cut short by Liza who was on her way and already talking: 'Oh my God, you're Doogie, aren't you? I mean, hello. Is Merrie with you?'

'Er no. She'll be here in a few days.' Doogie looked a bit startled. He probably hadn't had this much young person interaction in years.

'I'll go call her. Amazing dog, by the way.' She was back off into the house, soon to be followed by the other two.

Netta waited for them to disappear inside. 'You did know my daughter and your daughter are friends, didn't you?'

'Yeah, yeah.'

'Sorry. She can be a bit full on if you're not used to it.'

He sat back down. 'No, it's fine. It's just a bit of a shock.'

'How do you mean?'

'She's just like you were at that age. Except for the hair colour. You were a lot darker, except when you had your Debbie Harry streaks.'

'I suppose so. I forget. I don't think I was so, you know, out there.'

'Yeah, you were.'

'Was I?'

He laughed. 'Yeah, you were very out there.'

Netta thought about the pouty scowls and giggled. Yes, she probably was.

Fred came bouncing through the interconnecting garden gate and stopped in front of Spike. That could only mean someone was home next door. While the two dogs did a bit of macho sniffing of each other's bits, Netta looked to see who had let him out. It was Frank. He ambled towards them, smiling. Then he spotted Doogie and his smile froze.

She decided the best way to tackle his rigidity was to adopt a casual, I know nothing, approach. 'Frank, Doogie's come to stay for a while.'

'Oh, right. Good. Great. How are yer, Doogie? Good to finally meet you.' His hand shot out, somewhat robotically, it had to be said.

Doogie scratched his head then shook Frank's waiting hand. 'Yeah, you too mate. You, too.'

14

USURPED BY THE NEMESIS AND HIS DOG

Shit and double shit. This was the stuff of nightmares. Frank's worst nightmares. Doogie Chambers was here and Frank, like an idiot of the highest order, was pretending this was the only time they'd met. But what else was he supposed to do? He hadn't told Netta yet that his road trip had taken him to the place where Doogie lived. He should have told her at the time, but it had been too excruciating to admit that he'd been so low in confidence he'd taken to stalking her ex-lover. Although it wasn't really stalking. It hadn't even been his idea to go there. His brother and cousin had suggested it because it was a great location. They were unaware of its significance and Frank had just gone along with it. He'd planned to tell Netta when he was feeling so good about himself that he could shake off the shame, and he'd been so close. Just another couple of weeks and he'd have got there. But then Colin Grey happened, Doogie Chambers had come back to haunt him, and Netta was going to find out from someone else. Because Frank was sure Doogie recognised him. He just wasn't saying so. Yet.

His face was beginning to ache from all the smiling. It was funny how it didn't hurt so much when you actually meant it. 'Right, well, I've some stuff to do. I'll leave you two to catch up.'

'Okay. Will you be over later for dinner?' said Netta.

'Not sure yet. We had a big lunch.' For some reason Frank's hand had taken to patting his stomach. 'Can I let you know?'

Netta's lovely forehead wrinkled. 'Sure. I'll speak to you later then.'

'Yeah. For sure. Well, I'll be... Good to meet you, Doogie.' Had he already said that? He thought he probably had. What an eejit. He extricated himself with as much dignity as he could dredge up, which wasn't much.

Fred took another sniff at Doogie's dog, Spike, but he was batted out of the way by Betty. He let out a surprised yelp and sloped away with Frank. Back inside the house, they caught each other's eye. Fred's crestfallen expression said it all. They'd been usurped.

Frank gave the dog's ear a scratch. 'Don't let it get to you, fella.' He reminded himself that he was new man Frank now and maybe he should take his own advice. 'Will we go for a walk and a pint?'

Fred's head immediately took on a more jaunty stance. He'd said the magic word. Walk, not pint. The pint was for Frank's benefit. They set off for the park, neither of them looking back. After chasing a few sticks, Fred seemed to have recovered his joie de vivre. Frank might have done so too if something hadn't just occurred to him. Doogie had brought his dog with him. That must mean he wasn't rushing back up to Scotland any time soon.

. . .

A long walk and a couple of pints at his favourite pub, the Hope and Anchor, had sorted him. Frank suspected that the beer had played a large part in the sorting. Tomorrow, he'd probably find that the feeling of being sorted was an elastic one. In the days to come, there was every possibility it would be stretched to the point of snapping. But for today he was back to being new man Frank, embracing whatever life threw at him. So what if the man he suspected was the love of Netta's life was staying with her? So what if her other ex, Colin Grey, that snake of a man, was living with him? Frank was chilled. Netta loved him. She'd told him that numerous times. And yes, Colin might be a sneaky, slimy, manipulative bastard, but Frank could handle him.

He checked the time. Colin would probably be back by now. Arthur had been taking him to the allotment regularly. Frank didn't know if it was helping Colin, but it did have the advantage of tiring him out. He'd been here five days and every night, as soon as he finished his dinner, he was away up to bed. That suited Frank. Most days he was over at Netta's but on the occasions he was in his own home, he didn't want to share his space with a person like that. Although to be fair, Frank hadn't seen much evidence of anything other than a man who'd lost everything, including his self-respect. The bruising had cleared up though. Netta mentioned that Colin had tripped on the stairs or something which seemed an odd thing for a reasonably healthy and fit man to do, unless he was plastered. Anyway, Frank had seen him in his underpants the other day and the bruises were pretty much gone. It had been a rainy allotment day and Colin had slipped in some mud. As soon as he got in he took off he stripped down to his underpants in the hall, so's not to make a mess and Frank was treated to the almost-full body experience. It wasn't the prettiest sight. But then, who was he to talk?

The strangest thing about Colin was his lack of interest in painting. From what Frank knew about him, he was always the one for spouting on about how important his art was to him. Admittedly, that information had mostly come from Netta with a bit thrown in from Liza, but you'd have thought that he would have, at least once, picked up a brush and had a dabble. It wasn't as if the offer to use the studio hadn't been made several times over, but it was like the room was a no-go zone. Not once, to Frank's knowledge, had Colin entered it.

He unclipped Fred's lead as they walked down his path. Once inside, he listened for signs of life, but the house sounded empty. He called out Colin's name. Nothing. Frank checked his messages. Netta had sent him one earlier saying they were having a barbecue, if he was interested. He'd sent back some lame excuse about being busy and giving her and Doogie some time together. She hadn't replied. He was beginning to think he'd upset her again.

From the kitchen window, he could see the barbecue was in full flow. Doogie Chambers was in the middle of it all, lapping up the attention.

He heard the front door open and close. Colin walked in from the hall. 'I thought you'd be next door.'

Frank turned to walk away. 'It's been a long day. I fancied a night off.'

'Looks like you're missing out on a party.' Colin peered through the window. 'Is that—?'

'Yes.'

'Oh for fuck's sake.' Colin turned, pushed past him, and went back out through the front door.

15

COLIN, THE MAN WITH A PLAN

For fuck's sake. Colin was at the limit of his endurance here. The limit! And now this. Doogie Chambers! Doogie fucking Chambers. She was rubbing his nose in it, the bitch. The absolute, out-and-out bitch. His arms pumped. His heart pumped. Everything about him was pumped. Colin was one pumping, throbbing mass of indignation, stomping down the street at near Olympian speed. He had nowhere to go but he couldn't have stayed there watching them having fun at his expense. If he had a car, he'd just get in it and drive, but there was no car, because Arianne had stolen that too. So there was nothing else to do but walk. He could have taken a bus, but Colin didn't do buses. He had his limits.

Before long he found he'd arrived at the allotments. He didn't know why he'd ended up here. It wasn't exactly a place of comfort, more one of daily endurance. And for what? In the vain hope his daughter might acknowledge his effort? She had not. In the even vainer hope that his son might recognise how much he'd been humbled? He had not. No one had made the slightest effort to say anything positive, except for

Clyde, and that was only that his digging had improved. Still, he was here now, and someone had left the gate unlocked.

The place was nearly empty. Just a few diehards left. Everyone else had gone home for their dinner. Colin kept his head down and followed the path towards the thicket hedge. He shouldn't be here really. Not without Arthur, his geriatric minder.

'Back so soon?'

Colin looked up and saw the woman who'd come to get Arthur on that first day. What was her name now? Ursula, that was it. 'Can't keep away.' He said it with a little laugh, keeping it light-hearted so she didn't guess he was here without permission, and kept walking before she asked where Arthur was.

Once he got through the hedge, he relaxed a little. They hadn't cut it back yet so he was invisible on this side. They'd left the chairs outside the shed earlier. He took one of them, his body still jittery with the shock of seeing Doogie Chambers, the man who'd ruined his life.

The first ever time Netta had spoken to Colin, he couldn't believe his luck. He'd been a nerdy accountancy student then and she'd been the girl all the guys wanted, the kind that floated around campus unaware that half the male population of Manchester University were having fantasies about her. When he saw her at a party, he already knew more than he should about her but he hadn't even registered on her scale. She was too much in love, really madly in love, with the one and only Doogie Chambers. As luck would have it, she'd had a big bust up with him that night and, even though he knew she looked down on him, Colin grabbed his chance and clung to it by his fingernails. Her friends hated him, her parents hated him, but he didn't care, because he loved Netta Wilde so much, nothing else mattered.

She didn't go back to Chambers, and Colin thought he'd won the biggest prize ever, the gold medal of gold medals. Because he'd won Netta Wilde, the most perfect woman he'd ever known. If she'd thought the same of him, or even if she'd liked him just a tiny bit, they'd probably still be married today. But she didn't. He wasn't funny, or smart, or cool enough. He liked the wrong music, wore the wrong clothes, said the wrong things. In other words, he wasn't Doogie Chambers.

When the children came along, it looked like their marriage might just make it. He was a good father and for a while, he thought she'd actually found some respect for him. But he'd reckoned without human nature. A work project had taken her back to Manchester, and back to him. Six months of working half the week there and half the week in Birmingham. Six months with Doogie Chambers. That's all it took to ruin everything. The thing was, he may never have found out if she hadn't got pregnant and lost the baby. Not Colin's baby. She'd hardly looked at him, never mind touched him, since she'd been pregnant with Liza. Two years of being shunned like a leper. Then, he gets called to the hospital and told his wife's had a fall and she's lost the baby. If he hadn't had the kids, he'd have probably done something to hurt himself. When she said who the father was, there were only two people he wanted to hurt. But he wasn't a violent man, and Chambers wasn't around anymore.

A flash of blue caught his eye. Ursula was making her way towards him, her path a bit easier than the last time she'd taken it. She was wearing the same dress she'd worn on that day and was carrying something. As she neared him, he could see it was a wine carrier and two glasses.

'I was about to open a bottle of wine, and I thought it would be very selfish of me to drink it alone when you're sitting here pondering on life. Unless you prefer to be alone, that is.'

Actually no, Colin didn't want to be alone. He'd had more than enough of that. 'I couldn't think of anything better than watching the sun go down with a nice glass of wine.'

She gave him a smile that showed a set of perfectly even, white teeth. 'I can't promise it'll be nice. It's pot luck at the corner shop, whatever's chilled in the fridge. But it will be wine and there will be a sunset.'

She sat in the next seat and gave him the bottle to pour while she held the glasses. They each took a sip and only winced slightly. 'I've had worse,' she said.

Colin thought about a revolting elderberry wine Arianne once brought back from one of her retreats. He'd been forced to drink it to keep her happy and spent almost a week on, or with his head down, the toilet. 'So have I.'

Ursula looked out beyond the furthest thicket hedge. 'It's lovely here. Samuel and I often used to sit here at this time, admiring the sky and talking through our day.'

'The guy who had this allotment? You were—?'

'Friends, yes. Great friends. I still miss him. He'd be happy to see his patch being reworked. Are you a keen gardener, Colin?'

So she knew his name then. Colin wondered what else she knew about him. 'Not really. I just come because...' He stopped, not sure what to say.

'Because you're in between things,' she said with no trace of irony on her face.

'Yes, that's a good way of putting it.'

'Many of us come for the same reason.'

'Is that why you come?'

'Not when I first started coming, but I think it is now.' She ran her fingers through her long, grey hair. She was a beautiful woman, but it didn't seem to matter to her. She reminded him of Netta in that way. She turned to him and smiled, the skin around her pale blue eyes wrinkling a little. 'Can you face some more?'

'Sorry? Oh yes, why not.' He'd been too busy trying to work out her age. He topped up their glasses and took a guess at early sixties.

'It doesn't taste so bad after the first half glass. Look, the sun's almost gone,' she said.

Colin turned back to the dying sun, a fireball descending into the Earth's core. It would be good to paint such a scene. Except he wasn't painting anymore, and even when he did, he didn't paint that sort of thing.

'I'm afraid I'll have to throw you out soon,' she said. 'Do you have somewhere to go?'

'Yes. Do you?'

'Yes, thank you.' She said it with a little laugh, and he thought of Netta again.

'Don't take this the wrong way but I could be anyone. I could be someone, you know, very bad. You should be careful.' His head felt woozy. He'd drunk the wine too quickly on an empty stomach. He assumed that was why he was jabbering on and patronising a woman who was probably older and wiser than him.

'Yes, you could be, which is why I called Arthur to check if you were harmless before I approached you.'

He sighed. 'What did Arthur the Great say?'

'As long as you don't open your mouth.'

'Hah.' That was quite funny. In fact, it was the funniest thing he'd heard in ages. Colin laughed, and suddenly he couldn't stop.

. . .

He was on a bus. Colin, the man who didn't do buses, was actually on a bus. He'd walked Ursula to the corner of her road and hopped on one before he changed his mind. Because Colin was also a man with a plan. He was going home. Proper home. Not Netta's. Not Frank's. His own home. Fuck the lot of them, he'd had enough.

It was only when he got to his drive that he realised he was another kind of man. One who'd recently downed two thirds of a bottle of wine and several cans of gin and tonic, purchased from the supermarket in the village. He wasn't drunk. Well, he was possibly a teeny bit drunk. But sometimes, a person needed a bit of help.

Having reached the door without too much issue, Colin rang the bell. It was opened by a great tank of a man, not muscular as such, but big and wide. It was unmistakably the man Colin had seen in the window on the day Arianne had thrown him out. 'Yeah?'

'I want to come in. This is my house. I want to come in.'

'Fuck off.'

The door slammed shut. But Colin hadn't splashed out on all that Dutch courage just to stand here and get a door in his face. No. Absolutely not. He rang the bell again, and when no one came, he hammered his fist on it and demanded to be let in.

The door was flung open so fast it bashed against the wall. Despite his insobriety, Colin thought of his plasterwork. But not for long, because there, in all her tracksuit bottomed glory, was Arianne, her eyes flashing wildly, her face purple. Behind her stood the big man. She jabbed Colin in the shoulder. 'I told you to keep away.'

He was suddenly reminded of their last argument and all the arguments before that, and he wobbled, both inside and out. But then he thought of Liza. If she were here, she wouldn't put up with this. He steadied himself and looked Arianne in the eye. 'This is my house. I want you out.'

'And I want you out.'

'I am out, but I shouldn't be. You should be out.'

'Well I'm not getting out, so piss off.'

'No, you piss o——' Before Colin could finish, a fist came for him, caught his left eye and finished it for him. His feet got in the way of each other, and he tumbled over, smashing the side of his face against the ground as he hit it.

Arianne stood over him, flexing her hand. 'I warned you, Colin. Next time, I'll set Byron on yer.'

'Anytime, babe. Anytime,' said big, bad Byron, as the door closed once again.

Colin scrambled up and stumbled away. He was no longer a man with a plan. He was just a man with a very sore face.

16

AN INFURIATINGLY COOL SHOWDOWN

It was the penultimate day of Frank's teaching career. Penultimate half day actually, seeing as he only taught on Wednesday mornings. The summer term was ending on Friday but tomorrow was his last working day, then that was it. He would no longer be an English teacher. The decision he'd made after that life-changing road trip was finally happening. He felt good about it. A wee bit nervous too, but the overriding sentiment was cautious optimism.

He stepped out into the garden to finish his coffee. It was too beautiful a morning to be inside. Fred pattered around, leaving his mark on every available bush or post. It was probably something to do with having another dog on his patch, all this excessive spraying. Spike was in Netta's garden, his eyes following Fred. Only the sound of Netta's kitchen door opening made him look away. Frank hurried back into the house, not yet ready to face whoever it was that was emerging.

Back inside, he listened out for Colin but heard nothing. After a final pat on the head for Fred, he left for work.

. . .

Frank was back home by one. He treated himself to a beer with his healthy lunch and took them both into the garden. Fred came out with him and stretched out by his feet. If the morning had been grand, the afternoon looked to be even more so. He closed his eyes and thought of all the things he was going to do now that he was free. Decorating the house was an absolute must. It hadn't been touched since long before his wife, Ellen, had died and none of it was to his taste. Except that is for Robyn's old room which had been purple until last month when he'd painted it pale blue. Obviously, decorating wasn't going to be his only activity, but it was high on the priority list. Mainly because it represented another step towards being new-man Frank.

A low growl from Fred made Frank open his eyes. Spike was in Netta's garden again. Frank's hand dropped down to Fred's back. 'Ah come on now, Frederick. Don't be like that. The fella's just being friendly.'

'It's the testosterone.'

Frank looked over the low fence, although he needn't have. He already knew it was Doogie Chambers. 'He's been neutered. I thought that was supposed to make them less aggressive.'

Doogie shrugged. 'Couldn't say. As far as I know, Spike's still intact but he's as soft as they come. He's feeling a bit sorry for himself. Betty's been having a go at him. All right if we come over?'

For a nanosecond Frank contemplated telling him that it was not okay, maybe even telling him to feck off back to Scotland. But it was just a nanosecond. 'Sure. I've beer in the fridge if you want one.'

'Yeah, why not.' Doogie came through the gate, trailed by

Spike who eyed Fred nervously.

When Frank came back with the beer, Fred and Spike appeared to have settled their minor differences and were lying next to each other. 'What did you do?'

'Nothing. They worked it out for themselves. The accountant not in then?'

'Colin? I don't think so. He's probably gone to the allotment with Arthur.'

'Cried off apparently.' Doogie took a battered tobacco tin out of his pocket and pulled out a ready rolled smoke. 'Okay?'

At Frank's nod, he lit up. Within seconds, the pungent hue of weed filled the air. Oh, so it was that kind of smoke. Frank tried to remember the last time he'd smoked weed. A long time ago, for sure. Definitely before Robyn was born, although he couldn't pinpoint an exact date. Doogie took a draw then snapped open his can without saying a word. The guy was so cool it was almost intimidating. Almost? Yeah, right.

'I can put it out if it bothers you,' said Doogie without looking at him.

'It doesn't bother me. I used to smoke it all the time. I've done drugs.' What in God's name made him say that? Was he one first-class nob, or what?

Doogie gave him the side-eye. 'Well done.'

Frank squeezed his eyes shut, then opened them again. Doogie was still there, smoking his joint, sipping his beer, looking cool. He on the other hand just looked like a total dickhead.

Doogie slid the tin across the table to him. Frank opened the lid. Inside was another ready rolled joint next to the lighter. He stared at them, his fingers hovering. 'It's been a long time.'

'No problem.' Doogie flipped the lid closed and went to

pull it back towards him.

Frank felt himself shrinking just a tiny bit. He couldn't back out now, could he? 'No. I was just saying, I'm a bit out of practice.'

Doogie let go of the tin. 'Knock yourself out then, bud.'

Frank lit up, took a drag and coughed. Shit, this stuff was strong. He took another. Not so bad. After the third, he was actually feeling quite mellow. 'Netta didn't tell me you liked to smoke this stuff.'

'She didn't tell me you like to paint Scottish beaches either.' He was clearly referring to the place they'd last met. Frank didn't like the way the corner of the man's mouth was turned up, like he was well aware he'd got one over on him.

'It was just coincidence. The other fellas I was with wanted to go there. I didn't know you'd be there.' That was only half of a lie. He'd guessed Doogie might be there after he'd agreed to go.

'Got it.' The look on him. Like he knew Frank was talking shite. Jesus, this guy was infuriating. 'I don't like to.'

'Huh?' Frank took another draw on his smoke.

'I don't like to smoke it. I hardly touch the stuff these days. I just needed a de-stresser.'

Oh. So, things got to Doogie the man too? He was a mere mortal after all. 'Anything you want to talk about?'

'Nope.'

'Okay then. So, we'll just sit here and de-stress together, will we?'

The man opposite remained silent. Infuriating. Fucking infuriating.

'About Scotland. I'd appreciate it if you didn't say anything to Netta. I haven't mentioned that we've met before. I've been meaning to—'

'Mate, she already knows.'

'You told her.'

'Didn't need to. She already knew. Cheers for the beer.' He stubbed out his smoke with his foot and went back through the garden gate with Spike at his heels.

Netta already knew? Shit.

He awoke to the sound of music coming through the open window. Steele Pulse, at a guess. Frank was lying on his bed. How he got here, he couldn't remember. He didn't even remember finishing the joint, but he must have done. His head was booming, and he felt sick. He needed to drink something fresh and clean. Tentatively, he eased himself off the bed and went down to the kitchen.

He felt marginally better after he'd drunk a pint of water. Well enough to look for his phone and his dog. The phone was on the worktop, so not too hard to find. He noticed he'd missed two calls from Netta. She'd left a message asking if he was having dinner with them tonight. The French windows in his studio were still open. He must have left them like that when he crawled off to sleep. The music was coming from Netta's garden. All the family was out there, including Geraldine and Arthur. Fred was sidling up to his new friend Spike, and Netta was doing the same with her old lover Doogie. He'd been betrayed on all sides.

He was aware of someone behind him, but he didn't turn round. A few more steps and Colin was next to him, watching what he was watching. 'You feel it too, don't you?'

'What?'

'Inadequate.'

Frank looked out at Netta and Doogie. They looked so damn good together; you couldn't feel anything but inadequate. For a brief moment, he had a window into Colin's world. He almost felt sorry for him. But then he remembered that this was the way Colin operated, sowing seeds to make you doubt yourself and others, and the window closed. He was not going to let that man into his head. He was going to go out there and he was going to show Colin Grey and everyone else that he was more than fucking adequate. 'I have no idea what you're talking about.' He turned to look Colin in the eye. And what an eye it was, bloodshot and surrounded by purple. 'What the hell happened to you?'

17

OH, COUNTRY BOY

From where she was sitting, Netta could see Frank in the window, although she didn't think he'd noticed she was watching him. A figure stood behind him, half cloaked by the shadow that had fallen in the kitchen as the sun had shifted to the side of the house. It was Colin. She knew his outline, even though it didn't stand so tall these days. She couldn't see him properly in the shade, but she could tell he was watching them. And so was Frank.

She was doing her utmost not to let Frank's behaviour get under her skin, but it irked her that he was being so childish about Doogie's visit. It irked her very much. In fact, her feelings were running very high in the being irked department at the moment. Her life had been overtaken by people who were irritating the hell out of her. Naturally, Colin was a given. She expected nothing less from him, but at least he'd been confined to next door, so she wasn't bumping into him every minute of the day.

Second on the list after Colin was Frank. All this skulking around, pretending not to have met Doogie. Not to mention the sulking. And what about that crap about having a big lunch yesterday? So rude.

And talking of Doogie, he wasn't entirely innocent of all charges either. Turning up on her doorstep without so much as a warning message, and for what? To hang around all day smoking weed seemed to be his only objective. The man was fifty-six for fuck's sake. It was about time he grew up.

And then there were the minor characters in the niggle area. Her parents, gushing all over Doogie like he was the prodigal son returned. Liza, who seemed to have conveniently forgotten she was the only reason Colin was still here. As far as Netta was aware, her daughter hadn't even been over to see him since they'd moved him over to Frank's. Betty was doing her head in with her mood swings. One minute she was snapping Spike's head off, the next she was canoodling up to him. And only this morning, Will had accused her of chucking his favourite old sweatshirt away. And now Frank was spying on them! What was wrong with these people?

She saw Colin move up to the side of Frank. Something didn't look right about him but at this distance, it was hard to put her finger on what it was. He and Frank were talking. It was only a short exchange, but it had set Frank off out the door. He was coming their way.

Still feeling rather peeved that he'd been ignoring her calls and messages, Netta said nothing. Never one to miss an opportunity, her mum spoke first: 'Hello, Frank. We were wondering where you'd got to.'

'Sorry, I had a few too many at lunchtime. I was sparked out. Stupid of me.' If Netta wasn't mistaken, a look was exchanged between him and Doogie. 'Net, could I have a quick word?'

Oh, so now he wanted to talk? 'What is it?'

'Could we just…?' He gestured to the kitchen.

Netta let out a loud and crisp sigh to convey her irritation with him and tramped off in the direction of the kitchen, aware that she too was in danger of being a touch childish herself.

'Sorry I missed your calls. I really was asleep,' he said, as soon as they were inside.

'Okay. Is that it?'

'It's Colin. He's got a black eye.'

'A black eye?'

'Uh huh. He won't say how he got it.'

'He won't…' Netta screwed her eyes up tight. For God's sake. 'Right. Come on. Let's go and take a look at him.'

She strode purposefully through the garden with Frank trailing behind her, ignoring enquiries from the family, and stopped so suddenly in Frank's kitchen that he bumped into her and almost knocked her over. 'Where is he?'

Frank shrugged. 'I guess he's gone back up to his room.'

'Stay here.' More purposeful striding took her to Robyn's old room which had temporarily become Colin's. Although, it had to be said, not as temporarily as she'd have liked. She banged on the door. 'Colin, are you in there?'

In reply, she heard the sound of something scraping against the door. She tried to open it but it was stuck. He'd pushed something against it. 'Colin, if you don't open this door I'm going to call your parents.' Well that was a threat she hadn't expected to come out with in a million years. Neither, it seemed, had Colin. There was more scraping and then the door handle turned.

Netta let the door swing open. Colin was facing her. No wonder he hadn't looked right when she'd seen him through the window. He had the most enormous shiner. Even though Frank had warned her, it was much worse than she'd imagined. The eye was swollen, and one side of his face was full of cuts and grazes. She took a moment to get over the shock of it. 'Have you been to the hospital?'

'It's nothing.'

'It is not nothing. I'm taking you to A&E.'

'There's no need. It's just a few bruises.'

'Colin, we are going now. For once in your life, just do as I say.'

Netta ate a bag of broken crisps that had come from the vending machine in the hospital waiting room. She was starving and tried not to think of the barbecue chicken she could have eaten ages ago if she hadn't insisted on bringing her ex-husband here. Three hours they'd been here. The chicken would be long gone by now.

Colin came out of a set of double doors, a piece of paper in his hand. He looked such a pathetic, mournful creature, her heart began to tug. Christ, what was happening to her? Everything was topsy turvy and all of her reactions were about-face. 'All done?'

He nodded. 'No lasting damage. The blow wasn't hard enough to break anything.' He held up the paper and she saw it was a prescription. 'Painkillers. Heavy duty.'

'Do you need them tonight?'

'No. They gave me something already.'

'Okay, let's go home,' she said, even though she knew it wasn't Colin's home and never would be.

When they got into the car, Colin's stomach rumbled loudly. 'Sorry.' He was so coy it made her think of the first time they met. Manchester, 1987. It was a crappy party, full of accountancy students. She'd only been there because she was hiding from Doogie and because Claire had heard there'd be lots of free booze. Colin had been manning the record player and she'd asked him if they'd got any Clash. He looked as if he didn't know what had hit him. It was quite sweet. He wasn't so well-practised in the art of manipulation then. He was probably putting it on now.

'When did you last eat?'

He scratched his head. 'Er, this morning, I think.' Yes, he was definitely putting it on.

'Let's stop for fish and chips.' Then, in case he thought she was mellowing, she added: 'I'm hungry too.'

It was a nice balmy evening and still light. Netta wasn't ready to go home yet, so she suggested they ate in the park. She was in no mood to face the questions that would inevitably meet them on their return. Mainly because she only had questions herself and it was easier to ask them here. 'How did it happen?'

Colin picked at his fish. 'I'd rather not say.'

'I need to know, Colin.'

'Why?'

'Because Liza's concerned about you.'

'Ah. Liza's concerned about me. No one else then?'

'Isn't that enough?' Who else was he hoping for? Surely not her. Will, maybe.

He turned to her, the trace of a smile on his lips. One side of his face was so swollen, it was painful to look at him. He'd been good looking back in 1987. Not in the same way as Doogie had been, but attractive all the same. She'd stopped seeing him as anything other than vile long ago, but in truth, he'd aged well. Until now. 'You have curry sauce on your chin.' He pointed to a spot on his own chin. 'Just here.'

She found a tissue and wiped it away. 'Gone?'

'Yep. I was just thinking about those weekends when we

were still at Manchester. Do you remember when we'd come back to Birmingham? You'd take me to a club. Snobs usually. Afterwards, we'd go to that chip shop in Hurst Street, by the Powerhouse.'

'What made you think of that?'

'Must be the fish and chips.' He kicked a fallen chip towards a crow waiting eagerly for cast offs. 'It was like another world to me.'

'It was just a club.'

'I wish you wouldn't do that.'

'What?'

'Belittle me. You were always belittling me. I had a different upbringing to you, Net. I couldn't help seeing the excitement in your world.'

That was rubbish. She never belittled anyone. She'd have told him so too, if he hadn't been such a wreck. 'They've moved Snobs now. Did you know?'

'I heard. Closer to the chip shop.'

'The chip shop went years ago.'

Colin wrinkled his nose, and the less damaged side of his face attempted a resigned smile. 'I so hate the present day.'

Netta laughed. 'Eat your chips before they get cold, country boy.'

He threw another chip to the crow. 'You haven't called me that in a long time.'

She didn't answer. She was thinking about when she used to call him that all the time. She always thought he liked it but perhaps she was wrong.

'I miss those times. I miss Will.'

Both of those statements came as a surprise and she had nothing to say in response, except: 'Oh, Colin. What are we going to do with you?'

18

OUTRAGE IN EQUAL AMOUNTS

It was almost ten-thirty by the time they arrived home. When she got out of the car, Netta was faced with the unusual sight of two men waiting in windows for her. Two lovers, one past and one present at two separate windows, in two separate houses. She was too tired to speak to either of them but speak to them she must, because there was still one burning question that needed to be answered. And since Colin wasn't giving her any kind of answer at all, she needed to ask them.

Frank opened his front door. Of course he would, why wouldn't he? For all his stupidity about Doogie, he'd been golden about Colin. As far as she knew, anyway. Doogie on the other hand remained in the window, predictably aloof. Wasn't that always the way? Well, he could wait. Frank had made the choice for her.

He stepped back to let them into the hall. 'How did it go?'

'Nothing broken,' said Colin.

Frank shoved his hands in his pockets. 'Can I get you both something to eat?'

'We got fish and chips.' It was a harmless enough thing to say but she felt ridiculously disloyal for saying it.

Frank cast his eyes downward. 'Oh.'

And there, in that one small word was the reason why she felt bad. 'We were both starving,' she said, in an effort to redeem herself.

'Righto. A drink then? I have beer, wine, whisky.'

'Better not. I've had some strong painkillers,' said Colin.

'Right,' said Frank. 'Tea then?'

Netta was already on her way to the kitchen. 'Tea would be perfect.'

Colin nodded, a little too eagerly for it to come across as natural. 'Yeah, I could murder a cuppa.'

Frank clapped his hands together. 'Tea it is then.'

They filled the wait for the kettle to boil with nothing talk – the long wait in the hospital, Frank's big day tomorrow. It was all meaningless chatter aimed at masking their embarrassment. And it was clear, they were all embarrassed, even if they were each embarrassed about different things.

Colin picked up his mug of freshly made tea. 'I think I'll take mine up to bed. I'm shattered.'

Frank looked relieved. 'Will I tell Arthur you won't be going to the allotment tomorrow?'

'Thanks. I could do with another rest day.'

'Shall we take this in there?' Frank gestured towards his studio.

They went in and Netta closed the door behind them.

'He won't come in here. He never does,' said Frank.

She joined him at the little table by the French windows. 'Really? I'd have thought he'd like being here amongst all the art.'

'You'd have thought so, wouldn't you? Has he said anything about what happened?'

'He refuses to say. I wondered if you knew anything about it.'

'Not really, no. The first I knew of it was just before I came outside to you. He was fine the last time I saw him. That was yesterday evening.'

'So it wasn't you then?'

'Of course it wasn't me.'

'Only I know how he gets under people's skin. I just wondered—'

'Well wonder no more. I didn't touch the fella. If it was anyone around here, it was probably yer man Doogie.'

'Why? Why would it be Doogie?'

Frank shuffled in his seat. 'He just seems the sort.'

Netta's hackles rose sharply. 'And what sort is that, Frank? The black sort?'

'Jesus, no. That's not what I meant at all. How could you think such a thing? You know I'm not like that.'

'What did you mean then?'

'He can be sinister, the way he looks at you. Like he's trying to work out the best way to rip your head off.'

'Sinister. I see. And is that the way he looked at you when you met him on the beach by Grace's farm?'

Frank's mouth clamped shut. He went to pick up his mug then, seeming to change his mind, clutched the top of his legs and looked at his lap.

She stood up. The chair clattered to the floor. 'I think we'd better leave it at that, don't you?'

He looked out into the garden. Clearly, he had nothing to say. He'd already said too much.

Her own house was empty, with the exception of Doogie and the dogs. 'Where is everybody?'

Doogie leaned against the door frame. 'Your mum and dad went home, and the kids went to the pub.'

'The pub? Their dad has a face like a busted football, and they've gone to the pub?'

'Yep. They waited until you messaged to say he was okay though. It's not like they left as soon as you were out the door.'

She brushed past him and went into the lounge. Even now, the closeness of him made her hairs stand on end. 'Did you punch Colin?'

He laughed. He actually laughed. Until he saw she wasn't joking. 'You're serious. Why would you...? Hang on, has he accused me of assaulting him?'

'No. He won't say what happened. I'm just trying to eliminate you from my enquiries.'

'Your enquiries? You're fucking kidding me, right?'

'I just have to know.'

Doogie kissed his teeth. He was fuming. Absolutely raging. She could tell by the look in his eyes and the thin smile on his lips. This was his way of containing things. She knew that, but somebody who didn't know him, like Frank, might see it as sinister. 'You have to know. Gotcha. All right, Miss fucking Marple, let's just look at the evidence, shall we? One, I haven't left your house since I got here yesterday. Two, the closest I've got to Colin the Wanker was half an hour ago when you pulled up outside. Three, I am not a violent man. I do yoga, for fuck's sake. And even if I was, why would I beat the guy up when he's obviously lost any will to live? Where's the fun in that? And four, how could you even think that? You prick.'

'Oh, I'm a prick?'

'Yeah, you are. Now calm the fuck down. You're upsetting the dogs.'

Netta dropped down onto the sofa. One by one, the dogs came in from the hallway to sit by her. She ran her hands along their backs until she was more like her usual self. 'I'm sorry.'

Doogie sat next to her. 'Was that for me or the dogs?'

'Both. But just for the record. You did used to get into fights, and you always came out on top.'

'Yeah, when we were kids. And "for the record" I only got into fights because other people started on me.'

She put her head on his shoulder. It was true. To her knowledge, he'd never started a fight. 'If it makes you feel better, I asked Frank as well.'

He put his arm around her. 'And how did he take it?'

'He was equally outraged.' She thought it best not to mention that Frank had pointed an accusing finger at him.

'I'm not surprised. I mean, he's a bit of a dickhead but he seems like a decent guy.'

She slapped his thigh. 'Frank is not a dickhead. Okay, he can be a bit of a dickhead sometimes. But in a nice way. Anyway, you hardly know him.'

'I wouldn't say that. We bonded this afternoon over a beer and a smoke.'

So that was why Frank had been sleeping it off, he'd been on the old wacky baccy.

'And we got on okay when he was camping on Grace's farm.'

'Ah. You did remember him then? Does he know, you know?'

'Yep. And he knows you know too. I told him.'

She put her head in her hands. 'So did I.'

19

THE THING ABOUT NETTA WILDE

Time was, Doogie enjoyed nothing more than lying in until late in the morning. Moving to Scotland changed that. Actually, getting involved with Grace changed that. It was hard not to feel a prick of conscience when the person you were sleeping with was getting up before dawn to milk the cows. He rolled over in bed and checked the time. Six-fifteen. She'd be collecting the hens' eggs now and thinking about her breakfast.

When he'd moved to Scotland, he'd wanted to get away from Manchester. His mum's family came from the west coast. Although they'd moved to Glasgow when his grandad was young, the Macraes liked to remind you of their roots. Doogie's uncle had a holiday cottage close to where his great-grandparents and the rest of the Macrae clan had lived. His grandad had stayed there for the last six months of his life, before the cancer finally took him. Doogie had put in a lot of time getting to know the old man in those six months, spending weeks there, just the two of them. Before then he'd always disliked the miserable old bastard, but a

begrudging fondness had gradually crept in, and he'd been
genuinely gutted when old Dougal Macrae took his last
breath.

He didn't return to Scotland until years later. He'd been
on the run from the life he hated and the person he hated
even more. Himself. He'd lost Netta for a second time to Colin
the Wanker after she walked away from him. He'd accidentally become a father with Claire, probably his best friend in
the whole world, and he'd abandoned her and their daughter.
Sure, he provided for them financially but physically, he was
gone. That was the point he was at when he'd offered to drive
some musician friends up to the Highlands to record an
album. They'd stayed near Sanna Bay. It was further north
than his uncle's place, but as soon as he got there, Doogie felt
the pull of his roots. That same connection with the other
half of his heritage just wasn't there. When he was younger it
had been an ongoing source of resentment. These days he
didn't let it bother him. Mainly because he refused to think
about it.

Within months of that trip, he'd sold up and moved there.
At first, he'd rented the cottage from Grace. Eventually, he
persuaded her to sell it to him. They got to know each other
and their relationship grew from being occasional bed part-
ners to something else. He thought about sending Grace a
message and decided against it, because where would that get
them? Absolutely nowhere. She only wanted to hear one thing
from him. The one thing he was having difficulty saying.

To take his mind off home, he tiptoed down Netta's
creaky old stairs. Maud was in one of the armchairs. He
couldn't see the other two, but he could hear whining and
growling coming from the back of the house. It sounded like
Betty was getting aggressive again.

He stopped dead in the kitchen doorway. The growling

was coming from Spike, and he was only shagging the shit out of Betty. 'For fuck's sake, Spike. Get off her.'

Spike gave one last push and climbed off Betty who didn't look too unhappy. He wasn't exactly hanging his head in shame either. Although, with the full extent of his manhood on display, it looked like he had plenty to be proud of.

'Put it away before anyone else comes down, you dirty get.' Doogie opened up the back door and shoved Spike outside. Betty tried to follow but he grabbed her collar and held her back.

'I think she wants to go out.' Netta padded along the hall in her bare feet. He hadn't heard her come down.

'She's been having another go at Spike. I thought I'd keep them apart.'

'I don't know what's wrong with her lately. She's usually so easy going.'

'She's not in season, is she?'

'She can't be, she's not bleeding.'

'Ah right, can't be that then.' Thank fuck for that. Except, he was sure they were properly doing it, and dogs weren't like humans. They didn't properly do it for fun.

'What are you up to today?' said Netta.

'I've got a meeting to go to. A client. I thought while I was in the area we could do a face to face.'

'Oh great. Talking of meetings, I'm going to invite Mum and Dad over for dinner. Frank as well, if he can make it. We need to talk about Colin.'

'Okay. You want me to stay away?'

'No. I want you to be there. I've been thinking about what you said last night about him having lost any will to live. I think we need to do something before it's too late.'

We? Was she forgetting how much he and the accountant couldn't stand each other?

'I know you don't like him.'

'Maybe try something a bit stronger, Net.'

She rolled her eyes. 'I know you loathe and detest him, but you have to admit, even you're beginning to feel sorry for him.'

'I'm not. I am so not. All right, I'll come. I'll be back late afternoon.'

Doogie held the door of the car open for Spike. 'I'm still mad at you, you frisky fucker, so don't think this is a treat or anything.'

Spike gave him the sad eye and slunk out. There were already two cars on the wide drive. He'd parked behind the smaller one. Doogie rang the bell. He had a key, but he didn't want to surprise them. They normally had plenty of notice when he visited.

His stepdad, Clive, answered the door. 'Oh my word! What a lovely surprise. And you've brought Spike. Julie, it's Doogie.' He threw his arms around Doogie and Doogie relaxed. Clive had that effect on him. Considering his mum and Clive had only got together when Doogie was in his mid-thirties, it was crazy how easily he'd become the dad figure in his life.

Doogie's mum came into the hall. 'It is you. I thought I was hearing things. Is Merrie with you?'

He kissed her and gave her a hug. 'No, Mum. A few days yet.'

She pushed herself away from him. 'Everything all right with you two?' She still hadn't forgiven him for not telling her she was a grandmother until Merrie was sixteen. Merrie was twenty now and Doogie suspected forgiving him was never going to be on his mum's to do list.

'Everything's good.'

'So you're staying for a while then?'

'I'm er, I'm staying with friends.'

Her eyes became two slits. 'Which friends?'

'Netta.'

She gave him a look only mothers could get away with. 'Netta? Again?'

'It's not like that.'

'Isn't it? Is that why you can't look me in the eye, Dougal? And what about Grace? Does she know you're staying with Netta?'

Clive took her arm. 'Darling, I expect Doogie's got a lot to tell us. Perhaps we should move into the conservatory.'

His mum glared at him, her eyebrows shifting upwards. Doogie tried to glare back but as usual, it was a lost cause. Even if he'd had no intention of telling them about the whole messed-up situation at Netta's house, he was going to have to tell them now.

'It sounds as though this Colin needs a friend,' said Clive.

'It sounds as though this Colin's an arsehole,' added Doogie's mum.

'That's very true, darling. It certainly does sound like he's been an arsehole. In the past, at any rate. But I guess that's all the more reason why he needs a friend.'

'I suppose so. And if we cut all the arseholes out of our life, where would we be then, eh Dougal?' She gave him another of those looks. Plus, she was still calling him by his full name. She was probably still annoyed about the Netta thing.

Doogie tutted. 'Was that a question, or an accusation?'

She was doing the Macrae stare now. Doogie thought of his grandad who could make you crap your pants with that stare. And even though he was way too old to be bothered by it now, he still shrivelled slightly under his mum's uncompromising attention. He decided to change the subject. 'Can Spike stay with you for a bit?'

'Of course,' said Clive. 'We'll take good care of him.'

'Why can't he stay at Netta's?' said his mum.

'He's getting a bit over friendly with Netta's dog.'

His mum arched her eyebrows again. He knew what she was thinking. Like dog, like owner. He turned to Clive. 'Can a bitch get pregnant if she's not in season?'

Clive frowned. 'I wouldn't know. I'm a doctor, not a vet. I do know one though. I'll ask.'

Doogie let himself in with the spare key Netta had given him. A delicious aroma of something cooking filled the air. He followed the sound of the radio in the kitchen and found Geraldine standing in front of the table with her hands in a big bowl. She looked up at him and then around him. 'Is Spike not with you?'

'I left him with a friend. He was annoying Betty.'

'Oh I see. I'm making steak and mushroom pies for dinner. Nearly done with the pastry, then we can have a nice chat.'

She put the ball of raw pastry into the fridge and washed her hands. 'Right we'll leave that to chill for a bit. Shall we go into the breakfast room? We won't go in the garden in case Colin's out there.'

She asked him to make her a cappuccino in the coffee machine. He took it in and sat down with her. 'Have you seen Colin then?'

She shook her head. 'No. I expect he's keeping a low profile. Have you?'

'Only last night, from a distance. His face looked pretty bad though.'

Geraldine picked up her cup. 'I never took to him, you know. I always felt bad about that. I suppose I thought it had in some way contributed to him being such a – I'm going to say it – bastard to my Netta.'

Doogie smiled. 'I don't think that was the reason.'

'I know that really, but you know how it is when you have dark days.'

'Yeah, I do.'

'We always hoped you'd come back and whisk her away from him. Save her from disappearing into that soulless shell she'd become. Little did we know.'

'I tried. She didn't want me.'

Geraldine placed a hand on his arm. 'I know, sweetheart. Is that what you're doing here now? Trying to save her? Come on, love, you don't think anyone believes that story about fancying a change, do you?'

'Merrie told me. She keeps in touch with Liza. They talk.'

'Those girls and their talk. Never stop. It was good of you to want to protect her.'

'I couldn't let him hurt her again.'

'I understand. You feel you let her down last time. But you didn't really. She wasn't ready then. When she was, she found a way back on her own. That's the thing about Netta, she doesn't need anyone to save her. She's very self-sufficient.'

Doogie couldn't stop a heavy sigh escaping from him. 'I know she is.'

She squeezed his arm. 'That doesn't mean she wants to do everything on her own. She still needs friends. And I'm glad you're back in her life. As a friend.'

20

ALL IS NOT FORGIVEN

After last night, Netta wasn't sure if Frank would come to the family meeting. They'd said some pretty strong things in the heat of the moment and when she'd messaged to invite him, his response had been short but not exactly sweet: *I'll be there.* On top of that, it was his last day at college. He might have had other plans. Bugger. It was his last day. It should be a happy occasion, and she'd spoiled it for him with her half-cocked accusations. Although he had made it easy for her with his own accusations and shady behaviour.

'You're going to wear a hole in that spot,' said Neil.

'What?' She looked down at the work surface she'd been cleaning for the last, however long. 'Sorry. Lost in thought.'

'Wanna share?'

'Wanna listen?'

He took the cleaning cloth off her. 'Always.'

'Well, Colin looks like he's had seven kinds of crap knocked out of him and I spent most of last night with him in A&E. When we got back, I had a row with Frank and, just to round the night off perfectly, I went home and had a pop at

Doogie. It seems like the only person I'm not annoyed with at the moment is Colin. I'm actually beginning to feel sorry for him. And that is the most worrying development in all of this.'

'Wow!'

'Exactly. Two weeks ago, everything was rosy. Colin gets thrown out of his house and suddenly everything is not.'

'Is it all Colin's fault then?'

She threw him a scathing look. 'Of course it is. It's always Colin's fault. If he hadn't been here, I wouldn't have accused Frank and Doogie of beating him up.'

'You accused them of beating him up? Ouch.' Neil did an extremely over the top wince. It wasn't the response she was hoping for.

'What else was I supposed to think? Colin wouldn't tell me who'd done it, so I assumed he was too scared to say. I put two and two together and...' She caught Neil's wide eye. 'Yes, all right, I can see now that I was completely wrong. But in my defence, Frank's been behaving very oddly and Doogie's ... well, he's just being Doogie.'

'In that case, who can blame you?' At first glance, Neil's face appeared serious but the twinkle in his eye was giving her notice that he thought the situation rather amusing.

'You're not helping as much as I thought you would, Neil.'

'Oh I don't know. We've already established you might have been a bit over zealous with your allegations.'

'Yes, yes, okay. Any other observations, perhaps less painful for me to hear, that you'd like to pass on?'

'Hmm. I guess it's worth looking at Colin's injury in a different way. It could just be coincidence. I mean he might have been mugged or got into a fight with some random. Why don't you cast the net a bit further than home and try to pin it down to a time and place?'

'So that is actually a good idea. We've got a family meeting tonight. I'll run it by everyone then.'

'And Frank. Perhaps try to understand why his behaviour's changed.'

'Oh I know why it's changed.'

'Yeah, but do you understand why?'

'Yes. Probably. Maybe not entirely.'

The house was full when Netta got home from work. In the kitchen, her mum was cutting a hefty portion of steak and mushroom pie and lobbing it on a plate full of vegetables. She put the plate on a tray along with a pot of gravy and shouted: 'It's ready, Liza.'

Liza came in and picked up the tray. 'Shall I tell Frank to come over?'

'Yes please. Dinner's going on the table now so come straight back.' She gave Netta a cursory glance. 'It's for Colin. Much as I dislike him, I can't have him wasting away.'

The table was soon loaded with the remaining pie and another that was untouched, and all the trimmings to make a big feast. If they were going to have a meeting, it was to be done on a full stomach. It was her mum's way. Whatever problem needed to be solved, there was always an appropriate food accompaniment to help find the solution.

Frank came back with Liza. He hung around the kitchen, not looking at Netta and generally getting in the way. Doogie was in the lounge talking to her dad and Will, so he was naturally going to avoid retreating to there. When her mum called everyone to the table his relief was obvious. And so probably was Netta's.

It was only when the dogs assembled around the table, as

they often did when food was in the area, that Netta noticed an absence. 'Where's Spike?'

'I left him with a friend for a few days to give Betty a break,' said Doogie.

'I didn't know you had any friends in Birmingham, besides me.'

'Well, it's a client really, the one I met with today, but he offered.' Doogie cut into a roast potato. Another one who couldn't look at her.

'Right, okay. Does he live far?'

'North side of the city.'

'Oh, so near your mum then?'

'I think so. He didn't say where exactly. We met up in the city centre.'

Still not looking at her then? Netta fixed him with a hard stare until he was forced to raise his eyes just long enough for her to make it clear she could see right through him. He loved that dog. There was absolutely no way he would leave him with someone whose address he didn't even know. Something else was going on here. It was just a pity she didn't have the time or headspace to try and work out what. 'You didn't have to do that on Betty's account. I thought she was getting on a lot better with him.'

'Just a few days and I'll fetch him back. When did you want to have the meeting?'

'Let's get dinner out of the way first, shall we?' said her mum.

Frank cleared his throat. 'I have to go out later. I'm meeting friends for a drink.'

Netta tried to catch his eye. 'I don't think it'll take too long. How was your last day?'

'Great actually. Really nice.'

He was smiling for everyone else's benefit, not hers. So was she. 'Great.'

The plates were cleared and everyone had settled back down at the table, including Will. Netta sat next to him. 'You know you don't have to be here, don't you?'

'Yeah, but no one minds if I stay, do they?'

'Of course not.'

Netta's dad clapped his hands together and everyone stopped what they were doing and looked up at him. 'Right. Let's get started then. Over to you, Nettie.'

'Yes. Right. Thanks Dad. The thing is, I'd hoped that Colin being here would help him to sort things out with Arianne, but that hasn't happened. If anything, his state of mind seems to have gone downhill and I'm worried. I am worried about Colin.' There, she'd admitted it. She looked around the table for reactions. Her gaze was met by a host of impassive faces which came as no surprise. It wasn't as if any of them, aside from Liza, could say they liked Colin enough to care. Not even Will.

'Me too.' It was the person Netta least expected it to come from. Her mum.

'I suppose I am too, a bit,' said her dad. 'I thought he was perking up at the allotment. He was getting on quite well with Ursula. And Clyde was tolerating him. But this black eye business has stopped him coming.'

'About that black eye. Does anyone have any idea how it might have happened?' Netta glanced at Frank who immediately folded his arms and set his mouth into a straight line. She looked away. 'No? Okay, so I was thinking. Actually it was Neil's suggestion. We should try to piece together Colin's movements to see if we can pin down a time and place.'

Frank pulled his arms in even tighter. 'Why?'

'I, that is, Neil and I, thought that by doing that we could try to get to the root of Colin's problem and really start to help him. Of course, it could have been a random attack but I'm not so sure.'

'That's a great idea.' It was Doogie. He had a sarcastic smirk on his face. At least he didn't call her Miss Marple again.

'What makes you think there's more to it?' said Will.

'Because it's not the first time I've seen bruises on him. The first week he was here, I bumped into him as he was coming out of the shower. His back was covered in them.'

Liza shot forward in her seat. 'Oh my God. Why didn't you say before?'

'Because he asked me not to say anything. He didn't want to upset you. He said he tripped on the stairs at his house.'

'Ursula saw him at the allotment on Tuesday evening. Apparently, he was fine when he left,' said her dad.

'What was he doing there?' said Netta.

Frank coughed again. 'He left the house just after Arthur dropped him back. He was upset.'

'He was perfectly all right when I left him,' said her dad.

'I don't doubt it, Arthur. He er, he saw something that upset him,' said Frank.

'What?' said her mum.

'Me?' said Doogie.

Frank nodded.

Liza tutted. 'I thought he'd gotten over all that. That's what he told me.'

Netta's attention shifted to Liza. So they must have discussed it then? At some point in the last few years, Liza and Colin must have had a conversation about her and Doogie. She wondered what had prompted that. She saw that everyone else was watching Liza too. Perhaps they were all thinking the same thing.

'He probably thought he had, but it can be harder than you think to get over stuff like that.' The communal focus shifted to Doogie. This time, Netta was sure they were all thinking the same as her. What made him say that? Frank looked like he'd already decided the answer to that question, and he didn't like it.

Her mum pulled them back to the matter in hand. 'Right, so we know Colin was okay when he left the allotment on Tuesday night, and no one saw him again until yesterday evening when he got back to Frank's. So that leaves the rest of Tuesday night and yesterday unaccounted for.'

'I'll ask Ursula when he left the allotment. Thinking about it, she might be able to get more information out of him. I think they had a good chat the other night.' As if catching the surprise in the room, her dad added: 'She's that kind of person. Not an enemy in the world.'

'You do that, Arthur,' said her mum. 'Let's get him back to the allotment then. Liza, that's where you come in. When we've finished here, go round and talk to him.'

Liza raised her hand in a salute. 'I get it. Turn on the emotional blackmail.'

'Exactly. Now then, I think while he's in such a vulnerable state he needs minding properly. Frank, you can do that while he's in your house, can't you?'

Frank looked like a rabbit who'd only just realised the headlights were almost on top of him. 'I guess so.'

'Lovely. Doogie, the other part is where you come in.'

Doogie frowned. 'Me?'

'Yes, love. You. I know you like a bit of gardening yourself so it shouldn't be too much of a hardship to keep an eye on Colin while you do it.'

'Er—'

'Mum, we've just established that Colin's still harbouring a grudge over Doogie,' protested Netta.

'Yes, I know. So Colin needs someone to guide him through that. And who better than the man he hates most?'

Doogie looked unconvinced. 'I really don't think that's gonna work.'

'You did say you wanted to help.' Her mum gave him one of her sweetest smiles. She'd backed him into a corner, probably of his own making because he must have been stupid enough to offer assistance in one of their little chats.

'Yeah but—'

'But?' A Geraldine Wilde eyebrow was raised and it was pointed at Doogie Chambers.

Doogie took the hint. 'Okay then.'

With the meeting concluded, Frank was on his way out the door. Netta followed him into the front garden. 'About last night.'

'It's forgotten,' he said, when clearly it wasn't.

'Okay. Where are you off to?'

'The Hope and Anchor.'

'Lovely. Do you want me to come with you?'

He shook his head 'It'll just be college talk, and you have your visitor to entertain.'

That was a bit too snidey for Netta's liking. 'Right. Well you go then.' She did an about turn and marched back inside the house, muttering under her breath: 'And fuck you.'

21

THE AVOIDANCE OF SHAME

Colin chewed on the last mouthful of the dinner Geraldine had sent over for him. He hadn't realised how hungry he was until he'd started eating it. There'd been a packet of crisps around mid-morning but other than that, he'd not eaten. It was surprising how easy it was to forget food when your heart wasn't in it. And let's face it, his heart hadn't been in it for quite some time. Still, if anyone was going to revive his interest in that area it was going to be the ex-mother-in-law. He'd say one thing for the old bat, she could make a mean pie. It was good of her really, especially considering how much she hated him. And there was no doubt in his mind that she did hate him. When he and Netta first got together, he'd tried his utmost to get on with Geraldine, but it was a waste of time. She'd wanted Chambers for a son-in-law, and he was never going to be a good enough replacement.

They were all in there now, in Netta's house. A family meeting. He'd overheard Liza talking to Frank, like he had some kind of parental privilege over her. He'd wanted to burst into the room and shout: 'Hey, I'm the daddy here,' but he couldn't even be arsed to do that. And anyway it would have made him look like a complete and utter wanker. Colin the Wanker. Chambers called him that. Another thing he'd overheard, this time through an open window. Netta probably called him that too. Although, last night in the park with her. It had been special. When they'd got back he'd gone up to bed and had a quiet little cry. Pathetic really, but that was the state he was in right now.

He washed and dried his dinner things and put them on the side ready to go back next door. It would be easy enough to drop them over but of course, he wasn't allowed. He was like a prisoner on parole, except that rather than be sent back to prison if he broke the rules, he'd be thrown out. This place of Frank's was like a prison. There was no heart to it. Unless Netta or Liza came round, which wasn't that often. It was no wonder Frank spent most of his time next door.

The dogs were spilling out into the two gardens. The meeting must have finished. It was about him, he supposed. What are we going to do with Colin the Wanker? Unfortunately, he had no insight of his own to share with them in that regard.

The little dog, Maud, walked up to the house. Colin pressed himself up against the kitchen window to see her better. She stopped at the French windows waiting to be let into the studio. He took a step towards it. No, he couldn't go in there. He turned away towards the hall, just as Frank was coming in with his own dog, Fred. 'I'm away out. I'm leaving Fred here. Liza's coming over soon.'

'Is she coming over for any particular reason?' he asked, although he knew it would be to pass on some new directive that they'd decided would be in his best interests.

'To check you're okay, and to talk to you about going back

to the allotments. I'll be late, so can you let Fred into the garden a couple of times?'

'Sure.'

'You won't forget him though, will you?'

Colin sighed. 'No, I won't forget him.'

He watched Frank go past Netta's, then stop and turn back for someone. It was Will. Colin's heart missed a beat. A huge great sob came from somewhere within. He put his hand across his mouth to stop it coming out as he watched his son strolling along with Frank.

He turned away and with Fred at his heels, went upstairs to his room. Flopping down onto the bed, he pulled Will's sweatshirt out from under his pillow and breathed in its mildly bitter scent. There had been a time when his son and daughter loved him unquestioningly. There had been a time when he'd been on top of the world. And there had been a time when he'd thought he was untouchable.

'Dad, you in?' The sound of Liza's call made him jump.

'Yeah. Give me a minute.' Colin put the sweatshirt back in its hiding place behind the pillow and wiped his eyes. Then he went downstairs to see what fresh hell the family Wilde had dreamed up for him.

Frank and Liza were looking at paint charts when Colin came down in the morning. 'Liza's helping me choose the colours for the bedrooms. They haven't been touched in a long time.' There was no need for Frank's explanation. The lack of upkeep was quite evident. As was the lack of housekeeping.

Liza gave Colin the kind of smile that was worth getting up for. 'Grandad's next door. He'll be here in a minute.' She was so like her mother sometimes. The only thing she'd inherited from him was his fair hair.

Back in their university days, Netta bleached the top layer of her dark hair, à la Debbie Harry, and she'd wear this little pink tutu over the skinniest, tightest jeans, along with a Clash T-shirt. Sometimes, when he was having trouble with what Arianne rather disparagingly referred to as his manhood, he'd think about that and bingo, he'd be going like a train. He found the T-shirt in the loft after Netta had moved out and had made the mistake of showing it to Arianne. Before he knew it, she'd bought the exact same one. She'd done it to show him how much better her body was than Netta's. But a voluptuous fifty-year-old can never get away with the kind of style a skinny twenty year old can, and as always, she'd missed the point. It was about the person, not the clothes. Not that he dared tell her that. Obviously.

It was slightly longer than a minute but not much more when Arthur emerged from Netta's house. Liza virtually pushed Colin down the path to meet him. She'd laid it on really thick last night and he'd had no option but to agree to go back to the allotment. He'd already lost one child and he damn well wasn't going to lose the other. Besides, he was sick of looking at Frank's poorly maintained walls and he couldn't stand the thought of being around all day while the two of them did their pseudo father-daughter painting love-in.

When he saw Chambers walking down Netta's path, Colin halted. Liza gave him another nudge, but he refused to move. 'I think I might have forgotten to say Doogie was going too,' she said. 'You're cool with that, right, Dad?'

Well, obviously, he wasn't cool with that, and she bloody well knew it. He'd been conned by the one person he thought had his back.

'Dad? You are going to go, aren't you? You're not going to shame me.'

Colin pressed his lips together. There, she'd gone and

done it, used the word shame. Young people speak for embarrass me, let me down, disappoint me. Whatever. It was all guaranteed to make him feel even worse about himself. 'Of course I'm not going to shame you. Looking forward to it.' Hmm, maybe that was much. She'd know for certain he was lying now.

'Amazing.' Liza hugged him. And then she shoved him into Arthur's arms. 'He's all yours, Grandad.'

'I'll follow in my car,' said Chambers.

At least Colin didn't have to share the same space as him. At least they didn't have to fight over who was going to sit in the front, because Colin knew who would win that particular argument, and it wasn't going to be him.

'Right you are. Colin, why don't you go in with Doogie, in case we get split up? As you know the way.'

Liza nodded in a kind of egging on manner. Fuck. He was up shit creek without a paddle. Colin gritted his teeth. 'No problem.'

Chambers gave him a look as they both got into the car. If Colin had to describe it, he would have said it was sinister. There was every chance he wouldn't get to the allotment alive. Liza was beaming at him. Well if he died today, at least he could go to his final resting place knowing he hadn't shamed her.

Chambers hadn't even switched the engine on when Arthur began to pull out. Colin fixed his mouth into a rigid smile, aware that Liza was still watching him. 'Shall we?'

Chambers started the car up. 'Do me a favour, shithead. Don't say another fucking word.'

22

THE TASTE OF DEAD AND ROTTING THINGS

Colin had spent the whole of the way with his heart in his mouth. Only when they parked up at the allotments, did it begin the journey back to its rightful place. He'd survived the drive in one piece, despite having to go against the instruction not to say another word when they'd missed the turning. Not that Chambers had threatened him with violence, but you never knew with him, did you? Back in their uni days, Chambers hung around with the sort Colin's mother would have called the wrong type, the lowest of the low. Mind you, in Mother's eyes, most people were the wrong type, including Netta. And as far as Colin was aware, Chambers didn't do anything shady, unless you counted the drug taking. But then, at least half the student population were doing that. Even he'd tried it once. No, the main thing about Doogie Chambers, his USP, was that he was tough. The kind of tough that didn't need to do anything to make people wary of him. The kind that made timid types, like Colin, crap their pants with just one look.

Arthur was out of his car looking all bright eyed and

bushy tailed. 'It's a fine day for it.' The man was a veritable
fountain of optimism. Nothing ever seemed to bring him
down.

'For what exactly? What thrills do you have in store for us
today?' Colin caught a warning shot from Chambers and
decided it would be safest to park the sarcasm.

Arthur laughed. 'Wait and see. I'll show Doogie round.
You can come too if you want to, or you can wait for us over
there.'

'Thanks, but I already know where the compost bins are.'
Shit, he'd succumbed to sarcasm again. He could feel Chambers's eyes boring into him. He tried to pull it back with an
inoffensive smile. 'I'll go straight over.'

The path took him past Ursula's allotment. She was there,
prodding the dirt between rows of something vegetable-like.
Today, she was wearing cut-off shorts and a jade-green vest,
showing off tanned, sinewy limbs. It occurred to him that she
moved like someone who was used to being in the spotlight
and he wondered what she'd been in her past life. It also
occurred to him that Chambers was like that too. Ursula, with
her bright clothes, seemed to embrace it. Chambers on the
other hand was much more low-key. When they were young
he'd worn the kind of clothes that were subtle, timeless, and
understated. From what Colin had seen of him in the last few
days, his style hadn't changed that much. He still dressed like
someone who didn't want to stand out. It was a waste of time
though. Chambers was the sort who always got noticed. Not
just for his good looks which were still very much evident,
unfortunately. It was everything about him, from his graceful,
straight-backed elegance to his restrained menace. You
couldn't not look at the bastard without wishing you had just
an ounce of his magnetism.

Colin registered no shock in Ursula's expression when she

saw him. Arthur must have told her what to expect. 'You're back. Good.'

'Yes, Arthur the Great's roped me in again I'm afraid.'

She laughed. It was girlish but natural. 'I'll come over with you.'

There'd been some work done in the two days he'd been away. The first allotment was clear now and a little path was visible between that and the neighbouring patch, a small corner of which had been dug.

'Samuel's patch is looking good. Nearly ready for someone new to take over.' Ursula sounded almost sad as she said it.

'It looks pretty much done.'

'Not quite. We have to clear the shed first.' She pulled out a key from her pocket. He expected her to unlock the door, but she sat down on a chair, the key still in her hand.

He sat down too, remembering the few hours he'd spent with her the last time he was here. 'I enjoyed it the other night. Watching the sun go down. It was so nice and peaceful.'

'So did I. The thing that happened to your face, was it after you left me?'

He nodded.

'Who did it to you?'

'I'd rather not say.'

'Okay. We should watch the sun come down again soon, don't you think?'

He looked at her serene face and in spite of everything, felt as if he were floating on a sea of calm. He wanted to stay here watching that face. The stillness of it. The wonderful, wonderful stillness.

But all too soon, Arthur was here with Clyde and Chambers. Clyde pushed his straw trilby back. 'Man, what a sight. I hope you don't have any hot dates lined up, boy, because they's gonna run a mile from you. We got some more help, Ursula.'

Chambers stepped forward and smiled. 'Hi. I'm Doogie.'

'Hello. I'm Ursula, in case you haven't guessed.' Ursula was transformed. The serenity was gone. She was aglow. Fuck. She fancied him.

'You got the key?' said Clyde.

'Yes.' She held it up. 'Ready?'

Clyde nodded. She put it in the lock. It turned fairly easily but the door was stiff and neither Ursula nor Clyde could move it. Colin stepped forward but Chambers got there before him. One hard shove from him and it was open. Chambers and Clyde stood aside to let Ursula go in first. She hesitated in the doorway, closed her eyes for a moment, then opened them and stepped inside. A minute later she was back out, cobwebs in her hair. 'It's just as he left it.'

Clyde put his head around the door. 'With a lot more mess. Samuel liked to keep it clean and tidy. He'd be mad as hell to see it in such a sorry state.'

'We'll soon get it cleaned up,' said Arthur.

Colin peered into the shed. It had a window that was covered by closed curtains but there was enough daylight coming through the open door to see the place was full of cobwebs and dust. The wall on one side had two shelves above a table loaded with pots and other indiscernible shapes. At the back was a small wooden cupboard with more things on top of it. Next to it was a wicker chair. 'Yes, shouldn't take you long.' He turned back round to the others and realised they were all staring at him. 'What?'

'We were hoping you'd say that,' said Arthur.

'Me? You want me to do it?'

Arthur pushed a broom in his direction. 'Well you don't look as if you could handle a spade today.'

'I'm not sure he can handle a broom today.' Clyde had a big smirk on his face and Chambers was grinning from ear to ear.

Colin was quietly fuming. He was about to tell them to shove their fucking broom when Ursula touched his arm: 'You don't mind, do you? It's just that it's too painful for Clyde and me.'

He gave himself a few seconds to take her in. She wasn't laughing at him or taking the piss, she just wanted his help. It had been a long time since anyone had asked for that. He took the broom from Arthur. 'Not in the least.'

Colin was not a fan of spiders or creepy crawlies of any kind. He didn't exactly run from them like a big girlie, but they turned his stomach. Although the one he was looking at now did actually make him want to run out of the shed screaming. It. Was. Huge. With fangs! Yes, fangs. He was certain they were fangs. The only thing stopping him from doing that very thing was the knowledge that they'd all laugh at him. They were out there now, doing manly activities. Chambers was ripping through the soil and turning it over like it was a cake mix instead of heavy, claggy dirt held together with a thick tangle of roots and weeds. Ursula was watching his lean, muscular body flexing, a big smile on her face. She didn't look quite so in need of help now.

She turned and waved. He waved back, embarrassed that she'd caught him. She strolled up to the shed. 'How are you getting on?'

'Fine. Just taking a breather from the dust and the spiders. There's a massive one on the curtains. I'm building myself up to dealing with it.'

'Let me see.' She smiled. Not the kind of smile she'd been giving Chambers. More the pitying kind.

Colin immediately regretted his confession. 'There's no need.'

But she was already in there, arming herself with a pot and an old newspaper from the table. In no time, she had the eight-legged mutant secured inside the pot and set it down on the ground outside.

Chambers came over to see the prisoner set free. 'Fucking hell, that's one ugly bastard. I hate spiders.'

Colin felt a little less hopeless knowing that the man wasn't entirely invincible. 'Me too,' he said, only afterwards wondering whether he'd transgressed the "don't say another word" rule again. If he had, Chambers didn't seem bothered by it. Perhaps he was softening. Maybe it was the realisation that they now had two things in common. Netta, and a hatred of spiders. He resumed the shed clearance with renewed vigour.

The first to go outside were the curtains, now that they were safe to approach. Next went the wicker chair which freed up enough room for manoeuvring around the small space. Now that he wasn't putting all his concentration into big, hairy spiders, Colin caught a whiff of something unsavoury. There were no obvious contenders on the shelves, table or cupboard tops so it had to be inside the cupboard itself. He opened the door and the smell of something dire and rank hit him so hard, he had to run back out into the fresh air before he puked.

Chambers was the only one out there now. He slammed his spade into the ground and left it there. 'Another spider?'

Colin tried to answer but he was bent over, involuntarily dry retching. So Chambers took it upon himself to go inside.

A minute later he was back out, spitting to clear his throat. 'How long did they say the guy had been dead?'

'A couple of years, I think.'

'That explains it. Get a bin bag.' Chambers pulled off his T-shirt and tied it across his nose and mouth.

Colin tried not to look at his strong, healthy torso. He tried not to think of his own puny frame in comparison. Height wise there wasn't much difference between the two of them, but Chambers had looked after himself. Colin had not. He knew it and, as he took off his own top to do the same, he could tell Chambers could see it too.

They crouched down in front of the cupboard. Colin could see an open carton of long-life milk, the life of which had long run out; the remains of some kind of foodstuff; a jar of hardened instant coffee; a tin that presumably held dried up tea bags, and a dead rat, its burst open carcass wriggling with maggots.

'Open the bag,' said Chambers.

He opened it wide while Chambers picked up the least offensive items with his gloved hands, then took a small shovel to the rest. When it was empty, they carried the cupboard out into the sunshine and left the door wide open.

Chambers put his T-shirt back on. 'That was fucking revolting.'

Colin tied a knot in the bag and shuddered. 'I feel dirty.'

Chambers spat into the dirt. 'Yep. I need something to get rid of the taste.'

'I'll take this straight to the bins and see if there's any tea going.' Colin looked out for the others on the way to the bins. He couldn't see them on either Arthur or Ursula's allotments. Clyde's pitch was tucked away in the furthest corner, too far to see. He remembered the corner shop Ursula had mentioned

the other night and went in search of something to rid them
of the taste of dead and rotting things.

When he got back, Chambers was in one of Arthur's chairs,
looking at his phone. 'You took your time.' He said it without
taking his eyes off the phone.

'I couldn't see anyone for the tea, so I went to the shop. I
got hand sanitiser to make us feel slightly less disgusting and
these.' He held up a four pack of beers. 'Not much choice,
only cheap lager or even cheaper lager.'

Chambers took a can. 'Mate, anything will do right now.'

Colin took a swig from his can, not quite believing he was
here. In 2003, Doogie Chambers had stolen the most precious
thing in his life from him and here they were, twenty years
later, sharing hand sanitiser and cheap lager. And the strange
thing was, it didn't feel wrong.

23

PRISCILLA SWEETING GETS A LETTER

Doogie opened up a second can. He was drinking with Colin the Wanker. How fucked up was that? He'd always imagined it would be Frank he'd be sharing a cold one with, but Frank was the one behaving like a prize prick and last night, Netta had asked Doogie to look after the man who'd done his best to ruin her life. Fucked up didn't even begin to describe it.

He leaned back in the chair. The sun was quite strong now. He didn't mind working in the heat, but he preferred it cooler than it was today. He'd got used to Scottish weather. You did get heat up there, but hardly ever as oppressive as this. The wanker was starting on his second can. He'd have to keep an eye on him. The guy was skinnier than a whippet. A second can might just be enough to knock him out.

Two things had happened while he'd been waiting for Colin the Wanker to come back. Arthur had messaged to say they'd gone to Clyde's to collect some more tools, and Doogie had gone back inside the shed. It was only out of interest really, to pick up some tips. His vegetable garden back home wasn't that different to having an allotment, and Clyde had told him this Samuel guy had been one of the best. So he'd been nosing around the shelves looking at the way things were set up when he saw the plastic wallet hidden behind some seed boxes. It was one of those like a big envelope with a press stud that closed the flap. His dad used them a lot when Doogie was a kid. They kept his papers clean when he was checking on his building sites. He used to give them to him for school. He probably gave them to Doogie's half-brothers and sisters as well. Doogie never asked. But that was why he'd taken the wallet down. It reminded him of his old man. Now he was wondering whether to tell Colin the Wanker what was inside.

'The others have gone to pick up more tools.'

Colin the Wanker nodded. 'That'll be why I couldn't see them.'

Doogie slipped the wallet out from behind his back. Might as well tell him. He'd find out soon enough when the others got back. 'I found this inside.'

Colin the Wanker opened the wallet's flap. 'A letter.'

'Yeah, it's addressed to someone. Mrs P Sweeting. Read what's on the back.'

'To be opened only in the event of my death. Bit dramatic. Do you think she's Samuel's wife?'

Doogie shrugged. 'Could be. Clyde and Ursula might know.'

They didn't have to wait long to find out. The others were soon back with food, drink and heavy duty cutters for the overgrown hedge. 'Any idea who she is?' asked Doogie.

'It's Priscilla, Samuel's wife. I can't believe this has been here all this time,' said Clyde.

'We wouldn't have known it was there. We pretty much locked the place up and left it straight after he passed,' said Ursula.

Arthur scratched his head. 'Strange place to leave such a letter.'

'Not for Samuel,' said Clyde.

Ursula sat down on the old wicker chair. Its cobwebs stuck to her hair and clothes, but she didn't seem to notice. 'He must have known he was dying.'

'So what do we do with it?' Now that he'd asked the obvious question, it seemed to Doogie that the two people who should have an answer weren't in possession of one. They just looked at each other with faces that were unreadable.

It was left to Arthur to say something: 'I didn't know Samuel, but it seems to me that he wouldn't have written it if he hadn't wanted his wife to read it. And I think even if as many as ten years had passed, my Geraldine would want to see it.'

'Your Geraldine is not Priscilla Sweeting,' said Clyde. 'But I see what you mean.'

'You're right, of course,' said Arthur. 'Do you know if Mrs Sweeting still lives at this address?'

Clyde nodded. 'She does.'

'Maybe we could call on her then. You and Ursula, as she knows you, and we shouldn't go mob-handed.'

Clyde gave Ursula another one of those unreadable looks. 'That's not a good idea, Arthur. Better if someone else goes.'

'Oh. Okay. Well you know best, Clyde. Shall I go then?'

'No. She'll spot you as one of us from a mile down the road. I think it should be him.' Clyde pointed to Doogie. 'I suppose the other one could go as well. As back up. Well, back up might be expecting a bit much. More like a distraction. But definitely Doogie. She'll open the door to him.'

.   .   .

Fucking hell. What had he got himself into and who was this Priscilla Sweeting? Fucking Godzilla from the sound of it. Whoever or whatever she was, Doogie and Colin the Wanker were on their way to her house. According to Clyde it was only a short walk away. What he'd actually said was it was a short run away, as if he was expecting them to have to make a sharp exit. If Mrs Sweeting was as old as Doogie thought she was, he'd have no problem outrunning her. He wasn't so sure about Colin the Wanker though. Maybe that's what Clyde meant by a distraction. Sacrificing the wanker for the greater good. The greater good being Doogie.

'She's probably a perfectly harmless old lady,' said Colin the Wanker as they approached Mrs Sweeting's house. Annoyingly, he seemed to think they were on proper speaking terms now that they'd cleared out the rotting rat corpse and the putrid milk. Doogie knew it had been a mistake to accept his lager.

'Yeah? In that case, you can do the talking.' He rang the bell and pushed Colin the Wanker to the front.

The door was opened by a tidy looking elderly woman, her grey-white hair somehow at odds with her dark, almost wrinkle-free skin. Colin the Wanker did a creepy smile. 'Mrs Sweeting?'

She gave him a quick once over. 'I'm not buying anything.' Then she slammed the door.

So much for a distraction. The wanker sighed and stepped out of the way.

Doogie tried the bell again. The door half-opened. The old lady stood, one hand on the door, the other on her hip. 'What you want?'

'Are you the widow of Samuel Sweeting?' He hadn't meant to blurt it out but this old girl was fucking scary.

'Who wants to know?'

'We've been helping to clear out Mr Sweeting's allotment shed. We found a letter addressed to Mrs Priscilla Sweeting.'

'What kinda letter?'

'It was marked to be opened in the event of his death,' said Colin the Wanker.

'We didn't open it,' said Doogie.

'You'd better come in.' She let Doogie into the hall. 'Not you.' She slammed the door shut in Colin the Wanker's face and held out her hand.

'Are you Mrs Priscilla Sweeting?'

She made a soft hissing sound. 'Of course I am. Fool.'

Doogie held out the plastic wallet. 'Sorry it's taken so long to get to you. They've only just started clearing it out.'

'What's that dirty thing you giving me? You couldn't clean it first?'

'Sorry. I'll take it out, yeah?'

'You asking me or telling me?'

'I'll take it out.' He removed it from the plastic wallet and held it out for her.

She looked at it, her arms folded. 'Clyde Wilson send you?'

'Yes.'

She took the letter, turned it over and read the back. 'You can go now.'

Doogie nodded. 'If there's anything—'

'There's nothing. Be gone.'

Colin the Wanker was waiting on the pavement for him. 'Everything okay?'

'Yeah.' Doogie set off for the allotment with Priscilla Sweeting still on his mind. There was something about that old woman that unnerved him.

24

A WOMAN WITH OPTIONS

Netta was managing a stall at a private market today. They didn't usually do these little markets anymore. Now that they had enough regular orders, they didn't need to. But this was a special favour to their longest and most loyal customer who was trying out a new venture, a Saturday morning market at the back of his café and deli in Moseley. It was a showcase of the producers that supplied his small empire of delis around the Midlands. They weren't expecting much from it, so she and Neil had agreed to split the day between them. She was doing the first shift. Neil was pencilled in to take over later. She wasn't entirely on her own though. Will had offered to keep her company, although he'd spent most of the time on his phone. 'It's quieter than I thought it would be,' he said, while still scrolling.

'It's new, and it's still early. People will probably start drifting in soon. You don't have to stay if you don't want to though.'

'No, I want to stay. Just saying, that's all.'

'At least it gives us a chance for a chat. We haven't had much time for that since you got back. I've been meaning to ask how you feel about Doogie being here.'

Will put his phone away. 'Dunno, I haven't really thought about it. Fine, I guess. I like him. Does that count?'

'Yes it does.'

'I like Frank too, by the way. He's great.'

'Okay. That's good to know.'

'Yeah, I mean, he really is great. I wouldn't mind if you two decided to move in together or get married or anything. Just so you know. I mean, that's entirely your decision. Obviously. And if you decided you preferred Doogie, that's absolutely fine too.'

'Well, it's nice to know I have your blessing should I decide to opt for either of them as my live in lover or husband, but I feel duty bound to tell you that I'm quite happy with my current situation.' Not exactly true, she had been happy with her current situation until her current situation changed and unleashed all sorts of mayhem. 'Do you want to serve this lady?'

'Sure,' said Will, looking ever so slightly sheepish.

Thankfully, a flurry of newly arrived customers put paid to any further discussion of options with regard to Netta's love life. She didn't normally subscribe to conspiracy theories, but she was beginning to think that the younger generation of her family and Frank's, were definitely conspiring to get them hitched. But if there had been any possibility of that before all this madness, and she wasn't sure there had been, then there wasn't now. Although it would appear that Doogie wasn't entirely off the cards as an alternative. From Will's point of view anyway.

The flurry soon died down and by the looks of Will, he

was building himself up to another revolutionary suggestion on the marriage front. In classic Will style he looked at his feet, then up and out into the distance. *Here we go.* She readied herself. But her preparations were unnecessary. His expression changed to a frown. 'Arianne's over there.'

Netta looked across the room and there was Arianne in an unusually pink and frothy ensemble. This was a new look for her. Usually, she wore spray on jeans and a tight T-shirt. Quite often, it was a Clash T-shirt, just like one Netta had worn back in her student days which, to Netta's mind, was always a bit suspicious. Not today though. Today she looked like an ageing ballerina who'd let herself go rather badly. Arianne hadn't noticed them. She was too pre-occupied making doe-eyes at the man whose hand she was holding. He was a big man. Big and round with a big, round, bald head and a shaggy beard. But, give the woman her due, he was at least fifteen years younger than her.

They were almost on top of the stall before she noticed Netta and Will, and unfortunately for Arianne, her new man was showing an interest in Neil's speciality Caribbean pickle. She grabbed his T-shirt and tried to pull him away. 'Leave it, Byron.'

But it seemed Byron had a mind of his own. Far from leaving it, he picked up a jar to read the ingredients.

'It's an old recipe from my partner's husband's family.' Netta put a spoonful on some crackers. 'Would you like to try it?'

'I would,' said Byron with an enthusiastic nod. Clearly his taste in pickle was better than his taste in women.

She held out the plate of crackers for him. 'And how are things with you, Arianne? Still living illegally in my ex-husband's house?'

Byron almost spat out his cracker. 'Oh. You're—'

'Yes, that's me. The woman who's having to put her ex-husband up because your lady friend seems to think it's okay to steal his property.'

Other than swallowing the remains of his cracker loudly, Byron seemed lost for words. Sadly, Arianne wasn't: 'I've put a lot of love into that house. That's worth a lot.'

Will stood up to his full height. 'Not in the eyes of the law.'

'Who the fuck are you?' Byron had found his voice.

'I'm Will Grey. Colin's son. I'm also a lawyer.'

Arianne grabbed Byron's arm. 'What about the abuse I've had to put up with? You can't put a price on that either, I suppose.'

'What kind of abuse are you alleging has been meted out to you?' said Will.

'Domestic.'

'Can you be more specific?'

'Not at this moment. Tell Colin, he'll be hearing from my solicitor.'

Netta let out a heavy sigh. 'So you keep saying.'

'Well this time I mean it. And tell him I don't appreciate him threatening me on my own doorstep either, and nor does Byron.'

'Don't you mean *his* own doorstep?' said Netta.

'No, I do not. Leave the chutney, Byron. We're going.'

They watched Arianne storm off, dragging Byron behind her. Netta rubbed Will's arm. 'You put the wind up them with that legal speak. Well done you.'

'It was all bluff. I mean, I'm not actually a lawyer. Just someone who's studied law.'

'I think you got away with it. It was very good of you to stand up for your dad like that.'

'I don't like to see people taken advantage of. I don't buy that domestic abuse line either. I guess you do though?'

'I don't know. I want to think he's changed but, you know.'

'I get it, and I understand why you think it's a possibility. But from what I saw when I was living there, I'd say it's more likely to be the other way round. And I've seen Dad a couple of times this week from a distance. He looks terrible. Can you imagine him threatening Arianne and that guy?'

Of course, it had been a good while since Will had spent any time with Colin and Arianne so he could be mistaken, but Netta remembered Liza had said pretty much the same thing. Perhaps there was something in it. 'Not really. But something has just occurred to me. I wonder if he went there on Tuesday night. That's when he got his black eye, according to Grandad's friend, Ursula.'

'You think Byron might have hit him? Do you believe in karma?'

'No. Do you?'

'Nah. Although, I guess some people might think Dad deserves it.'

A few names immediately sprung to mind. Not hers though. 'No one deserves to be treated like that. Not even your dad.'

When Neil came to take over, Will went into town to meet Belle and do some shopping for their impending holiday. Netta took a slightly circuitous route home via Colin's road and a brief stop outside his house. It had been just over two weeks since she'd been here last, and she was curious to see if anything had changed. The only obvious difference were some purple voile curtains covering the lounge windows.

Colin would be horrified if he saw them. Perhaps he already had.

Frank pulled up in his car just as she arrived home. They hadn't spoken since Thursday evening. Not even a message had crossed between them. That wasn't normal.

He took some tins of paint from the boot of his car. She took a food shop out of hers. They met in the middle of both cars.

'You're decorating again,' she said, unable to think of anything better.

'Yep. The small bedroom this time. Working my way up to the bigger rooms.'

'Good plan.' She wanted to invite him in for coffee or even to invite herself over to his but for once in the entire time she'd known him, there was a barrier that she didn't know how to cross. It might have helped if she knew what the barrier was or why it was there, but she could only speculate on both of those things because the barrier wasn't hers. It was his.

'I'd better get these in.' He smiled but it wasn't Frank's smile. Someone had snatched her Frank away and left this silly, proud idiot in his place.

'Are you coming over to dinner tonight?'

'I thought I'd stay in with Colin. Got to do my bit to help with his recovery.'

'Right. Okay. See you tomorrow morning then.'

'Sure.'

She let herself into her empty house and put her shopping away. Then she poured a glass of chilled wine, put her feet up in the garden with her phone and started a ranting message trail with her old friend Claire. She would have called her, but she didn't want to be overheard by whoever was in Frank's house.

Her message rant concluded, and her wine finished, she fetched herself another glass and put her feet back up. If Frank wanted to be an arse, let him be one. She had better things to do than worry about him. She was a woman with options. All kinds of options. According to Will anyway.

25

TWO OLD DRUNKS

Frank knew he was behaving like a first-class eejit, but he couldn't seem to stop himself. Last night, he'd vowed to sort out this ridiculous mess with Netta. On Wednesday night, he'd been angry that she could accuse him of so many things in the space of a few sentences. Truth was that he was still annoyed, but it had gone too far. People were beginning to notice. Liza, in her own inimitable way, had asked him yesterday what was up. Naturally, he didn't tell her but it did make him realise it was time to grow up, take the moral high ground and all that. Although that last bit didn't sound particularly grown up, now that he thought about it.

So there he was, all set to hold out an olive branch and then she pulled up with that attitude, like it was all his fault. He should have been thinking about how much he was missing her, even though she was just a few feet away. Instead he was thinking about how she was comparing him to Doogie and wondering just how badly he was coming off. New man Frank? What a joke. He was just the same self-conscious fool hiding away from the obvious. Doogie Chambers was here for one thing only. To take Netta away from him. He'd as much as said so at the family meeting with that comment about it being hard to get over stuff. Hard to get over Netta is what he meant. So he'd come back for her. And Frank was just standing by and letting it happen.

He busied himself preparing the small bedroom for its makeover. When that was done, he put on some music and made a start on dinner for two.

Colin came in just as he was preparing the rice. He sniffed the air. 'Mmm, that smells good. Curry?'

'Yep. Chicken.'

'Excellent. I haven't had a decent curry in ages. Have I got time for a quick shower? I'm filthy. Been cleaning out a dead man's shed. Hasn't been touched for two years.' He was extremely jaunty for a beaten-up homeless man who'd spent the day carrying out an unenviable task.

'Yeah, no problem.'

When Colin came back down, he was even jauntier. 'Anything I can do?'

'You can get some bowls and cutlery out.'

'For how many?'

'Two.'

'Okay.' He said it in that way people did when they wanted you to know they were in the middle of working out what was going on.

Frank ignored the inference. If Colin was hoping he'd spill the beans he was out of luck. 'D'you want beer or wine?'

'You can't beat a cold beer with curry.'

'My sentiments exactly. Can you get some out of the fridge?'

Frank set the food out on the table and refused to think about how wrong it felt to be getting on with Colin Grey.

Colin heaped curry and rice into his bowl and wolfed it

down. 'This is really good. There's something about curry and chicken that works so well, isn't there? I used to love the chicken bhuna at the Rajdoot. Have you tried it?'

'No. I'll make a point of trying it next time I'm in there. Have you not been in there yourself lately?'

'No, it's been off limits for about a year now. Meat and fish for a lot longer. Arianne and her mad theories. She insisted on cooking everything herself.'

'It's possible to make some great veggie meals these days.'

'Not if you're Arianne it isn't. She can turn a slice of hot buttered toast into a lump of charcoal coated with an oil slick.' Colin ripped off a piece of naan bread and used it to scoop up more curry. 'Which reminds me, Netta's cooking's improved. Her culinary skills weren't exactly as dismal as Arianne's, but they were a bit basic. I generally did the cooking.'

Frank stopped eating and gave Colin the evil eye. 'I guess that was because you weren't working all the hours to pay the bills and feed and clothe the family.' The cheek of the fella. In spite of all that he'd done to Netta, she'd taken him in, and this was how he repaid her.

'I didn't mean it as a criticism. She really couldn't cook. It didn't bother her. She found it funny. We both did. We'd have a good laugh about it actually.' Colin took a slow drink of his beer. 'This might come as a surprise to you, Frank, but we did laugh quite a lot in the early days. We did actually get on. By the way, why aren't you over there tonight?'

Frank carried on with the evil eye. He wanted Colin to know he could see that he was twisting things around to suit his own ends, just like Netta said he would. Well Frank could do that too. He could twist with the best of them if he had to. 'I thought you might want some company. It must be lonely over here on your own, night after night.' He wanted to add unloved and unwanted but that was a twist too far and Frank wasn't that cruel.

Colin's expression changed to a satisfied smirk. 'Oh I get it. You don't want to be over there. It's him, isn't it? Chambers.'

'Not true.' Shit. The twisty fecker had seen right through him.

Colin leaned back. 'Any chance of another beer?'

'Help yourself. I'll have one too.'

Colin flipped the tops off the beer bottles and handed one to Frank. 'I understand how you feel.'

'Is that so?' It was a strange kind of duel this. The two of them were dancing around each other verbally, both saying things and not saying things but still conveying the meaning.

He rolled the beer bottle in his hand. 'Personally, I tend to measure my life before and after the second coming.'

Frank snorted. 'You getting all religious on me?'

'The first coming was before she met me, when she was with him. The second was when he came back and took her from me.'

'She's not a possession,' said Frank, even though he'd been thinking virtually the same thing not that long ago.

'I know that. It was a figure of speech. Besides, it's not possible to possess Netta. Not even Chambers can do that.' Colin emptied his beer bottle and took out two more from the fridge. 'You should have seen her back then. She was sublime. Perfect in every way. But different, you know? Not like beauty-queen perfect. Different-planet perfect. Funny and quirky and so, so beautiful.'

'I can imagine.' Frank didn't like the way the conversation was going but he felt compelled to stick with it.

'So was he, unfortunately. Perfect, I mean. The kind of guy you'd expect to be a film star or something. Good looks and brooding intensity. You know the sort. What's that term? Golden couple. They were a golden couple. Everyone at uni wanted to be them or be with them, but they were in their own orbit. I don't think it was deliberate. They just didn't notice anyone else, except the chosen few, like Claire. The rest of us mere mortals could only look on in awe. Even when they broke up, they were totally consumed by each other. It was frightening to watch from the sidelines.' Colin stared at the bottle in his hand, his earlier jauntiness all gone.

'Sure, it was all a long time ago. People change,' said Frank, the doubts already piling up in his head.

'They do. Not so sure about them though. I knew she was having an affair. You can tell, can't you? They leave little traces, the unfaithful. Changes in behaviour, the smell of someone different on them.'

'I couldn't say. Ellen, my late wife, had an affair and I didn't have a clue.'

'Then you weren't paying attention, my friend. Maybe I wasn't either because I didn't, for one minute, guess who she was having the affair with. I had to wait until she was in the hospital, having just lost his baby, to find out.' He raised his bottle in the air. 'The second coming.'

They'd run out of beer and had moved on to wine. Two old drunks sitting on the floor in the living room, sorting through Frank's records.

Colin picked out an Undertones album. 'Can we play this one next?'

Frank remembered Netta saying how Colin only pretended to like her music to wheedle his way into her affections and that, given the choice, he preferred eighties pop. 'I thought Rick Astley was more your style.'

Colin giggled and hiccupped at the same time. 'I suppose Netta told you that? It was when I met her. I'd led a sheltered life. Very much under the parents' thumb. But contrary to popular opinion I like lots of different music, including punk. And by the way, there is nothing wrong with Rick Astley.'

'The man's an icon.' Frank was slurring, but at least he was sitting upright which was more than could be said for Colin who was almost lying down. There was a question he'd been wanting to ask all evening. If he didn't ask now, the opportunity would be lost. They'd be too far gone. 'Why don't you paint anymore?'

Colin shrugged. It made him slide down further so that he was very nearly horizontal. 'I don't know. I just know I can't do it.'

'Can't do it as in physically unable, or can't bring yourself to?'

'Dunno.' His eyes were almost closed now.

'C'mon. I want to show you something.' Frank pulled him up. Together they stumbled into the kitchen.

When they got to the studio door, Colin came to an abrupt halt.

Frank gave him a gentle tug. 'You won't want to miss this.'

Colin shook his head. 'Can't.'

'It's only in there.'

'Can't. Can't go in.'

Frank put his arm around him. 'I've got you. It's okay.'

It needed some persuading but eventually, Colin let Frank lead him into the studio. They took small, slow steps and stopped in front of a head and shoulders portrait.

Colin opened his eyes wide. 'It's me.'

'Yep. What do you think of it?'

'It's very good. You're very talented.'

'Not me. Liza.'

'Liza?' His voice faltered. 'Is that how she sees me?'

'It's an inspired painting.'

'Yes, it is.' He let out a single sob.

'You know, it would mean the world to her if you painted alongside her.'

'It's all cockeyed this, isn't it? Our kids shouldn't have to take care of us. At least not until we're old and infirm.'

Frank remembered all the times when his own darling girl, Robyn, had looked out for him when he was at his lowest. 'It doesn't always work that way, Colin. Sometimes you have to let the people who love you take over.'

Colin rubbed his eyes. 'What about the ones who don't love you? What are you supposed to do with them?'

26

THE PORTRAIT OF COLIN GREY

Colin had been having a nice dream about him and Netta on their wedding day. Or Annette as she'd been to him then. The vicar was just about to pronounce them man and wife when he woke up and found her looming over him. Maybe looming was an overstatement, but she was in his room which came as a shock. 'Could you not have knocked?'

'I did, but you didn't answer.'

'So you just barged in.'

'Pretty much, yes. You look as bad as Frank. Were you two on the pop last night?'

'In a manner of speaking, yes. Is there something I can do for you?'

'The others have taken the dogs for the Sunday morning walk. I thought we'd have a chat.'

Colin put his head in his hands. 'Oh God no, not a chat.'

The corners of Netta's mouth twitched. 'I'll make you a strong coffee.'

He threw on some clothes and went down to the kitchen

where coffee was waiting for him. The little dog, Maud, was with her. Thanks to his hangover, the room seemed brighter this morning. Brighter in the sunny sense of the word that this. The kitchen itself was rather dull and tired and in need of a good revamp, much like the rest of this house. If there was one thing Colin had learned about Frank O'Hare during his stay here, it was that he was not a man who cared too much about appearances. Especially when it came to his home. Shabby chic it was not.

Dust particles floated before his eyes. It made him think of the shed he'd spent the last few days cleaning. Ursula had already gone by the time he'd finished yesterday which was disappointing because he wanted to see her face when she first went in.

'We can sit outside if you like. There's no one else at home.' She meant Will. It was safe to go out there because Will wasn't at home. In truth, Colin was feeling a bit too delicate to face the sunshine, but he should take the opportunity while he was able to. And anyway, the smell of stale curry was making him feel sick.

'No one? Has Doogie gone for the walk as well then?' He was thinking of Frank, imagining how hard that would be for him. Frank hadn't admitted it last night, but Colin could tell, Chambers was stirring up all sorts of emotions in him too. And like he said last night, he understood. Frank had obviously thought he was making trouble. If it had been a year or so ago, his assumption would probably have been spot on. But a lot had happened since then and frankly, Colin didn't have the energy for trouble. He'd actually been trying to show a bit of empathy, but it was lost on Frank. Naturally. Like everyone else, Frank had long ago formed an opinion of him that was not for changing.

'Doogie had something else to do. It's just us. Shall we?'

Netta had clearly decided not to wait for his answer and already had the back door open.

They sat on a bench in the shade. It was nice to be out here in the fresh air, not worrying that he was going to offend someone's sensibilities by simply being here. He let his hand slip down to Maud and she pushed her head against it.

Netta smiled, more at the dog than him. 'She has a sense for people who are struggling. She must think you need a friend.'

He had a sudden flashback from last night, that portrait of Liza's, and took his hand away. It was bad enough that his daughter pitied him. He didn't need it from a fucking dog as well. Not taking the hint, the dog leaned against his leg. Colin considered pushing it away, but Netta caught his eye and he thought the better of it.

'I was doing a market in Moseley yesterday. I saw Arianne again.'

'Oh.' He supposed it had to happen. Netta was always doing markets in the area and Arianne, with her obsession for so-called natural foods, was bound to bump into her at some point. 'Was she on her own?'

'No. Someone was with her.'

'A big guy? Name of Shelley?'

'Byron. Wrong romantic poet.'

'Right. English was never my strongest subject.'

'You know about him then?'

'Only recently found out about him.'

'When, Tuesday?' She was putting two and two together and was about to make five.

'No. She told me about him the last time we spoke. Right before she blocked my number.'

'How did you know he was a big guy?'

Bugger. He'd given too much away. Stupid of him. No

point trying to backtrack now. He'd only dig a hole for himself. 'I've seen him.'

'On Tuesday?'

He let out a short sigh. It came out like a huff. 'Yes.'

'Colin, did he assault you?'

He thought about letting her think it was Byron but knowing Netta, she'd be all for calling the police and then he'd have to admit the truth. 'No. Can we just drop this?'

'It was Arianne, wasn't it?'

He was about to get up and walk away but the little dog jumped onto his lap. 'Can you tell your dog to get off me, please?'

'I'm afraid she has a mind of her own. I can't make her do anything.'

'She's a dog. They're supposed to be able to obey simple commands.'

Netta shrugged. 'Try telling her that. So, it was Arianne who did that to your face then.'

'It was an accident.'

'And the other bruises on your body, were they accidents as well?'

'Yes. I told you, I tripped on the stairs.' Colin's throat tightened. Invisible walls were closing in on him and taking the air away.

He felt her hand on his arm, her touch making the walls retreat. He could breathe again. 'How long have you been having panic attacks?'

'I don't have panic attacks. It's just a touch of hay fever.'

'Your heart's pounding. You feel like your chest and throat are shrinking, and there's no air left.'

'It's not like that at all,' he said but the walls were already closing again.

'I understand what it feels like.'

He moved his arm away. No she didn't. How could she?

'Shall we just sit here quietly?' she said.

'Yes, please.'

He let her take his hand. The little dog leaned up against his chest. Colin stroked its fur and listened to the sound of the world turning around him. He rested his head on Netta's shoulder and closed his eyes. How long was it since he'd been this close to her? Close enough to breathe in the scent of her. Close enough to feel her strong, steady heartbeat. Too long. Far too long.

He didn't know how many minutes or hours they'd stayed there on that bench. Time had stopped. All he knew was that his peace had been broken by the noise coming from Netta's house. The dog walkers were back. Maud slipped off his lap and he stood up. 'I'd better go back inside. Don't want to upset Will.'

Netta still had his hand. 'He's going away at the end of the week. If you want to, you can come back to stay until he gets back.'

'I think I'm good staying with Frank, if he doesn't mind. But I'd like to come over sometimes, if that's acceptable.'

'Yes, it is. You know I'm here when you're ready to talk?'

He nodded and went back into the house before he did something stupid like try to kiss her.

The stale curry odour hit him again as soon as he returned to the kitchen. Last night he'd been salivating at the thought of it. It didn't smell quite so tasty now. He scraped the dried-up leftovers into a bag and took them straight out to the bin at the front of the house.

A pretty girl with long blonde hair was going through Netta's gate. She waved at him as she walked down the path, and then he realised who she was. It was Belle, Will's girl-friend. He'd only seen her once before, about a year ago. Coincidentally, that had been the last time he and Arianne had been to the Rajdoot. Frank's daughter had come down with some friends from Edinburgh and there was a big party of them taking up the back of the restaurant. That girl had been there too. Kelly. Colin struggled to understand the hold that young woman had over his ex-wife and children. He'd tried his utmost to sow seeds of doubt in Liza's head about her, but all it got him was a warning to back off and a label. Snob. Apparently, he was a nasty snob. It was the only time he thought Liza might fall out with him.

He gave Belle a little wave back, threw the bag into the bin and scurried off before Will opened the door to her. Back inside, he tackled the dirty dishes, wiped round the worktops, and opened the windows to get rid of the remaining smells. He'd enjoyed talking to Frank last night. He'd probably said too much though. He didn't have any male friends. He didn't have any friends at all really. Arianne had been his friend once. They'd met at an art class not long after the second coming. He'd gone there for something to take his mind off Netta and Chambers. He'd always been good at drawing and painting, but it was just a hobby, until it became something to be. Something Netta might respect. What a waste of time that had been.

He looked through the open door to Frank's studio. Last night, he'd made it across the threshold, gone in there and seen Liza's painting. And what a painting. Frank had said it was inspired and it was. But it was also devastating. He needed to see it again. He needed to feel it.

He forced himself into the room, closed his eyes and breathed in. No curry smells here. Just paint, layer upon layer of it filling the room, filling his nostrils, reminding him of the person he used to be. Underneath it all, there was a different smell lingering in the air. White spirit.

The last time he'd set foot in his own studio, the day he finally gave in, was nearly three months ago. There'd been an argument because he'd turned down his usual summer residency at Lake Como. He'd known there'd be hell to pay: Arianne loved those retreats, but he'd had no choice. What good was an art teacher whose hands shook every time he got close to a canvas? She was in a rage, knocking over his paints, throwing things. And then she saw a glass jar filled with white spirit. When she'd done with venting her anger, Colin cleaned the room up, closed the door and didn't go in again.

He reopened his eyes and looked around Frank's studio. It was a small room, but Frank had managed to cram in three easels, a bench for his paints and a little café style table with two chairs. The easels each had canvases and there were another four finished paintings leaning against the wall. Frank occasionally exhibited at the same gallery as him, so he was familiar with his work. It was impressive. Wild and natural. Nothing like Colin's style.

He stopped in front of Liza's portrait. Now that he was looking at it sober, he could appreciate it properly. It was good. More than good. It was amazing. His daughter was an amazingly talented artist. How had he not known this? If anything, she was too good, because she'd captured the real Colin Grey. Not the one he wanted to be but the one he truly was. A sad, and angry man with a broken past and no future. Nasty and bitter, with all the kindness emptied out of him. That's what they'd done to him, his ex-wife and her lover. He needed to remember that instead of getting all sentimental.

Colin backed away. He had to get out of there. Away from this room, this house and the one next door. He needed to be with someone who didn't know him.

27

ARTHUR SPEAKS OUT

Luckily, Clyde was near the entrance talking to someone. Colin called out to attract his attention. Clyde acknowledged him but didn't come over straight away. That was a little annoying, but Colin knew he had no choice but to wait. He'd been coming here long enough to know Clyde would see to him when he was good and ready, and he would not be good and ready until he'd finished his extremely long and drawn-out discussion on sweet potatoes.

When he was done, the old man ambled over to the gate. 'What you doing here? Arthur doesn't come on Sundays.'

That was another thing he'd come to understand about Clyde. Not only could he talk for England, he could hold a grudge for it, too. It didn't matter that Colin had never done anything bad to him personally. It was enough that he'd offended Arthur and Geraldine. 'I was at a loose end, so I thought I'd carry on with the digging.'

'Arthur know?' For all his conversational expertise, Clyde didn't usually waste too many words on him.

'I don't think so. Should I have told him?' He was trying to play the innocent. Probably a waste of time since the miserable old sod had no interest in his innocence.

Clyde took off his hat, scratched his head and clicked his tongue. 'Okay, you can come in. I'll let Arthur know.' He fished around in his pocket and pulled out a familiar key. 'Use one of the spades in Samuel's shed. Give the key to Ursula when you're done.'

'Oh, is Ursula here?' A sudden tingly feeling pranced across Colin's chest.

'Ursula's always here.' Clyde unlocked the gate and let him get a few steps along the path before calling out: 'And no funny business.'

Colin took a deep breath. Fucking Clyde and his proxy grudge. He stuck his hand up to acknowledge the instruction and carried on walking. 'Scout's honour.'

The route through the thicket hedge was less of a squeeze since Arthur and Clyde had been cutting it back while Chambers had carried on with the digging. There were two allotments fully dug now, a third one half done and one final untouched patch. It was all coming together nicely. Not long till it was finished, and he'd have no need to come here. He wondered what new punishments his ex-in-laws had planned for him then. Perhaps they just hoped he'd be gone before they had to think of any.

Ursula was sitting on the wicker chair which was still getting an airing outside the shed. She had her eyes closed and hardly seemed to be breathing. Colin stopped far enough away not to disturb her and waited for them to flicker open. She smiled. 'You've come.'

'I thought I'd get on with the digging. Clyde says I should give you the key when I'm done. I've finished tidying it up, by the way. I suppose you already know that.'

'No. I haven't been inside yet. I thought I'd wait for you to show me. Can I see now?'

'Sure. You go first.' He unlocked the door and stood back, unable to believe his eagerness for approval from this woman.

She stood in the centre of the small shed and clasped her hands together. 'It's lovely. Just as Samuel would have liked it. You've brought him back to us. Thank you.'

'It was my pleasure.' His cheeks were instantly flooded with an intense and unforeseen heat. He looked down at his scruffy trainers and curry-stained jeans and wished he'd remembered to tidy himself up before leaving the house.

Colin was employing the double digging technique that Clyde and Arthur had taught him. You had to dig a trench to the depth of a spade and put the soil to one side, then dig out another layer in the same trench. Then you had to put the first lot of soil back in and cover it up with the second layer. It was overkill in his opinion, but he didn't want to be accused of not doing the job properly. Especially as Chambers was a star at it. You might know.

Now that he was doing something, he was feeling better. Talking with Ursula had helped. They'd only spoken about the allotment and her friend Samuel, but it had been a refreshing change not to have to analyse his own life in the forensic detail everyone else seemed keen on. He stopped digging and examined his work so far. Not bad. He was getting better. Take that, Chambers, you absolute total out and out bastard.

His thoughts turned to Will's lovely girlfriend, Belle. How gracious it was of her to acknowledge him. Will might be pretending he didn't exist, but she'd waved to him. He hadn't been invisible to her. She might persuade Will to give him another chance. You never knew. It was important to stay positive and not give up on hope.

Liza was his great hope. When everyone else had turned away from him, she'd carried on loving him. She saw something in him that no one else did. Although, judging by that portrait it wasn't necessarily what he wanted her to see. Last night, Frank said it would mean a lot to Liza if Colin painted with her. That was bullshit, because she could have painted with him any time she came to stay at his. Mind you, was it any wonder she didn't with Arianne hovering over them like some demented earth mother gone bad? All the same, Frank was probably just trying to make him feel better, or easing his own conscience for stealing someone else's daughter. One or the other. Still, Frank was a good sort really. Not many men would let their partner's ex move in with them. Colin hadn't fancied it at first, but it had worked out for the best. He couldn't stay at Netta's now. Not just because of Will, or even because Chambers was there. It was just too much. Too many feelings being aroused. Feelings that should have been shut off a long time ago.

Colin heard a movement by the hedge. He looked up and was disappointed to find it was Arthur. He'd been hoping for Ursula. He stopped digging. 'I thought you didn't come here on Sundays.'

'I've been sent on a mission to make sure you're still alive.'

He threw his arms out. 'Yes, still alive. Very much not dead.'

Arthur marched past him towards the shed. 'Geraldine's sent food and drink. She seems to believe that if you don't top yourself first, you'll die of malnutrition.'

'I thought she'd be happy to see me six foot under.'

'Yes, but not on her watch.'

'Charming.'

Arthur chose a folding chair. 'Do you want it or not?'

Colin took the wicker chair. 'Yes.'

'There's cheese and pickle, or ham and mustard.'

'I'll take the ham, if I may. I've been a bit meat-deprived lately.' Colin bit into the sandwich. Oh but it was tasty. So very, very tasty. Aside from these last three weeks at Netta's and a defiant veggie breakfast on the morning Arianne locked him out, he'd spent the last year living on the kind of slop that even vegans would turn their noses up at. If that didn't show commitment to a relationship, he didn't know what did. But even that wasn't enough. Well, he hoped Byron was enjoying her signature yellow mush as much as he had. The overgrown, sock-stealing twat. If she hadn't blocked him, he could have asked her for the recipe and knocked some up for Frank to use for his decorating. It would make great wallpaper paste.

Arthur poured out two coffees from a flask and handed one over to him.

'Thank you.' Colin's mouth was full of food. He couldn't shove it down fast enough. He was like one of those little orphans from a Charles Dickens novel. If he could leave his mouth empty for long enough, he'd probably start singing about food, glorious food.

'Don't thank me. I'd happily leave you to starve.'

Just occasionally, Arthur's affable mask slipped, and a darker side emerged. Colin remembered one time in particular. 'You slashed my tyres once. I watched you doing it from the bedroom window.'

'Count yourself lucky. I could have done a lot worse than that.'

Count himself lucky? Fat chance. 'I don't feel very lucky.'

'That's because you're a greedy, selfish prat who only ever thinks of himself.'

'Don't hold back, Arthur, whatever you do.'

'And another thing. Ursula's a nice lady. If you hurt her, I'm perfectly prepared to slash them again.'

'Very noble of you but in case you haven't noticed, I don't have a car anymore. It's been stolen from me, along with my house.'

'I'll wait till you've got one again.'

'You're old, Arthur. I can wait longer than you'll probably live before getting another one.'

'Don't be so sure. By the look of you, I'll outlive you.'

Colin fished around for a cheese and pickle sandwich. Dairy was another unacceptable luxury under Arianne's regime. 'You can be quite unpleasant sometimes, can't you?'

'Oh I can get much more unpleasant than this, believe you me. So if you're planning to do the dirty on my Netta again, think long and hard about it because next time, I won't hold back.'

'I'm not planning to do the dirty on anyone. Not even you, Arthur.'

Arthur shook his head. 'So you stood there and watched me rip your tyres open? Why didn't you come outside and try to stop me?'

Colin thought about it for a moment but didn't have an answer. Not one he was prepared to share anyway. 'Don't know.'

'Huh. I expect it's because you're a slimy coward with no backbone. Not too scared to destroy helpless women though, are you?'

Ah. It seemed he hadn't needed to worry about sharing because Arthur had worked it out for himself. The cowardly bit anyway. The rest was absolute twaddle. 'If you're referring to Netta, she was never helpless.'

'She wasn't. Not until you got your claws in her. Do you

remember when I did it? It was the same day you threw her out.'

'I didn't throw her out. It was a family decision. The kids wanted it too.'

'If you think I'm going to believe that, you're even more delusional than I thought you were. She came to us a broken woman on that day with no desire to live. You did that to her. We thought we were going to lose her.'

'I didn't know that.' Colin's thoughts shifted back to earlier when Netta had asked him about panic attacks. The way she described them, she'd completely nailed it. And the thing she said about understanding how it felt. Perhaps she really did understand. Had he really done that to her? Had she really not wanted to live?

Arthur looked at him as if he were a filthy, disgusting reptile. 'Yes, you did. It was exactly what you wanted.'

It wasn't, but there was no point in trying to explain. 'I'm sorry.'

'No you're not. You're never sorry. It's always someone else's fault with you. I rue the day she met you. She'd have been much better off with Doogie.'

'You do know the reason she dumped Chambers and went out with me was because he cheated on her, don't you?'

Arthur shook his head. 'I'm not interested in your smears. Doogie would never do anything to deliberately hurt her. He's above all that. You though. You're not even fit to stand in his shadow.'

Finally. The truth was out, and it was hardly a shock. If she had only chosen Chambers instead of him, their darling daughter would have been saved. Never mind that Colin had loved her with every fibre of his being. Or that she'd practically crucified him when she turned her back on him. Never mind any of that. The only thing that mattered was their

Netta's happiness. And as far as Arthur and Geraldine were concerned, Colin had never been the one to deliver that. No matter how hard he tried, it was never going to change. Because the only man who possessed those superhuman qualities was Doogie Chambers, the man of steel, the man of honour and integrity. The man who stole his life from him.

28

DOOGIE AND THE TOUGH OLD GIRL

Doogie was resting his stomach after the big Sunday lunch his mum had laid on. Spike was leaning against his legs. He'd hardly left his side all morning.

'He's missed you,' said Clive.

Doogie rubbed the top of his dog's head. 'It's probably home he's missing. He's used to roaming wherever he wants.' Spike wasn't the only one. They'd only been in Birmingham five days and Doogie was already starting to get that hemmed in feeling that usually came when he'd reached his tolerance threshold for city living. It was a threshold with a low setting.

'When are you going home?' said his mum.

'Not sure yet. Will you be okay to keep him for a bit longer?'

'Yes, no problem,' said Clive. 'But while I think of it, you should be out of the danger zone by the end of the week. I spoke to my vet friend. Dogs can have what they called a silent heat. That means they don't show any outward signs, like bleeding. If your lady dog was at the mating stage, that lasts for ten days at the most, so you should be in the clear by next weekend at the latest. Unless Spike's already been successful, that is.'

Spike's ears pricked up at the mention of his name, then he rested his head on Doogie's knee. If he hadn't seen it with his own eyes, Doogie would have said Spike was way too innocent for that sort of thing, but there was nothing innocent about the way he'd been giving it to Betty. 'If I'm still here by next weekend, I'll take him back. I'd better go. Gotta be somewhere.'

'Where?' said his mum.

'Gonna visit an old lady.'

'Which old lady?'

'No one you know. I only met her the other day. I'm just gonna look in on her. Make sure she's okay.'

He stopped outside Mrs Sweeting's house and cut the engine. He didn't know what he was doing here really. But he was here now, and the old lady was standing in the window. She'd seen him.

She had the door open before he reached it. 'What now? You got more letters?'

'No. I was passing. I wanted to see how you were doing after the letter.'

'Oh you wanted to see, did you? Well take a good look. There. Now you've seen you can go back to them old friends of Samuel and tell them Priscilla Sweeting is doing just fine.'

The door was about to swing shut on him. Doogie put his hand out to stop it. 'They don't know I'm here.'

She pulled it back open and looked him up and down. 'Well don't stand there messing up my step, get in.'

He edged past her. The top of her head just about reached his chest. She looked tiny against him but that didn't make her any less fierce. She closed the door behind him. 'In there.'

He went into the living room. It was a decent size, but it was crammed with furniture and ornaments. She pointed to a big sofa overloaded with cushions. 'Sit. I'll make tea.'

He sat down and looked around the room while he waited. One wall was covered with family photos. His eyes searched for one that might have Samuel in it. There was nothing on the wall but he spotted a framed picture on the mantelpiece. He got up to take a closer look and saw it was an old wedding photo. Behind it was the letter, its envelope still sealed.

Mrs Sweeting came in with a tray. 'That what you here for, to snoop around?'

He slunk back to the sofa. 'Sorry. I was just curious to see what Mr Sweeting looked like after everything I've heard.'

'What you heard? What them say?'

'That he was a good man and a good friend. A really nice guy, and a great gardener.'

'Pah. That's not much for a lifetime.'

'I wouldn't mind that for a description of my life.'

'Then you're a fool. Tek a biscuit.'

'I'm fine thanks. I had a big lunch.'

'I said tek a biscuit.'

Shit, this old girl was tough. Doogie picked out the smallest one.

She kept her eye on him to make sure he ate it. 'It's good. I make them myself. You look a bit like him. Did they tell you that?'

Doogie shook his head, his mouth still full of biscuit.

'That's probably why they sent you.'

That made sense. It was no wonder Clyde had been so sure the old woman would open the door to him.

'Not as handsome as you, though. Where's your weaselly friend?'

'We're not friends. I was just looking after him.'

'What are you, some kind of social worker?'

'Just trying to help out.'

'You want to help out, you can cut my hedge for me.'

Doogie hauled himself out of the overstuffed sofa. At last, something he could get right. 'No problem.'

Her tongue clicked. 'Not on the Lord's day. Come back tomorrow. Ten o'clock. Don't be late. Don't be early either.'

He left Mrs Sweeting with a promise to be there at ten o'clock sharp and drove around until he found a park. He picked a quiet bench to make some calls. The first was to Merrie. She preferred video calls. He didn't mind them. They'd only been seeing each other for about four years so looking at his daughter's face was still a novelty for him.

She popped up on the screen. 'Hiya. Where are you?'

'In a park. On my way back to Netta's.'

'How's it going with Liza's dad and everything?'

'Sort of okay, I think. Julie and Clive were asking about you this morning.'

'I'll message them later. I'll be there in a few days, so I'll see you all then.'

'You haven't told your mum I'm here, have you?'

'No. Oh shit, she's coming. I better go. Laters.'

Doogie caught a glimpse of Claire in the background, seconds before Merrie cut the call but she probably didn't see him. He didn't like asking Merrie to keep secrets from her, but he knew Claire too well. If she found out he was here, she'd go apeshit.

The thing about Claire was that she was very loyal and

protective towards the people she loved. She'd been Netta's friend before she'd been his. They'd only really become close after she'd fallen out with Netta over Colin the Wanker. For a couple of years they were more than friends, but it wasn't until they'd agreed to split and had a final shag for old times' sake that they accidentally made a baby together. It was around the same time that Netta had turned up in Manchester again. He hadn't known he was about to become a father until after Netta had walked out on him. He hadn't known that he almost became a father for the second time until years later when Claire and Netta reconnected. So now the two women were best mates again and Claire's protection radar was on high alert. She also knew everything about him and Netta. So, if it came out that he was here, along with the wanker and Frank she'd be on his case for making a bad situation worse.

With bad situations still on his mind, he called Grace. She answered quickly. That was good. 'I'm in the middle of something, what is it?' Okay that wasn't so good.

'Nothing. Just realised we hadn't spoken for a while.'

'Uh huh, and?'

'How are you?'

'Busy. Too busy for small talk. Are you still in Birmingham?'

'Yeah. Merrie's coming up later in the week.'

'And is that the only reason you're still there?'

'No.'

'Don't call me unless it's to say you're coming home. Then we can talk.'

On the way back to Netta's, Doogie had a message alert on his phone. He was hoping it was from Grace, although he knew that was pretty much an impossibility after their call. If Grace was mad at you, she was mad at you until you gave her a reason to stop, and saying he wasn't coming back wasn't the reason she was waiting for. He'd always liked that about her, that certainty. He'd never had it, which is probably why he managed to fuck up every relationship he'd ever had. You'd have thought he'd have learned by now, but here he was, still making the same old mistakes.

He pulled up at Netta's and checked his phone. As he'd guessed, it wasn't from Grace. It was from Merrie:

Mum knows. Netta already told her.

Shit, of course she did. What kind of a dickhead was he not to realise Netta would have been speaking to her? He tapped out a message back:

How angry is she, on a scale of one to ten?

I'd say twenty. I tried to explain why you were there but you know what she's like.

Netta's dad pulled up behind him. Doogie still found it strange calling him Arthur. He'd always been Mr Wilde when he'd visited before. He'd only been a kid back then though. If things had worked out with him and Netta, they'd have eventually progressed to the stage where it was natural to call him Arthur. Maybe they'd be so far along the scale of familiarity that he might even be calling him Dad. That would have been the stuff of his dreams at one time. Except none of that happened, thanks to his own stupidity. And now Doogie was back here, trying to behave like there hadn't been a gap of more than thirty years since the days when he thought Mr Wilde was probably the best dad in the world, and trying to act like he didn't still hold the man in awe.

Doogie and Arthur got out of their cars at the same time. Colin the Wanker took longer to drag his arse off Arthur's passenger seat. He smiled at Doogie. For some reason, he seemed to have got it into his head that they were friends. Doogie didn't return the smile but that didn't stop the wanker from talking to him: 'I've been up at the allotment. Done a bit more digging.'

'Right.'

'Yeah, it's really starting to take shape now.' The wanker looked down at the ground.

'Great.' Doogie turned to Arthur. 'I can't come tomorrow. I've got something on.'

Colin the Wanker looked like he wasn't too unhappy about that. 'Is it work?'

'Not exactly.' Now it was Doogie's turn to look away, except he was more for looking over a person's shoulder than shoegazing.

'I'll see you tomorrow then, Colin.' Arthur stared at the wanker until he got the message.

'Oh right. Yes, okay. I'll bugger off then, shall I? My presence not required.'

'Exactly. Try to get through the night without doing any harm to yourself or anyone else, won't you?' said Arthur.

'Rest assured, I'll do my utmost not to cause you any further trouble.'

'Everything okay between you two?' said Doogie, when Colin the Wanker had gone.

'Things haven't been okay between us two for years, but if nothing else, becoming his minder has loosened my inhibitions when it comes to speaking my mind. I'm a liberated man, Doogie. Everything all right with you?'

'Yeah. About tomorrow, I'm going to cut Mrs Sweeting's hedge. I just didn't want to say in front of him.'

'Enough said. I must have got it wrong, I thought she wasn't very welcoming.'

'She wasn't but I dropped by today, to see how she was. The letter must have come as a shock.'

'And how was she?'

'Still unwelcoming. But she did ask me to come back to cut the hedge, so I guess I'm growing on her.'

Arthur went straight off without going into the house. Poor guy probably wanted a quiet night in without having to babysit a man he couldn't stand. Doogie felt bad about not stepping up more, especially as that was why he was supposed to be here.

As he walked up the path, he got a message from Claire ordering him to call her. Yeah right, like that was gonna happen.

Netta was in the garden with Frank. They had faces on them like an old married couple who just about tolerated each other. From what she'd told him about their relationship, it wasn't how Doogie had expected them to behave. He guessed it was the current situation that was screwing things up with them. Only thing he couldn't pin down was whether it was him or the wanker that was doing the screwing up.

Netta looked as if she couldn't decide if she was happy or sorry to see him. Her face eventually settled into a smile so that probably meant she was happy. 'Hi. Good day?'

'Yeah. You?'

'Sort of.' She flashed a look at Frank. 'I've found out something worrying about Colin.'

'What, just the one thing?'

She did an eye roll. 'I think it was Arianne who gave him the black eye.'

Doogie took a seat. 'Okay.'

'Okay? Is that all you have to say?'

'What do you want me to say? The guy's had it coming for

years. He probably tried to do the same to her that he did to you, but she wouldn't stand for it.'

'Oh and I would, I suppose.'

'I didn't say that.'

'No, but you insinuated it.'

'You misinterpreted it.'

'No I did not.' She jumped up and stormed off into the house.

Doogie scratched his head. 'What is it with that woman?'

Frank shrugged. 'I have no idea.'

29

THE REAL SAMUEL SWEETING

'Tek a biscuit.' Mrs Sweeting shoved the plate under Doogie's nose. He didn't really want one but after yesterday, he decided it was best to just take it.

'You want tea, coffee or lemonade?'

'Tea's fine.' He'd have said water but as far as he could see, Mrs Sweeting was easily offended and he'd already offended one woman in the last twenty-four hours. Actually two, if you counted Claire whose calls he was avoiding.

He was standing next to the hedge, juggling some ancient garden shears, the biscuit, and the T-shirt he'd just pulled off because he was sweating, while trying to decide whether he was supposed to sit in one of the green plastic garden chairs.

The old lady came back out with two drinks. She put them on the sun-faded but spotless green plastic table, sat down and pointed to a chair. 'Tek a seat.'

That was his question answered then. He left the shears on the grass and sat down.

He hadn't even finished the biscuit before she pushed the plate over to him. 'Tek another one.'

'I should be getting back on. It's a big hedge.'

'Is it too much for you?'

'No. There's just a lot of it and you've only got these old shears. It's gonna take a while.'

'You got somewhere to be?'

He shook his head. 'No, I was just saying.'

Mrs Sweeting nodded at the plate. 'You got time for a break then.'

Doogie sighed and took another one. Now he had one and a half biscuits to finish. Actually, they were pretty good. They tasted like fig rolls. It made him think of Mary who'd lived next door to them when he was a kid in Nottingham. She'd loved fig rolls. Whenever he went round there, which was a lot, she used to have a packet waiting for him. They were a little family, his mum, Mary and him. When she died, it was like losing a nana.

'I suppose you'd better tell me your name,' said the old woman.

'Doogie. Doogie Chambers.'

'Doogie? That your real name?'

'It's Dougal. Dougal Macrae Chambers to be exact. But I usually go by Doogie.'

'Hah! I can see why. Where you from?'

'Nottingham originally, but I live in Scotland now. Right up in the Highlands.'

'What's a man like you doing living all the way up there?'

'I like it. My family's from there. My mum's side that is.'

'And what about your father, where's his family from?'

'St Kitts. He's moved back there now.'

'You see him much?'

'Not really.' Fucking hell, this was like being under interrogation.

'You don't get on.' It wasn't a question, so Doogie didn't feel the need to answer.

'I said you don't get on?'

Ah, so it was a question then. Doogie shrugged. 'We're not close.'

The old woman sat back in her chair and folded her arms. She was waiting. Doogie knew what she was waiting for and even though he didn't want to, he found himself giving it to her. 'He had another family. He lived with them. Me and my mum had to fit in around it, until she decided she'd had enough.'

'And you felt left out?'

'I suppose so, when I was a kid. I don't really think about it now.'

'That so. Well you're lucky it hasn't affected you. It's hard for a boy to grow up without a father. It's hard for girls as well, but boys need a man around.'

'Only if he's the right kind of man.' Doogie was thinking about Arthur Wilde and his stepdad, Clive. They were the right kind of men. It wasn't that his dad was a bad man. He paid his taxes, never broke the law and tried to behave like a real father, but he had too many conflicts. Conflicts lead to casualties. And the casualties always seemed to be on Doogie and his mum's side. They were always the ones having to drop everything because Nevin Chambers had turned up without notice, having found an hour to squeeze them in between his other commitments. Doogie was always the one who had to go to his dad's other house and mix with his other family, even though they teased him for being too white and even though his dad's wife hated his guts.

Mrs Sweeting swilled the tea around in her cup and watched it slopping from one side to the other. 'Them people at the allotment, they all think Samuel was the right kind of man.'

'Wasn't he?'

She put the cup down. 'Let me tell you about Samuel. Not their Samuel, my Samuel. He was a waste of space. We had four children. Three girls and a boy. You'd think being a father to that many kids would keep a man occupied, wouldn't you? But not Samuel. He had another family as well, and he preferred their company to ours.'

'He had another family?'

She clucked her tongue. 'Not that kind of family. Them friends of his at the allotment, they were his family. He spent every spare minute with them. His precious vegetables meant more to him than his own children. You know, he'd bring home a few peppers and tomatoes and put them on the table like he was God on the sixth day. Never mind that his son was smoking pot and his daughters were tekking up with unsuitable men. All he cared about was the allotment association. And that woman.'

'Woman?' Doogie already had a fairly good idea which woman she was referring to but he asked anyway.

'Ur-su-la. I told him, you think me an idiot, you think me can't see the way your eyes light up at the mention of her name? She was welcome to him. Let him waste her time. Mine was already full-time tekken up with keeping my kids out of trouble.'

'Are they all right then, your kids?'

'You could say that, but no thanks to Mr Samuel Sweeting. The pastor sorted my boy out. He's an estate agent now in Milton Keynes. He visits me every month and cuts the hedge. You've saved him a job. The two oldest girls are divorced and the youngest never married. They're very intolerant in that regard. I suppose that was one thing Samuel did for them.'

She threw the last of her cold tea into the flower border. 'You'd better carry on, Doogie.'

He picked up the shears. 'Yeah. Thanks for the tea and biscuits, Mrs Sweeting.'

She nodded. 'You can call me Priscilla.'

She was warming to him. The thought made him smile. 'Priscilla.'

'You do remind me of him a bit.' She held his eye for a minute then snatched up the plate. 'But I won't hold it against you.'

'Did you read the letter?' he said, as she started to head back into the house.

She stopped but didn't turn back to him. 'Not yet. Me probably won't bother.'

30

THIS IS HOW IT WOULD HAVE BEEN

Netta was in the lounge, on the phone to Claire. 'The thing is, I'm not really sure why Doogie's here. Has he said anything to you?'

'I haven't spoken to him. I've tried, but he's ignoring my calls. I could pump Merrie for information, but it doesn't seem fair,' said Claire.

Netta moved the phone a bit further away from her ear. They'd been talking for over half an hour, and it was starting to feel sweaty and clammy. 'No, it wouldn't be right. I'm going to have to ask him myself at some point. Not that I haven't already, but he keeps giving me that rubbish about fancying a change.'

'Have you tried his mum?'

'I don't know her number and I haven't spoken to her for years. Not since our uni days. It would be a bit weird if I called her up to check whether her son was lying to me or not.'

'True. I don't really know her either, thanks to Doogie and his secrets. The poor woman didn't know she had a granddaughter until he finally decided to step up and become a proper dad.'

'Anyway, she's on holiday which is why he's staying with me.'

'Really? She called Merrie last night. Must have been from wherever she's staying. Actually, thinking about it, I might introduce myself next time I'm up there. Now that she's playing a part in my daughter's life, we should get to know each other better.'

Netta heard a car pull up out the front. She checked through the window. 'Good idea. He's just come back. I'd better go. I'll keep you informed.'

She opened the front door to let him in and eyed the carrier bags in his hands. 'Been shopping?'

'I thought I'd cook tonight's dinner. A thank you for putting up with me. Is that okay?'

'Sure. Are you going home then?'

'No, not yet. Unless you've had enough of me?'

'Don't be daft, of course I haven't.'

Now would have been the perfect time to ask him what he was sticking around for, or even why he'd come in the first place, but she'd hesitated too long. He already moved past her and was on his way to the kitchen. 'Merrie's coming in a couple of days so I'm sticking around for a bit longer. Do you think Frank'll be coming over for dinner?'

'I don't know. I'll check.'

'Cool. I'll take a shower first. Been doing some gardening for an old lady.'

'Anyone I know?'

'Don't think so. You know that letter we found at the allotment? It's the lady we delivered it to.'

'Oh, that's nice of you.'

'Not really. I just…' He screwed his face up.

'Just what?'

'I dunno. You remember my dad's wife, Monique?'

'You hated her.'

'Yeah. Priscilla, the old lady, reminds me of her.'

'Oh! But you're still helping her out.'

'I know. Mad or what?'

The doors to Frank's studio were wide open and Fred was lying across the gap. He lifted his head wearily, as if it was too much effort. Netta patted it as she stepped over him and he let it flop back down to the floor. She could hear music coming from upstairs. Frank had said he was painting one of the bedrooms, so she guessed that's where he was. It was all part of his new life plan, now that he'd retired. It began with putting his own stamp on the house he'd neglected for years and spending more time on his art. He'd shared all that with her when he'd returned from his epiphany-style road trip at Easter. Was it really only a few months ago that everything had seemed so straightforward and simple? And was it only yesterday that she'd been sitting in the garden, wondering who this man was that she'd been sharing her life with?

It had been his reaction to the revelations about Colin and Arianne that had done it. She'd told everyone when they got back from the walk. Will's lack of surprise came as no surprise given that he'd already hinted at something along those lines. Liza had also suggested it, but she still blamed herself, despite everyone's assurances to the contrary. Netta's mum and dad said very little, but it was highly likely they thought Colin had it coming. Frank had said almost the same thing, word for word, as Doogie. Maybe it was because his late wife, Ellen, had been quite unstable that Netta had assumed he'd have some sympathy for Colin. She'd assumed incorrectly. When

Frank had said it, she'd been annoyed. Partly at his lack of sympathy, but mostly because he'd managed to insinuate that she was somehow less of a person than Arianne for not putting up more of a fight with Colin. She'd let it ride when he said it, but all afternoon, she could feel the aggravation festering like a simmering pot.

It took Doogie to make her erupt. Wasn't it always the way? He was probably the only man she ever really lost it with. That was how it worked with them. But it didn't feel like a bad thing. It felt like an honest thing. Within an hour of him saying it, they were friends again. That didn't stop her resenting the suggestion that she was weak, but for some reason, her resentment had settled entirely on Frank. Perhaps it was because the way she and Doogie dealt with differences was big, loud and fast. But she and Frank didn't have that confrontational aspect to their relationship. Frank wasn't an arguer. The boat didn't rock. But keeping it on an even keel had its own risks. Unspoken words were in danger of festering if left unsaid. Back to that simmering pot again.

A painting caught her eye as she made for the kitchen. It wasn't Frank's usual style, but the subject was unmistakeable. It was Colin. She moved nearer to get a closer look, then wished she hadn't. She did a sudden, sharp intake of breath. It was the eyes that got to her. Fear, despair and exhaustion with a hint of cruelty and spite. The sum parts of Colin Grey right now. Just looking at it filled her with sorrow, and when she saw the initials in the bottom corner, she almost cried. It wasn't Frank who'd painted it. It was Liza. She pulled herself away before it got to her completely and went to find Frank.

As she reached the top of the stairs, she saw him in the room opposite. He had his back to her, running a roller up and down the wall. Van Morrison was turned up loud and he was singing along, unaware that she was watching him. She smiled, despite herself and stayed there until he turned and saw her. He grinned at her and her heart swelled. But she'd caught him by surprise, and it was an all too brief unguarded moment. Within seconds his expression had changed and this time, her heart shrank just a little bit.

'It's looking good,' she said, all at once feeling embarrassed.

'It'll need another coat but definitely an improvement.'

'Are you coming over for dinner tonight? Doogie's cooking.'

'I thought I'd stay in. Keep an eye on Colin. After what you said yesterday about him and Arianne.' It was obvious he'd just reached for that last bit because it was a handy excuse.

'Okay then. If that's what you want.' She took a step down, then remembered that simmering pot. 'How long are you going to keep this up?'

'Keep what up?'

If that blank face was him trying to make out, he didn't know what she was talking about, it was a pretty poor attempt. She moved her head slowly from side to side. 'I'm going. Let me know when you've grown up enough to talk this over like an adult.'

She went back out the way she came, careful to avert her eyes as she passed the shocking portrait. Her emotions were already up in the air, she didn't need to fuel them further.

Doogie was in the kitchen, chopping up vegetables. 'Is Frank coming over?' he said without taking his eyes off the food.

'No.'

He looked up at her then. 'You all right?'

She nodded, breathing in short, angry breaths.

He put down the knife and wrapped his arms around her.
'Frank, or Colin?'

'Frank.' She rested her head against him.

He held her tighter. She slid her arms around his waist.
This is how it would have been if things had worked out for
them. There would have been no Frank, no Colin. Just her
and Doogie. But life was never that simple, was it?

31

WHAT IF AND WHAT WAS

It was warm enough to eat outside. Liza, Will and Belle were all at home, so it was dinner for five. It should have been dinner for six, but Frank was too busy being obstinate to join them. It didn't seem to bother the kids that he wasn't there, so Netta was determined that it wasn't going to bother her either.

Doogie was surprisingly relaxed in the company of her children. After she'd married Colin, she'd sometimes fantasised about her and Doogie never splitting up. In her dreams they'd be living in some trendy flat in London. Never did those dreams include children. When they ran into each other again in Manchester, the affair was inevitable, and the fantasies changed. This time she dreamed about her and Doogie bringing up Liza and Will. But a dream was all it was. Because she knew Colin would have done everything in his power to stop her taking the children away from him, and she was certain that Doogie wasn't ready to have kids in his life. So when she found out she was pregnant, she finished it. She broke his heart in order to save her own. Except that no one was saved, and here was Doogie Chambers behaving like a family man who'd always had kids in his life. If she'd been brave enough back then to leave Colin, perhaps this would have been exactly how it was.

Colin was featuring a lot in her thoughts lately. Too much really. It was funny. In all the time she'd known him, she never really felt like she actually knew him. To be honest, she hadn't really wanted to scratch beneath the surface, because for the best part of their married life and even after they'd divorced, the surface was unpleasant enough. But that top layer was gone. Shattered by Arianne, she suspected. The man who used to be her husband had been stripped bare, and now Netta had no choice but to see Colin as if she were seeing him with fresh eyes. He was a thing to be pitied. He'd loathe that if he knew. Probably accuse her of belittling him again. Had she belittled him back then? If she had, it hadn't been intentional, but then we could all say that about the distasteful things we've done. If Colin ever actually admitted the things he'd done to her were wrong, he'd probably say he hadn't meant to be so malicious. She should hate him really. She used to. But hatred is such an exhausting state to exist in, and besides, she had cared about him once. Enough to marry him and have his children. Maybe that was why she couldn't turn her back on him now.

'Hey, Mum, you wanna come into Kings Heath with us?' said Will.

She dragged herself back into the conversation. 'Sorry?'

He rolled his eyes and laughed. It reminded her of Colin when they first moved in together. He used to do the same whenever she had one of her many cooking disasters. There was no edge to it then though. Back in those days, she could do no wrong.

'Do you want to come to the pub?'

'Oh no, thanks. I've had a long day. You go ahead.'

'Okay. Doogie?'

Doogie shook his head. 'Nah, I'm good, thanks man. Cheers for asking though.'

They stayed in the garden after the young people had gone. Just her, Doogie and the dogs. From where they were sitting, she could see the back of Frank's house. She wondered if he was watching them now. Perhaps the two of them were. Frank and Colin, both watching together. She couldn't decide which one of them disliked Doogie the most. You'd think it would be Colin, but it was hard to judge lately.

'They're great kids,' said Doogie.

'They are, but they're not really kids anymore.'

'I guess not. Do you know what I was thinking earlier?'

She shook her head. She didn't want to know. Because whatever it was, it was going to churn her up.

'I was thinking, what if you and me had stuck it out? What if we'd worked things out with Colin over the kids, would we be a family now?'

Yes, she was right. She was churning up. 'Well, Liza would have been happy to have Merrie for a sister.'

'If I'd been around to look after you, she might have had two sisters.'

She put her hand up to stop him. 'Don't.'

He sighed. 'You wanna know what else I was thinking?'

The answer, of course, was not if it had anything to do with their baby. All the same, she couldn't bring herself to say it.

'I was thinking that if Will and Liza hadn't had Colin around, they'd be different people. Maybe not so great.'

'Okay. I wasn't expecting that. Does that mean you're warming to him then?'

'Fuck no. I still think he's a manipulative wanker. I'm just saying he probably wasn't a complete bastard when it came to the kids.'

'Well, that's all right then. I was worried you'd gone soft for a minute.'

His phone rang. He picked it up off the table. 'Sorry, I need to…' He gestured towards the house.

'Work?'

He nodded and answered the call as he walked inside. It was a lie. She'd seen the name that came up. It was Mum.

She got up and paced around the garden. Doogie was no better than Frank. He talked about Colin being manipulative, but he wasn't averse to playing a few mind games himself.

She turned and saw Frank looking on from his studio. Right. That was it. She strode through the gate into his garden and stood on the other side of the French windows. Frank shifted uncomfortably, and well he might. He opened the door, somewhat reluctantly she thought. Her hands found a place on her hips. 'Is there a problem?'

'No, I was just checking the weather.'

'Oh right. Only it looked very much like you were spying on us.'

'Spying? That's a bit melodramatic, isn't it?'

'What would you call it then?'

'I wouldn't call it anything.'

Her arms magically folded themselves together. They had a life of their own now that she was back in angry-woman mode. 'Where's Colin?'

'I dunno. He hasn't come back yet.'

'I see. So you've been skulking in here alone, like some seedy peeping Tom.'

'I didn't want to interrupt your tête-à-tête.'

'Our tête-à-tête? You know, I never really had you down as the jealous type, Frank. I thought you were far too modern a man for that. Looks like I got you wrong. Glad I found out before it was too late.'

'I'm not the jealous type,' he called after her as she stormed off for the second time that day.

She spun back round. The hands were on the hips again. 'Is that so? Well from where I'm standing, you're looking pretty fucking jealous. And I'm not having it. I am not having it at all.'

32

CLOSE ENCOUNTERS OF THE RUNNING KIND

This was absolutely not how Frank's new life was supposed to begin. There should have been celebrations, partying and such like. Actually, not partying, seeing as he'd specifically requested no partying. But a quiet dinner, a toast to acknowledge the end of one life and the start of another. That would have been nice. And what had he got? Well, none of the aforementioned. Obviously. The best Netta could muster was allegations, followed by more allegations. Without a doubt, this new life of his was all going to shite.

He was feeling awful. Hardly surprising given that he'd not slept a wink all night. By rights he should still be in bed, trying to catch up, but that would have been a pointless exercise because after yesterday's personal attacks, there was no way he'd be dropping off any time soon. Attacks which were completely unfounded, by the way. According to the woman who was following her ex-lover around like a love-struck teenager, not only was he behaving like a child, he was also consumed with jealousy. How dare she? How fucking dare she? And as for her complete U-turn with regard to Colin?

Unbelievable! One minute she's having a pop at him for feeling sorry for the fecker and the next, she's giving him evils, just for saying what Geraldine and Arthur were obviously thinking. And Frank absolutely stood by what he'd said. Because maybe, just maybe, Arianne had given Colin a robust dose of karma. Not that Frank condoned violence and not that Colin was ever violent towards Netta, as far as he knew. But maybe for once, the man would see what it was like to be on the receiving end of a malevolent force. Although it had to be said, it didn't look like Colin was showing any contrition in that regard whatsoever.

Frank put on his trainers. Malevolent forces or not, he was going for a run. Even if he did feel like a mangled turd, he was not going to let this business ruin his journey to fitness.

Fred was waiting at the front door, just in case Frank was thinking of going without him. He was a good running mate, as long as he didn't get distracted which was a reason enough to go early before the park got too full.

Frank kept his eyes straight as they trod the few precarious steps from the house to the street. It was too early for anyone to be leaving Netta's, but you never knew. He started with a steady jog and kept it at that pace all the way to the park. Once he'd let Fred off his lead, he picked up speed. When he'd first started this running business, he'd barely made it around the park without having to walk part of the way. Now he could do three or four laps without feeling tired. For a man who was never previously disposed to any kind of sport, that gave him a peculiar sense of pride.

The park was as empty as he'd hoped it would be. Just a lone runner on the other side of the loop and a woman with a little dog that Fred showed no interest in. The runner was going at a decent pace. It wouldn't be long before they lapped Frank, but that didn't bother him. He wasn't into all that macho competitive rubbish, especially when it came to exercise. Before all this madness, he'd have said he wasn't into it in any shape or form, but now he wasn't so sure.

He was three-quarters round his first lap when the other runner caught him up. Fred, who until then had been running at Frank's side, peeled off and turned his attention to the person who was just a few paces behind.

'All right, mate.' Doogie Chambers slowed down and gave Fred some fuss.

Bollocks. He should have paid more attention before it was too late to head right back out of the park, unspotted. Frank wasn't sure whether to stop and acknowledge the man's presence or carry on. He opted for carrying on, went a few paces, then changed his mind and stopped. 'I didn't realise it was you.'

'Same here. Mind if I join you?'

'I might slow you down.'

Doogie shrugged. 'Slow's fine. This a new thing for you, is it?'

Frank started up again. 'Uh huh. Trying to get fit. You been running long?'

'Most of my life. It's an easy way to stay healthy and it's a good time to do some thinking.'

'I wouldn't know. My thinking's mostly whether I'll get around before my lungs collapse.'

'You'll get past that. Then you can let your mind drift off to other things.'

Frank immediately began imagining the sort of things Doogie's mind would drift off to and most of them involved Netta. Although technically, Doogie did have a partner. 'How's Grace doing?'

'She's okay. Busy with the farm and the tourists.'

'Nice lady. She reminded me of Netta.'

'Interesting.'

Frank was expecting him to say something else, but he didn't, he just carried on running without even breaking his stride. He'd said it to make it clear that he could see right through the fella, but now he felt like a bit of a nob for saying it and he was in something of a dilemma as to what to say next.

Doogie saved him the pain of further digging himself into a hole. 'Net was a bit pissed off with you last night.'

Ah right, so he'd taken the pain away with one hand and given Frank a different pain with the other. Talk about devious. And they said Colin was a sly fecker. 'I don't think that's any of your business.'

'Got yer. Only I thought, as we were talking about our women, it was okay to mention it.'

'Well it's not.'

'I guess not. Just so we're clear, it's also not okay to suggest that I'm only with Grace because you think she bears a passing resemblance to Netta.'

Yet again, Frank was the one left feeling like a nob. He was out of his league here, but he still couldn't let it lie. 'Okay. But I don't get why you're here.'

'Not my problem, mate.'

No, Frank didn't suppose it was. 'Point taken,' he said begrudgingly.

'Yeah? Take this point as well while you're at it. It's not me that messes with Netta's head. Stop being a dick and focus on the real problem.' Doogie slowed down. 'Try thinking that one over. I'm heading back. See yer.'

Netta's car was gone by the time Frank got home. She normally went to the foodbank on Tuesday, so it was a bit early for her to have left, but she sometimes popped into work beforehand. Frank was relieved. After running a few extra laps, his earlier anger had fizzled out. Now he was only mildly indignant. Although the source of his indignation was hard to pin down. Sometimes it was Netta, sometimes it was Doogie, and sometimes it was Colin. One way or another, they all had their part to play. Much as he'd wanted to ignore Doogie's advice, he had done some thinking and had come to the conclusion that he didn't agree with him. Whether Doogie believed it or not, he was messing with Netta's head. So was Colin. That went without saying. But so was Frank, and before he could face her, he had to face himself and work out why.

He opened the front door and let Fred off his lead. Colin was moving about upstairs. He'd come back late, long after Frank had gone to bed. He had no idea where Colin had been, but it probably wasn't somewhere good.

Liza appeared on the drive, just as he was about to close the door. 'Hey. I've been looking out for you. I wanted to check it was okay to come round and finish off that painting later.'

'Of course it is. You don't need to ask.'

She shrugged. 'I didn't know, what with you and Mum falling out and everything.'

'Oh, she told you that, did she?'

Liza snorted. 'Of course not. We kind of guessed though. Is it Doogie?'

'No.'

'Dad then? Something's making you weird.'

'You think I'm being weird?'

'Er, yes!'

'I don't think I'm being weird.' He was about to say it's everyone else but one look at her face changed his mind.

'Frank, in what way do you think your behaviour is

normal? Wait. Oh my God, you don't even know you're doing it, do you? You have so got to look at yourself in the mirror right now. And I thought my dad was in denial. I'll be over around eleven. Maybe use the time to think about it, yeah?'

Frank's lips clamped together. He was aware that his brow probably looked like a newly ploughed field. So far this morning, he'd been called a dick and a weirdo in denial. And apparently, he needed to think about what he'd done. Quite a day of it, considering it wasn't even eight-thirty.

33

GO, TEAM NETTA

Frank liked to jump in the shower straight after a run, but Colin had beaten him to it. It was yet another annoyance to add to his tally of annoyances that morning. He went up to his bedroom and did some stretches while he waited. Colin was still in the bathroom when he'd finished stretching, so he stripped down to his shorts and checked himself out in the mirror. Not that he was vain or anything but since starting this healthy lifestyle, he liked to keep track of the size of his paunch on a regular basis. It was definitely slimming down. When he'd been staying at Grace's farm on that Scottish trip, he'd been painting on the beach when he saw Doogie out running. The sight of him moving like a gazelle across the sand had been enough to blast Frank's confidence to pieces. Next to Doogie Chambers, he'd felt like one seriously fat old fuck. He still had a way to go before he was properly fit, but he was on the right path now. He'd liked to have said standing next to Doogie no longer made him feel like an inferior species, but he wasn't quite there yet.

At last, Colin vacated the bathroom. Frank grabbed a

clean towel and zipped in. He muttered a curse when he saw the empty shampoo bottle. Fucking Colin got through shampoo like nobody's business. What the hell did he do with it? He went to the back of the cabinet for his secret stash of the special stuff he kept for when Netta stayed over and felt a twinge of regret stabbing his heart. He thought of last night, those gorgeous eyes of hers flashing at him, blue like a summer's midnight and so angry, and wondered if she'd ever stay over again.

Colin was making coffee and toast. Frank poured some granola into a bowl, went to the fridge and did another silent curse when he pulled out the milk. That too was nearly all gone.

Colin gave him a guilty look. 'I'll go to the shops this morning and top up on supplies.'

'Aren't you supposed to be at the allotment?'

'No, not today. Arthur has something on. I may go later on my own.'

'Liza's coming over around eleven to finish your portrait.'

Colin nodded.

'You were late last night.'

'Keeping tabs on me?'

'No. I happened to be awake.'

'Don't worry I was staying out of trouble.' The petulance of the man. You'd think he was fifteen not fifty-something. It would have come as no great surprise if he'd stormed off to his bedroom in a strop. As it was, he slugged down the coffee and made himself another one with the last of the milk.

Frank bit his tongue, picked up his breakfast and went outside to eat it in the sunshine before any more grievances could be added to the tally.

You might know the other bane of his current life was out there. Over in Netta's garden, Doogie was walking up and down, talking on the phone, a cup of something hot in his other hand. Probably coffee. Doogie Chambers was making coffee with Frank's machine. The machine that Netta had bought specifically for him. There you go then. More fresh outrage. He just couldn't get away from it.

Doogie finished his call and stood for a few minutes, staring into space. Then he walked up to Frank and sat down next to him. Frank noted he hadn't asked if it was okay to do so. That tally was getting pretty long now.

'You know, we should be working together.' Doogie put his mug down on the table.

Frank couldn't resist a sneaky look. As he suspected, it was coffee. Fecking cheek of the man. 'In what respect?'

'To get shot of that wanker. You do want to get rid of him, don't you? I know I do.'

Colin let out a loud cough. 'I'm only in here. I can actually hear you.'

Doogie kissed his teeth. 'Well then get out here, wanker.'

'I can't. Will might come out.'

'He's gone to his girlfriend's.'

Colin came outside. 'And if you don't mind, I'd rather you didn't call me a wanker.'

'Accountant wanker then.'

'How about cutting out the wanker bit altogether? And for your information, I stopped being an accountant years ago.'

Doogie pushed a chair towards Colin with his foot. 'Yeah, I know.'

Colin pulled the chair a bit further away and sat down, not looking entirely comfortable. All the same, he couldn't seem to resist the sarcasm: 'Oh I see. It was just a little joke, was it?'

Doogie turned his head towards him. Frank couldn't see his expression but, judging by the way Colin shrank back, it was probably sinister. 'When are you going back to your own house?'

'Surely you're not bored of me already?' Colin was clearly trying to brazen it out. In Frank's opinion, that was a mistake.

'Mate, I've been bored of you since the first time I laid eyes on you.' Ouch. Frank almost felt for Colin.

Colin flinched then tried to hide it with a sneery little laugh. 'Kick a man when he's down, why don't you?'

Doogie sucked the air through his teeth again. 'The problem with wankers like you is you see being down as an opportunity. You'll do anything to milk every last drop of sympathy out of Netta and bleed her dry.'

'I won't. You've got me all wrong. It's not like that.'

'It had better not be. Because if you try to fuck her up again, I'm coming after you.'

So that was what Doogie was doing here. Word must have got to him, and he was here to protect Netta. He was doing the job Frank should have been doing, if only Frank hadn't been behaving like a nob of the highest order. He gave Colin his hardest stare which arguably was probably nowhere near as hard as Doogie's, but he was new to this intimidating looks business. 'And I'll be right beside him.'

Colin stood up and stuck his fist in the air. 'Go, Team Netta.' Then he hotfooted it inside, presumably in case Team Netta battered the living daylights out of him.

A few minutes later, they heard the front door slam. 'He'll be back. He's got nowhere else to go,' said Frank.

'We need to get him back into his own place.'

'You're right, but I don't know how. He seems to be happy with the current arrangement.'

'He's not the only one. Everybody's getting a bit too used

to the current arrangement. It's like they've accepted him being here. You know what I mean?'

'I do.' Frank hadn't seen it before, but now that he'd had it pointed out to him, it was obvious. Everyone was just getting on with things as if it was the most natural thing in the world to have Colin here. Including Netta and including him. And the thing was, the more they got used to it, the easier it was for Colin to get inside their heads and spoil everything. And one thing was plain to see, he'd already got into Netta's head. 'If we're going to change things, we need to get Netta back onside.'

'Yeah. So I guess that means you're going to have to apologise to her then.'

Ah. Frank hadn't thought of that.

34

THERE WERE ALWAYS TWO SIDES TO A STORY

Shits, the pair of them. Thick as bloody thieves. Foolishly, Colin had thought he and Frank were getting along just fine. Saturday night, when they'd got drunk together, had felt like a turning point. Not that he could remember everything that was said, owing to the huge amount of alcohol he'd drunk, but he was fairly sure they'd reached an understanding. And while living with your ex-wife's new partner, being banned from seeing your oldest child, and having to put up with snide remarks from your ex-parents-in-law wasn't ideal, Colin was actually beginning to enjoy the camaraderie of sharing with another guy. It was almost like being back at uni. Although the guys he shared with then weren't really the kind of people he'd wanted to spend time with. Needless to say, he'd dropped them as soon as he left Manchester. But Frank was different. He actually liked Frank. Frank would have been the kind of housemate Colin would have given good money to share with at uni. Trust Chambers to take it all away from him. Again.

He was heading for the allotments. He should be shopping to replace all the things he'd used up really but fuck that.

202202202202202202202 HAZEL WARD

Frank could do his own shopping. He could take his new best
mate with him. Bastards.

A retired couple who had an allotment near Ursula's let
him in. He couldn't for the life of him remember their names,
but they knew his. He wondered what else they knew about
him. Had Arthur and Clyde spread the word that he was a
nasty piece of work? Hah! If they wanted to see a nasty piece
of work, look no further than Doogie Chambers. There was
absolutely no way that man hadn't committed GBH on some
poor unfortunate sod at least once in his life. No way. Colin
had never actually seen Chambers lay a finger on anyone but
there'd been rumours at uni. Which was why he'd kept well
clear of him. The only time he and Chambers had ever
spoken was the same night that Colin spoke to Netta for the
first time. Chambers had been at that party too, looking for
her. He'd said one thing to Colin: 'Don't even try, mate. You
couldn't handle her.' Well, look who proved you wrong,
Chambers. Look who got to live the dream. For a while,
anyway.

It was the worst day of his life when he found out about
their affair, even though he'd already guessed she was being
unfaithful to him. Like he'd said to Frank, you can spot these
things. When they told him at the hospital she'd lost the baby,
he actually felt gutted for her. Not that she was the most
maternal woman you could hope to meet. She'd only had Liza
and Will because he'd nagged her to death. He'd wanted children. He'd really, really wanted children. So when he found
out about the miscarriage, he felt bad for her, and he'd been
convinced he'd have taken that child on and raised it as his
own. Because he loved her. He loved her so much the weight
of it nearly crushed him sometimes. He'd have forgiven her.
He'd have done anything to have her love him. But then she
told him who the father was, and everything changed. The

love was gone, at least he thought so at the time. In its place was anger. More anger than he could deal with. It was like he'd fallen into a black hole of vengeance.

Colin passed Ursula's allotment, went through the gap in the hedge and sat down in front of Samuel Sweeting's shed. If it had been anyone else but Chambers, they might have stood a chance. But it wasn't and sometimes even now, Colin felt that weight coming back to crush him. Arianne picked up on it soon enough, which is why she sometimes lashed out. Perfectly understandable. Hadn't he done the same when he'd been hurt? Except he'd taken a more subtle approach.

He saw a flash of electric blue. Ursula. She was wearing that dress again. 'I thought it was you. I wasn't expecting anyone here today.'

'I just needed to get out of the house.'

'Do you want to borrow a spade?'

He surveyed the remaining patch of tangled weed. One more day and it would all be clear. He'd have no excuse to come back. What would he do then? 'No. I'll leave it for today. I'll just sit here for a while, if you don't mind.'

'No problem. I was about to go home. I have some jobs that need doing.'

'Anything I can help with?' He didn't know why he'd said that. All he really wanted to do was sit here on his own and be still.

She let her head drop to one side and frowned slightly. 'I have to take some things to the tip. I suppose I could use an extra hand.'

Ursula's house was like a big white square box with large, black-framed windows and a flat roof. Although he didn't know a lot about architecture, Colin knew of a style that was similar to this. It was called Bauhaus. It was the kind of house he'd dreamed of living in before everything had gone pear-shaped. It was not the kind of house he'd expected to find Ursula in. He'd imagined her living in a little terraced villa or a cottage, possibly with roses around the door.

She seemed to read his thoughts. 'It was built by my late husband.'

'He was a builder?'

'An architect.'

The interior took his breath away. The downstairs was a wide expansive room that was partially divided by screens. A wall of glass overlooked a large garden. The space inside seemed vast and every bit of it was filled with light. Plain white walls were accentuated by modern artwork that looked like genuine originals. Every piece of furniture was in the classic modernist style. Expensive, stylish, but not necessarily comfortable.

'I like your house,' he said.

'All my husband's design. I can't take any credit for it. He died six years ago. It's still as he left it.'

Colin looked out onto the garden. It was immaculate. 'How do you manage to keep it so tidy?'

'I have a gardener. I've no interest in it. It's just window dressing to me. I prefer my allotment.'

'So gardening was your husband's thing?'

She gazed out of the window. 'No. Order was his thing. Order and control. Everything in its place. If you look closely, you'll see each tree and plant in the garden has been placed where it is for visual effect. It's not really a garden. It's a beautifully landscaped prison.'

'You don't like it?'

'I can't stand the garden or the house. That's why I'm selling up.'

'You're moving?'

'The board's going up tomorrow. Which is why I need to go to the tip. I've been clearing out a lot of baggage.'

Ursula showed him to the garage which was set apart from the house. Inside was an old Volvo estate and a lot of boxes and bags. 'Everything on the left is to go to the tip. Everything on the right is for the charity shop.'

They did the tip first and then cleared out the charity shop donations in a couple of trips. Ursula parked the Volvo back up in the garage and locked it up. Normally she drove a newer car, one of those little Fiats, but Colin thought the Volvo suited her better. 'Nice old car,' he said.

'It was my husband's pride and joy. He'd spend hours polishing it and tinkering with it, refusing to let it give in to age. A car should be allowed some scruffiness as it gets older, don't you think? I've helped it along a bit since he went. I like to think of it as small acts of defiance. Are you hungry?'

'Er, yes, I suppose so.' He was still trying to work Ursula out and the sudden change of subject caught him off guard.

'How about lunch? There's a nice Italian restaurant nearby.'

'That sounds great.' For a few seconds, Colin entertained the idea that she might be suggesting something other than a friendly lunch, but that was as long as it took to dismiss it as fanciful. In his heart, he knew a woman like her wouldn't be interested in an ugly, skinny arse no-hoper like him. He was quoting Arianne there. It was one of her favourite quips if ever he was stupid enough to mention Netta. Still, he was glad he'd spent so long in the shower that morning. It was important to be presentable. It was important to be positive too, which was exactly what he'd said to himself last night as he lurked in the shadows watching Arianne and Wordsworth, or Byron, or whatever the fuck his name was, smooching up on his sofa, in his lounge, in his house. Bastards. The world was full of them.

They went for the fixed-price menu, both opting for spaghetti bolognese for their main course. It was perfectly adequate. In times gone by, Colin would have been a bit disappointed by it but these days, even adequate was enough to set his taste buds off like fireworks.

The bottle of Sauvignon Blanc they shared wasn't bad for the price and they both agreed, it was definitely a step up from the last bottle they'd shared. Ursula was good company but then, he already knew that. It seemed she could talk about anything, but she could also listen. She asked about Colin's art. He replied, falteringly at first, then gradually opening up. For the first time in months, he felt connected to it. Not enough to want to paint again, but at least enough for him to feel some nostalgia for it.

It was hard to recall when he'd last spent time over a bottle of wine and a meal, just talking to somebody who didn't abhor him. And it had been such a long time since he'd actually enjoyed the company of others. Such a long time since he'd wanted to know more about a person. 'Do you mind if I ask about your marriage?' he said.

'That depends on what you're about to ask,' she replied.

'Forgive me if I'm prying, but was it happy?'

She sighed. 'It was neither happy nor unhappy. It was just empty. I take it your marriage to Arthur's daughter was unhappy?'

'Ah well, that's a long story. Suffice to say, one of us was ecstatically happy until they found out the other was very much not.'

Ursula both frowned and smiled at him. 'That's very cryptic.'

'Sorry. I suppose I'm still bitter about it. But Arianne was there when I needed someone. She looked after me.' Up to a point, but Ursula didn't need to hear about that. No one did.

'I had my allotment friends. They filled the emptiness.'

'Especially Samuel? Sorry I didn't mean to imply anything was going on between you.'

She laughed. 'I know. Shall we go? I have a few more jobs to do at home.'

They crossed the road, towards Ursula's house. Once over, she turned to him. 'Thank you for today. I'd forgotten how nice it was to have company.'

'Me too. I've enjoyed it. I can come and help some more, if you want.'

She shook her head. 'These are personal jobs I need to take care of.'

He smiled to mask his disappointment. 'I understand.'

'What I said about my marriage. It wasn't the only thing that was empty. So was I. Perhaps if I hadn't been, I would have realised how unhappy I was. But it's hard to feel anything when you've been completely broken. You see my husband's need for control wasn't just over the garden, or the house, or the car. It was over everything, including me. He had ways of shaping people. Such ways. I think you know a bit about that too.'

'What do you mean?' So he'd been right. Arthur had been telling her about him and as usual, it would only be one side of the story.

'I thought… Arianne.'

'Oh Arianne. She has her moments but not that. No.'

Her eyes narrowed a little, but her face soon softened.

'Then it's my turn to apologise. I was mistaken. See you tomorrow?'

'For sure, yes.'

He waited at the bus stop and kept his eyes on her as she walked down the busy street. To his surprise, Arthur's words popped up into his head, the ones about how he'd broken Netta. It was true, he had wanted to crush her but he'd never wanted her dead. He'd just wanted her to see him.

Ursula finally disappeared into the distance. Such a lovely lady. He wondered how she'd managed to saddle herself with a husband like that. Although, there were always two sides to a story, weren't there? And then it occurred to him that there was only one side that mattered. It just depended whose side you were on when it came to which one that was.

35

THE ONLY SIDE THAT MATTERED

Colin buried his head in the pillow. It was just gone four a.m. No time to be awake. No time to be asleep either, according to his brain. It was Ursula. He'd dreamed about her in that stark, sterile house filled with stark, sterile objects. He'd seen her in that meticulously landscaped garden, wearing her bright blue dress. She'd been digging, her lean muscular arms taut with the effort. On her feet, she wore Athenian style sandals. Dirt was stuck in between her toes. Her toenails were black, but she paid them no heed.

She'd carried on digging until she was so far down, he'd only been able to see the top of her head. Frightened he might lose her, Colin had called out to her to be careful. She'd hauled herself out and beckoned him over. 'Look what I found.'

The hole had been deeper than he'd imagined. Too deep to see the bottom. In the time between her climbing out and him walking over, it had filled with something liquid. Not water. Too dark and thick. A small white speck had been just about visible far below the surface. He'd squinted to get a better look and saw that it was getting bigger, but that was because it was floating upwards. As it got closer to the surface, he'd been able to make out a roundish shape. A ball? The liquid had been dark red against the pale shape. Like blood in fact. And what was that shape? Oh fuck. It was a head. And as it had bobbed on the top of the well of thick red blood, Colin saw that it was his head. Its eyes had opened, and it was silently screaming one word. Help.

He was glad to be awake now. Frightened to close his eyes in case he drifted back into that awful nightmare. He retrieved Will's sweatshirt from under his pillow and pushed his face into it, glad to inhale its comforting odour. Was it too early to get up? He couldn't just lie here with that dream still fresh in his mind.

He crept downstairs, careful not to wake Frank. Colin hadn't seen him since yesterday morning. After lunch with Ursula he'd gone to a pub and waited there until it was dark enough for another night of spying on those bastards who were squatting in his home. Frank must have been in bed when he'd returned.

Fred emerged from the little room Frank used as his studio. Unlike everyone else, Fred was indiscriminate with his affection. Colin liked that about him. That was the knowledge he was beginning to gather about dogs. Generally, they were pretty decent companions. Even that dog that belonged to Chambers was happy to accept a scratch behind the ear from him. Come to think of it, where was that dog? Colin hadn't seen him in the garden for a while. Fred made a whimpering sound. Colin put his finger to his lips. 'Shh. You'll wake him up.' The dog's eyebrow whiskers lifted, then he went back into the studio.

Colin ran the cold tap to fill a glass with water and just about caught a glimpse of orange fur disappearing into the hedge. A fox probably. Netta had said they had them here. He occasionally got them in his own garden. Arianne sometimes left food out for them. Unsurprisingly, it was rarely touched. Even foxes had their standards.

Fred was whining again in the other room. Colin stood in the doorway and twisted his head around to see what the fuss was about. Another fox was on the other side of the glass looking at Fred who was looking at it, his tail wagging. Dogs. Indiscriminate. The fox fixed Colin with a stare that seemed to go on forever. Eventually, it turned and stalked off in the same direction as the other one. Colin shuddered. First the head, now the fox. The morning was turning out to be very unnerving.

Liza's portrait caught his eye. Frank had said she was finishing it off yesterday. He didn't want to see it really, but he knew he had to face it one more time. He held his breath and stepped inside. The smell of drying oil paint and white spirit hit him as he got closer to it, and he was reminded again of the last time he was in his own studio. Determined to block it out, he focussed on the painting. He could see where she'd made the changes. She hadn't overworked it, but it had a more finished, less spare look to it. As an artist, Colin preferred the unfinished version. It was more raw somehow. As the subject, he hated both versions equally. No, that was wrong. He didn't hate the painting. He hated the man in it. Everything about him was loathsome, but the eyes were the worst. Mean and unloving. It wasn't Liza's fault; she'd just painted what she saw. It wasn't all his fault either. He was a victim of circumstance. If only people could be made to understand that.

He turned away, went back upstairs and locked himself in the bathroom where he threw up.

· · ·

Arthur was his usual aggravating chirpy self when he came to pick Colin up. Possibly even more than usual. Colin didn't want to imagine what he and Geraldine had been up to that would make him so happy. Liza had once told him that they still had a good sex life. Although why they thought it appropriate to share that with her was more than questionable. Sex wasn't a word that came up in his own parents' house. Neither did love for that matter. They hadn't shared a bed in years. He was pretty sure his father had had affairs though. Colin didn't agree with it. It was true that he'd been having relations with Arianne by the time he'd asked Netta to leave, but it wasn't really an affair. It couldn't be an affair when your wife had already cheated on you. And anyway, Netta had already left the marriage mentally. She just lived in the same house. It had been a kindness to put her out of her misery and ask her to go.

He climbed into Arthur's car. There was no sign of Chambers, or his car. 'I take it Chambers isn't coming today?'

'He'll be along later,' said Arthur. 'I hear you've had a few late nights recently.'

'Two, Arthur. I've had two. News travels fast in these parts. I can just imagine the messages flying back and forth, lighting up your dreary days.'

'You know, Colin, you really are quite obnoxious, aren't you?'

'Yes I am. Especially when I've had very little sleep.'

'Something playing on your mind? Conscience perhaps?'

'My conscience is clear, thank you.' Colin knew he was stretching the truth a bit. For example, he knew he'd been adulterous with Arianne. And he also knew the way he'd treated Netta had been wrong. But it had been under extreme provocation. He was as much a victim as she was and as he'd realised earlier, people needed to hear his side of the story.

That was why he was going to explain it all to Ursula when he saw her.

Ursula was already at the allotments. He was glad to see she had a yellow dress on. The thought of her in the blue dress would forever be associated with that vivid memory of his bodiless head screaming for help. Although he did note she was wearing sandals that while not strictly Athenian, were definitely strappy.

'You're an early bird,' said Arthur.

'There are some people coming to view my house this morning. I'm staying out of the way. Are you okay, Colin? You look worn out,' she said.

He willed himself not to look at the sandals, or to think of her digging that bottomless pit of thick red blood. 'I had a disturbed night. Otherwise fine.'

'Okay. I'll see you later.' She treated him to another of her serene smiles. Yes, definitely a lovely lady. If anyone was going to understand, it was going to be Ursula.

Because there was only the last patch that needed digging, Arthur left him to get on with it while he saw to his own allotment. Colin wasn't in the mood for Arthur's sanctimonious carping. Neither was he in the mood for Chambers and his threats, so the absence of both suited him. He started digging, pleased that he was going to be able to finish this project by himself. It would be rather nice to say that he'd completed something. He hadn't been able to say that in ages.

Ursula came to see him at the point where tiredness was beginning to slow him down. The warm wind whipped her loose dress against her, wrapping it around her bare legs and forcing the spare cloth to float behind her like a sail. The outline of her pants and bra were just about visible through the thin cotton as her body formed a barrier that stopped the dress floating away completely. Standing on the edge of the loose soil that he'd just turned over, she held up two mugs. 'Coffee. I thought you might need a pick-me-up.'

His eyes shifted to her feet. The soil had fallen between her toes. He told himself it was nothing. Not at all connected to his nightmare.

The coffee was strong and black. It sent him a little light-headed and a bit shaky. It was the caffeine burst attacking his sleep-deprived nervous system. That, and the anticipation of what he was about to say. With no one else here, he couldn't have asked for a better time to bare his soul. 'The things you said yesterday about your husband. I've been running them around in my head.'

She frowned. 'That's not what stopped you sleeping, is it?'

'In a way I suppose. Do you think he meant for you to be so… hurt.'

'You mean so broken.'

Yes, he had meant that, but he couldn't bring himself to say it since Arthur had used the same word to describe the way Netta had been when Colin and the children had asked her to move out. 'Do you think he realised what he was doing?'

'That's an interesting question.' She paused for a minute. 'When we first married, I thought he didn't know he was doing it. He'd say little things that hurt but make a joke of it, like poke fun at what I was wearing, or something I said. You can imagine the sort of thing. It built up from there really. I just accepted it as one of his silly little quirks and changed the way I was to stop it. It's easier sometimes to do that than to fight it, isn't it? Except once I stopped doing the thing he didn't like, he'd find something else that wasn't acceptable. It was only when I came here and talked to someone about it that I understood how controlling he was. By then, it was too late for me to do anything but ride it out. I just spent as much time here as I could, which he ridiculed, but I think he saw it as a way to keep me quiet. He didn't know this place and these friends were my quiet revolution.'

'The person you spoke to, was it a therapist?'

She smiled. 'You could call him that. I spoke to Samuel. He helped me to see what was going on.'

'I think sometimes it's possible for people to do wrong things for all the right reasons.'

'What kind of things?'

'The kind of things your husband did.'

A set of wrinkle lines appeared on her brow. 'What are you trying to say, Colin?'

'I may have done the same things to Netta, my wife. Ex-wife. Arthur must have told you.'

She shook her head.

'He seems to think I broke her.' He laughed. He didn't mean to, but it was the nerves making him do stupid, crass things.

'You broke her.' It didn't sound like it was a question, more a confirmation of what he'd said, and yet her expression was undeniably questioning.

His heart was thumping. He'd gone too far, said too much. But to say no more would only make it worse. He had to explain. 'It was never my intention to do that. I was just so angry and hurt. The thing she did to me. Her and Chambers. Doogie. You know, Doogie? The thing they did. It tore me apart.'

'What thing? What did they do?'

'They had an affair. She was having his child, but she lost it.'

'She lost the child?' Her hand reached for her mouth. 'Oh the poor woman.'

She wasn't getting it. She was focussing on the wrong thing. 'You don't understand. I'm trying to say, it was me that was broken first. They broke me. Everything I did after then was their fault. I can see it was wrong, but I had a good reason. I had extenuating circumstances.'

'No. I don't think so. There is never a good reason. I didn't finish answering your earlier question. I don't know whether my husband meant it or not, but I don't think it matters. What matters is what he did. The same applies to you.' She stood up.

'Please don't go.' Colin reached for her arm, but she was already too far away.

She shook her head. 'I can't stay.'

'It wasn't my fault,' he called after her, but she passed through the gap in the hedge without looking back.

Devastated. Colin was devastated by her lack of compassion. He went back to his spade and shoved it in the ground, pulled it back out, tipped off the soil, and repeated the process. He told himself to keep going. It was important to do that and not let things get to you. But every movement was an effort, and he wanted to be sick again. And the walls. The walls were closing in once more. He dropped the spade and walked out with his head down, past Ursula's allotment, past Arthur's, past the retired couple who'd let him in the other day. The gate at the entrance was closed. He climbed over it rather than have to speak to someone. He'd messed up big time. He should never have said anything. Now he'd lost the only person he could talk to. The only person other than Netta.

36

THE NUB OF IT

This morning, Netta had received a message from her dad telling her Colin had left the allotment in a hurry. It was something to do with that woman, Ursula. He'd promised to let her know when or if Colin returned. She hadn't heard from him since. But she couldn't think about that now. She had more pressing issues on her mind. She'd just had a message from Kelly who was currently in Australia, asking her if she needed to come home to help with the Colin problem. That could only mean Liza had been pouring her heart out on one of their long chats which, in turn, could only mean Liza was struggling. Netta replied to say there was no need, but she appreciated the offer and made a mental note to sit down and have a heart-to-heart with Liza when she got home.

Before that, she had something else to deal with. Frank had phoned an hour ago to ask if they could meet when she finished work. She'd said yes. Not necessarily because she wanted to see him. She wasn't angry with him anymore, but she was troubled, and she didn't have any space left in her head for yet more trouble. But whatever was going on with him needed to be sorted before they reached the point of no return.

She pulled into the car park of the pub they'd chosen. It wasn't one that either of them frequented usually which made it good and neutral. She couldn't have done this at his usual haunt, the Hope and Anchor.

Frank was in the beer garden. He stood up as she approached the bench. 'Is here all right for you? We can go inside if you'd rather?'

'Here's fine.' She was thinking it was quieter and more private. Easier to talk, and easier to storm off to her car if the need took her.

'What'll you have?' He was still standing. Actually no, he was hopping, from one foot to the other like a nervous rabbit. Not that she'd ever seen a nervous rabbit doing that particular thing, but that's what she imagined one would do if it were nervous.

'I'll have a spritzer please. Plenty of soda and just a small wine in it. I'm driving.' And also, she wanted to keep a clear head.

It took him a while to come back. 'It's busy in there,' he explained, even though she hadn't asked for an explanation.

'Good job we decided to stay out here then.'

'I guess so.'

He had flecks of light blue paint on his fingernails. It reminded her of the first time they met when she came to view the house. They'd been splatted with oil paint then. Frank had been kind and courteous. She'd thought him a nice man and quite attractive in a scruffy and ramshackle way. Nothing like the other men in her history as far as looks were concerned. Perhaps that was why she fell for him, although she hadn't been looking to fall for anyone. Maybe that was the secret to the best love affairs. They sneaked up and took hold of you before you had a chance to back away. With Doogie, a flame burst into life from the first moment she set eyes on him, and it was still burning. She knew that now. With Frank, it was different. More of a gentle, laid-back heat. Like having a radiator humming along in the background but being able to turn it up a notch or two when you wanted it. She wondered if that nice, kind man was gone forever and whether that would spell the end of them.

She pointed to the paint flecks, unable to bring herself to think about it any longer. 'I like the colour.'

He looked down at his nails. 'I did scrub up before I came out, honestly. I'm such a scruff.'

She wanted to smile but that would have given the impression that everything was all right, and everything was definitely not all right. 'You said you wanted to talk.'

'I wanted to say sorry.'

Well that was a good start. 'For what?'

'Let's start with my stupidity and take it from there.'

She resisted the smile again. Far too early. 'Go on.'

'I know I've been behaving like a total dickhead.' His eyes met hers. 'A jealous dickhead at that. I don't know what got into me.'

He'd been on the right track up until that last point, but no, she wasn't buying it at all. 'No, I'm sorry but that won't do. I think you know exactly what got into you.'

Frank looked at his fingernails. He'd been busted and it was obvious he knew it. 'You're right, I do, but I'm kind of embarrassed to admit it.'

Netta didn't need to say a word. Her raised eyebrow with an accompanying huff was enough to convey her feelings.

He rubbed the back of his neck. His eyes scanned the beer garden and finally settled on hers. 'I panicked. I thought I was going to lose you, and I panicked.' This was uncomfortable for him, she could tell.

'Is that why you stopped coming over?'

'I suppose so. I tend to go into ostrich mode when I panic. The old head in the sand thing. I'm trying to face things properly but it's hard. I'm not great with conflict.'

'So who did you think you were going to lose me to?'

'Doogie.'

It went without saying that she knew that already. She just needed to hear him admit it. 'Did you come up with that idea all by yourself, or has Colin been helping it along?'

'A bit of both. Colin throws in the odd thing here and there, as you've probably guessed, and it doesn't help having him in the house, but it's mostly me and my insecurities. I'm sorry I didn't tell you that I saw him in Scotland. I was in a bad place, confidence-wise, at the time. I meant to tell you when I came back but I was embarrassed again.'

Poor Frank. Bad behaviour notwithstanding, she could understand how Doogie might threaten a man's ego, if that ego was teetering on the edge of extinction. 'How's your confidence now?'

'Pretty much non-existent, if I'm honest.' Still teetering on the edge then.

'But I don't understand why. This can't be all because Doogie's here.'

'Doogie the good-looking cool guy who's living under the same roof as the woman I love you mean?'

'Doogie, cool? You really don't know him, do you? The man's terrified of relationships and he has an allotment in his garden.'

Frank leaned backwards and finally looked like he was beginning to relax. 'I've heard gardening is the new cool.'

'Not from me you haven't.'

He took her hand. 'I'm sorry. I've been such an idiot.'

Netta gave him the smile she'd been holding back. 'Yes, but you're still my idiot.'

'Am I? Even after acting like a first-class twat?'

'You're just about managing to hang on by your paint-flecked fingernails, Mr O'Hare.'

He put her hand to his lips and kissed it. 'God, I love you, Ms Wilde.'

'I love you too, you first-class twat.' She felt a weight lifting ever so slightly, one that she hadn't realised was there until now. There was a long way to go yet but with Frank at her side, there was every chance she could ride through the chaos that inevitably came with Colin and get back to something approaching normality. With Doogie on the other side too, she supposed. But Doogie was never a hundred percent with anyone and anyway, he had his own agenda going on. She hadn't worked out what it was yet, but she was about to get some help in that regard. Before then though, there was something she needed to clear up with Frank. 'Do you think I'm weak?'

'Not at all. Where did that come from?'

'Something you said on Sunday. You and Doogie both said pretty much the same thing about me not doing enough to stand up to Colin.'

'That wasn't what I meant. Jesus Christ, Net, is that what you think I think of you? I would never think that. And for the record, I don't believe Doogie does either.'

'How do you know, have you asked him?'

'No, but we've had a little talk.'

'Oh, a little talk. About me?'

He took a sip on his pint. 'Get over yourself, Wilde, you're not the only thing we have in common.'

Netta's face broke into a grin. 'Oh my God, I can't believe

I just heard you say that. Come on then, what else do you have in common?'

'Running. We both run.' He frowned. 'Scotland. We both love the place. And we both want to get Colin back in his house.'

So now she'd got to the nub of it. Frank and Doogie had joined forces out of necessity, and the primary reason was to get rid of Colin. She'd hoped for a more noble purpose, but she'd take this one. It wasn't ideal but it could be the start of something good. As long as they didn't hang Colin out to dry. In spite of their past, Netta couldn't do that to him. Because it was clear Colin was a man who needed friends and in the absence of any other volunteers in that capacity, she'd stepped forward.

37

A COMPLETE LACK OF REDEMPTION

Frank had walked to the pub, so Netta gave him a lift home. 'Are you coming over for dinner or are you having another quiet night in with Colin?' she said.

'I'm coming over. Colin hasn't been the best of company lately. In fact he hasn't been there at all.'

'So I hear. Has he said where's he's been?'

'No. He seems to be all in one piece though, so it doesn't look like he's been starting any fights.'

Colin starting a fight? Never in a million years. 'Fighting isn't really his style. His retaliation is a bit more underhand. I suppose I'd better go and look in on him. Dad said he left the allotment rather abruptly this morning.'

'Yeah, I heard. You go in. I'll see if he's back yet. He wasn't when I left earlier.'

She was surprised to find dinner preparation underway. She was even more surprised when she saw that the preparation was a family effort. Liza, Will and Belle were all in the kitchen doing bits of this and that. Doogie was there too, doing something with rice. He winked at her. 'All right?'

'Yeah. All good. Something smells tasty. Will there be enough for Frank?'

'Plenty.'

She caught his eye. It was obvious he knew where she'd been. Frank must have told him when they had their talk.

Will waved her over. 'Mum, you have to see this. It makes the best fried chicken. We've been testing it out.'

'Testing what out? Oh.' A beast of a machine was throbbing away on the worktop. 'What is it?'

'An air fryer.' She hadn't seen him this excited since the pups were born.

'Where did you get it? It looks expensive.'

'I bought it. It's a present,' said Doogie.

A present. Surely a box of chocolates or a bunch of flowers would have sufficed? Not so it seemed. Apparently a massive, fuck off nonsense gadget was exactly what she needed. He'd bought her a dress once, during their affair. How times and people change.

'We chose it though,' said Will.

Doogie nodded. 'They did. Which is why it ended up being so big. Sorry. I can take it away if it's too much.'

'No!' shouted the younger branch of the family all at once. It looked like she was stuck with it.

'It's absolutely fine,' she said, at the same time wondering how you actually cleaned such a thing. Perhaps when all the fuss had quietened down, she could find it a permanent space in the pantry, next to the spiraliser that Liza had been so keen on, for about a month.

Frank came in as they were laying out the food. 'Is that an air fryer?' His eyes were like little bright buttons. It seemed he'd found something else he had in common with Doogie.

'Do we need to take some of the food over to Colin?' she said.

'He's not in,' said Frank, without taking his eyes off the new gadget.

When they'd finally exhausted the subject of air fryers, which took some exhausting, Doogie told them they'd finished off the allotment project today so there was no need to go back.

'Oh I nearly forgot, I spoke to Nan earlier. They're coming over at seven to talk about Dad,' said Liza. 'Sorry, I was just so buzzing about the air fryer.'

Well, at least Netta had one reason to be grateful to that horrendous monstrosity. If Liza had been having a moment of crisis about Colin, it had been temporarily displaced by the promise of limitless supplies of fried chicken.

'It's seven now,' said Belle, just as the door knocker went.

Liza giggled. 'Good job I remembered just in time then.'

Netta's mum and dad made a beeline for the new equipment. 'That's one of those air fryers, isn't it?' said her mum.

'Yes, Doogie bought it for us. Shall we sit down?' said Netta, already sick of air fryers, although quite surprised that her parents had heard of them.

'I've been doing some research on them. We're thinking of getting one,' said her dad.

Of course they were. As usual, her mum and dad were way ahead of her on pretty much anything and everything. 'Shall we leave this discussion until later? Liza said you wanted to talk about Colin.'

Her dad took a seat at the kitchen table. 'Well, as I mentioned in my message, Colin took off without a word. I thought he was probably tired. He'd said something about not sleeping last night. Although that didn't explain why he couldn't have told me he was going, but then that's Colin all over.' He looked at Liza and Will. 'Sorry, kids. Anyway, I left it for an hour and then called Liza to see if he was back.'

'So I checked at Frank's and dad wasn't there,' said Liza.

'He hasn't been back all day,' said Frank.

Netta's dad leaned forward and rested his arms on the table. 'I spoke to Ursula. I've mentioned her before. She's a widow. Very nice woman. Had an allotment for years. But I digress. Colin and Ursula get on quite well. Not in that way but you know, they're friendly. They sometimes have chats. I saw Ursula heading towards the patch where Colin was working and then the next time I looked, he was gone. So, when Liza told me she couldn't find him, I asked Ursula if she knew where he was. Apparently, he'd said something to her that she didn't think went the way he was expecting it to go.'

'Oh my God. Did he come on to her? Eww,' said Liza.

'No, nothing like that. She wouldn't go into all the details, but she said it was something about you and him, Nettie. Something to do with the way he'd treated you. She got the impression he'd expected her to be more sympathetic. Those were the words she used. But you see, he'd picked the wrong person if that was the case. I haven't known Ursula for long, but I do know her husband was very controlling. Ringing any bells?'

'Do you think Colin tried to make it sound like it wasn't his fault?' said Frank.

'I think so, yes. Naturally, Ursula told him straight there could never be an excuse to behave like that. The thing is, she'd already told him about her husband. You'd think he'd have cottoned on, wouldn't you? Anyway, she left him and shortly after, she saw him climbing the gate to get out. Didn't even ask someone to unlock it for him.'

'Ursula was a friend of Samuel's. The old guy whose patch and shed we've been clearing,' said Doogie.

Her dad nodded. 'That's right. According to Clyde, they were very close friends. Apparently, she was a timid, frightened thing when she first got an allotment. It was Samuel who brought her out of herself.'

There was a rawness in Netta's throat. Like she'd just vomited, but she hadn't. It was just the rawness. A few hours ago she'd been seriously considering befriending the man who'd almost irretrievably damaged her. And now what? He was using their story and twisting it as he always did to his own ends. What a fool she'd been to think he had any sort of redemption in him. And was he trying to get his claws into this Ursula now? It was no wonder Arianne lost it with him. If she actually did. There was every chance all that was put on too.

She suddenly felt hot and dizzy. She needed to get away without causing alarm. 'I just need to pop to the loo. Why don't you all explain the fried chicken process to Nan and Granddad? Let them have a go with it. Or something.' And with that she shot upstairs before anyone could stop her and locked herself in the bathroom.

She lay down on the floor and curled up like a foetus, her heart thumping against the cold, hard tiles. It felt oddly comforting. Droplets of water settled in the corner of one eye and trickled out of the other. Not tears as such. It was just the anger pushing them out.

Her phone went off. She pulled it out of her back pocket and almost laughed when she saw who it was. His ears must have been burning. 'Where are you?'

'Not far away. I'm just not ready to come back yet.'

'Why? Because of what you said to Ursula?' She could hear the sound of traffic in the background. He must be somewhere busy.

'I was just trying to tell her my side of the story.'

'Uh huh. I suppose that's the one where I deserved everything you dished out, is it? Did you tell her how you threatened to take the children away from me if I didn't toe the line? Did you tell her how you constantly reminded me what a filthy, disgusting, whore and an unfit mother I was? Did you?'

'I don't remember it that way.'

'No? Well then tell me how you remember it, because I am dying to know exactly how you can twist this one around.'

'It's not important now. I wanted to ask you something.'

Netta wiped her eyes. The anger was in full flow now. 'What?'

'Did you try to kill yourself?'

Her heart skipped a beat, then another. 'Who told you that?'

'It doesn't matter. Please tell me. Did you?'

'No. I thought about it, but a kind stranger talked me out of it.'

'Was that, was that the morning we asked you to leave?'

'Yes.' She thought she heard something like a sharp intake of breath mingling with the traffic sounds, but she could have been mistaken. 'Colin, you need to come home.'

'Yes, I'll be back later. There's just a few things I need to do first.'

'Like what? Colin?' He'd hung up. Netta tried to call him back, but it went straight to answerphone.

38

A FOOL AND HIS CHOICES

Doogie parked the car some distance from his destination and walked the rest of the way. He was still smiling at Netta's reaction to that air fryer. He knew it was a mistake to buy it but the kids had ganged up on him as soon as he mentioned he'd like to get her something. It was so funny to see her pretending to like it. When they were together, she'd have told him straight out it was a shit present. But she was different now. More considered. Staying in her house with her family had opened his eyes to a different side of her that he was still getting used to. She'd gone over to Frank's for the night now that they were back on speaking terms. They'd wanted to spend some time on their own, but they were also waiting for Colin the Wanker to come back. Doogie hadn't fancied staying in with the kids. There was only so much bollocks TV you could take. Besides, he had a need to be alone for a while. All that people interaction was doing his head in.

The bars and cafés in Moseley were loud and busy. You'd have thought a Wednesday night would have been quieter. And there were so many cars. Before he moved to Scotland, he loved loud, buzzy places like this. But there was no space here. It was all so claustrophobic, and he was beginning to go stir crazy. Why else would he be doing mad things like running errands and gardening for a crabby old girl who reminded him of Monique, his dad's nasty bitch of a wife? And why else would he be tramping the streets looking for Colin the Wanker?

He cut across the road while there was a lull in the traffic and followed the same route he'd taken that morning. Liza had given him the address. It was something they'd cooked up between them, seeing as Colin's ex didn't know him. He'd watched the house, just to see what she was up to, if she had any patterns, went out at certain times. That sort of thing. This morning, he'd seen a big guy, who was carrying too much weight to be a threat, leaving and coming back a couple of hours later. He'd made a note of the times. The woman hadn't shown her face, but he saw her moving about inside. He'd do the same thing tomorrow before he went to see Priscilla Sweeting. She had more jobs for him.

He was here on a hunch tonight. Frank had said Colin the Wanker had been out late for the last few nights. To Doogie's mind there weren't many places he'd be likely to go to. He'd already tried the allotment, and Liza said he wasn't all that into pubs. So now that it was dark, Doogie was guessing there was only one place he'd be.

He kept to the opposite side of the road to the house, his eyes searching leafy bushes and the kind of dark places a man could hide in. He'd done it himself once, after Netta had ended their affair. He hated that word, affair. It sounded seedy. Dirty. Netta had lived with Colin in a different house then, but Doogie had hidden away in one of those dark places watching her. He'd been fully intent on knocking the door and begging her to come away with him, but something had stopped him.

So instead he'd stayed there watching and wanting. It had been seeing her kids, Liza and Will. He couldn't take her away from them. He knew what it was like to have a distant parent, and Colin the Wanker had looked like he was a good dad. Better than he could ever be anyway. So he'd decided Netta was better off without him and walked away. If only he'd gone through with it. If only he'd had the courage to be a different man. Because even from across the road and through glass, he'd seen that Netta was hurting. And he'd known that Colin was just another version of Monique, so it was obvious he'd want to hurt her some more.

He thought about what Geraldine had said to him a couple of weeks ago, about how he felt he'd let Netta down. If she'd said he was ashamed of himself for being a coward and walking away without fighting for her, that would have been closer to the truth. He had no way of knowing if he'd have convinced Net to go with him, or if she had, that things would have worked out, but at least he'd have tried. If nothing else, he'd have saved her from Colin. And it was fine for Geraldine to say there was no need for him to protect her but try telling that to his conscience. Try telling it to his gut instinct. And try telling it to his heart.

A figure stumbled out from a gap between two houses. He remembered from this morning that it had been a gully of some sort. Sure enough it was Colin the Wanker, and he was doing his flies up. He was obviously pissed because he fell over a bin. If he carried on like that, he was going to either get himself arrested or beaten up again. Doogie considered rescuing him and taking him home. But then he remembered the way Netta had looked when she came back down from the bathroom earlier on. The wanker had called her, and she'd been crying. Fuck it. The guy was a bastard. Whatever happened, he had it coming to him. He went to find a park where he could lie down, look at the stars and imagine he was in Scotland where he belonged.

He was up and out before anyone else came down. Netta's car was outside, so he assumed she was still next door. Doogie couldn't decide how he felt about Frank. He seemed like an all-right kind of guy, but all that sulking shit was pretty childish. If you had a problem, you should either say it or let it go. That's how it worked with him and Netta. Him and Claire as well. Actually, that was how it worked with him and Grace. Had worked. Until he'd fucked things up. Yeah, right. And there was him calling Frank childish.

But it wasn't the sulking that was his main problem with Frank. It was the thing he'd said about Grace. In Doogie's opinion it was low and below the belt. The kind of thing he'd expect from Colin the Wanker, not the man Netta chose to be with. Either her judgement was way off, or Frank's decency had been skewed by recent events. Both of those scenarios were possible.

It niggled him though, because it was true that Grace bore a passing resemblance to Netta, which was exactly why he'd resisted getting involved with her at first. She'd been the one to make the first move. And the second, and the third. In fact, she'd made all the moves. Doogie had been like a nervous animal, scared of human attachment. Initially, it had just been about the sexual release for both of them. He didn't ask but he guessed she'd exhausted all the other available options, there weren't many in that small and remote community. In the warmer months when the tourists came, she'd sometimes hook up with a passer-through. But she kept coming back to him. He rarely slept with anyone other than her. Not because he had particularly strong feelings for her but because he didn't want the contact.

As they got to know each other better he found that aside from the slight similarity in looks, Grace was nothing at all like Netta. She was straightforward, blunt to the point of rudeness sometimes. You only had to be with her for a while to get how connected she was to the land and her roots. It was impossible to pull them apart. Doogie liked that about her. But the thing he liked most about Grace was that she didn't understand him at all, and she made no effort to change that. She didn't care what made him tick. For her, it was all about his actions. The whys behind them weren't important. It was a refreshing change, and he came to love the way it made him feel like a new and different person with nothing to hide.

Two summers ago she announced that she was his alone. He said it was the same for him. He didn't one hundred percent mean it, but she wouldn't have known that because she couldn't see into his soul. Unlike Netta who could do it with one look.

It was raining this morning, so he parked the car near enough to the house to be able to see it from inside without being noticed. Colin the Wanker wasn't there anymore, so he'd either gone back to Frank's or he was sleeping it off in a cell or a hospital bed. Doogie didn't care which.

After a while, the guy came out of the house and followed the same route he'd taken yesterday. An hour later, a woman with big blonde hair and big everything else came out and walked past the car. Doogie smiled to himself. There was no way anyone was going to accuse Colin of having a partner who reminded them of Netta.

The woman came back not long after with a bag of shopping, and the guy returned at about the same time as yesterday. So a pattern was beginning to emerge. Doogie stayed until around midday. Priscilla was expecting him in half an hour, and he didn't want to keep her waiting.

The old woman opened the door. 'You're late.'

'Only five minutes. The traffic was bad,' said Doogie.

'That don't make you any less late.'

'You got somewhere to be?'

She scowled at him for a minute then her face wrinkled into a smile. 'Cheeky monkey.'

Mary used to call him that when he was a kid. He felt a snag from somewhere deep inside, a feeling that was long buried. He'd loved that old lady as much as he loved his mum. Possibly more so when he was little, seeing as she was the one who let him get away with anything and kept him topped up with fig rolls. He still liked a fig roll to this day.

'I suppose you've been wasting your time at that allotment again.' Priscilla had her arms folded and one eyebrow arched. Doogie half-expected her to slip into a rant, until he realised, she was teasing him.

'Not today. We've finished the project now. Samuel's patch is cleared and the shed's tidied up, ready for someone else to take it on.'

'I tek it you've removed all trace of him.'

'Nah. Ursula said the shed's exactly as it was when he was there.'

He saw a flash of hesitation in her eyes when he said Ursula's name. He shouldn't have mentioned her, but it was too late to take it back. Priscilla's jaw was already set. Her playful teasing eyes had narrowed. 'Well she would know.'

'I can take you there if you like. So you can see it before someone else takes over.'

'What makes you think me want to waste me precious time going there?'

'I dunno. Closure I suppose.'

'You believe in all that claptrap?' Priscilla looked him up and down like he'd just walked something disgusting into the house and once again he was reminded of Monique. Although in Monique's eyes, he would have been the thing that was disgusting.

'Not really, but—'

'Well don't say it then, fool. You want a sandwich?'

'Go on then. I'm starving.'

'Wait in the living room. I'll bring it in.'

Doogie noticed Samuel's letter was still on the mantel-piece. The sound of clattering crockery told him it was safe to go in for a closer look, so he checked to see if it had been opened. It hadn't. No great surprise there.

The crockery fell silent, and the kettle had finished boiling. He moved some of the cushions away from his place on the sofa, sat down, and pulled out his phone as if he'd been occu-pying himself with it the whole time. There was a message waiting for him from Merrie:

Hey D, I'm on my way to Birmingham. Probably see you tomorrow, if you're around.

He never knew whether the D stood for Doogie or Dad. Doogie, probably. It was unlikely she thought of him as her actual dad. That honour would have gone to Claire's husband, Dom. He was okay with that. It was just his mum he felt bad for. Another act of cowardice on his part had left her without the official title she would have loved.

Priscilla brought in a tray of sandwiches and tea. She glanced at the letter before giving him the once over. 'You look happy. Got some good news?'

'My daughter. She's coming to see me.'

'You got kids?' She seemed surprised.

'Just the one.'

'She don't live with you?'

'Nah. I kept away until a few years ago.'

'What you do that for?'

'I thought she'd be better off without me.'

'What kind of damn fool thing is that to say? Are you completely stupid?'

'Yeah, I think I must be.' Trust Priscilla to say it like it was.

'You know what I think, Dougal? I think you've made some very bad choices.'

Doogie grinned. She was so right. Pity it took till now to have it pointed out to him. 'Oh Priscilla, I really wish I'd met you twenty years ago.'

'I would have scared the life out of you.'

'I know.'

She eyed him over her teacup for what seemed like longer than it probably was. 'Fetch it over here.'

'Fetch what?'

'The letter. You think I don't know you check it every time you come in here? If you want to see it so bad, go and get it.'

Doogie sighed and fetched the letter. He held it out for her. Priscilla stared at it like it was a thing from outer space. 'Read it.'

'Me?'

'Yes, you. Read it.'

He opened the envelope. Inside was a single sheet of paper. It looked like it had been torn out of an exercise book and someone had tried to tidy the rough edge with scissors but had made a bad job of it. He cleared his throat:

My dear Priscilla,

I should have been a better husband and father. I tried, but I gave up too quick.

I'm sorry.

Samuel x

Priscilla still had the teacup in her hand. 'That's it? Not one single mention of love or forgiveness?'

Doogie turned the letter around for her to see. 'He's put a kiss on there.'

'Sixty years of marriage and that's all I get? One kiss and I coulda been better.'

'I think by saying sorry he's implying he's asking for forgiveness.'

She put the cup down. 'Oh you do, do you? And what would you know?'

39

I GAVE UP TOO QUICK

Priscilla's list of jobs kept Doogie busy all afternoon. She'd stayed mostly out of his way. He'd assumed he'd annoyed her again but by the time he'd finished, she seemed to have got over it enough to present him with a new list. He wondered what her kids did for her when they visited. Maybe she didn't want to ask them. Although from what he'd seen of her, that was unlikely. He didn't want to judge though. It wasn't as if he ever offered to do jobs for his mum and Clive when he visited them. It wasn't deliberate, it just didn't occur to him. They were younger than Priscilla. His mum had been really young when she'd had him. Younger than his own daughter was now. He never really thought of her as old, but he guessed it wouldn't be long before that changed. Clive was about the same age as his mum, and he kept himself fit. His dad though was about ten years older. Since Doogie hadn't seen him in a long time, he had no idea how he was doing.

There were more cars in Netta's road than usual. It had probably been a through-road, once, but the one end was blocked off now. It wasn't close enough to park for the shops on the main road, unless you liked walking, so you didn't seem to get a lot of visitors here. He recognised Arthur's car parked next to another one that looked sort of familiar. Netta's door opened, and he instantly remembered where he knew the car from. Oh fuck. The cavalry was here, and she didn't look very happy.

Claire was blocking his way into the house. 'Surprise!' If it was supposed to be a friendly greeting it didn't come off as one, but then it was unlikely that friendly had been her intention.

He decided the best approach was to style it out. He put on an expression that made out like he was pleased to see her. 'What are you doing here?'

She stepped out onto the path and pulled the door to. 'Take a wild guess.'

'Er, no. Can't think of anything.'

Doogie loved Claire. They'd been friends for so long they knew each other inside out. He credited himself with knowing pretty much all there was to know about her. And one thing he knew above everything else was you didn't want to make Claire mad at you. Because when she was mad at you, it was impossible to tell which way she was going to go. She could scream and shout. She could throw things. She could be so angry she couldn't speak. If she was really, really mad at you, she could be all of those things one after the other. And boy did she look really, really mad right now.

She came to within a few inches of him. 'What the fuck are you playing at?'

'Don't know what you mean.'

'Don't give me that shit. You haven't just turned up on Netta's doorstep because you fancied a change. You're up to something.'

She poked her forefinger into his chest. He backed away

slightly. 'I heard what had happened with the accountant wanker. I thought she might need some support.'

'She's got Frank for that.'

'I know but…'

'But what? You here to make a play for her while she's at her most vulnerable?'

'Don't be stupid, Claire.'

She was in his face again. 'How come I'm the one being stupid all of a sudden? It's not like I dropped everything to drive four hundred miles, like a knight in his four-by-four charger to save an old girlfriend from the clutches of her evil ex-husband, is it? And while we're at it, Merrie confessed to telling you, so let's have less of the "I heard" crap, shall we?'

'Is Merrie here as well?'

'No, she's at my mum's. I told her she had to stay away until I'd spoken to you.'

'It's not her fault.'

Claire looked like a big cat ready to pounce on something, and the something in question was him. 'I know that, shit-head. I'm putting this all on you. You can see her tomorrow when you go to pick Spike up from your mum's.'

He was about to tell her she'd got it wrong about Spike, but she flashed him a warning shot right between the eyes. 'Don't you dare try to lie your way out of this one. I have spoken to your mother. Yes, Doogie, I have actually spoken to Julie, the woman who can do no wrong. So I know you've been feeding Netta lies. Which leads me back to my first question, what the fuck are you up to?'

'I'm here to stop Netta's ex doing what he always does.' He pressed his lips together. That was all she needed to know for now.

A loud cough made them both turn. Frank was on the

other side of the fence. 'How are yer, Claire? Great to see you.'

'Frank. Lovely to see you too. Netta says you've been stuck babysitting Colin. You poor sod. You coming in?'

'I am.' Frank nodded at Doogie. Doogie wondered how much he'd heard.

'Come over then. There's a proper family council going on.' She let Frank pass then gave Doogie more evils. 'This isn't finished.'

The whole family was inside, except for Will and Belle. Netta seemed on edge. Doogie saw her glance at him when he walked into the kitchen behind Frank and Claire. If Claire knew he'd lied about his mum being away, then she probably did, too. There was going to be a fallout of some kind. He could feel it brewing. He wasn't exactly in the best of moods himself after Claire had said that about his mum being the woman who could do no wrong. She'd called her that before, back when he and Claire had been together. Usually because he'd refused to introduce them, or to tell his mum that she was a grandmother. He'd been a mess at the time, and it was just one more complication he could do without. He'd known then it was immature and selfish. It hadn't stopped him doing it though. That was the coward in him again. Sometimes, when Doogie thought about all the years he'd wasted, he wanted to howl.

'We can't find Colin. He didn't come back last night, and his phone's switched off,' said Netta.

The others seemed to be aware, so he assumed she'd said it to bring him up to speed. 'Have you tried the allotment?'

'He hasn't been there since yesterday,' said Arthur. 'I've got everyone on high alert. If he turns up I'll know about it straight away.'

'Actually I saw him last night, watching his house. He was pissed up.'

'What were you doing at his house? Never mind, what did he say?' said Netta.

'Nothing. I didn't speak to him. He seemed to be okay, so I left him there.' Yeah, all right, he probably wasn't okay but so what? Doogie was no good Samaritan. Especially when it came to Colin the Wanker. Claire was eyeballing him. He looked around the room for a friendlier view and landed on the shiny new air fryer. That was better than nothing.

'We should check the hospitals. And his road. And the pubs,' said Netta.

'We'll go to his road,' said Arthur.

'I'll come with you,' said Liza.

'I'll call round the hospitals,' said Frank.

Suddenly everyone was busy running around in different directions. Doogie reached into his pocket for his car keys. 'I'll try the pubs.'

Claire pulled him back. 'No, I'll try the pubs. You stay here with Netta.'

So that was the way it was going to go then? Just him and Netta. People were moving around them, getting their things together to set out on their searches but all Doogie could see was Netta, her endlessly deep, dark eyes full of hurt. He'd been right, there was going to be a fallout.

His mind took him back thirty years to the day she'd found out he'd been seeing someone else. A girl he'd met while they were on one of their legendary break-ups. To him she was just a friend who'd been helping him discover his Black roots, but as usual he'd let things go too far and it got complicated. He'd tried to keep them separate, but Netta had seen them together on that day and that had been the end of everything. His hopes, his dreams. Everything. She'd had that look in her eye then, right before she told him he was toxic, and she hated him. Right before she told him never to talk to her again. Later that day, she met Colin the Wanker.

Frank was the last of them to go, and then it was just him and Netta and a load of dogs, none of which was his. Doogie shoved his hands in his pockets and waited.

'So I hear your mum isn't on her holidays. I hear Spike is with her, not some random business acquaintance.'

'No, she's not, and yes he is.'

She put her fingers against her temple, like she had a headache that needed clearing. The headache, of course, was him. 'I don't understand. Why did you lie?'

'Because I thought you wouldn't let me stay here if you knew I'd got somewhere else to go.'

'But why would you want to stay here with all this Colin stuff going down? I'd have thought the further away the better would suit you.'

'I wanted to be close to you.'

'Because of Colin?'

He went to say yes, but he held back for just a moment too long, and she caught it.

'It's not because of Colin, is it? Claire said there was more to it.'

'Claire knows shit.' He'd gone in too hard. He could tell by the look on her face. He should have known better than to criticise Claire.

'Oh really. Why don't you tell me then, Doog? Tell me what you're really doing here.'

'I'm here to protect you.'

'To protect...' She interrupted herself with a laugh. 'From what? From Colin? Or Frank? You know what, don't bother to answer. It doesn't matter. I don't need anyone's protection. I can protect myself.'

'I'm sorry, I just thought… Forget it.'

'You thought it was the perfect excuse. You're not telling me the whole truth, are you?' She grabbed hold of his arms. 'Tell me why you're really here, and don't give me any bullshit this time.'

'It's Grace. She wants to get married.'

'Oh!' This time it was her turn to hesitate. 'That's great, isn't it?'

He didn't answer. He was looking at those fucking eyes of hers again, thinking about how they were giving away her true reaction.

'Are you going to?'

'I don't know.'

She turned away from him. 'You should. You should marry her.'

And just like that Doogie was transported back in time again. This time to their affair when she'd go cold on him for no reason other than to keep him at a distance. The anger rose in him now, just as it did then. 'I don't need your permission.'

'So what are you doing here?'

'I don't know.'

'Well then, you're no use to me.'

She was right, he was no use to her. He was no fucking use at all. He turned and walked away. And all he could think about was Samuel's words: *I tried, but I gave up too quick.*

40

LIT FUSES AND A TALL ORDER

The front door closed and Doogie was gone. He hadn't taken his things with him so presumably he'd be back at some point. Where he'd gone, Netta didn't know. He wouldn't go to Merrie in case he bumped into Claire, so that left his mum, Julie Macrae. Although thinking about it, she probably hadn't been Macrae since she married Doogie's stepdad. Netta wondered if Doogie had told her where he'd been staying. She'd lay money on Julie being completely in the dark about the marriage proposal. She herself would still be blissfully unaware of it if she hadn't forced it out of him. Right now, that would have been her preference.

She couldn't understand why she was taking it so badly. It wasn't as if there was a future scenario where she and Doogie fulfilled the destiny she'd mapped out for them all those years ago as a girl. Jesus. Over thirty years and she could still feel the way her heart stopped the first time their eyes met in that grotty pub in Manchester. She could still taste their first kiss, still sense the way his body pressed against her the first time they had sex. The scent of him.

The feel of him. She didn't really think about it on a day-to-day basis but sometimes, when he got close to her, it was like she'd never moved on. Was that what how it was for everyone with their first love? She'd like to ask someone, but what if they said no? What if they thought she was some kind of weirdo obsessive who was hanging on to the past? She could always ask Claire. It wouldn't be so bad if Claire thought that. Actually, Claire probably already did think that.

When Netta was younger and a lot more naive, she had a thing about Doogie being her Heathcliff. She'd imagined their love going on forever. Beyond death even. Just like it did in *Wuthering Heights*. But that was before years of living a real life. Experience had since taught her that kind of love was strictly for romance novels. It was nice sometimes to drift into the world of romance. As long as you didn't forget it was fiction and the reality was much harder, much less noble. She, for instance, wasn't in the least bit noble. She, for instance, should be thinking about Grace and how she was coping with the man she loved running off as soon as she dropped the M word into the conversation. And was she? No she was not. Because she was too busy wondering whether she could let Doogie go. There you go then. Not very noble at all. Especially since she'd made her choice twenty years ago. She'd let him go then. Walked away without giving him the chance to choose, ignoring the great chasm that was cleaving her heart in two. People thought it was Colin who broke her. He certainly finished the job. But it was leaving Doogie and losing their baby that had started it. And if Doogie really didn't need her permission, why had he come to her? Netta didn't know the answer to that, unless it was because he wasn't sure if he could let her go either. Perhaps he was just as selfish and ignoble as she was.

A message came through on the 'Colin watch' group chat they'd set up. It was from Liza:

Dad wasn't at his house. We're going to start on the pubs.

A minute later, Claire sent a list of places she'd already tried. Shortly after, Frank messaged to say he'd had no joy with any of the hospitals. Then Will called: 'Mum, what's going on?' He was at Belle's, about to go on holiday, but he'd seen the group chat.

'Your dad's gone AWOL. He didn't come back on Wednesday night. It's nothing to worry about. We're just taking precautions.' She decided not to tell him that Doogie had seen Colin spying on his own house. No need to spoil Will's holiday before he'd even gone.

'Are you sure?'

'Yes, absolutely. He's probably just found someone else to stay with. We'll soon have him back under supervision.'

Will let out a heavy sigh. 'Mum, what are we going to do about him?'

'I don't know, darling. But we'll work something out.'

'Do you think I should talk to him?'

'Only if it's right for you. You won't be able to get hold of him at the moment. I've tried but I think his battery's flat. Have a think about it while you're away and decide when you come back. Just promise me you won't let it ruin your holiday.'

'I won't. I love you, Mum.'

'I love you too, my darling. Now go on and have a great holiday. It'll be your last one before you have to surrender to the dreaded nine to five, so make the most of it.'

She met Frank in the back garden as he was coming to hers. 'Will's just phoned. The messages got him worrying. I played it down to put his mind at rest. I didn't say anything about Doogie seeing Colin last night.'

'Very wise. No point in sending him off in a panic. Are you all right? You look a bit wound up.'

'Yes, all good.'

'I saw Doogie going back out again. Has he gone to look for Colin?'

She searched Frank's face for a clue as to his motive for asking the question. A few days ago she'd have said he was trying to find some dirt on Doogie, but now he looked more confused than anything.

'You don't have to say if you'd rather not,' he said.

Yes, there was always that option, but they'd only just made up after all that silliness and distrust. 'He didn't say where he was going. We had words.'

'I see. I overheard him and Claire talking earlier. I couldn't help it. I walked out the door and they were in the middle of it. I'm guessing your words were about the same thing.'

'I expect so. He hasn't been entirely truthful with me. It seems he's sort of on the run.'

'Has he broken the law?'

'No, not that kind of on the run. Grace wants to get married. It looks like it was enough for him to do a Doogie.'

'What's a Doogie?'

Netta did a mime that involved her running on the spot, getting into a car and driving off.

He looked amused. 'Ah, I see. Will he come back, do you think?'

'Eventually. When he's stopped being angry with me.'

'Are you angry with him?'

'He lied to me, Frank. Of course I'm angry. I expect it will blow over though. We're like a couple of lit fuses, me and

Doogie. We flare, we blow up and then it's gone. Mostly anyway.'

Frank kicked a half-chewed tennis ball across the grass, sending the dogs scooting after it. 'Is that how you'd prefer our relationship to be?'

'God no. It'd be totally exhausting. Although I would appreciate you being more open when things bothered you.'

He smiled. 'That's quite a tall order, but I'll do my best.'

'That's all I ask.' She kissed him, glad that he was here for her again.

Two more messages came through to advise of more non-sightings. Netta sighed. Colin was despicable, but that didn't mean she wanted anything bad to happen to him.

Frank shook his head. 'Where the hell is he?'

41

YOU NEVER ASK ME

Colin was probably having an out-of-body experience. If he wasn't, then why was he looking at his own face? Oh God, don't say he was having another of those fucking nightmares about his disembodied head again. That would just about be the last bloody straw. He closed his eyes then opened just one. Yes, it was him, with one eye open and one closed. He was about to let out a loud scream when he realised that he was looking into a mirror. A dirty, grungy, greenish mirror. He was lying in front of it on something soft, verdant and damp. And a big fat slug was slowly progressing along his arm. He shook the slug off and sat up. Where was he? A garden. Yes, definitely someone's garden. But whose? Not Netta's or Frank's, although it did look strangely familiar.

'Adam, there's someone at the bottom of the garden.' Shit the bed, it was his neighbour, Jude. He was next door to his own house. 'Colin. Is that you? Adam, I think it's Colin.'

Adam and Jude. Not his type of people but useful to have as friends. Although they didn't look too friendly right now. Perhaps they'd gone over to the dark side and cosied up to

Arianne. Before they could reach him, Colin scrambled over the fence and dropped into the thorny bushes that formed a border between the back of their houses and a small park. He picked himself up and scarpered as fast as he could.

It wasn't long before the pain in his side forced him to stop running and find a bench to catch his breath. He was such a mess these days, although two days of drinking and sleeping rough didn't help. The bench was in a play area. He used to bring Liza and Will here when they were small. He'd push them on the swings and chat to the other parents. Nice people like him. Decent people. That's how he saw himself then. He didn't know how he saw himself now. He was undefinable.

There was a half-empty bottle of wine underneath the bench. He picked it up. Malbec. He was quite partial to a Malbec. All the same, what kind of person would leave that sort of thing in a kiddies' play area? What kind of thoughtless monster? A flash of recall made him realise he was that monster. He'd come here last night, after drinking in places his old self didn't even know existed. Awful places, but at least no one would think to go looking for him there. If they were looking. His battery was dead so he had no idea. For all he knew they could be glad to see the back of him. Most of them would definitely be glad to see the back of him. Except Liza. She wouldn't give up on him.

Colin took a swig from the bottle. How he'd ended up in his neighbours' garden was anybody's guess. His memory was mostly a blank since that call with Netta on Wednesday. The events before then were clear. The discussion with Ursula, her walking away from him. He remembered leaving the allotment and pounding the streets for hours without any real thought to where he was going. He'd ended up in Cannon Hill Park sitting by the lake, going over Ursula's assessment of her husband and him: "What matters is what he did. The same applies to you." Then he'd recalled what Arthur had said about Netta not wanting to live and a terrible, terrible thought had crossed his mind. What if these people were right? What if it really didn't matter how others had treated you? What if all that mattered was your own actions?

The call to Netta had set his mind at rest a little. She hadn't tried to kill herself, only thought about it. Well we could all say that, couldn't we? He'd been on his way back to hers when he'd phoned, but the other things she'd said about the way he'd treated her had sent him into another tailspin. The last thing he remembered was settling in with a large gin and tonic somewhere in the back streets of Balsall Heath, assuring himself that she'd been exaggerating to make him feel bad. Just how many he'd had after that was way beyond his recall. And yet no matter how much he drank, there was still that nagging doubt in the back of his head that wouldn't go away. Because even though he couldn't remember what he'd been doing, Colin couldn't forget what he'd been thinking, over and over again. All that really matters is what you've done.

He put the bottle to his lips again and the Malbec slid down his throat, into his otherwise empty belly. But he'd glugged it too quickly and half of it came back up again with a choking cough. He wiped the red trickles from his chin, the accountant in him mentally clocking up the waste percentage.

A young woman was watching him from the other side of the playground. She had a small child with her but she wouldn't let go of its hand. She was wary. Of him. She was wary of him. Suddenly shamed by his appearance and his behaviour, he stood up and bowed his head. 'I'm so sorry. I'm not myself today.'

He found a bin on Moseley Road to leave the wine bottle in. No doubt one of the alckies that hung around the green would find it. Good luck to them if they did. They might as well kill their livers with something decent for a change.

A bus that took him in the direction of Netta's house turned up as he passed the stop. He'd get that and walk the rest of the way. With any luck, they'd all be out by the time he arrived.

Colin was just a few streets away from Netta's. It had taken him longer than expected to get here because he'd been forced to leave the bus early on account of the other passengers turning their noses up at him. Yes, he was aware that owing to the fact he hadn't washed for two days and had slept on a bed of compost, he smelled. But did people have to be so rude? To make matters worse, the sun was a bastard this morning and he was sweating profusely.

Just in time, he spotted Frank's car coming his way and dove behind a hedge. At least he'd dodged having to face his ex-wife's current lover. Assuming she hadn't run off with Chambers yet.

He managed to get safely inside Frank's house without further incident. First of all he'd have a coffee to sober up. Then he'd get cleaned up and go round to finish that last patch of allotment. He wasn't really in a fit state to do it but it felt important that he finished it off himself. And Ursula might be there. She might even talk to him if she saw him doing something good.

He made the coffee and drank it so quickly he nearly scalded his throat. He tipped back a glass of water, but his thirst seemed to know no ends and his need for more coffee became desperate.

He heard the front door reopening and Liza appeared in the hallway, her eyes blazing. 'Dad, what the fuck? We've been searching everywhere for you. We looked all over the place yesterday and people are still out looking this morning. Where have you been?'

'Here and there. I needed some space.'

'To do what exactly? Drink yourself stupid and get into fights?'

'I haven't been in any fights.' Not as far as he could remember anyway.

'So what are those new marks on your face?'

He touched the fresh bumps and scratches. He was sure he'd remember if he'd had a fight. There was blood on his fingers. Of course. It was his emergency escape from Adam and Jude's. 'I got caught up in a bush with sharp thorns.'

He held out his arms to her and she came closer then stopped and covered her nose and mouth. 'Oh my God, you stink so much.'

'Oh, you don't like my new image?' It was good that he was making light of it. It was important to retain a sense of humour.

She moved to the other side of the kitchen. 'I don't know what's going on with you, but it's gone far enough.'

'I'm just going through a hard time, darling. I'll be all right soon.'

'I'm not talking about all of this.' She waved her hands at him. 'I'm talking about the things you said to that lady at the allotment. Ursula.'

'Ursula? What has she said?'

'Enough.'

'It's not true.'

Liza tutted. 'That's you all over isn't it, Dad? You don't even know what she said and you're already denying it.'

'No, you've got the wrong end of the stick, darling. I tried to tell her about the things that happened between your mum and me but she didn't understand.'

'Okay, so what did you tell her?'

'I said I'd done bad things. I tried to explain the extenuating circumstances.'

'Wait. Extenuating circumstances? What are you talking about?'

'Your mum and Chambers. Their affair.'

Liza walked away. For a minute, Colin thought she was leaving but then she came back. 'Nothing, I repeat, nothing that mum and Doogie did excused the way you treated her. Or us.'

'Us?'

'Yes, us. Me and Will. You used us to get to her. You forced us to take sides.'

'No, darling, no. I asked your mum to leave because she'd broken us up. We talked about it, the three of us. We agreed. You were just a kid. You're misremembering.'

Liza ran at him and pushed him. The shock and the force of it sent Colin reeling backwards. 'Will you listen to yourself? You didn't ask her to leave, you ordered her to. In the middle of a crowded fucking restaurant. And then you made out that we all wanted it. You hadn't even told us but you made us choose between you and her.'

No she was wrong. She was wrong. She was missing the point. 'All right, yes I did tell her to go, but I did it for us. For you, me and Will.'

She shook her head slowly. 'You did it so you could move Arianne in. You did it for yourself. We were just the excuse you pretended to have. All that money you stole from Mum? You stole it for yourself. And don't pretend it wasn't theft. It doesn't matter which way you try to fake news it, you took money from her that wasn't yours to take. I don't blame Will for despising you.'

'He, he despises me?'

She laughed. It was angry and mean and not in the least bit like his lovely, sweet daughter. 'That's all you care about, isn't it? What Will thinks of you. You never ask me what I think of you.'

'I don't need to, I've seen your painting of me.'

She stared at him, her disgust so very, very obvious. 'I hated you that night you made us your accomplices. I hated you both for different reasons, but I stuck with you because I had to stick with someone. Mum and me are cool now. But you, Dad. You. I have tried so hard with you but you're just so fucking selfish. So I'm giving up on you. Frank's been a better dad to me than you've ever been. I've only known Doogie a few weeks and he's already beaten you into third place. And just so's you know. Yes, that portrait is exactly how I see you. Nasty, cruel, mean, deceitful, evil and absolutely fucking pathetic.'

42

THIS WASN'T HOW IT WAS SUPPOSED TO WORK

Colin was in the bathroom, retching. His stomach was empty, and the toilet bowl was full of something that resembled gone-off blackcurrant cordial but was in fact, pure Malbec. How many bottles had he drunk in the last two days? He had no idea. Almost everything was still blotted out. He wanted to blot out the last half hour as well, but that was never going to happen. Liza had left but her fury, her frustration and her words would always be etched in his memory. He didn't think he would ever forget the day his daughter told him exactly what she thought of him. She'd given up on him. The one bond he thought was unbreakable had turned out to be already broken. And it was all his fault. That was what she'd said, wasn't it? Everything. Crushing Netta. Making Will despise him. Using them. Ruining all their lives. All of it was his fault. Liza hated him and she had every right to. How could he possibly go on now?

He splashed water on his face and caught the sight of himself in the bathroom mirror. His forehead and cheeks were marked with dark scratches, forming lines of dried blood. His wine-stained lips, teeth and tongue looked like something out of a horror film. His clothes were disgusting, and his hair was lank and greasy. He'd considered himself something once. Turned out that something was nothing more than a pile of vile, unpleasant shit who'd ruined the lives of everyone he'd ever loved.

He went into the bedroom and put his phone on charge, then took out his son's sweatshirt. It wasn't true that he only cared about what Will thought. Liza was wrong. But she was right about the other thing though. Will did despise him. Colin had been hiding from it but now that Liza had said it, he couldn't deny it any longer. His son despised him and his daughter hated him. When you came down to it, they were just two words that meant the same thing.

It took a while for his phone to spring back into life but eventually a steady round of ping, ping, pings let him know that he'd missed numerous messages regarding his whereabouts. Not that they actually cared. Not really. They just didn't want his expiration on their consciences. He buried his head in the sweatshirt and began to cry.

A single isolated ping made him look up. This had to be a more recent message. Perhaps it was Liza saying sorry. He was almost too scared to pick it up and find out, but he reminded himself it was important to stay hopeful and opened it tentatively.

Naturally, it wasn't from Liza. It was from Arianne, taunting him for sleeping in Adam and Jude's garden. That was it, he'd just about had enough. Colin let out a raw, agonising squeal. He was going to show them he had feelings too. And he was going to start with Will.

He grabbed the sweatshirt and went down and out the back, through the gate into Netta's. There were sounds of movement coming from inside the house, but he couldn't see anyone. The door was locked. He banged on it and set the dogs off barking. 'I know you're in there. Come out and talk to me. That's all I ask.'

The door remained closed. The dogs continued to bark.

'I'm your father. I demand to speak to you.' Still no one came.

He picked up a stone and threw it at the window. The glass cracked. 'Do you see what you've driven me to? No? Well, look at this. Look what I'm doing now. Despise this.' He tore at Will's sweatshirt and ripped it down the front, then ripped it again so that it became two uneven halves. 'I am someone. I deserve to be spoken to. I deserve to be seen.' Colin sank to his knees. 'I deserve to be pitied.'

The door opened as he curled into a tight ball while unstoppable tears erupted from him. All at once, he was surrounded by a pack of whining dogs. A pair of feet stopped in front of him. Colin looked up and let out a loud sob. If it had been anyone else but Chambers…

Chambers crouched down to his level. 'The kids aren't here, mate.'

Colin wiped his nose. 'I was hoping to catch Will.' It was a ridiculous thing to say, bearing in mind that he had snot running down his blood and wine-stained face and was still holding two halves of the sweatshirt, but that was the least of his worries right now.

'He went on holiday yesterday. Come on. Let's get you in.' Chambers took his arm and helped him up.

Netta's lounge was as cosy and inviting as ever. He could have lived in a house like this if he hadn't insisting on controlling everything in their home. If he'd forgiven her, they might have found happiness again. His children would still love him and everything would be just fine.

Chambers put a mug of tea down on the coffee table.

'Hot and sweet. My mum always says it's good for shock and she used to be a nurse. You know we've all been out looking for you?'

Colin wiped his eyes. The tears were slowing now. 'Liza said.'

'I saw you on Wednesday night, outside your house.'

'Well that accounts for one night then. I have vague recollections of sitting on a park bench last night with Mr Malbec for company, but the only thing I know for sure is that I woke up this morning in my next-door neighbour's back garden.'

'I've had a few nights like that myself. Not so much recently though.'

'Perhaps you went through your existential crisis earlier in life.'

Chambers was trying to hold in a smile. He was human after all. 'Yeah, I did. I burned everything I had that belonged to the woman I loved on Crosby Beach and sat over it all night like it was a funeral pyre, smoking weed.'

'Sounds a lot cooler than my meltdown.'

'It wasn't cool. I regretted it two days later. Drink your tea.'

'Was it Netta? The woman.'

'It was.'

'She does that to you.'

This time he grinned. 'She so fucking does. What did you burn of hers then?'

Colin picked up his tea. A tear plopped into it. Ridiculous bloody emotions. 'Nothing. What I did was much worse.'

'I know.'

'You broke my heart, the two of you.'

'You broke mine twice. The first time she chose you and the second when she went back to you, so it looks like we're even. Although technically, I guess you owe me one.'

Oh. Colin had never thought about it like that. He'd only ever looked at it from his side. 'Have you come to take her away?'

There was that grin again. The one that told him he was an idiot and a wanker. 'She doesn't want me, Colin. She doesn't want you either, so don't be getting ideas. It's Frank she loves now.'

'Frank's a nice guy.'

'Yeah. Bastard.' He caught Colin's eye and winked.

'No, I think that might be me actually. I think I'm a bastard.'

Chambers stood up. 'Finish the tea. You need to take a shower and clean your teeth. You look and smell like shit. Then you need to get some rest. When you're better, we're gonna make a plan.'

'To do what?'

'To sort out your existential crisis.'

The whole of Colin's body sighed. This wasn't how it was supposed to work. Chambers was his mortal enemy, not his saviour. He wanted to cry again. 'Why are you being so kind?'

Chambers shrugged. 'Because even bastards deserve to be pitied sometimes.'

43

THE SERIOUS STEPDAD CRUSH

Netta was at the foodbank, helping out in the job club they'd set up not long after she'd first started volunteering here. Back then, she used to give interview advice, but it had been so long since she'd had one of those sorts of jobs that she was out of touch. These days, she left that to the volunteers who came in from her old firm and she stuck to form filling and helping people find the right outfits to borrow for their interviews.

She was just finishing off taking someone's details when Neil signalled to her that she was needed. She let someone else take over and went over to see what the problem was.

'Liza's here,' he said. 'She's upset. Fliss has taken her over to a quiet room in the church.'

She speed-walked over to the church that the foodbank was attached to, cursing herself for putting off that heart to heart talk she'd been meaning to have. What kind of a crap mother was she?

The door to the quiet room had been left open and she could see Liza and Fliss, the vicar's wife, talking. Liza looked

like she'd been crying. Netta crouched down by her side.
'What's happened?'

'It's Dad. I've had it with him. I'm just so fucking angry.'
She gave Fliss a sheepish look. 'Sorry for swearing in church.'

Fliss assured her it wasn't a problem and left them alone.
Netta sat down in the vacated chair and held her daughter's
hand. 'He's turned up then?'

Liza nodded. 'He looks so bad. I think he's been sleeping
rough and drinking. We had a fight. He was being his usual
self and not taking responsibility for his actions, and I just lost
it. I ripped him apart. I told him Will despised him and I
hated him, and he was evil and a shit dad.'

'Oh my poor sweet girl, it's okay.'

Liza sniffed back a sob. 'The thing is though, Mum. He
looked really, really upset when I left him. But I was just so
mad.'

'He'll be all right. We'll sort it.'

Netta's phone rang. She pulled it out of her back pocket.
It was Doogie. He hadn't come back last night. He was probably calling to apologise now that he'd cooled off.

'Take it,' said Liza.

She answered the call. 'I haven't got time right now for a
chat.'

'I'm calling about Colin. He's had a meltdown but he's all
right now. My mum and stepdad came over. Clive's a doctor.
I'm worried about Liza though. I think they had an
argument.'

'She's here with me. A bit upset but otherwise all right.
Will you stay with him?'

'Yeah, yeah. He's in Will's bed. I'll keep an eye on him.'

'Is it Dad?' said Liza.

Netta ended the call. 'Yes. Doogie must have gone home

and found him in the middle of a meltdown. He's taken care of him and he's resting in Will's bed. I'll collect my things and we'll go. Why don't you drop a message out to the group chat and let them know he's safe and sound?'

'Okay. Mum, do you think if Doogie hadn't turned up he might have done something?'

'No, I don't. You mustn't think this is on you, Liza.'

She frowned. 'But it sort of is, isn't it? Maybe it was about time though. Maybe I had to tell him the truth to make him see.'

The last time Netta had seen Doogie's mum, she'd had gorgeous, long, naturally red hair. It was shorter now and there was more silver than red but as soon as Julie smiled at her, the years slipped away.

'Well this is turning out to be quite a momentous day. For the first time since he was a wee boy, that one's asked for my help, and now I get to see you again. And if that's not enough excitement, I'm about to meet the mother of my granddaughter.' Julie looked over Netta's shoulder. 'And you have got to be Liza. You look just like your mum did the last time I saw her.'

'Yeah, people say we look alike,' said Liza.

Julie gestured towards the man standing behind her. 'This is Clive, my husband.'

Clive shook her hand. 'Hello, Netta.' It was a formal gesture, but it was done in a warm and friendly way. That would be his doctor's training kicking in.

Netta took him in, this clean-cut, quietly spoken man. Everything about him was understated. He was nothing at all like Doogie's dad. Nevin Chambers had been loud and flashy. Not in a negative way, but he was definitely the kind of man who filled the room with his presence. When he was around, you knew about it.

'Shall we move from the hall so we can talk more freely?' said Clive.

'How about the living room?' said Doogie.

Clive touched Doogie's back. 'Perfect.'

She didn't know whether it was the touch or the one single uttered word, but a look temporarily settled on Doogie's face that she didn't think she'd ever witnessed in him before. Adoration was the only word she could think to describe it. Quiet man or not, Clive had achieved something that Nevin Chambers had never been able to do.

Clive positioned himself in front of the fireplace. 'He's going to be all right. He's very dehydrated and I doubt if he's eaten anything substantial for two or three days. He's been on quite a bender, but I think he'll survive with some rest. By the look of him, he's been through the wars.'

'He doesn't drink a lot normally,' said Liza.

'I think he's been having a rough time with his partner. She may have lashed out at him,' said Netta.

'That would explain it. He's rather underweight for his frame and height. Just an observation. It's probably nothing. When he's up to it, I'd suggest a proper medical. I can recommend someone who'll do it quickly, and reasonably, if necessary,' said Clive. 'Well, we have to go. We're meeting Claire. Doogie, call me if you need to.'

'Are you not going with them?' said Netta.

'Not this time. Anyway, I've got to keep my eye on Colin. Clive's given me instructions.' Doogie looked to Clive and all at once he was a little boy hoping for approval. He got it. Clive returned the look with one that was so genuinely full of affection and pride, Netta's heart almost burst with love for him.

'I'll go and look in on Dad,' said Liza, after they'd gone.

Netta went into the kitchen and filled the kettle. She didn't really need a drink but making a tea in times of crisis was the thing people did, wasn't it? British people anyway. There was a bundle of cloth on the table that looked a lot like Will's favourite old sweatshirt. The one that had been missing for a while. She picked it up and found it was indeed the sweatshirt. In two rather unequal halves. Then she noticed the kitchen window was cracked.

'Colin did that,' said Doogie.

'How?' She had visions of him putting his head through it.

'Threw a stone, I think. I was upstairs. I saw him tear the sweatshirt up though. I don't think he was thinking straight. He was in a bad way.'

'It's Will's. Was it genuine, d'you think? You never can tell with Colin.'

'It was genuine. It wasn't something you could put on.'

'That bad then?'

'Yeah.'

She carried on making the tea that she didn't really need or want. 'So, Clive's lovely.'

'Yeah, he's okay.'

Okay? Yeah, right. Doogie the hard man was fooling no one. There was definitely a serious stepdad crush going on there. The big softie. 'He's nothing like your dad.'

'No, he's not.' He ran his finger along the back of a chair, caught her watching him and stopped. 'I really wasn't here to get your permission. That's not what this was about. I promise.'

'Okay. Can we talk about it another time? When Colin's not having a nervous breakdown.'

'Sure. I just wanted you to know.'

She opened the door to let the dogs in from the garden. Spike loped in first. 'Spike's back.'

'Yeah. I need to tell you something. There's a chance, a slim chance, Betty might be having Spike's babies.'

Netta closed her eyes and let out a long, weary sigh. 'Oh you're just full of fucking surprises, aren't you?'

44

THERE WOULD ALWAYS BE LOOKS

Frank had wanted to rush over as soon as he saw Netta return with Liza, but he'd stopped himself. Doogie had everything under control, and he'd only be hanging around like a spare part.

He'd been out looking for Colin that morning when Liza's message came through that he was back. He'd come straight home, expecting Colin to be there. But of course he wasn't. Just as he'd been about to panic, Doogie was at the door. He'd left Colin with his stepdad. A doctor, apparently. When Frank heard what had happened, he was shocked. Colin must have been in an awful state. Probably for weeks. You didn't just explode like that on a whim. At that moment, a small cloud of guilt had deposited itself in Frank's psyche. He should have seen it coming. He should have been on the alert, but he'd been too busy with his own infantile jealousy. He'd been given one job, to look after Colin, and he'd failed miserably. He was one first class, self-absorbed dickhead.

Doogie's mum and stepdad had left a while ago and Fred was scratching at the back door. Frank let him out, followed him into the garden, and carried on through to Netta's kitchen. She was in there on her own.

'How is he?' he said.

'Sparked out. Clive gave him something to help him sleep.'

'I wanted to come over earlier, but I thought you'd a houseful already. I didn't want to get in the way.'

She took his hand. 'You'll never be in the way. Don't ever think you'll be in the way.'

He was about to kiss her, but Liza was suddenly in the doorway, her face full of angst. She threw herself on him. He let go of Netta's hand and put his arms around her. 'It's all right, darling girl. Everything's going to be all right.'

'I don't know how it can be,' she sobbed.

Doogie was next to come in. He stood behind Liza completing the circle around her.

'We're going to make it be,' said Frank. 'We're going to put him back together. All of us.'

Doogie nodded. 'We have to help him get back into his house, but he's not strong enough for that yet. He needs building up. He needs to get his head straight.'

'You're both right,' said Netta. 'But we can't do this on our own. We'll have to call in the big guns.'

Geraldine and Arthur were round within the hour. Geraldine had even bought a lemon drizzle cake for them to discuss tactics over. 'Just a small slice for you, Frank. I don't want you going off the rails, health-wise.' You could always rely on Geraldine to keep you grounded.

Arthur leaned forward on the table and slid his fingers together so that it looked like he was praying. 'We'll help out in whatever way we can. Although Gee's the one with the experience when it comes to mental health.'

'Well, I went through the mill and came out again with the help of therapy. It's experience of a sort, I suppose,' said Geraldine.

'It's the best we've got at the moment, Mum,' said Netta. 'Also, he needs building up. Clive says he's underweight, and you are by far the best cook in the family. No offence to anyone else here.'

'None taken,' said Frank.

'We need to get him checked over by a doctor, to make sure there isn't another reason,' said Doogie. 'He's probably just not been eating but Clive said it was best to check.'

'Very sensible. That will stop us all worrying.' Arthur's eyes fell on Liza. God love him, he was trying to put her mind at rest.

'And when he's strong enough, what do we do then? He can't stay here in limbo forever. It's just not good for him. Besides, Arianne has stolen his house,' said Netta.

Frank noticed Liza and Doogie exchanging looks. 'Actually, me and Doogie started working on a plan before all this happened. He's been watching the house.' She nodded at Doogie.

'Yeah. I've been checking for any patterns to their movements. The guy she's living with goes out in the mornings at around half nine and comes back just after one. I don't know about afternoons. I'm only doing mornings,' said Doogie.

Smart. Frank wished he'd thought of it. 'What do you have in mind?'

'We thought we might be able to work out a way of getting in there when Arianne's on her own,' said Liza.

Netta clapped her hands together excitedly. 'Stage a coup. I like it.'

'Clever girl,' said Arthur.

Liza blushed. 'Thanks, Grandad, but it was mostly Doogie.'

'Nah, she's the brains behind it. I'm just the one with the incognito spying experience.' Doogie's eyes flittered over to Netta for an instant. There was a coded message there. Frank was sure of it.

'How exciting,' said Geraldine. 'Looks like we're pooling our experience. And Arthur, I think we've found you a job. You can do a spying shift. So can you, Frank. Doogie can teach you the tricks of the trade so that she doesn't spot you. Will they need to wear dark glasses, Doogie? She might know their faces.'

'Probably not. They just need to keep a low profile,' said Doogie.

'Shame. Arthur looks rather a hunk in dark glasses.'

Doogie smiled and shook his head. He wasn't used to Geraldine and Arthur's little flirtations with each other yet. 'Okay, well I guess if it's sunny.'

'Excellent. Let's work out the shifts for the next week,' said Arthur. 'We can start tomorrow.'

Frank, Netta and Doogie were sitting in the garden, sharing a bottle of wine. Liza had gone round to her friend's to pour her heart out. Colin was still dead to the world, but they were taking it in turns to check on him.

'It feels like the start of something good tonight,' said Netta. 'Not just because we might actually be getting some-where with Colin. But you two. Look at you. You're working together. You're getting on.'

Doogie laughed. 'Fuck off, you patronising cow.'

She jabbed his arm. 'Don't ruin it, nobhead. Oh, by the

way, Frank. It seems Betty might be with child. Apparently, Spike's been getting amorous which was the real reason idiot-features here took him to his mum's.'

'Yeah, who knows, Spike and Betty might be able to go where me and Netta failed.'

She raised her eyebrows. 'Not funny, Doog.'

'It is a little bit though, isn't it?'

'Not even a tiny bit,' she said, but her mouth was twitching.

She was different with him. Playful. Teasing. Girlish. Frank hadn't noticed it before, but that was probably because he'd excluded himself from their company up until now. Doogie was a different man too. Softer. Less composed. Less sinister.

Frank noticed how they held each other's gaze for a heart-beat too long. Long enough for him to feel like he was on the outside of something looking in. Something special that he'd never be a part of. He was reminded of something Colin had said about them: 'They were in their own orbit. I don't think it was deliberate. They just didn't notice anyone else.' At last he got what Colin had been trying to tell him, and he understood that there would always be moments like these, there would always be looks. And with that fresh insight he also realised that if he wanted Netta in his life, then he had to make room for Doogie too because their feelings for each other weren't ever going to diminish. Frank just had to decide whether he could accept that. Because if he couldn't, he would almost certainly lose her.

45

AND SO DECREED OVERLORD CLAIRE

The door to Frank's breakfast room was open. Doogie wasn't sure whether to knock or just step in, so he stood outside on the paving, looking in. He could see a load of paintings in there. Some on easels and some stacked up against the wall. It looked cramped. He wouldn't be able to work in a room like that.

He noticed the wallpaper was coming away in one of the top corners. The paper itself was tasteful, obviously expensive, but dated. The woodwork was badly in need of attention as well. Grace's house had been like that when he first got to know her. Parts of it still were. He'd managed to persuade her to let him sort out some of the rooms, but she'd absolutely refused to let him touch her office and the little sitting room at the back of the house. The office had been her dad's once, and the sitting room had been her mum's favourite place for working and relaxing. Both had died before Doogie arrived on the scene. Grace said she felt connected to them in those rooms and there was no way she was going to let him take that away from her just because he had a need for clean lines and open spaces. It wasn't really a need, but it was fair to say he felt more comfortable without the previous generation's clutter in his face.

Frank appeared in the doorway between the breakfast room and the kitchen. 'Morning. Come in.'

Doogie stepped in and walked around the edge of the room, wary of knocking a canvas over. He hadn't really been looking at the paintings, art wasn't his thing, but then he saw one of Colin and he stopped. It was... How would he describe it? Raw. Exposed. Shocking. His main work was marketing, so he knew an arresting image when he saw one. This was an arresting image.

Frank stood behind him. 'It's good, isn't it? Liza painted it.'

'She's talented.'

'It's her best yet.'

'You and Liza are pretty tight, yeah?'

'I guess. She's a great girl. I have a daughter of my own though. She lives up your way.'

'Yeah, Netta mentioned it. She said you practically brought her up on your own. How d'you do that?'

Frank frowned. 'I didn't really have a choice. My late wife wasn't very present. Then she wasn't here at all. You just get on with it and hope it turns out well in the end.'

'And did it? Turn out well, I mean.'

'Yeah, it did. How's it going with your daughter?'

'All right, I think. Hard to tell. I wasn't very present either for most of her life.'

Frank probably knew that, but he didn't say. 'You're making up for it now though, yeah?'

'Trying to.'

'That's all you can do, try your best and hope it turns out well in the end.'

'I suppose so. I'm going to do my shift at Colin's house now. Net's already left for her market stall. Liza's on her own with him until Geraldine and Arthur get here.'

'I'll go over and keep her company.'

'Cheers. I'll be back late afternoon. I'm meeting my daughter when I'm done spying.'

'Good luck.'

'Well I might see Claire, so I'll probably need it.'

Doogie parked up outside Claire's mum's house. It was in Kings Heath, not far from Geraldine and Arthur's. The morning had been uneventful. Neither Arianne nor the guy, Byron, had left the house. It had been boring, but it had given Doogie time to do some thinking about life and love, and families. They were curious things, families. They didn't always look like one from the outside. When he was a kid, his family had been small. Just him, his mum and Mary from next door. He didn't see his Scottish family enough to feel part of them and he'd never been allowed to feel part of his dad's family. Monique saw to that. At uni, his friends had been a sort of family. In truth though, he'd always been a loner. Netta saw that in him. No one ever really got him like she did. Not even Claire. And no family ever made him feel he belonged as much as Netta's had. Maybe it was because she was part of it. Or maybe it was because Arthur and Geraldine got him too.

Merrie was on her way down the path. 'Mum's on the phone. Quick, let's get outta here before she finishes talking.'

'Is she still really mad at me then?'

Merrie stuck her head to one side and closed one eye, like she was thinking really hard. She looked really sweet when she did that. 'Not sure. Probably. She's always a bit mad at you, isn't she? Even when there's nothing to be mad about.'

He laughed. 'I guess.' Claire was another one he could have been happy with, if only he'd given them the chance. 'Let's walk.'

'Okay.' She slipped her arm in his. 'We can go into Kings Heath.'

Doogie felt a twinge of regret for all the walks he'd missed over the years. He imagined being on the receiving end of that sweet look of hers if he'd had to tell her off for being naughty. It was just as well he'd missed them because he'd have been a complete walkover. She'd have gotten away with anything. 'How did it go with Julie and Clive yesterday?'

'Oh I'm calling them Nana and Grandad now. Mum has officially sanctioned it.'

'Yeah?'

'Yeah. Well she suggested it'd be nice if I did. So I think we can say it went well. I wish you could've seen Mum though. She was on her best behaviour so's not to scare them off. So hilarious watching her trying not to swear. The effort was intense.' She was funny too, his daughter. In the early days of them getting to know each other, she'd been shy but now that she was more relaxed around him, her personality was beginning to show. It had only taken a few years. Not bad for a person who'd inherited his genes.

'I can imagine. She'd like that, your nana. It wasn't her fault she missed out on knowing you.'

'I know. I think it might be cool to meet my biological grandad some time as well though. What do you think?'

'I haven't seen him myself for a long time. We're not really close.'

She rolled her eyes. 'Is that like code for I haven't told him about you, Merrie?'

'Yes.'

'Honestly, you are so useless. It's a good job Nana's told him.'

'You're kidding me? I thought she didn't speak to him anymore?'

'Well she does now. Looks like you're not the only one with secrets. He wants to meet me. So when you're ready. Just say the word. Only don't leave it too long because Nana says he's well old.'

'Oh you want *me* to take you?'

'Well I'm not going on my own, am I?'

'I'll see what I can do.'

She kissed him in the cheek. 'Thanks, Dad.'

Doogie felt a blush coming from his neck upwards and told himself to get a grip. It was just a display of affection from his daughter. Yet another thing he'd missed out on. Hang on, did she just…? 'Did you just call me Dad?'

'Yep. It's another thing Overlord Claire has decreed. Is it okay?'

Dickhead that he was, he could feel a lump forming in his throat. 'It's more than okay. I'm not sure I deserve it though.'

'No, you don't, but I'm giving you a second chance.'

He tried out an awkward kiss on the top of her head and nearly missed. She laughed. 'You're not very good with emotions, are you?'

He blushed again. She was observant as well as funny. 'No. I guess I bottle them up. Sometimes with disastrous results.'

'Was I a disastrous result?'

'No. But walking away from you turned into one. Somebody recently told me I'd made some bad choices. Leaving you was probably the worst.'

'Is that your way of saying sorry?'

There was that lump again, making his throat sore. 'Yes.'

'I've been waiting for that.' Merrie stopped and opened her arms. 'Come here, idiot.'

Doogie took a step closer and let her wrap her arms around him. Tentatively, he put his around her.

'I won't break you know,' she said.

He squeezed harder.

'You're a bit goofy with that whole hermit thing you've got going on, but I think I love you, Dad.'

'Okay.'

She tutted loudly. 'This is the point where you're supposed to say I love you too Merrie, my incredibly stunning, amazingly witty daughter.'

He wiped his eyes which were inexplicably damp. 'Sorry. I love you too, Merrie, my incredibly stunning, amazingly witty daughter. I really, really do.'

'Hmm. Better. You can buy me lunch now. And we can talk about our trip to see Grandad Nevin.' She took his arm again and pulled him along in the direction of the High Street. 'Do you think Grace would like to come with us?'

'Not sure. Grace is upset with me. I don't know if I can fix it.'

She frowned. 'Do you know what Mum says about you?'

Doogie could think of a lot of things Claire might say about him. None of them good. 'What?'

'You're a compartmentaliser. You like to put people into boxes and keep them separate.'

'She's right. I am. A lot of the time I do it without even realising.'

'Ever thought about opening up the boxes and setting all those people free?'

Yes, he had, but he wasn't sure he'd be able to cope with the fallout. He wasn't sure if everyone else would cope either, especially with all this Colin crap going down.

46

THE POWER OF CHICKEN SOUP

'Well, you look a bit of state, I must say.' Geraldine was standing by the bed with a tray of something that smelled rather delicious.

Colin had no idea when the last morsel of food had passed his lips, touched his tongue, or slid satisfyingly into his belly. Although given that he'd lost several days at least, that didn't count for much. For all he knew, someone could have force fed him a whole roasted pig during his dark period, although his stomach was suggesting such a theory was highly implausible. That particular organ was screaming out to be satiated.

Geraldine moved the tray closer. 'Do you think you could manage a bowl of homemade chicken soup?'

'I'm pretty sure I could eat a vat of it.'

'Let's start small. We can build up to a vat later.' Did Colin detect a smile from the old girl? Well, well. Things must be bad if even Geraldine was being nice to him.

She rested the tray on his lap and the aroma of chicken hit him. And was it tarragon? Yes, he believed it was. He spooned it in too quickly and some of it dribbled down onto his chin. Oh but the creaminess of it. It was divine.

'Steady on, you'll make yourself sick. Take some bread with it.' Geraldine sat on a chair that had mysteriously appeared at the side of the bed since he'd been asleep.

He wiped the stray soup from his chin. 'Sorry. I'm very hungry and this is so good. You're a damn fine cook, Geraldine.'

'It has been said before. Take it slowly.'

Colin tried, he really tried to take it slowly, but it was like he'd been taken over by some gluttonous, ravenous animal. Even when he got to the bottom of the bowl, he was scraping his spoon around it and mopping up the dregs with the last chunk of gorgeously crusty bread.

Geraldine wrestled the tray off him and put it on the floor. 'Let it settle now. I'll bring you more later.'

Colin lay back on his pillow. He didn't want to wait. He wanted more this very minute. But his stomach was already fighting him. A huge burp came out of nowhere.

'That's because you ate it too fast,' said Geraldine.

'Sorry.' He closed his eyes in the hope that she might take the hint and bugger off. When he opened them again, she was still in the chair, hint not taken. 'Are you going to just sit there and watch me?'

Geraldine crossed one leg over the other. 'No. I'm going to sit here and talk to you.'

He closed his eyes again. 'I'm tired.'

'So am I. I'm tired of having to look after you but we are where we are.'

He sighed. 'You're really into this tough love stuff, aren't you?'

'More of the tough, less of the love when it comes to you, Colin. But the family seems to think I'm your best bet, so you're stuck with me. And unfortunately for me, I'm stuck with you.'

'Best bet for what?'

'Redemption.'

Redemption? If only that were possible. But Colin knew it was very much out of the question. For the last twenty-four hours, his mind had been into overdrive. It didn't matter whether he was awake or asleep, his past life had been constantly flashing before him. Except that it was as if he'd been looking at another life that belonged to someone who was not at all nice. Someone whose daughter thought he was nasty, cruel, mean, deceitful, and evil. Not forgetting pathetic. A man who'd used his children and driven his ex-wife into considering suicide. But of course it wasn't someone else's life. It was his, and he was not worth redeeming. 'I think I'm beyond that, Geraldine. I've taken a look inside the eye of this particular beast, and I can only see darkness.'

'That's a bit melodramatic, if I may say so. No one is beyond redemption. You've taken a step in the right direction by recognising what a horrible person you've been. We can build from that.'

Well that was a backhanded compliment if ever he'd heard one.

'We're all rooting for you, Colin. We all want you to get better.'

'You mean you all want me to be better. There's a difference.'

'I suppose we want both. Surely you don't want to stay like this forever? I've been through something similar and believe me, it just gets worse and worse until all you want to do is lie down and wait for death.'

Now who was being melodramatic? Colin had heard about Geraldine's problems from Liza a few years back. He'd pretended to be sympathetic to get in Liza's good books but secretly he'd taken some pleasure in it. That was the kind of nasty git he was. Of course, he hadn't realised quite how bad it was at the time. He'd like to think if he had known, he'd have been kinder. But in his heart of hearts, he knew he wouldn't have been, because he didn't have it in him to be a kind person. 'I'm sorry you had such a bad time.'

She smiled at him. It was a little sad, he thought. 'It was the best thing that happened to me. I had family and friends, and a wonderful therapist who pulled me through it. I'm so much happier now. I'd recommend seeing a therapist by the way, but in the meantime, you'll have to make do with me.'

'If I talk to you, can I have some more soup?'

'Yes.'

'Okay. What do you want to talk about?'

'Tell me what happened with Arianne.'

Bam! Right in the gut. Could have been worse, he supposed. She could have asked about Netta. 'She lost interest in me.' He closed his mouth. Enough said.

Geraldine had a funny look on her face. Completely impassive and yet expectant. 'Where did you meet her?'

'Oh right, you want to go that far back. It was at an art class. Life drawing. She was the model. She painted as well. Not very well but we can't all be Picasso, can we? Some of us used to go for a drink afterwards. She came along and we chatted. It wasn't that long after I'd found out about Netta and Chambers, I mean Doogie. I was feeling pretty low. She cheered me up. We were just friends for a long time, but before you ask, yes, we did eventually have, you know, relations while I was still with Netta.'

Geraldine didn't even flinch. She still had that look on her face. 'So she moved in with you, in the course of time. Were you happy?'

Hmm. Were they? 'I think so. Mostly. For a while. The kids were a problem for her. I sometimes think she was jealous of them. Almost as if she didn't want to share me. I don't think Will ever really took to her. Liza tried harder but when she made up with Netta she had somewhere else to go, didn't she?'

'Why did it go wrong, do you think?'

'As I said, she lost interest in me. And she went a bit odd. Well, I suppose she was always a bit erratic. Terrible mood swings. But it went off the scale with the pandemic. Lock-down was an absolute car crash. She was completely over the top about hygiene. She rallied afterwards though. Especially when we went to Italy for my summer teaching retreats. But when we got back from last year's, it was like a switch flicked on inside that demented head of hers. All of a sudden, she turned into a vegan maniac. Actually, I'm doing vegans a disservice. She wasn't even a proper one of them. She wouldn't let us anywhere near anything she hadn't cooked herself. And let me tell you, Geraldine, she is a shit cook. I couldn't even sneak out for a crafty veggie breakfast because she'd be sniffing me for signs of betrayal as soon as I got in. And if she thought I'd transgressed, she became a demon.'

'What would she do when she turned into a demon?' said Geraldine.

Colin picked at his fingernails. 'You know what she did.'

'Tell me.'

'She'd throw things, hit me. A few months ago, she smashed a glass jar on my chest, here.' He showed her the scar. It didn't hurt anymore, unless he thought about it. Mostly he didn't think about it. Unless he caught the smell of white spirit.

'Did you speak to anyone when it happened? Go to the doctor or a hospital? Or the police?'

He shook his head. 'Too ashamed.'

Geraldine leaned forward and took his hand. 'I know that feeling, Colin. But that particular shame isn't yours to carry.'

'Meaning there are other shames that are?'

'You tell me.'

'I…' The words wouldn't come out. He wanted to cry now, but he couldn't do it in front of Geraldine.

'Shall I get you some more soup, love?'

'Please.' His lips trembled and the tears had come before she'd closed the door behind her.

47

A ROBBERY OF SORTS

It was Sunday. Colin knew that because earlier, he'd heard the dogs going mad in the garden. That meant Netta's family and friends had come for their Sunday morning dog walk. Geraldine had stayed behind for another of their talks after which she'd brought him a sausage sandwich and a pen and notepad.

He ate the last bit of crust from the sandwich and licked the plate, his tongue greedily lapping up the fat juices and brown sauce that had oozed out of the soft, fluffy bread. The little dog, Maud was on the bed next to him. She did not look impressed by his antics. Perhaps she'd been hoping to do the same herself.

Colin lay back and shut his eyes, savouring the taste and reliving the last few moments of porky goodness. It was like he'd been given the keys to a sumptuous banquet after being fed nothing but grit all his life. Every time he ate one of Geraldine's offerings, it was as if he was tasting real food for the first time. Each meal was a voyage of delightful discovery.

Unfortunately, there was no such thing as a free lunch. Or breakfast, or dinner for that matter. The ex-mother-in-law demanded payment, and the payment required him to bare his soul. Not that she explicitly demanded the baring of souls, but it just seemed to happen. In another life, Geraldine would have been a therapist or one of those agony aunts. She was so damn good at getting you talking. She never used to be like that. The old Geraldine, the one before her breakdown, had been scared of her own shadow and would rather have sewn her mouth up than have a meaningful conversation. But she was a different woman now. No wonder Arthur was always so chirpy.

Yesterday afternoon, they'd talked again over a slice of delicious lemon drizzle cake. She'd told him why she'd gone to a therapist. Just came out with it with no trace of emotion. She'd even hugged him when his own emotions got the better of him again. He'd talked about Liza and Will and what he'd done to them. Geraldine told him how hard it had been for her and Arthur to stand by and watch him systematically destroy Netta. He'd cried again then but there was no hug to comfort him that time, which wasn't exactly a surprise.

This morning, they'd talked some more about Arianne, and he'd told her about the night before she locked him out. It had been a relief to let it out but to his humiliation, he'd ended up tearful again.

The argument had started over dinner. If you could call that slop she insisted on serving up, dinner. It was more like regurgitated bird seed. They'd been having the same thing all week and frankly it had been making him sick. He literally couldn't keep any of it down. Bizarrely, Arianne's cooking didn't have the same effect on her. If anything, she was getting fatter. When she'd demanded to know why he hadn't touched it, he'd explained it didn't agree with him. Her response had been to smash the lot, plate and all, over his head. He'd got up calmly, because it was important to stay calm when these things happened. Then he'd locked himself in the bathroom and taken a shower.

He'd been halfway across the landing, on his way to put on some fresh clothes when she came out of Liza's room. She'd let the door swing open so that he could see she'd wrecked it. For the first time in a long time, Colin had seen red. He could take a lot, but to do something so spiteful to Liza, that had been his breaking point. Yes, he'd screamed obscenities at her, but who could blame him? He didn't touch her though. Not one finger did he lay on her, even though he'd wanted to. But he told her to get out, and it was enough for her to lay hands on him. The shove had been so quick and unexpected, it had knocked him off his feet. He remembered tumbling down the stairs and that was it. He'd woken up later in the dark. She'd left him there and gone to bed. Colin had slept on the sofa that night. In the morning, still bruised and angry he'd gone to a café to eat some proper food and plot his escape or rather, Arianne's eviction. Unfortunately, she'd already made her own plans.

His reward for this morning's talk and yet more tears had been the sausage sandwich, with a promise of quiche for lunch, made by Netta's friend, Neil. It was a speciality of his, apparently. Colin remembered Neil's husband, Chris, being kind to him that first Sunday after he'd come to stay here. Netta had some nice friends. She'd come out of their marriage rather well in the end. But if anyone was going to survive living with a bastard it was going to be her. She had the kind of determined inner strength that you could never really break. He'd tried. He could admit that to himself properly now he'd seen the light that had been switched on for him. But seeing it was one thing. Dealing with the glare was quite different.

Colin picked up the pad. Geraldine had told him to use it if anything occurred to him, or even if he just felt like writing down his thoughts. He wondered what she'd think if he wrote down, I am a bastard. She'd probably agree.

Little Maud gave him an expectant look that reminded him of Geraldine. 'Any suggestions?' he said. The dog licked his hand. She could probably taste sausage. 'I'm not sure that's particularly helpful.'

Maud snuggled up closer to him and rested her head on his leg. Her action provided a flash of inspiration that was worth noting down:

Arianne – shoulder to cry on.

That's what she'd been in the first place. He hadn't been attracted to her. He just needed a friend. Someone to pour his heart out to while he healed. But she'd got under his skin and poisoned him against Netta. She fed his suspicions and fear. Not that he was blaming her. She'd been pushing against an open door. She might have encouraged the things he did but the responsibility was all his.

He wrote something else down:

Pay Netta back.

Then he realised that if someone read that they might think he was up to his old tricks again. He crossed it out and added new words in its place:

Make amends with Netta.

The voices downstairs signalled the return of the dog walkers. It must be nice to be in a little community like that. The kind where people care about you. No one cared about him like that, not even his parents. With them it was more a case of popping out a few sprogs to ensure the family name continued and then having as little to do with them as possible. If he hadn't been tied to them by blood and an unrelenting sense of obligation, he'd have cut them out years ago.

There was a knock at the door. 'Are you decent?' It was Arthur. Chirpy chappie Arthur.

'As decent as I'll ever be, Arthur.'

He came in with a mug of tea. 'Gee thought you might want this.'

'Thank you. That's very kind of her. She's being exceptionally kind to me. Especially considering.' He was going to say especially considering how much she hates me but for now, he was allowing himself to pretend she was doing all of this because she had a teeny tiny place in her heart for him. It was nonsense but it was the only thing he had to cling to at the moment.

It was nice to see the ex-father-in-law again. Other than Doogie's mother and stepfather, who were not at all as he'd imagined they'd be, he'd only seen Geraldine since the incident. Not long after Doctor Clive had dosed him up with sleeping tablets, he'd thought Liza had come into the room but that might have been a dream. Or wishful thinking.

Arthur sat down in the chair. 'She's a kind person. She can't bear to see someone suffering. She'll get you right, Colin. In fact, we're all working together to get you right.'

'I see.' He didn't really but he was sure Geraldine would explain it to him when the time came. 'I don't suppose that includes my children.'

'Yes, it does. Liza anyway, but Will's been keeping up to date.'

'Really? I thought they'd both—'

'You're their dad, Colin. They worry about you.'

'It's not a given, Arthur. Being someone's dad doesn't automatically mean they will care about you. I know that for a fact. I, for example, can't stand my father.'

'That might be so, but if he was ill, you'd be at his bedside like a shot.'

'Okay, Arthur. I give up. You're right and the world is just rosy.'

'You're being sarcastic again.'

'Sorry. I've got this notepad here. After you've gone, I'll write a hundred lines. I must not be sarcastic.'

The ex-father-in-law raised his eyebrows, in contrast to his mouth which was very much on a downward trend. Colin had done it again. He sighed. 'I apologise for being a despicable shit. Believe it or not, I am trying not to be.'

'Apology accepted. I actually came up to give you some news. Ursula's accepted an offer on her house. She's talking about going away for a while.'

'Oh. That was quick. I suppose it's a very desirable house.' His heart felt oddly heavy. Even though he knew he'd blown it with Ursula, the thought of her going away was crushing. 'Did she say where she was going?'

'Wales. To stay with friends. In a commune.' Arthur's eyes were wide, as if to say, imagine that.

Colin's eyes matched Arthur's. He hadn't seen that coming at all. Although he could actually see Ursula fitting into a commune quite nicely.

'And we've got some people interested in those allotments we cleared.'

'Great. I think I'll be well enough to come and finish that last bit off tomorrow or the day after.'

'No need. Doogie's already done it.'

'But…' He wanted to say that patch was his to finish but his lip was already trembling.

'There, there now. Don't be upset. It was only a few weeds.'

'I know. I just… I just wanted it to be me that finished it. And now he's robbed me again.'

'Who's robbed you?'

'Chambers. I've been robbed.'

48

THE MAN WHO COULDN'T CRY

With it being Sunday, they'd agreed not to keep watch on Colin's house, so Doogie was taking it easy in the kitchen after the dog walk. Arthur had gone up to see Colin and give him the news about Ursula. He was now back in the kitchen looking a bit worried. 'I've upset Colin.'

Geraldine had been putting together sausage and bacon sandwiches, along with Neil, until that moment. She stopped, leaving half a sausage stuck on the end of the fork she was holding in mid-air. 'How have you managed that?'

'Was it the news about Ursula moving?' said Doogie.

'I don't think so. He seemed to take that fairly well. It was the allotment.'

Doogie frowned. 'Ursula's allotment?'

'No. The one we've been digging up. He was upset because you finished it. He was muttering something about you robbing him again.'

Geraldine tutted and put the sausage down onto a slice of bread. 'I'd better go up and see him.'

Doogie put his hand up to stop her. 'It's all right, I'll go. I think I might know what this is about.'

He pushed the bedroom door open. Colin was stroking Maud. He was also crying. Not sobbing and wailing like he'd been doing on Friday when he had his meltdown, but quietly. Long silent tears were rolling down his cheeks and falling from his jawline. It was an uncomfortable sight, but Doogie couldn't just walk away. He closed the door behind him. 'All right, bud?'

Colin kept his eyes on the dog. 'Not really, no. You've done it to me again.'

There was a chair next to the bed. Doogie took it and leaned forward onto the edge of the quilt. 'What did I do?'

'I wanted to be the one to finish the digging.'

'I'm sorry. I just did what Arthur asked me to do. We didn't know it was important to you. Why didn't you say? We'd have waited if we'd known.'

Colin pulled a couple of tissues out of a box on the bedside table. They were the mansize variety that promised to be extra-large and extra-strong. 'Because I was embarrassed to admit that something so simple meant so much.'

'Why did it mean so much?'

'Because it was a good thing to do, and I wanted to prove that I could do something good. It's all right for you. People think you're a nice guy. They like you. I wanted to be that guy for a change. But you took it from me.'

Doogie was stunned into silence. That was some seriously fucked up shit the accountant was coming out with.

'Look, I'm sorry about this.' Colin pointed to his tears. 'I don't seem to have any control over it. My emotions are completely off the scale at the moment. I do actually know I'm being pathetic.'

'I'm the other way. I can get angry, but crying? No. Not in a long time.' Unless you counted yesterday with Merrie. But a lump in the throat and a bit of dampness around the eyes didn't really match up to Colin's outbursts.

'That's a good thing, isn't it?'

'I dunno. I suppose it helps sometimes to cry.' He was thinking of Merrie laughing at his inability to handle emotion. It wasn't funny really. It was tragic. He might not want to be breaking out in tears all the time, but what about the other emotions? What about sadness, or happiness, or unadulterated joy? Surely it was better to deal with those than to coast through life like nothing touched you? Except things did touch Doogie. That was why he hid from them. Or ran away. A hermit, Merrie had called him. He didn't want her seeing him in that way.

'Geraldine seems to think it helps. I'm not so sure,' said Colin.

'Anyway, I thought you hated digging.'

'I thought so too, but it's quite therapeutic when you get into it. And as I said, I was focussing on the end point rather than the gruelling bit in the middle.'

Doogie smiled. 'Yeah, it's very therapeutic.' When he got back home, his vegetable garden would need some serious work. He wondered if Grace had been picking the sweetcorn. It would be starting to ripen now. She liked it barbecued, coated with a special sauce he made. He'd picked up the recipe on his second and last visit to St Kitts. He wondered if Grace was missing him. He'd been on the verge of calling her so many times, but she'd told him not to ring unless it was to say he was coming home, and it wasn't time to go home yet. 'Maybe you should get an allotment.'

Colin blew his nose. 'I don't know if I'm an allotment person. I don't know what kind of person I am anymore. I know what kind I used to be, and I certainly don't want to go back down that road again. The rest is a mystery.'

'You'll figure it out. Listen, I'm sorry I robbed you. I guess that makes us even now.'

'I hardly think you digging up a bit of soil is on a par with the woman you loved choosing me and then me setting out to destroy her.'

'It's all relative.'

Colin's tears had stopped. He was smiling. 'Nice try, mate.'

'You heard about Ursula going to a commune?'

'Yes. Have you seen her since Wednesday?'

'Nah, but I might see her tomorrow. I'm taking Priscilla Sweeting to the allotment. I've been doing some odd jobs for her. She wants to see the place where Samuel died.'

'You're brave.'

'She's not so bad when you get to know her.'

'I could say the same about you.'

Doogie winked at him. 'Steady on, bro. I'm not good at emotions. You should go and see Ursula before she leaves.'

'I'll think about it. I'd like to apologise to her.'

'Also, you should know. We're working on a plan to get your house back, but I don't think anyone's asked if that's what you want.'

Maud looked up at Colin and cocked her head to one side. Colin smiled and scratched under her chin. Doogie thought he was never going to answer, but then he said: 'I don't know. I think I'm afraid to walk back in there.'

49

THERE ARE MORE WAYS TO BE
UNFAITHFUL

Priscilla was dressed up in what looked like her Sunday church outfit. She always looked smart, but today's extra effort was noticeable. She was wearing a wig. What with that and the make-up, she looked younger.

Doogie held out his arm for her. 'You're looking mighty fine today, Priscilla.' He hadn't meant to sound like he'd just stepped out of a cheesy seventies TV series. It wasn't the kind of thing he'd say in real life, more the kind of thing his dad used to say to his mum, back in the day. He'd been thinking a lot about him since Merrie brought him up. That was probably why it had slipped out.

Priscilla fixed him with a stern glare. 'Don't think that gives you the right to flirt with me, young man. I'm very particular about who I receive amorous remarks from.'

He winked. 'Does that mean you've got someone you're less particular with then?'

Her face creased. 'There might be a certain widower at church I exchange pleasantries with. And no, it is not Clyde Wilson before you start getting ideas into that thick head of yours. That man hasn't seen the inside of God's house since him buried his wife. This gentleman is cut from much finer cloth.'

'No chance for me then?'

She slapped his hand. 'Absolutely none. I got very high standards these days. Are we going, or are we going to talk nonsense on my doorstep all morning?'

'We're going.' He offered his arm up to her again.

She batted him away like she was swatting a fly. 'I'm not an invalid. I can walk down my own garden path without falling over.'

She waited while he opened the passenger door for her, then sat in the seat and put her handbag on her lap. Doogie gave her time to do the seatbelt up before closing the door. When he got inside the car himself, he noticed how very upright she was. She was holding the handbag so tight he could see her knuckle bones through her skin.

'I'm not that bad a driver,' he joked.

'Shut up your foolish mouth and drive,' she said without looking at him.

By the time they pulled up outside the allotment gates, beads of sweat were showing on Priscilla's forehead. She wiped them away with a tissue.

'Are you sure you wouldn't rather have your son or daughters with you?' said Doogie.

She shook her head. 'They'd make too much of a fuss. I'd rather do it with you.'

'Okay. When you're ready, I'll call Clyde. He's going to let us in.'

She took a compact out of her bag and began to powder her face. 'Will she be in there?'

'I don't know. Probably. I think she's there most days. Are you sure—?'

'Stop asking me if I'm sure.'

'I don't know if this helps but according to Clyde, Ursula and Samuel were just friends. They didn't, you know—'

'Have sexual intercourse? No, it does not help.'

No, he didn't think it would, but it was worth a try.

'There are more ways to be unfaithful than sex. Sex is just the tip of the iceberg. Remember that, Dougal. It might help you make better choices in the future. You can call Clyde now.'

Well that was him told off then. Doogie stepped out of the car to make the call.

Clyde came to get them straight away, his dog Colonel a few paces behind him. He was wearing his usual straw trilby, but he looked neater than he usually did. He must have dressed up for the occasion as well. Even Colonel looked as if he'd been given a brush.

Clyde pushed his hat back. 'Hello, Priscilla. Nice to see you again. How you doing?'

She acknowledged him with a tight nod. 'Surviving, Clyde. What about you?'

'Surviving, Priscilla. I'll take you up there.'

'No.' She pointed to Doogie. 'He can do that.'

Doogie could see the sweat beads had returned. He offered her his arm again. This time she took it.

Ursula wasn't on her allotment. It would have been awkward if she had been. Presumably the same thought had occurred to her. The path that ran through the gap in the fence had been cleared properly now so it was an easier walk up to Samuel's shed. They stopped outside. 'This one was his,' he said.

'I know.'

'Sorry, I thought you hadn't been here before.'

'I haven't. His old dada used to have a shed just like this one.' She touched the battered old wicker chair that had been left outside. 'He even had one of these. The family had a bit a land back home in Jamaica. Not much, but enough to grow a few crops. Samuel used to help him. He missed it when we came here.'

'It's not locked, if you want to go inside.'

'In a bit.' She let go of his arm. 'Leave me now.'

'Okay. I'll come back in half an hour. I won't be far away if you need me though.'

'If you see her, tell her come.'

Doogie nodded and walked back up the path. When he got to the hedge, he looked back. Priscilla was still standing facing the shed, her hand on the old wicker chair.

There was a bench on Ursula's allotment. He sat down on it and pulled out his phone. Merrie had left a message to say she and Claire were coming over to Netta's tonight for dinner. Doogie thought about Colin facing his demons, his emotions running wild. He thought about boxes, and his own demons, and what Priscilla had said about there being more ways to be unfaithful than sex. He needed to call Grace.

'Hello.' Her voice was sharp. She often sounded that way on the phone, even when she didn't mean to be, but Doogie reckoned this time, she meant to be.

'Are you in the middle of something?'

'I'm always in the middle of something, and I'm a bit shorthanded at the moment.' It was a dig at him not being there to help her out.

'What are you doing?'

'Believe it or not, I'm in your garden trying to keep the weeds down.'

'There's no need to do that.'

'Why? Are you coming back to do it yourself?'

'Yeah. Soon.'

'How soon?'

'Not sure yet. I have a couple of things I need to finish off. I'll explain when I get back.'

'Explain? That'll be a first.'

'Yeah well, I'm unboxing.'

'I haven't a clue what you're talking about.' Her voice softened. That was a good sign.

'It'll make sense, I promise. Have you tried the sweetcorn yet?'

'I barbecued some for our campers on Saturday. It would have been better with your special marinade, but they loved it as it was.'

'Yeah? That's good.'

'I'm gonna go now. Unless there's anything else you want to say?'

He had loads of things he wanted to say, but not here on the other end of a line. Not in this alien city. He wanted to sit down on an empty beach with her, watching waves crashing on white sands. He wanted to look up at vast blue skies and talk until his voice was hoarse and the heavy load of unspoken words had lifted. 'No. I just wanted to…' *Say it. Say you just wanted to hear her voice.*

'Okay. Let me know when you're done down there. Don't take too long.'

'I miss you, Gracie.' Fuck. She'd gone.

He was aware of being watched. Ursula was on the pathway. She was wearing that bright blue dress that looked so good on her.

'I hope you don't mind me taking a seat. Priscilla wanted some time alone,' he said.

'Not at all. Is she all right?'

'I think so. She'd like to speak to you.'

'I see. I suppose it's about time. I have a little stove inside if you'd like to brew up some tea. We may as well make it civilised.' She handed him the key to her shed then went off towards the hedge.

Doogie left it a while before making the tea, to give them time to talk. Clyde turned up as the kettle was boiling. 'Got enough water in there for one more?'

'Don't know if there's enough cups.'

Clyde opened up a cabinet at the back of the shed. 'Ursula keeps extra in here. Everybody comes to her for tea and sympathy. I don't know who we'll go to when she leaves us.'

They carried the tea through the hedge, along with a tub of biscuits that Clyde had supplied. Priscilla and Ursula were sitting talking. Priscilla was in the old wicker chair. When they saw Doogie and Clyde, they stopped.

Doogie handed Priscilla a china mug that he'd found in the cabinet. Geraldine had told him tea tasted better in a china cup. He couldn't tell the difference himself, but he thought Priscilla would appreciate it. 'We can go away again,' he said.

The old woman eyed the cup and frowned. 'Stay.'

He held the tub out to her. 'Tek a biscuit.'

She arched one eyebrow. 'That's a terrible accent. Didn't your father teach you nothing?'

Doogie grinned. 'Not really, no. I can do a better Scottish accent though. Do you wanna hear it?'

'No, I do not. Fool.' She was smiling now.

Clyde laughed. 'I knew you'd like him.'

She turned to Clyde. 'Oh did you? I thought you'd just sent him to vex me.'

50

LOVE THE BONES OF YOU

When they finished the tea, Priscilla asked them to wait for her by the hedge. Clyde and Ursula went through it and stood on the other side, but Doogie kept her within his sight, worried that the uneven path might be too much for her.

She turned her back to him and faced the wicker chair and the shed. Her head was bent, and her hands clasped in front of her. He realised she was praying. She stayed in that position for a few minutes, then she took something out of her bag and stuck it into the wicker weave. Was it a Jamaican flag? The object was small, and it was hard to tell from this distance. When he looked away from it, he saw that she was coming towards him. He rushed forward to help her back to the better path.

Priscilla allowed Clyde to escort her out. They stopped occasionally for Clyde to point out different plants to her. She was a lot more patient than you'd imagine. She almost seemed to be enjoying herself.

Doogie and Ursula followed a few paces behind. 'Arthur told me about Colin's breakdown. How is he?' she said.

'He's going through a bad patch at the moment, but I think he'll get through it.'

'I'd like to see him again before I go away.'

'I'll tell him. He wants a chance to say sorry to you.'

'Then we should make it happen.'

They'd reached the car. Doogie held the passenger door open for Priscilla. She nodded at Ursula. It wasn't exactly friendly but probably the nearest it was ever going to get.

Clyde helped her in. 'Goodbye for now, Priscilla. I might call on you after Doogie's gone back home. Just to check up on yer.'

'I don't need no checking up on, Clyde Wilson, but you can come. Just don't get any ideas.' She pointed at Doogie. 'Me got enough of that with that scallywag.'

The corners of Clyde's mouth turned up. 'I can assure you Madam Sweeting, my intentions are honourable. I'll be seeing you.' He shook Doogie's hand. 'Samuel can rest now.'

'What did that old fool say about Samuel?' she said when Doogie got back in the car.

'Nothing. Did you sort things out with Ursula?'

'Depends what you mean by sort things out. We talked. It was enough. That cup you gave me, where did you get it from?'

'Ursula's shed. Why?'

'It was one of mine. Samuel must have taken it there.'

Doogie sighed. Every time he tried to do something good, he fucked it up. 'I'm sorry. Do you feel better for going there though? Being able to say a prayer for Samuel, did it help?'

'The prayer wasn't for him. It was for me. I was asking the Lord for forgiveness.'

'I don't understand. Why do you need forgiveness?'

She pulled her bag up against her chest. 'Because I threw my husband out two days before he died. Samuel spent the

last days of his life in that shed when he should have been
with his family. If he hadn't been alone in that damn place, we
might have got him to a hospital and saved him. I took him
away from them.'

'But I thought you said he wasn't interested in them?'

'He wasn't. But that could have changed. Ursula said he
talked about us all the time. But he never talked *to* us, Dougal.
All he ever talked about was vegetables and that place. The
fool. The stupid idiot fool.'

'Look, Priscilla. Samuel made his choices and there's no
reason why you had to put up with them. You didn't do
anything wrong. You gave him plenty of time to change.'
Doogie was thinking of his mum. She'd been like Priscilla
once, waiting for his dad to be a different man. Until she
decided it was a waste of time and she was better off
without him. It couldn't have happened soon enough for
Doogie. The way she always played second fiddle to
Monique used to really get to him. So did the way his dad
kept everyone in their safe little boxes. Safe for his dad that
is. Doogie was the only one allowed to cross the divide. No,
that wasn't actually what happened. Doogie was the only
one *forced* to cross the divide. He'd been the one with no
choices. It was kind of ironic that he'd ended up doing the
same thing as his old man, given that he'd hated having it
done to him. 'My daughter and her mum tell me I'm a
compartmentaliser.'

'A what?'

'I put people into boxes. Keep them apart. It's a way of
not having to deal with stuff that's going on inside my head.'

'Hmm. And are you?'

'Yeah. I've always been that way. Do you think Samuel
might have been too.'

Priscilla clucked her tongue. 'That's all modern claptrap.

My generation don't do com-part-men-talising. We just get on with things.'

'Sorry.'

'And if he was one of them, the box he put his family in was the smallest one of all. The Lord probably forgave him for it, but I can't. No more fool talk now, Dougal. Tek me home.'

Doogie held the gate open for Priscilla and noticed for the first time that its hinges were loose. 'I'll sort that out for you next time I come.'

She patted his arm. 'God bless you. You're a good boy.'

He smiled to himself. It had been a long time since he'd been a boy, and even longer since he'd been blessed.

She opened the front door and made straight for the kitchen. 'I'll make us some tea.'

'I can't stay.'

'You got somewhere to be?'

'Yeah, I have actually. My friend's coming over.'

'Is she the one?'

Doogie frowned. 'The one?'

'The one who broke your heart.'

He leaned against a cupboard, winded. He'd said nothing to Priscilla about broken hearts, or Netta, or Claire. Or about Grace either. 'She's the mother of my daughter.'

'Did I ask you that?' Priscilla was giving him the steely stare now. She was sending him a message which basically translated meant cut the crap, I can see right through you.

'No. She didn't break my heart. I think I may have broken hers though.'

'Them bad choices?'

He nodded, too ashamed to look at her. 'Yes.'

'And the woman who broke your heart, is she a friend as well?'

'Yeah. I'm staying with her at the moment.'

'You still have feelings for her?'

'It's complicated.'

'You got no one else back up in Scotland?'

'Yeah, I've got someone. Her name's Grace. She wants to get married.'

'And what about you?'

Doogie shrugged. 'Like I said, it's complicated.'

Priscilla sent a puff of air shooting out through her lips. 'You're even more of a damn fool than I thought you were. No, it is not complicated. You either want this friend who broke your heart, or you want Grace. Or you want to be on your own. You make a choice. Just make it a good one that you can live with for the rest of your life.'

Doogie had spent the drive to Netta's thinking about choices. Priscilla was right and it wasn't really that complicated at all. It was just a matter of three simple choices. All he needed to do was decide which was the good one. The right one.

Merrie, Liza and Claire were in the garden. He couldn't see Netta. Merrie jumped up and gave him a hug. 'How'd it go with Priscilla?'

'Good. She nearly ripped my head off for suggesting Samuel might have been a compartmentaliser, but I think she'd forgotten it by the time we reached hers.'

He caught Claire's attention which wasn't tricky since the mention of compartmentalising had attracted her interest. 'Can I have a word?'

She went with him into the living room and folded her

arms. 'What?' Maybe she thought he was going to have a go at her for pointing out his faults to Merrie.

'This is going to sound stupid but go with it, okay?'

'Okay,' she said, slowly.

'I never said sorry to you, so I'm saying it now.'

Her head jerked back. 'Which bit are you saying sorry for? Abandoning your daughter? Stringing me along and pretending you were happy before abandoning me and your daughter? Or—'

'All of it. I've made a lot of bad choices.'

'Yeah. So Merrie tells me. Priscilla helping you see the light, is she?'

'It's a lot of things. The other thing I wanted to say was thank you. For not giving up on me and not letting me give up on Merrie. And for being my best friend.'

'Are you feeling all right?'

'Yeah, I'm good.' Doogie wrinkled his nose. 'I'm trying to follow Merrie's advice. I'm trying to open a few boxes and let the emotions out.'

'Fucking hell. You wanna be careful there, mate.' She looked him in the eye. 'We were shit lovers, but we've always been best friends, haven't we?'

'Yes, we have. Oh and thanks for suggesting Merrie should call my mum Nana. Mum's made up about it.' He tried to look away, but she matched the movement of his eyes with her head until the only place he could set them was back on her. 'She's calling me Dad now. She said that's down to you as well.'

'Uh huh.' Claire's mouth turned into a crooked grin. She was having a good time. That much was easy to see. It was a bit more difficult to predict how she was going to react to the thing he was about to say next.

'Thanks. It means a lot. So, I need to tell you the real

reason I left Scotland. Grace said she wanted to get married, and I panicked. I know, I know. Don't have a go at me.'

She took a step back. For a minute, he thought she was going to smack him one. It wouldn't have been the first time. 'Okay I won't have a go at you, but you are a prick. What are you gonna do?' He could tell then that she already knew and had had time to process it. Netta must have told her.

'I'm going to tie up the loose ends here and go back home to talk to Grace. Listen, I know we're not touchy-feely people but seeing as you've decided not to smash my head in, could I get a hug?'

She tutted and wrapped her arms around him. He held on, wishing she could have been the woman for him. 'I fucking love the bones of you, Claire Fogarty.'

'I love you too, you stupid prick. Always have and always will.'

He couldn't be sure, but he thought he heard her sniff.

51

AN OLD DECLARATION

Netta was standing in the hallway watching Doogie holding Claire in his arms. Or perhaps it was the other way round. Whichever it was, it was a very tender moment, and she was caught in the middle of it. She'd just come back over from Frank's. The girls had told her Doogie and Claire were inside, so she knew they were there. She just hadn't anticipated walking in on such an intimate moment. Not that she'd actually walked in on them. She was just standing outside their field of vision, observing, not sure whether to announce her arrival or quietly creep away. In the end she didn't have to do either because Doogie noticed her and pulled away.

'All right, Net?' He looked a little guilty in her opinion.

'Yeah. Just came to say dinner's nearly ready. Frank's cooked a curry over at his but we'll eat it over here so that we're not leaving Colin alone.'

'I'll give him a hand carrying it over.' He brushed past her as he went out. She caught a whiff of Claire's perfume on him.

Claire rubbed her arms. Her eyes were wet. 'Not like him

to ask for a hug. He's just apologised for leaving me and Merrie all those years ago. I think he's having a mini crisis.'

'Must be catching.'

She did a little embarrassed laugh. 'He told me Grace wants to get married. I didn't say you already told me last week, but he probably guessed.'

'Sorry we haven't had time to talk about it properly. It's been a bit chaotic here, as you can imagine. What do you think?'

'I think she's exactly what he needs.'

'I've never met her.' She knew she sounded indignant, but that was exactly what she was. Why was Grace exactly what Doogie needed and not her? Why had Claire, her oldest friend, never said that Netta was exactly what he needed?

Claire was watching her carefully. 'What do you think?'

'If he's going to do it, he should just get on with it and stop running away.'

'Net. Are we good, you and me?' Claire had seen right through her.

'Of course we are.'

'Because I wouldn't want you to think there was something going on with me and Doogie.'

'Never crossed my mind.'

'We're just mates. You know that, yeah? That's what we are, you, me and Doogie. Mates.'

'Always. It was just a bit awkward, walking in on you.'

'Awkward? Don't be a nob.' Claire squeezed her into a hug. 'If Doogie walks in on us right now, are you gonna think it's awkward?'

Netta pushed herself back. 'Well, obviously. Because knowing Doogie, he'd probably be having rude fantasies about the three of us in bed together.'

Claire roared with laughter. 'Fair point. I wouldn't put it past him.'

They'd finished off Frank's curry. Liza had taken Merrie into town. Somehow, they'd started talking about their old university days. Frank was next to Netta on the sofa, laughing at the things they got up to. He was indulging them, and she loved him for it.

'Where's that box of stuff you had from those days,' he said. 'There are some top photos of you three in there.'

'Oh it's in the loft. Colin brought my old photos and records over from his house ages ago. You won't want to see them,' said Netta.

Doogie and Claire stated chanting: 'Get them, get them.'

Frank pulled her up. 'Come on, I'll help you.'

They climbed the ladder up through the hatch. The sun hadn't gone down yet and a shaft of bright light was coming from the small window in the roof. It was more of an attic really. In times gone by, when the house and the area was a bit more grand, it had been the housekeeper's room. Since then, the staircase that led up to it had been replaced with a ladder and it had become a loft. When Netta had first moved into the house, the room had been full to the brim with decades of memorabilia. It was quite empty now, except for half a dozen boxes.

Frank sat down on a box and looked around. 'I still say this room would make a great studio if you put a couple more windows in.'

'Nice idea but I don't have the money to do that.' She scanned the room for the box she was searching for, her thoughts still a bit muddled about what she'd seen and heard earlier.

'You okay?' he said. 'You were a bit quiet over dinner.'

She sat back on her knees. 'Yes. Well, sort of. It's ridiculous really. I walked in on Claire and Doogie hugging, and it felt a bit weird. I don't know, it was like it was their thing and I wasn't a part of it. I mean, I know they obviously had a thing because they have a daughter. It's just…'

'You've just realised there are things about them that are theirs alone.'

'I suppose so.' That was half of it. The other half, the bit about her having a secret strop because Claire didn't think she was the perfect partner for Doogie, was not so easy to explain. Or admit. Which is why she was keeping it to herself.

'You'll get used to it. Just don't go off and behave like an arse in the meantime. That can get you into all sorts of trouble.'

He understood. Of course he did. He'd been going through the same thing himself. She'd just been too preoccupied to pick up on it. 'Oh Frank, I'm sorry. I didn't think.'

He kissed her. 'I still think you should convert this room into a studio.'

She slipped her hand around the back of his neck and kissed him. 'Maybe when I have some money. By the way, you're sitting on my box.'

'Oh my God, will you just look at us. What did we look like?' screamed Claire. 'Net, you're doing your signature pout in this one.'

'I think you look pretty good. You should see my old university photos,' said Frank.

'All right, bud.' Doogie was addressing the doorway.

Netta had her back to it. She turned to see Colin with the

tray she'd taken his dinner up on earlier. 'Sorry, I just brought my empties down.'

Doogie got up and took the tray off him. 'I'll take it. Come and join us.'

'I don't want to intrude.' He cut a pathetic figure in Will's track pants and T-shirt. They were hanging off him. Good job he was seeing a doctor tomorrow.

'Park your arse down there.' Claire pointed to the armchair Doogie had just left.

'We're looking at the stuff you brought over from yours,' explained Netta.

Claire pulled out a record. It was a single. 'Close to Me'. Netta had known which one it was as soon as Claire began to read the writing on the sleeve. 'Netta. Our first dance together.'

It was obvious she'd already reached the bottom of the message, even though she hadn't read it out. 'That's sweet.' She slipped the record back in the box and picked up another one. Claire had always loathed Colin but it seemed even she didn't have the heart to put the boot in anymore.

Colin accepted a beer from Doogie and was putting on a good show, but she could sense him faltering. He met her gaze and in her mind's eye, she saw the rest of the message without needing to look at the sleeve:

Love you always,
Colin xxxx

52

TALK OF LOVE AND FORGIVENESS

Being a Tuesday, Netta would normally be at the foodbank, but she was having the day off to take Colin to a doctor. She could have left the job to one of the others, but it was something she felt she had to do herself. They'd come to the one Clive had recommended. Colin hadn't wanted to go to his own in case he bumped into someone he didn't want to see. Arianne mostly, but there was also the possibility of Adam and Jude, his neighbours. Netta had never liked them, so she was happy to bring him across town. Besides, a private doctor was easier to get an appointment with.

Colin had been in there for absolutely ages, and she'd exhausted the waiting room's ample selection of magazines. There were, after all, only so many ways you could be told wide-legged pants were the new skinny jeans, and red lipstick was the new red lipstick. She'd even read an article about air fryers now that it seemed she was stuck with one. It was hilarious really when she thought about Doogie's legacy for her. Two doomed love affairs, one lost baby, a litter of pups and an air fryer. Well if nothing else, at least she'd be able to make nice chips.

She checked the clock and wondered, not for the first time, what they were up to in there. She avoided looking at the receptionist because there were also only so many ways you could say that no you did not require another latte and Danish. You didn't get this at your local GP. A leaflet on cystitis and a working toilet was as much as you could expect there, if you were lucky. But you got what you paid for, she supposed. If you could afford to spend money on this kind of treatment all the time, you'd want to feel like you were in a spa. She wondered how Colin was paying for it. Perhaps he still had money squirreled away somewhere. His ill-gotten gains from when he'd pretended to be a penniless artist and made her pay for everything. He probably built up a tidy nest egg then. She hoped Arianne didn't know about it because he was going to need it when they got him back home.

Colin came out of the doctor's room at last. She met him halfway but had to wait until they were back in the car before he gave her the details. 'The doctor thinks I'm undernourished and depressed. She's arranging other tests to rule out anything else. I have some supplements to help build me back up. I refused medication for the depression and said I didn't want a therapist.'

'How did she take that?'

'She didn't have much choice. I told her I'm managing just fine with Geraldine's help.'

'Fair enough. How do you think you'll get on when you don't see so much of Mum?'

'When you move me back into my own house, you mean? Doogie told me the plan. I've discussed it with Geraldine. When the time comes, she'll come to me, or I'll go to her. She said she'll be around for as long as I need her.'

Wow. Sometimes Netta wondered if her mother wasn't some kind of superhero in disguise. Or maybe a saint. She had to be one or both of those things considering how much work she was putting into helping a man she had such a massive grudge against.

Colin asked if they could stop somewhere for a walk. 'I feel like I've been cooped up inside for too long. I could do with stretching my legs.'

She took him to Edgbaston Reservoir. She hadn't been here since her mum was coming to the end of her therapy. It seemed appropriate somehow.

'I'm sorry about the record last night,' she said when they'd been walking for a while. 'I forgot it was in there.'

'That's okay. At least Claire had the decency not to finish reading it out. That would have been embarrassing.'

'Would it have been so embarrassing though? We all write stupid declarations when we're young.' She was thinking about a book she'd bought Doogie when he was still very much her Heathcliff. It was *Wuthering Heights*, naturally. She'd written something cringeworthy on the inside of it. *From one outsider to another*, if she remembered correctly.

'It wasn't stupid. At least, I didn't think it was at the time. Did you?' he said.

'No, I thought it was cute.'

'I'll settle for cute. Tell me something, truthfully. Did you love me at all?'

'Yes, I did.' If he'd asked her six years ago, or even six months ago, she'd have said no. But pain has a habit of warping your memories. For too long she could only think of the man he'd become. Lately, she'd remembered the shy, nerdy boy who wrote his undying love on a record sleeve. And yes, she had loved him. Not in the same way she'd loved

Doogie then. Not in the same way she loved Frank now. But she'd loved him all the same.

'I loved you so much,' he said.

'No, you loved the idea of me. Until it got too much.'

'Not true.'

'If you loved me so much, why did you want to change me? All those times you nagged me to make my dress and my language more appropriate. And what about refusing to call me Netta? You always called me Annette, even though I didn't like it. And I know you think I belittled you but you were on a daily mission to make me as small as possible. And all of that was before the affair. Afterwards, you just wanted to crush me.'

'I was an absolute bastard, and perhaps you were too much for me to handle but that doesn't mean I didn't love you. Please, don't take that away from me, Netta.'

She stopped walking and took his hand. 'If I ever belittled you or made light of your feelings for me, I'm sorry. But that was nothing to the way you treated me. From the moment you found out about me and Doogie you made my life unbearable.'

He looked at her hand holding his and touched it gently with his free one. 'I know. And the worst part of it is I enjoyed it. I can't begin to describe just how much disgust I have for myself right now.'

She searched his eyes for the lies that usually hid behind them but saw none. 'Colin. We're in our fifties now. It's time to stop suffering and move on. I forgive you. For all the things you did. I forgive you.'

'But I haven't done a proper apology yet.'

'I think you have.'

'I'm going to pay you back. All the money I took from you under false pretences, I'm going to pay it back.'

'And how are you going to do that?'

'I'm going to sell the house.'

'But you love that house.'

He shook his head. 'Not anymore. When I get back in, I'm going to put it on the market.'

She touched his cheek. 'You don't need to pay me back in money. You just need to be a better person.'

'I'm going to do both.' He blushed and couldn't look at her.

She was reminded again of that shy, nerdy boy she once thought was cute and she put her arms around him. A strange feeling came over her. Relief. How about that? Forgiveness must do that to you.

They were almost home and were just passing the road the allotments were on. She'd thought Colin was miles away, but he suddenly blurted out: 'Could you drop me here?'

Netta stopped the car. After his last visit, she wasn't so sure it was a good idea.

He must have sensed her hesitancy. 'I'd like to catch Ursula if I can, and she has asked to see me. I'll come straight back home afterwards, I promise. Geraldine will have my guts for garters if I don't.'

She relaxed. It couldn't do any harm, could it? 'Well you don't want to make the mighty Gezza angry.'

'I certainly do not. That woman is my lifeline. Where would I be without her counselling and her numerous pies?'

She let him out and drove on home. Claire had stayed over last night. She was heading back to Brighton today and Netta wanted to say goodbye to her.

She got there just as Claire was on her way out the door.

Doogie was with them. 'It's a pity you can't stay a bit longer,' he said.

'I've got to get back to work, husband and kids. You've got Merrie for a few more days. She'll kick your arse for me if it needs doing,' said Claire.

She gave Netta a hug. 'Hope things get sorted with Colin. I actually feel sorry for him. Don't know how that happened.' She prodded Doogie in the chest. 'Sort your life out you, before you're old and grey and nobody wants you.'

They waited until her car had turned the corner before going inside. 'Frank's just gone to take over from your dad at Colin's,' he said. 'Is now a good time to talk?'

53

THE PEOPLE WE COULD HAVE BEEN

'Is now a good time to talk?' he'd asked. Actually, no it wasn't. Netta was quietly battling all kinds of internal emotions, and she could have done with some time alone to process them. It had been talking to Colin earlier. So many surprises had come out of it that had set her mind racing. The first was the realisation that Colin still had feelings for her. She didn't know why she hadn't seen it before, but then she'd never been the most observant of people.

The second surprise was the recollection that she had once loved him. Not enough to be faithful to him when the opportunity arose for her to be with Doogie again, but that wasn't because she hadn't cared for Colin. It was because her love for Doogie had been such a destructive force that nothing else came close. That was how it had been back then. What worried her now was whether it was still the same today. Until he'd turned up on her doorstep, she'd managed to fool herself they were just good friends. But these last few weeks had given her a taste of what might have been and dispelled that particular myth. Now everything was chaos. Doogie was probably going to marry someone other than her, and there was every possibility she was in danger of being consumed by that force again. There was also every possibility the thing she had with Frank might not survive it.

Everyone had been trying so hard to protect her from Colin, no one had seen the real threat hiding in plain sight. Everyone except Claire that is. She knew. She'd understood the implications well before Netta. Why else had she come up from Brighton if not to save her from herself, and from Doogie?

Doogie was waiting for an answer to his question. 'I suppose it's as good a time as any,' she said, instantly fearing the words that might come spilling out.

They went into the lounge. The garden was too open to people arriving home unexpectedly. At least in the middle of the house they had the advantage of being aware of others before they were aware of them.

He stood in front of the fireplace, just as his stepfather had done last week. 'Like I said before, I didn't come here to get your permission to marry Grace.'

'I see.' She knew that of course. That wasn't the way he worked. But it didn't stop a shard of disappointment forming. 'So why did you come then?'

'I needed to think. It's too isolated up there. I'm in a nice safe bubble. Too easy to make a decision I might regret. I had to come away to get some perspective.'

'About your feelings for Grace, you mean?'

'Partly.'

She wanted to ask, if it was only partly about Grace then who or what else was it about? But she was silenced by that fear again.

He touched her fingers. She met his eyes and saw the longing in them. Not for her. Not in the way he used to long for her. But for freedom. He'd come to set himself free from her. He'd lied. He had come for her permission.

She moved her hand away. 'I love you.'

He closed his eyes for a minute. When he opened them again, they were wet. 'I love you.'

She felt tears stabbing the back of her own eyes. 'It's not enough though, is it?'

'No.'

'Do you think there'll ever be a time when we won't feel we took a wrong turn somewhere?'

'No. But maybe when we're too old to care anymore, it'll hurt less.'

'You think?'

'Not really. I was just trying to cheer you up.'

She laughed in spite of everything. 'Do me a favour.'

'Anything.'

'Hold me and don't say another word.'

He took her in his arms. She wrapped hers around him and rested her head against his shoulder. They breathed slowly and synchronously. She noted how well their bodies fitted together, even after all these years. Everything about them was made for each other, except the one thing that mattered. It wasn't that they didn't love each other. They did and they always would. But it was the wrong kind of love. The kind you couldn't live with.

His tears fell onto her face. They were even crying in time, that's how perfectly aligned they were. She pulled away and kissed his stained cheeks. 'It's okay, it's okay. We're going to be all right. We're going to be fine. You're going to be happy, and so am I.'

'You think?' he said mimicking her own words.

'Not really. I was just trying to cheer you up.' One corner of her mouth turned up and then the other.

He laughed. 'Look at me, Wilde. I don't do emotions. '

'Well you do now, Chambers.'

He shook his head. 'Give us a kiss, you mad cow.'

The kiss was long and delicious. She savoured it knowing it would be their last one like this. Tomorrow and for the rest of their lives there would only be friendly embraces. They probably both knew that, which is why they lingered too long.

He pulled away first, his eyes searching her as if he'd just seen her for the first time. 'Ah, Netta Wilde. The things we could have done. The people we could have been.'

54

A DAY OF SECOND CHANCES

Colin hung around the allotment gates for a while hoping to catch someone's eye, but he was out of luck. It was going to have to be another climb over. Fitting, he supposed, since that was the way of his last exit.

He was halfway over when a car pulled up. Clyde was in the driving seat, and he did not look happy. Colin climbed back down again and hung his head like a guilty schoolboy. Typical to be caught in the act when he was trying to do the decent thing.

Clyde got out of the car and let Colonel out. 'What do you think you're doing? Climbing over gates, a man in your condition. You think Arthur will be happy about that? And what about Geraldine? She'll do her nut.'

'You could always not tell them.'

Clyde sucked air between his teeth. 'You vex me bad sometimes, Colin. You know that?'

'I do, and I'm sorry, Clyde. I have a habit of vexing people. I don't always mean to. It just happens. I am actually trying very hard not to do any kind of vexing at all.'

'I'm thinking you need to try harder.'

Colin nodded his head. Words were unnecessary, and probably pointless when it came to Clyde.

Clyde unlocked the gate. 'Come on, Colonel.'

Colin could have sworn the big dog gave him an eye roll as he loped past him through the hallowed gate.

Clyde jerked his head a touch. 'Well come on then, if you're coming.'

He quick-stepped through before the old man changed his mind. 'Are you going to tell Arthur?'

'I'm still thinking about it. What you doing here anyway? We're all finished up there.'

'I wanted to see it now that it's been done. And I er, I was hoping to see Ursula.'

'You going to be upsetting her again?'

'No. Quite the opposite, I hope.'

'You better not be. Otherwise I am definitely telling Arthur. And Geraldine. She'll be the first to hear of it.'

'Understood. Can I go now?' That sounded sarcastic and Colin was trying really hard not to be either sarcastic or vexing. He added: 'Please' in an entirely non-sarcastic, non-sneery, non-vexing way. At least he hoped that's how it came across.

'Okay. But remember, I'm keeping my eye on you, and I got Geraldine's number on speed dial.'

Wasn't everybody's number on speed dial these days? He decided not to point that out.

Colin tried Ursula's allotment first, but she wasn't there, and the shed was locked up. Disappointed, he turned towards the hedge which had been cut back even further. Its height had been halved too, so that you could actually see most of

Samuel's shed. The wicker chair was still outside. A small piece of green paper had got caught up in the cane. As he got closer to it, more colours emerged, and Colin recognised it as the Jamaican flag. It was held in place by a stick, a bit bigger than a toothpick. Doogie had brought Samuel's widow here yesterday. She may have left it. He sat down in one of the other chairs. The flag made it wrong to sit in Samuel's seat. As if you were sitting on him.

With the weeds all gone, the space looked bare and vacant. Colin rather liked it that way. It fitted his current state of mind. The sun came out from behind a blob of cloud. That type of cloud had a name, but he didn't know it. His dad would have known. He was something of a cloud specialist. Which was precisely why Colin refused to remember any of them.

He closed his eyes. After too many days in bed, his busy morning had tired him out. Probably all those months of neglect and stress didn't help either. Still, he'd had a good talk that morning with Netta. She'd told him she'd loved him once which had made him a bit sad, but mostly deliriously happy. Rather ashamed too about all the other things. He wished she'd given him the chance to say sorry properly, but she'd given him a different kind of chance. A second one. She'd forgiven him and now his happiness was off the scale.

The sun on his face felt good. It felt optimistic, if he dare use such a word. 'Are you getting this too, Samuel?' So he was talking to ghosts as well as dogs now? He was officially off his rocker. He smiled. Yep, completely lost it.

When he opened his eyes again, he saw a shot of red over the top of the hedge. Ursula was wearing a new dress. She looked quite stunning.

'I like your dress,' he said when she was near enough.

She answered with a smile, but it was her eyes that gave

away all that Colin needed to know. She knew everything about his breakdown. Everything about him and Arianne too, probably. She had some flowers in her hand. 'Sweet peas. Samuel's favourite flower. I promised Priscilla I'd lay some for him.' She put them on the wicker chair and shut her eyes for a spell. Then she took the seat on the other side, so that it felt like Samuel was between them.

He waited for her to settle before starting: 'I shouldn't have made those assumptions about your husband. I knew really that what he did was wrong. Just as I knew what I did to Netta was wrong.'

She turned to look at him, her eyes impassive. 'Then why couldn't you say that?'

'I think because I'd built my life around it. The revenge. That was me. If I admitted it was wrong then there was nothing left for me to be.'

'And now that you have, who will you be?'

'Hard to say. I'm in a state of flux at the moment. Not exactly redeemed but not quite a write off. I have a very bossy lady keeping me in check.'

'Would that be Geraldine? She's a formidable woman.'

'She is indeed. Sadly, she's exactly what I need at the moment. I hear you're leaving.'

'Just for a few months while I work out who I'm going to be.'

'And what then?'

She shrugged. 'Who knows? I'm in a state of flux too. Come with me.'

Colin wrinkled his nose. 'To a commune?'

Ursula threw back her head and laughed. It was like watching a waterfall cascading. Fresh, vibrant and life affirming. 'It's not what you think. They don't sit around a pot full of lentils singing 'Kumbaya'. It's just a community of people who share a large house rather than be lonely. They have some spare rooms for visitors. It's near Snowdonia, the perfect place to work out where you're going next. We can do it together.'

Colin took in her dazzling smile, the mischievous twinkle in her eye, the gentle but strong nature of her and marvelled at how easy it would be to fall for this woman. 'It's not that I don't want to, Ursula, but I'm not ready for another relationship.'

'Neither am I. We're both still grieving. But I'm always ready for friendship.'

Friendship. Of course. How arrogant of him to assume that she would be desperate enough to want him. 'I'm an idiot. I'm sorry.'

'Don't be. You're still finding your way. Everything's upside down for you at the moment.'

'Can I ask who is it you're grieving for? Is it your husband, in spite of all he did?'

'No. Someone much dearer.'

Samuel, he supposed. It was obvious now that Colin thought about it. There was a sadness to her whenever she spoke of him

'And you Colin, who are you grieving for?'

'I don't know.' He looked out at the land in front of him. 'It seems empty here now that it's done.'

'Not empty. Resting. Waiting to be filled up again.'

Resting. Waiting. Yes, he could see that now.

He felt unusually positive as he walked back to Netta's. Ursula had that effect on him. He'd be sad to see her go, but they'd agreed to keep in touch and while she was away, he was going to mind the allotment for her. Yes, him. An allotment holder.

Imagine! It would be nice to see this commune that wasn't really a commune. If it really was full of lonely people, he'd fit right in. But he couldn't go yet. He was too dependent on this new family he'd somehow accumulated. He was thinking about grief. It hadn't been difficult to work out who Ursula was grieving for. It was harder to work out the source of his own grief. There were so many things to pick from. But one thing he did know. It wasn't Arianne.

'Is that you, Colin?' Geraldine called out to him as he let himself in.

He already had his foot on the stairs. 'Yes. Can't stop. I need to write something down.'

As soon as he was in the bedroom, he picked up the notepad. The first thing he did was put a tick next to: *'Apologise to Ursula.'*

Then he wrote:

Who or what am I grieving for?

He heard someone on the stairs. Probably Geraldine. If Clyde had called her, she'd be coming to give him a verbal clip round the ear. Maybe he'd show her what he'd just written. She'd have a field day with that one. The footsteps were getting closer. He hastily scribbled one more thing:

Not empty. Resting. Waiting to be filled up again.

The knock came on the door. Colin steeled himself. 'Come in, Geraldine.'

The door opened and it was Liza. It was the first time he'd seen her since she'd walked out on him on Friday. When he was fully awake at any rate. He still wasn't sure if she'd come to him when he was semi-conscious. He felt quite shaky, unsure as to whether it was nervous excitement or fear for what she might say to him this time.

'Hey. You're looking a bit better.' She was messing with her thumbs, twisting and turning them.

'I couldn't look any worse, I suppose. Sorry I was in such a state.'

'Can I…?' She pointed to the bed.

'Yeah. Sure.' He moved up to give her space.

'About the things I said to you—'

'You were right to say them. I needed to hear it. You were spot on about what an absolute swine I've been. I really don't know how you put up with me for so long. No one else did. You're wrong about me only being interested in Will though. I'm sure it looked that way. I think I got a bit fixated on him because I can't be around him. And I definitely took you for granted, but I promise I will never do that again. If you give me a second chance, that is.'

'Okay.' She took hold of his hand.

Colin's emotions were in turbo charge mode again. He pointed to the tears splashing on his cheeks. 'Ignore these. Your nan says it's good for me but frankly, I find it highly embarrassing.' She laughed. Laughter was good. 'Your painting is brilliant, by the way. Frightening, but brilliant.'

'Maybe I'll paint you again when you're all new and different.'

'That would be good. Perhaps wait until I look a bit less ravaged.'

'We could paint together, like I do with Frank.'

He shook his head. 'I wish I could say yes, darling. I would so like to be able to set up an easel next to my wonderfully talented daughter, but I can't. It just won't come. In fact, the idea of picking up a brush again makes me physically sick.'

Liza slid her arm around his waist and put her head on his shoulder. 'Let's just see how things go when you're back in your own place.'

'All right.' He didn't think that would change things but he didn't have the heart to tell her.

She let go of him and turned to face him. 'I've got something to tell you. Me and Merrie have been doing some undercover work. We've been following Arianne. You know like she makes out she's a vegan and all that? Well she's been buying meat and cheese, chocolate and so many things that are absolutely not vegan.'

'It'll be for that Byron guy. He looks like a meat eater to me.' He looked like a Colin eater too, given half the chance.

'Yeah, we followed him too. He works in a tattoo parlour further up Moseley Road. There's more. We've seen her eating food in cafés.'

'Are you sure, Lize? She stopped eating anything but her own cooking a couple of years ago.'

'Well she's back on it now, and guess what.'

'What?'

'We've seen her tucking into a big fat meaty burger. Twice!'

Colin's jaw went slack. A burger? The lying, deceitful bitch. No wonder she was getting fatter while he was withering down to skin and bone. He reached for the notepad and wrote:

Get my house back and throw Arianne out.

Liza read it over his shoulder. 'Go, Dad.'

'Yes, go me. But I just want you to know, this is not about revenge. I'm not doing revenge anymore. This is about facing my fears.'

55

ALL DONE AND DUSTED

Netta's kitchen was full. Everyone was here, including her mum and dad, Neil and Chris, and Merrie. They'd all been sucked into Operation Reclaim. No one could remember who'd given it that title, but it had stuck. If it had been up to Netta, they'd have gone to the police, but Colin didn't want them involved unless all else failed. She supposed she could see why. Involving the authorities might end up in court battles and Colin had been humiliated enough already. So here they were, devising a plan to get his house back and get rid of Arianne.

'So, I'm thinking I can call at the house to ask her about the garage conversion,' said Doogie.

'My studio, you mean? Arianne wouldn't know anything about it. It was done before Netta moved out. It was Netta who paid for it.' Colin looked a little shamefaced. Good. Netta had forgiven him, but it didn't hurt for him to be reminded of the man he used to be.

'Yeah, but I won't know that, will I?' said Doogie. 'I'll tell her I'm moving in around the corner and say I'm looking for someone to do mine. We've said hello a couple of times in the street now, so she'll think I'm from around there.'

Netta's dad slapped Doogie on the back. 'Oh that's very clever. What happens then?'

'I'll force my way in once the door's open.'

Colin shook his head. 'No, she'll probably do you for assault. Believe me, she wouldn't hesitate. I can't have that hanging on you, it wouldn't be right. But there might be another way. All the windows and doors are kept locked. When she's at home, she usually keeps the keys in a key cupboard in the kitchen. But the old pantry at the back of the house has a dodgy window. The catch has broken. You can't tell from the outside but all you have to do is lift it up. I've been meaning to get it fixed for months but never got round to it.'

'You don't think Arianne might have got it repaired?' said Frank.

'Highly unlikely. She doesn't know about it. I use the pantry to store paint and canvasses. She never goes in there. It's in between the doors to the kitchen and the studio, but it's an L-shaped hall, so as long as Doogie keeps Arianne talking at the front she won't see anything.'

'Grand. So if Doogie distracts Arianne while Byron's out at work, I'll climb in through the window and let you in by the back door,' said Frank.

'The window's too small. It'll have to be someone slim. I'll do it,' said Colin.

'Sorry, no. You're not going into that house on your own when she's in there. I can't allow it. I'll do it,' said Liza.

Colin moved his head slowly from side to side. 'Thank you, Liza, but I'm not letting you take the risk of being alone with that monster. I'm going in.'

Netta's mum put her hand up. 'Well I'm the smallest. I should go in.'

Everyone looked horrified, not least, Netta's dad. 'I don't think so, Gee. I'm afraid my foot is firmly down on this one. There could be all sorts of dangers in there and I don't like to harp on about age, but climbing through a window at your time of life could result in a broken hip. Or worse.'

'Oh for God's sake, I'll do it,' said Netta. And before anyone could protest, she slapped the table. 'Discussion over.'

The room went quiet. Everyone looked either straight ahead or at the two cakes sitting in the middle of the table. One chocolate, one coffee. Her mum had made them to help with the planning process.

Frank broke the awkward silence with a cough. 'Just to recap then. Byron goes to work. Doogie distracts Arianne. Netta climbs in through the window. What's next?'

'I'll creep into the kitchen, quiet as a church mouse, get the keys from the cupboard, and let you, Colin and Liza in through the back door,' said Netta. 'Merrie will keep watch from the street. Mum and Dad, Chris and Neil will be waiting in their cars, out of sight. We confront Arianne, bundle her out the door and Chris will change the locks.' Netta clapped her hands together. 'All done and dusted.'

Colin turned to Chris. 'You can do that, can you?'

Chris nodded. 'It's not difficult. My dad's a builder. I've learned stuff even if I didn't want to. I'll fix that window as well. Don't want anyone else climbing through. So when are we going to do it? It's just that the holidays are almost over, and I've got a couple of teacher training days next week.'

'Tomorrow?' said Colin. 'That'll be quite fitting as it will be exactly four weeks to the day, she threw me out.'

'Tomorrow it is then.' Netta's mum stood up. 'I'll get the

plates, and we'll have some cake. Extra-large slice for Colin. Extra-small slice for Frank.'

Colin threw Frank an apologetic look. 'Sorry, mate.'

Frank waved away his apology. 'Don't be. Geraldine knows what's best for both of us.'

Netta got up to help with the plates, just in time to hear her mum whispering in her dad's ear: 'You were very masterful then, Art. You should try it more often. It made me tingle all over.'

It sounded like her dad was going to find out what was best for him tonight. At least someone was getting it. It might have been four weeks since she and Liza had rescued Colin, but it was slightly longer since she and Frank had had anything remotely resembling carnal relations.

'Mum, have you got a sec?' Liza pulled her into the study.

Netta closed the door behind them. She had a feeling this was going to be something monumental.

'I might move back in with Dad for a bit if we do manage to get in tomorrow. I don't want to leave him there on his own.'

Okay, so not monumental exactly. Probably expected. 'All right, darling. I understand.'

'You don't mind, do you? I'll still come and see you.'

'Not at all. And we'll arrange cover for you so that you're not shouldering the burden all by yourself. We'll all chip in.'

Netta remembered the last time she'd slept in that house. It was the night Colin told her to move out and it hadn't been a happy experience. But things were different now, and this time she wasn't going to walk away from her family. This time they were in it together.

56

OPERATION RECLAIM AND THE BARBIE DOLL

Doogie checked the time. Byron had been gone for half an hour. He phoned Netta. 'All clear here. Merrie's gonna call Liza when Arianne opens the door. She'll keep the call going so you can stay updated.'

'Okay. We're in the park now. Almost at the back of the house.' She was out of breath. He imagined her running commando-style across the parkland carrying the folding ladder they'd taken with them. Although it was probably Frank doing the carrying. 'Ouch.'

'What is it?'

'Nothing. I just sat down and managed to get a thorn in my bum. We're there now. You can go.'

He cut the call. 'Time to go.'

Merrie was jiggling around in the passenger seat, a big grin slapped across her face. 'Yay. Operation Reclaim starts here.' She tried to fist bump him, but he was having none of it.

'Listen, Mer. This isn't like one of your computer games. It could get violent. Stay calm, focus on your job, and keep out of trouble. Don't come anywhere near the house until

Arthur and Geraldine are ready to take you in. Okay?' Chris and Neil were down as first back-up in case there was any aggro, so he figured Merrie would be safest with the old couple.

'Yeah, yeah. It is though. It's like an **RPG**. I'm the cool girl warrior going into combat against the forces of evil.'

'I have no idea what you're talking about but behave. I mean it. This is serious.' He'd only recently realised how geeky his daughter was. He loved that about her.

He left Merrie on the corner and walked the few yards to Colin's house. The living room curtains were open, but the window was covered by purple net. They didn't stop him seeing Arianne on the sofa, watching TV.

She noticed him walking down the drive and was up at the window before he reached the door. The nets parted and her head appeared between them, looking like it had been wrapped in purple chiffon, like those scarves old ladies used to wear when he was a kid. Doogie smiled at her and did a thumbs up. She disappeared and from the shadow on the door glass, he could see she was going upstairs. He rang the bell, hoping she wasn't looking out of the window for suspicious characters.

'Be there in a minute. Don't go away.' It sounded like she was shouting from the landing.

He glanced over at Merrie. She was watching him and talking on her phone. Suddenly, the door opened and Doogie was hit by a wall of perfume and hairspray. When she'd looked at him through the chiffon, Arianne's hair had been flat against her head. Now it was big, loose, and obviously brushed. He noted she'd also put lipstick on. She hadn't been looking out for trouble, she'd been making herself presentable. And she was pouting at him. It knocked him off course and it took a minute to get back on track. 'I er, I… Sorry to bother you, love. I know we haven't met properly.'

'Arianne.' Her eyebrows rose and fell. She finished off with another pout.

'Oh right. Nevin.' Fuck knows why of all names he'd picked his dad's. It must have been the stress of being hit on by an oversized Barbie doll.

'Lovely. So now that we've met properly, what can I do for you?'

'Your garage conversion. I was wondering who did it for you? I've bought a house around the corner and I'm looking to do some improvements. Bring the place up to scratch. You know what I mean?'

'Oh I do. It certainly adds value to the house. I've noticed you around a few times. Have you moved in yet?'

'Not yet. There's too much work needs doing. The builders are starting next week but they're a bit pricey, so I was looking for another quote for the garage.'

'Isn't everything these days? I think I know which house you mean now. Top end of the road? Red door?'

'Sounds like you know the area well.'

'I've been here a while. You get to know a place, don't you? Get attached to it. You from around here?'

'Not till I move in.'

There was a crash from the back of the house. Arianne's head spun round.

'So the garage. Did you say you could give me the number of the builder?'

'Sorry, Nevin. Did you hear that?'

'Hear what?' There was another noise, like something falling. So much for being quiet as a church mouse. Net must go to some pretty wild churches if she thought that was being quiet.

'That. I think I might have an intruder.'

'Nah. It's probably just a cat or the wind knocking something over.'

'I don't have a cat and none of the windows are open. And my partner's just popped out to the shop.' She took a step away from him, towards the back.

Doogie leaned his hand on the door and tried to look casual. 'The shop. He's not at work then?'

'No, he's having a day off.' She turned back to him and frowned. 'Do you know Byron then?'

'Not really. Just went into his shop the other day. Been thinking about getting a new tatt.'

She looked him up and down. 'Sounds like you've been thinking about getting a lot of work done, one way or another.'

'Yeah well, new house, new me. You know how it is with fresh starts.'

But Arianne wasn't listening anymore. She was on her way down the hall.

57

A SERIES OF PLANNING DEVIATIONS

Operation Reclaim was not going as smoothly as the plan had suggested. For a start, Colin had neglected to tell them that the bushes on the house side of the garden fence had grown somewhat since Netta had last been here. They were now the size of small trees, but not nearly as sturdy. She'd been the first one over the ladder and had subsequently sky dived straight into a prickly Pyracantha, tumbled through its sharp, spiky branches and landed in the middle of it with both her hands and clothes badly torn. The others had fared only slightly better. Their collective injuries amounted to a nasty gash on Frank's arm, a scratch on Liza's neck and several on Colin's face. Notwithstanding the damage, they had successfully completed phase one without alerting either Adam and Jude, the turncoat neighbours, or Arianne.

Phase two had not been without its issues either. Netta had quickly discovered she was not as slim as she thought she was. She would have to have a word with her mother about her obsession with cakes when all this was over; they were no good for people trying to extricate themselves from a tiny window.

For a while, she'd thought she was going to be stuck with her backside hanging out of the old pantry until the fire brigade were called. It was only an enormous shove from Frank on said backside that managed to shift her, head first into the tiny room. Or more precisely, into one of Colin's canvasses. Luckily it was a blank one. She knew how much the completed ones sold for.

As she prepared herself for phase three of their assault, her main concern was the noise. It was bound to have alerted Arianne. She held her breath for a while and listened. Doogie was still talking. All might not be lost just yet. Manoeuvring herself onto her rear end, she pulled the canvas off her head, scraping skin off her ears in the process.

The next thing to do was to stand up which was not easy in this small space. She gripped the shelves either side of her and hauled herself up. As she did so, her left hand pushed down on something. Oh. Her head came up to its level and she realised, too late, it was a tube of paint that was bulging under the pressure of her weight. Before she had a chance to change its course, a stream of red shot out at her. She turned away, just in time to avoid it hitting her square in the eye. It caught her hair and the side of her face. And then she fell forward and crashed through the door into the hall. Bollocks!

Netta jumped up, ran into the kitchen and searched for the key cupboard. It was exactly where Colin said it would be. But shit, there were so many keys in there. How was she supposed to choose? She grabbed a bunch with a pink fluffy pom-pom for a key ring. That had to be Arianne's master set. The first key she tried wouldn't turn and almost got stuck in the lock. With shaking hands, she tried another. No good. A third. No. A fourth. Still no good. How many fucking keys did the woman have?

Someone was running down the hall and she knew who

that someone was. 'You!' Yes, it was definitely Arianne. Netta turned back to the door and shoved a fifth key in.

Arianne was almost on top of her. 'Nevin, call the police. We've got a break in.'

Nevin? That was Doogie's dad's name. Oh thank God, the lock turned, just as Doogie was saying: 'I don't think so, love.'

She ripped the door open. Frank, Colin and Liza tumbled in to face the wrath of Arianne. It was four against one, but Arianne was going down fighting. She grabbed a saucepan. 'Get out of my house.'

Colin pushed past Netta. He was trembling. 'No. You get out of my house.'

Arianne raised the saucepan 'You pathetic little pig.'

'Don't you dare touch him.' Without realising it, Netta had jumped in between them. 'Don't you ever touch him again.'

Arianne stepped back. She had a sneery look on her face. 'This is what you've reduced yourself to is it, Colin? Hiding behind her like a snivelling coward. And her of all people. After everything she did to you.'

Just then, big burly Byron came thundering down the hall. 'Babe, what's going on?'

He wasn't supposed to be here. 'Why aren't you at work?' said Netta.

'He took a day off,' said Doogie.

'What? Who the fuck are you?' said Byron.

Doogie walked up to Byron until he was within inches of him. Netta was reminded of that time Frank had said he was sinister. 'Doogie Chambers. Mate, I think you'd better go and take your missus with yer.'

Arianne gasped. It must have been the name. She would have known it well. 'He tricked me, Byron. He forced his way in. Hit him.'

Doogie flexed his fists. 'You wanna try it, fella?'

Byron didn't look so sure. 'I'm a black belt in Ju Jitsu.'

Doogie looked him up and down. 'Let's give it a go then. I reckon I could knock you out with one punch, but even if you did manage to Ju Jitsu the fuck out of me, Frank here'll finish you off. Or those two behind you.'

Chris and Neil were in the kitchen now. Merrie was behind them. Byron was looking a bit unsure. 'You shouldn't go forcing your way into other people's houses.'

'It's my house. I pay the mortgage,' said Colin. 'I can come and go as I like.'

'But I thought… Babe, is this true?'

Arianne was clearly trying to force out a tear. 'It's as good as mine. I've earned it, having to put up with him.'

The big man threw his hands in the air. 'Fucking hell. I did not sign up for this. I just wanna quiet life. Do what you have to do, man. I'm outta here.'

'Byron, come back. Byron. Byron.' Arianne's begging was fruitless. Her man was gone.

It looked like phase three of Operation Reclaim was going a lot easier than the previous two phases. They just needed to bundle Arianne out the door and that was it. Job done.

But then Netta saw that Frank and Doogie were lunging towards her. Neil, Chris, Liza and Merrie were doing the same. A horrible rasping shriek rang through her ears. She turned towards it and saw Arianne coming for her. Then she saw the glint of metal. Arianne was just feet away now, the blade close enough to see her own reflection in it. They weren't going to make it in time. Netta knew she should back away but she was frozen. Suddenly, out of nowhere, someone grabbed Arianne's arm. It broke Netta's trance. She almost fell backwards into the man who'd saved her.

Colin finally let go of his grip on Arianne's arm when

Frank took over and Doogie prised the knife out her hand. He sank back onto a tall stool and hung his head.

Netta slipped her fingers between his. 'Are you okay?'

He lifted his head up. 'Are you?'

'Yes. I think it's time to call the police.'

He glanced over at Arianne who was still screaming and fighting. 'Yes. It is.'

58

AN OUTBURST OF THE CHOUX
PASTRY KIND

The police had taken Arianne away. It was over, although in reality, it was just the start of it. There were statements to be made, charges to be brought, possibly even court appearances. But Colin couldn't think about that right now. He was still reeling from the thought of what had just happened and what might have happened if his brain hadn't engaged in time to stop Arianne. He was shivering. The whole of his body felt ice cold. Netta was still holding his hand, and he realised he was gripping it too hard, but he couldn't let go.

Geraldine filled the kettle and switched it on. 'I think we all need a cup of tea to calm our nerves.' She was taking charge. Everyone else was too shell-shocked to speak. Even Doogie was looking less together than normal. He was talking quietly to Merrie, a protective arm around her. Colin looked on enviously. He'd like to be that sort of father again, strong and wise. If he ever really had been that kind of father.

On the wall behind them was one of Arianne's many "Important Things to Remember" slogans. This particular one was a hoot, given her recent behaviour:

'It is important to be kind.'

She'd printed them out and laminated them after listening to a series of crappy podcasts by some self-styled lifestyle, well-being and spiritual guru. There were loads of them stuck around the house covering a broad spectrum of witless theories. You couldn't even have a nice sit down on the toilet without being informed about the importance of having regular bowel movements.

Geraldine was opening and closing cupboard doors. 'Where do you keep the tea, Colin?'

'I'll get it.' Liza opened the cupboard where the tea was usually kept. A packet of biscuits fell out. She gave him a guilty look, as if it was her fault they were in there.

Colin noticed they were triple chocolate chunk cookies. His favourite. He used to buy them for a treat before Arianne went loopy. He thought of all the times she'd told him they were poison and were not under any circumstances allowed to pass their lips. He put on a smile. It was important not to let these things get to you. 'At least we'll have something to eat with our tea. I'll get the milk.'

He opened the fridge door and was as glued to the spot as Netta had been when she saw Arianne hurtling towards her with that knife. The fridge was literally stuffed with all the things Arianne had been denying him for longer than he could remember. Meat, fish, cheese, butter, cream cakes, proper wine and beer. It was bursting with them. The cookies were bad enough, but this? He closed the door. There was another slogan on the front telling him that it was important to keep your body free of toxic food and thoughts. Well bollocks to that. He was going to explode. For one day only, Colin Grey was going to fill his boots with toxic food and thoughts.

He opened the door again and took out a box of choco-

late éclairs. Without a word, he rammed first one, then two in
his mouth. The others were staring at him, but it was too late
to stop. The anger inside him was a burning fire and the only
way to put it out was by dousing it with a ton of cream-filled
choux pastries. It didn't matter that he wasn't enjoying it. It
was his small act of defiance. Like Ursula scuffing up her
husband's prized car. He picked out another one and was
about to stick it in his already full mouth when he saw Geraldine on her way to him. He shoved it in quick before she
confiscated it.

Geraldine took the box from him and slowly removed an
éclair. Then, she pushed the whole of it straight into her
mouth. Her cheeks were like a hamster with its pouches full.
She looked ridiculous, as ridiculous as he probably did. They
both started to giggle. Bits of chocolate covered pastry and
cream were all over the place, which made it even more
disgustingly funny. Soon everyone was laughing their heads
off with them. Someone even applauded. It might have been
Frank.

'How did that make you feel?' Geraldine said when the
last bits of éclair had left their mouths, one way or another.

He wiped himself down with kitchen towel. 'Awful. I feel
sick.'

'Me too. Let's have that tea.'

'You have the tea, Geraldine. I've got some clearing out to
do.' Colin opened a cupboard and emptied it of anything that
was health food related. 'Lying, evil cow. I never want to see
bulgur fucking wheat in this house again.'

He was three cupboards in when Neil joined him with
some shopping bags he'd found. 'Don't throw them out. I'll
take them to the foodbank.'

Colin stopped sorting. 'Yes, of course. Sorry. Selfish
of me.'

Neil put his hand on Colin's shoulder. 'No it isn't. Don't worry about it.' He reached into the cupboard and pulled out a big bag of yellow lentils, Arianne's torture weapon of choice. 'What about these?'

Coin shuddered. 'Take them away. You would not believe how much yellow-lentil slop I've been forced to endure in the last year.'

They kept going until they'd been through every cupboard. Colin surveyed the array of food laid out on the worktops. He was convinced they'd been untouched since the day Arianne had locked him out. She must have cracked out the good stuff as soon as Netta drove him away. He found a roll of black bags under the sink and tore some off for Neil. 'You may need more bags. And could you check the fridge? If there's any tofu in there, take it. Liza, Merrie, come with me. We have wardrobes and drawers to empty. The rest of you, search the house for dreamcatchers, banal slogans and any other hippy shit that woman's soiled my house with. And someone please take down those purple net curtains.'

59

FRANK'S SHIFTING PERSPECTIVE

Well that had been a day! Frank could not believe the madness of it. Operation Reclaim had taken a few unexpected turns but they'd secured the house. More importantly, crazy Arianne was out of harm's way. And yes, Frank was aware that he wasn't being very politically correct there, but the woman had been as crazed as a rabid dog. Frank had seen the whites of her eyes when she went for Netta. His response had been instinctive. He'd been aware that Doogie was also racing to save her, but Colin had beaten them to it. That was kind of appropriate really, and he didn't care who got there first, as long as someone had.

Talking of crazed, Colin was doing a pretty good impression of a madman himself at the moment. The fella had been shaky as hell, even after the police had left, but something had changed in him when he opened up the fridge to get the milk. An odd kickstart to a frenzy but there you go. Sometimes the strangest things can tip a person over the edge. That business with the éclairs had to be one of the maddest things Frank had seen in a long time. Geraldine was great the way she handled it. It was ridiculous and incredibly moving. Frank thought he was going to cry. Instead, he'd applauded. It seemed the right thing to do. All the same, the image of Geraldine's face bursting with cake and cream would stay with him for a long time. Without a doubt, she was the most amazing woman. As was her daughter who seemed to be taking her near-death experience in her stride. Not Frank though. The incident had shaken him to the core, and the prospect of losing Netta had shifted everything into perspective. He never wanted to have that feeling again.

Colin muttered something derogatory about purple curtains and pulled a laminated card from the wall as he marched out of the kitchen with Liza and Merrie following in his wake.

'He's lost it again, hasn't he?' said Doogie.

Geraldine picked up a black bag. 'At least he's not crying this time. Let's indulge him. Arthur, love, will you check the garden? I can see at least two wind chimes out there. I suspect they might fall into the hippy shit category. Also, they can be very grating after a while.'

Netta took another bag. 'I'll do the lounge and get rid of the nets. Doogie, can you do the dining room? Frank, would you do the studio?'

Frank opened the door to Colin's studio. He wasn't expecting to find anything offensive in here but it was a good excuse to look into another artist's workplace. He'd been in here once before in 2018, the year Netta became his neighbour. He'd come with her to meet an estate agent. She'd been threatening to sell the house if Colin didn't buy her out. Colin had been a

different man then. Nasty. Not dangerous like Arianne but
unpleasant, nonetheless. Frank had come along as Netta's
wing man in case she needed back-up. She didn't, of course.
Netta Wilde didn't need anyone really. But lucky for him and
the others, she allowed them to swim in her slipstream. He still
couldn't believe he'd almost lost her.

A film of dust had settled on Colin's paint and tools. It
looked like no one had been in here for a while, possibly
longer than the time Colin had been away. The beginnings of
a painting sat on an easel. It was another of the street scenes
that Colin did so well. Netta had admitted that they weren't to
her taste, but Frank could appreciate the work that went into
them. Colin was a good artist. Not in Liza's league, but then
neither was he. Liza would be a great painter one day, he was
certain of it.

He wandered over to a stack of finished paintings resting
against a wall. More street scenes and a few portraits. All
accomplished works. The stack to the side of it was covered
with cloth. Frank lifted it and found a painting of Birmingham on a rainy night. He flicked idly through two more,
then stopped, his mouth parting at the shock of this new
painting, the portrait of a frail and broken old man. He recovered and moved on to the next one. The same man but
younger. Next, another of him cowering in a corner. Then
another, and another. Six self-portraits of Colin in various
states of distress. They were Colin's private thoughts and
Frank knew he shouldn't have looked at them. It had been
wrong of him to carry on after he'd found the first one. He
covered them back up and left them in their hiding place.

He took a wider look around the room and saw that even
here in what was probably once Colin's sanctuary, the offensive hippy shit was evident. There were several laminated

cards dotted about. Just like the one Colin had torn down in
the kitchen, they espoused the importance of this or that. It
was quite bizarre. Like being caught up in one of those weird
cults. He removed them all. One final sweep of the room
yielded one tatty, cobwebby dreamcatcher in the window.
They were supposed to protect you from evil, weren't they?
Frank tossed it into the black bag.

Netta had taken Merrie and Liza home. Arthur and
Geraldine had left too. Liza would be back tomorrow but
tonight, Frank and Doogie were staying with Colin. Frank had
the feeling it would be some time before Colin would be truly
independent again. Neil and Chris had stayed behind too.
They didn't live far away. Neil had cooked dinner using the
food that Arianne and Byron had left behind. Now, they were
sitting around in Colin's not particularly comfortable living
room, drinking beers.

'Oh, I nearly forgot to give you your new keys.' Chris
threw them over to Colin.

Colin caught them and kissed them. 'These mean so much
to me. Thank you.'

'That's okay, bro. It really wasn't hard.'

'You said your dad's a builder. Mine was too. Retired now,'
said Doogie. 'He built houses from scratch. Small plots of two,
three or six. He was a self-made man.'

'He did well to come up the ranks like that. My dad's
always saying how hard it was in those days,' said Chris. 'Was
he a bling man?'

Doogie laughed. 'Fucking hell, yes. Rings and chains.'

'Yeah, my old man too. Did he get you on the sites? I tell
you, every summer holiday my mates were playing football in
the park and me and my brothers were hauling bricks.'

'Only once. It didn't work out well. My half-brothers did though. They followed him into the business.'

'When did your parents divorce?' asked Colin.

'They didn't. He was married to someone else. He never left his other family.'

'It happens,' said Chris.

'My dad used to take me into work with him,' said Colin. 'He was an accountant. Had a team of them. Told me that's what I was going to be. So I was. And I hated every minute of it. First chance I got, I ditched it to become an artist. Don't know what I'm going to be next. But I do know I've got people to help me work it out. That's new.'

Doogie bumped his can against Colin's. 'Take your time getting there though. Make it count.'

'Good advice. I will.'

Frank took a sip of beer. He'd never in a million years have imagined this scenario. He often spent time with Neil and Chris, they were friends, but chewing the cud with Colin Grey and Doogie Chambers was way beyond the boundaries of his imagination. Yet here he was. Somehow, they'd become friends. Family even.

His thoughts went back to 2018. Colin had told him he measured his life before and after the second coming, which was his way of describing Netta's affair with Doogie. If Frank had to measure his recent life, it would be before and after Netta's coming in 2018. He'd been alone, somewhat set in his ways, and missing his daughter. Then one day a shy, almost broken woman came to view the house next door and that was it. Netta Wilde walked into his life and changed it forever. And he knew it would carry on changing, because things never stood still with Netta. It would always be filled with people like Doogie and Colin. Like Neil, and like Kelly too, that sweet mixed-up kid with a whiplash tongue who'd adopted Netta as her surrogate mum. Their family would keep on changing because people were drawn to Netta Wilde, and she had a heart big enough for all of them. Including him.

60

UNPACKING THE BOXES

'Mum is so gonna wish she'd hung around for longer,' said Merrie. 'She's gonna be really pissed off at missing you being all-action hero.'

They were sitting in the waiting area of New Street Station. It was a vast open space with lots of people, benches and, curiously, a thirty-foot metal bull. Doogie pulled his attention back from the bull to the conversation. 'I doubt that very much. And talking about being pissed off, I'm still racked off with you for not listening to me about waiting for Arthur and Geraldine.'

'Ooh listen to you coming on so dad-like. Anyway, they were right behind me.'

'Only because they had to scramble out the car after you when you shot past them like a racehorse, according to Arthur.'

'Well I was scared for you when I saw Byron coming back.'

'You don't need to be scared for me. I can look after myself.'

'Well obviously I know that now, Mr Hardcore. Hey, can you teach me some boxing moves next time I see you?'

'Boxing moves? It's not like dancing, you know. Yes. All right. If that's what you want. I don't know what Claire will say though.'

Merrie crossed her long legs. 'Dad, I know you like, missed a few years, but I am twenty now. Mum is not the boss of me.'

Doogie laughed. 'Have you broken that to her yet?'

'Hell no. Oh, my train's here. I'd better go.'

He walked her to the barrier. 'Let me know when you're back home.'

'It's only Brighton.'

'I know but I worry.'

She took her bag off him. 'Huh. Where were you when I fell off my bike and broke my arm?'

She meant it as a joke, but he felt it all the same.

She kissed him. 'So you'll let me know how it goes with you and Grace?'

'Yes.'

'And you'll think about St Kitts?'

'Yes. Go, before you miss the train.'

She threw herself on him. 'I've decided. I do actually love you, Dad.'

'I love you too.' His daughter loved him. He'd been a terrible father, and she still loved him. He held her, not wanting to let her go.

She slipped away from him. He watched her going down the escalator to the platform, a massive grin on his face. Then she was gone, and he realised he was crying. He hoped she hadn't noticed. It wasn't fair to lay his emotions down on her. She deserved better than that. It occurred to him this was the second time the man who didn't do emotions was doing emotions. Something strange was happening to him.

On his way out, he took another look at the bull. It looked like it had been built out of spare parts. People were crowding around to watch it move its head slowly from left to right, then back again. Doogie walked away. This mad fucking city. He needed to get home.

He put his bag into the car and went back inside to collect Spike. He'd left him in the back garden to give him as much time outside as he could before the long ride home. He'd been in Birmingham a bit less than four weeks, but it seemed a lot longer. Doogie couldn't wait to get away, and yet he knew he'd miss it as soon as he was gone. Miss her.

If it had only been those three years at uni then it was just possible, he wouldn't be here now. When Netta dumped him that first time, he had probably stood a small chance of letting her go. Even though losing her had made him feel like he was no longer a whole person, Doogie reckoned he could have lived like that with a broken part somewhere in the place where the essence of him had been. In the ten years between then and seeing her again, he'd got used to it and had built a reasonably good life. Claire would have argued it was a life devoid of emotional risks and maybe it was, but it worked for him. And anyway, that wasn't all down to Netta.

It was the second time that really did it for him. Seeing her had been one of those coincidental things that change the course of your life. The minute he saw her, he was whole again. He knew it was a really bad idea to start it back up, but the need to be with her was too strong.

He soon found out she was still the same old Netta, but different. Still smart, funny and crazy bonkers mad. Still on a different planet to everyone else. But she was colder and harder. On the outside at least. Inside, she'd become so fragile.

It killed him to see her like that. He wanted to take her in his arms and never ever let her go. And that was it. That was why he couldn't pack her away and forget about her. Not even when she walked away for good, and he burned all the things she left behind on Crosby Beach. Not even when he had chances to be happy with someone else. He was spoiled goods. And everything that came after her was ruined.

When she did finally come to him again, as he knew she would someday, he'd patted himself on the back for not jumping into bed with her and being civilised about the whole thing. And he still hadn't been able to let her go. But Doogie was getting too old and too weary of living in the past. There comes a time in a man's life when he's earned the right to choose between what makes him happy and what makes him pine for something that was never really his. He was following Priscilla's advice and making a choice. He'd have to wait and see whether it was the right choice.

Netta was waiting in the kitchen for him. He'd hoped to get off before she woke up but he should have known she wasn't going to let that happen. She was putting a flask into an already full carrier bag. 'I've followed my mum's example and done you a food parcel for the journey.'

'I could have stopped on the motorway.'

'Don't deny me this one pleasure.'

He kissed the side of her head. 'I'll bring the flask back next time I come.'

She pushed the bag over to him. 'You never said whether you were going to marry Grace.'

'Because I don't know what'll happen when I get back up there.'

'I thought you had an open relationship. I didn't realise it was serious.'

'It changed a couple of years ago.'

'You never said. Why didn't you say?'

'Because it's none of your fucking business.'

She put her hand on her hip and dropped her head to one side. 'Charming.'

Her crooked smile almost took his breath away. Fucking hell. This woman. She did things to him that no one else could. If he'd been a believer, he'd be praying for the big man's help right now. 'You do know you're not the only woman in my life, Netta Wilde?'

'Er, clearly. I think Merrie is testament to that. And by the way, I still can't believe you copped off with my best friend as soon as my back was turned.'

'You mean years after you dumped us both.'

She folded her arms. 'All right, Chambers, don't rub it in.'

They laughed, then stopped, their eyes searching each other. He sighed. 'Net, I've gotta go.'

She nodded. 'I know.'

She walked him to the car and opened her arms for him. 'Claire's right you know. You do need to sort your life out. Commit to something.'

If only she'd given him the chance back when it counted. He pulled her into a hug. 'Sort out your own life, missus. All this living next door to your man business. I'm not the only one who needs to commit to something.'

She pushed herself away, laughing but there were tears in her eyes. 'Yes okay, Chambers. You can fuck off now.'

'Fuck off yourself, Wilde.' He kissed her for the last time, then got in the car and drove.

As soon as he hit Loch Lomond, Doogie began to relax. When he reached Glencoe, he stopped to breathe in the air and let Spike stretch his legs. They'd been on the road for most of the day. With the exception of Netta this morning, he'd said his goodbyes last night. He'd be back there later in the year for one of Betty's pups. He'd promised to take one. Although it wasn't confirmed yet that she was pregnant, all the signs were pointing that way.

He'd call in on Priscilla when he went back. Yesterday, after he'd taken Merrie to the station, he went round to see her. She was still refusing to forgive Samuel, and he got why. He understood the anger and the sense of betrayal. But he could also see it from Samuel's perspective. His own decisions were probably rooted in the same fears and inhibitions as Samuel's had been. And that was the most frightening thing. Because Samuel had known he'd let them all down. That must have been so hard to live with. Maybe even harder to die with.

Doogie took a photo of the mountains. Last night, Frank had told him about that road trip he'd had at Easter when they'd bumped into each other. He'd talked a lot about how he'd been bowled over when he stopped at Glencoe. He sent the photo to him.

A minute later he got a reply:

Lucky bastard.

He smiled. Yes, he was, but it had taken a trip to Birmingham to show him that. Frank was lucky too. Doogie hoped he realised exactly how lucky.

He took a detour that allowed him to stop off at his grandad's grave. It was in a small cemetery overlooking the sea. His uncle's cottage was only a mile away. His grandad had loved the sea. Even when he'd lost the strength to walk, he'd have Doogie wheel him down to the shore and they'd sit together watching the waves crashing. Sometimes they'd sit in silence, two generations of Dougal Macraes temporarily at peace with their demons. Other times they'd talk. Mostly about all the Macraes that had come before him. It was like the old man was on a mission to drum as much family history into him in the short time he had left. Because there was one thing his grandad was unequivocal on, Doogie was a Macrae, and this place was as much his heritage as any other Macrae.

Occasionally, they'd touch on old Dougal's thoughts on life and love. It was just after Doogie had lost Netta for the first time and he was still hurting. His grandad had helped him see the way through. For all his faults, old Dougal was the only man Doogie had ever talked to. Really talked to. And then just like that he was dead and Doogie was left to figure things out on his own again. Sometimes, life was a real bastard.

He found the grave nestled among the other Macraes, some dating back hundreds of years. It wasn't hard: he'd been plenty of times before. He wiped dust and salt off the head-stone with his sleeve and imagined his grandad's spirit sitting on top of it, giving him the Macrae stare. He'd probably be telling him what a big fucking mess he'd made of his life. Just like Priscilla. Come to think of it, maybe that's who she reminded him of. Doogie scanned the other graves, his family, then turned back to his grandad's imaginary spirit. 'I'm back, old man.'

It was almost eight by the time he pulled up outside his cottage. Spike ran into the garden sniffing everything and making his mark. Doogie opened the cottage door but Spike wasn't ready to go in yet. He was a dog for wide open spaces, not the confinement of four walls and big cities. So was Doogie. He dropped his bags inside, closed the door and walked up to the beach. Spike went the other way, up to the farm. He'd go up there soon enough but for now he wanted to feel the moist salty air on his face. He wanted to look out to the horizon and see nothing but sea and sky, hear nothing but the crashing of waves on white sand.

He stood on the sea's edge and breathed slow and deep. He was where he should be. He was home.

Grace appeared at his side. She slipped her fingers between his. They fitted perfectly. 'I thought I'd find you here. Spike came to let me know you were back.'

'He's missed home. So have I.'

'It's missed you. Are you hungry? We could have a barbecue here.'

'In a bit. First we need to talk.'

'Good.' She led him away from the water and pulled him down onto the sand. 'Talk.'

She was still annoyed with him. He could tell by her manner that he wasn't going to get off lightly. But that was Grace all over. She didn't take crap from anyone, not even the man she wanted to spend the rest of her life with. He loved that about her and he was going to tell her so. He was going to tell her everything. Because Doogie was ready to unpack those boxes now. He was ready to do emotion. She would give him a hard time, but he already knew by the way she'd held his hand on the shore that she would ask him again to marry her. And this time, he wouldn't run away. This time, he knew what his answer would be.

61

NOT EMPTY. RESTING

The morning sun was warming the back of Colin's head and casting glorious light on the neat rows of potatoes, carrots, and chard that were surrounding him. A little further away there were ripe tomatoes that needed picking. He'd do that shortly but for the moment, he was sitting on Ursula's bench counting his blessings. One week ago today, two seismic events had taken place. The first was the successful recapture of his house, along with his car. The second was Ursula leaving for Snowdonia. Colin was now a man with a house, a car and an allotment. The allotment was only temporary until Ursula returned or gave it up. Actually the house was temporary too but that would be up to him to decide when to let it go.

From where he was sitting, he could see Clyde talking to the retired couple whose names he still didn't know. He'd actually smiled at Colin this morning. Perhaps his new-found humility was finally wearing the old bugger down. His big dog, Colonel, was lying across the path, taking in the sun. Colin missed dogs. He'd never really liked them much, but they'd grown on him while he'd been living at Netta's and Frank's. Especially little Maud. Liza told him there was a possibility Betty was having pups. Spike, apparently. What was that saying about dogs being like their owners? He'd sent a message along those lines to Doogie when he found out. He'd received a reply telling him to fuck off. Typical Chambers. But there was a smiley face next to the words, so Colin knew he hadn't taken offence really.

How strange it was, the way things had worked out. Colin finally had real friends and one of them was Doogie Chambers. He supposed he should thank Arianne really, rather than have her locked up. He hadn't wanted to involve the police. The whole idea of it all coming out had filled him with dread. Not least because he knew exactly what his father would say. There'd be talk of him not being man enough etcetera, etcetera. The usual stuff. Mother would have been no better. She'd probably have had one of her faints and told him she'd never be able to face the WI again. All in all it would have been better if things had gone to plan, and Colin could have pretended they'd just gone their own separate ways. But Arianne had crossed a line. She could punch and kick him as much as she wanted to, but when she'd turned on Netta, he realised hiding from it wasn't an option. The woman was dangerous. She needed help. And if that meant having the world know what happened, so be it. He had family and friends to help him through it. Although probably not his own parents. Oh well. *C'est la vie.*

Talking of extraordinary workings out, Geraldine had become his new bestie. That said, she'd made it clear she still hadn't forgiven him for the way he'd treated Netta and never would. It was fair enough. He didn't think he could forgive himself for it either. He'd be seeing Geraldine later. They'd probably talk about the things he'd written in the notepad since their last talk. He'd been taking it everywhere in case something occurred to him. She was going on holiday in two weeks. Arthur was whisking her off to the Amalfi Coast. Colin had lined up a visit to Ursula while the glamorous granny was away. He was looking forward to experiencing life in a commune that was in no way a hippy commune. Although he'd already warned Ursula if he saw one dreamcatcher he'd be out of there before you could say yellow lentils.

He saw Arthur coming through the gate and lifted his hand to wave but stopped in mid-air when he saw who was with him. It was Will. Colin sat motionless but his heart was racing. His throat was dry and yet liquid was dripping from the roof of his mouth in the way it did just before you threw up. Arthur veered off towards his own allotment, but Will was on a different course. He was on his way to him. Colin held on to his knees. His palms were sweating. There was every chance he really was going to be sick.

Will stopped on the path in front of the bench. 'Hey, Dad.'

'Hey, Will. This is unexpected.'

'Got room for me?'

Will looked taller and broader than he remembered. He seemed to go on forever, but then Colin hadn't been this near to him for years. People said they looked alike. They did in a way, although Colin had never been that handsome. Never that self-assured either. Now that he looked closely, he could see Arthur in Will too. Those were probably the handsome parts. Colin had seen photos of Arthur as a young man and there was no denying he'd been a very good-looking chap. He patted the space next to him. 'Plenty.'

Will sat down and filled the space. Colin felt small and rather diminished next to him.

'How you doing, Dad?'

'I'm doing okay. I'm being well taken care of.' It was true, he was. Liza and Geraldine were making sure of that. He didn't want that to be a permanent solution though, especially as far as Liza was concerned. 'I'm sorry I tore up your sweatshirt.'

Will shrugged. 'That's okay. Belle's been going on at me for ages to get rid of it. Apparently it stinks.'

'I rather liked the smell of it. Listen, Will, there's something I need to say while I've got the chance. I am so sorry for all the things I put you and Liza and your mum through. I'm not asking for forgiveness because I don't deserve it, but I just wanted you to know that I can see how wrong it was.'

Will nodded. It was the best Colin could hope for and it was still more than he'd expected. 'Mum says you're selling the house.'

'I am. I'm going to use some of the money to pay back everything I cheated her out of.'

'Yeah, she told me. She said you don't need to do that.'

'Tough, because I'm bloody well doing it. Even if I have to feed fifty-quid bundles through her letterbox.'

Will grinned. 'Bit much but I applaud the sentiment. Will you be okay when Nan goes on holiday? I know you're seeing a lot of her, at the moment.'

'That's a nice way of saying I'm heavily dependent on her. Yes, I think I will be. I'm going on a little holiday myself. To Wales.'

'To stay with your lady friend, Ursula?'

'Well she's a lady and she's a friend, but she's not what I think you're implying.'

'She could be, though? When you've got over Arianne.'

Got over Arianne? Colin was long over her. Well before she lost her head. It would be more accurate to say got over the things she did. But then again, that wasn't the real reason. Ursula had named it. The reason was grief. The grief over the loss of his children was healing now, especially after this. But Colin was rapidly coming to understand his grief had many layers and many complications. And it would take a long time for the grieving process to be over. It was about love too. Love and grief. You couldn't have one without the other.

'The thing is, Will, I'm still in love with your mum. I think she knows that but I'd rather you didn't tell her, if you don't mind. I don't want to make a big thing of it. I know she doesn't love me but we're friends now and I don't want to spoil that.'

'I won't say anything. But I don't get it though. I don't get how you could have treated her so badly if you truly loved her.'

'Because I'm a bad person.' He could have lied or shifted the blame like he'd always done in the past, but that was not who Colin was now.

'You're different now though, yeah? You've changed.'

'I'm trying very hard, but I think maybe it's a bit like being an alcoholic. You have to fight your natural instincts to be a complete shit every day.'

Will smiled. 'Well Liza will soon tell you if you are. She's told me once or twice. I can help too. I could come and stay with you a couple of days a week. If you want?'

'I do want. Very, very much.'

'Cool. You don't mind Belle staying, do you? We're kind of living together in a currently homeless, living with our parents sort of way until we've got jobs.'

'I don't mind at all.' It was lucky Colin had finally got his emotions in check because if he was still blubbing at the drop of a hat, he'd be in absolute bits by now.

·   ·   ·

'Ready?' said Liza.

Colin did another round of the breathing exercises Geraldine had taught him, then nodded. 'As I'll ever be.'

She took his hand. 'Right, we're going in.'

In fact she pulled him in rather than allowed him to walk into his studio under his own steam, but he had done it. He'd crossed the threshold.

He took a look around and was pleased to see someone had removed Arianne's ratty old dreamcatcher and the mindless slogans. From now on he would decide what was important in his life.

Liza tugged at his sleeve. 'We're going to walk to the canvas and pick up a brush now.'

'Have you been taking lessons from your grandmother?'

'Just shut up and do it, okay?'

He took another long, slow breath. 'Okay.'

She let go of him when they were standing in front of the last painting he'd started months ago. The client had been waiting for it since then. Colin had several other commissions that he'd accepted before he'd become too frightened to paint. He'd promised Liza he'd try to complete them before deciding whether to give it up for good.

'Pick up the brush and just move it around the canvas without the paint.' Yes, Geraldine had definitely being giving her tips.

His hand shook as he chose a brush and lifted it to the canvas. He was sweating and he wanted to throw up again.

She put her hand over his. 'I'm here with you, Dad.' Together they moved the brush around. Circles at first, then strokes, long and short. Colin's hand stopped shaking.

'Do you want to try it with some paint?' she said.

'Not this one. I might spoil it. I'll get a fresh canvas. You start on yours.'

She moved over to the easel she'd set up next to his. He watched her painting for a while, admiring her technique and the lines that were forming. She was such a talent.

'Standing over me and doing nothing was not part of the deal,' she said.

'I know, I just love watching you. You're so good.'

'Go and get a canvas now!'

'Okay, bossy boots. God, you're so like your mother and grandmother.'

Colin took his painting off the easel and laid it against the stack of finished ones. The cloth covering the next pile had slipped a little. He put it back in place. Maybe one day he'd show the ones he had hidden in there to Liza. He'd explain to her how every time he tried to paint, all that came out was another account of his own personal hell. He'd tell her how he was so afraid of what might appear on the canvas, he didn't dare pick up a brush. Maybe one day. When he could face them again.

He went into the old pantry to get a new canvas and smiled when he saw the one with the Netta-shaped hole in the centre. He was going to keep that one as a reminder of the moment she stood between him and Arianne to save him. Even with twigs in her hair, arms scratched to pieces and vermillion paint running down her face, she was magnificent. He might frame it just as it was.

Liza glanced over at the blank canvas that he'd placed on the easel. 'Paint anything. It doesn't matter what.'

'I'm waiting for inspiration.' He looked around him and his eyes fell on his notebook to something Ursula had said about Samuel's patch. He'd written it down later and had returned to it time and again, underlining it each time.

'Still looking for inspiration?' she said.

'No. It's not a picture but it might be a start.'

He chose forest green, the colour of leaves and allotments and growth. Slowly and shakily he painted the words:

Not empty. Resting. Waiting to be filled up again.

62

WELL, I SUPPOSE…

It was mid-afternoon and Netta was in Frank's bed watching a spider spinning a web across one corner of the ceiling. She'd have liked to think normality had been restored but that wasn't true. The old normality had been consigned to the bin the day Colin came to stay. For a while everything got messed up. Then it got worse. Then it got better. And from all that a new normal had emerged. One in which Colin had become part of her family. Doogie too. Possibly Grace in the future as well. Who knew what was ahead of them?

On the plus side, carnal relations had been resumed between her and Frank. They'd been as good as ever, with maybe just a little extra spark after all that had gone on.

Saying goodbye to Doogie had been a lot harder than she'd thought it would be. She should have known, because saying goodbye to Doogie was always hard. It was like letting a part of herself go. She liked to think that in a parallel universe somewhere, there was another version of her and him leading the life they'd imagined they would, back when he was her Heathcliff and she was his crazy mad, one and only Netta Wilde.

She checked her phone yet again, hoping for a message to tell her that Grace had forgiven him and there was a wedding on the cards. It was his turn to be happy now and she wanted it so much for him.

There was no message from him but there was one from Liza saying she was coming home later. Yesterday, Will had been to see Colin and familial relations had also been resumed, which was a relief. He and Belle were staying over there for a few days and Liza was taking a break. The new normal. At least that got Netta off the hook in the staying-over department. It wasn't staying with Colin that bothered her, just staying in the house. It gave her the creeps. Not only because of the life she'd had when she'd lived there, but also because it was the place where she'd nearly met her untimely demise. No one was saying too much about that, but she knew they were all thinking it could have been the end of her. And although she didn't want to dwell on it herself, it had certainly made her stop and think. You only got one life, and all that. Also, it hadn't escaped her notice that it was Colin who'd saved her. Although, it had to be said, she wouldn't have needed saving if he hadn't got her into that situation in the first place.

Will had asked if she minded him staying there which was sweet of him. Right after he asked, yet again, if she and Frank were going to get married which was not so sweet of him. She didn't understand why the younger generation was so hung up on marriage. You'd have thought they'd have seen the mess their parents made of it and vowed to keep well away from it.

Frank put his arm around her. 'What are you thinking about?'

'I was thinking how everything had changed. I knew that

day I picked Colin up from his house that it would. I thought it was a bad thing.'

'Me too, but it's been all right really.' She pulled a face at him. 'Okay, I admit it was a bit shite for a while. All right, it was very shite for a while. But we worked through it. We beat it.'

'That's very upbeat and positive of you, Mr O'Hare.'

'That's me, new-man O'Hare. I'm an upbeat, positive kind of person these days. To be honest, I don't mind Colin and Doogie being around. Since Colin's been through hell, he's turning out to be a sweet guy. Doogie scares the crap out of me sometimes, but he's actually a really nice fella. And he was great with Colin.'

'He was, wasn't he? If we're being honest, I think I should tell you the kids keep talking about us getting married.'

'Oh, they're doing that to you, too? The sneaky wee feckers.'

Netta looked back up at the ceiling. The spider was still spinning. The wallpaper behind it was starting to peel away. Perhaps the web was the only thing holding it in place. 'Which room are you decorating next?'

'Probably this one, before the ceiling paper comes down on us. I've got some paintings to finish for my next exhibition first. I'm a bit behind. Do you want to?'

'What?'

'Get married.'

'Not sure. Probably not. You?'

'Ditto. Although, if we are being completely and absolutely honest, I wouldn't mind waking up next to you every day.'

'Getting under my feet?'

'Exactly.'

'I suppose we could just move in together. If we wanted that.'

'I suppose. I could crack on with the decorating once my exhibition was out of the way. Rent this place out. Just in case we change our minds.'

'Yes, you could. And I do have that nice big empty loft. You said yourself it would make a great studio with a few more windows.'

'We could get the stairs put back in. I've money put away for a rainy day that would more than cover it.'

'Really? Well, I suppose, when you put it like that…'

ALSO BY HAZEL WARD

The Netta Wilde Series – buy now in ebook and paperback.

Being Netta Wilde

Finding Edith Pinsent

Saving Geraldine Corcoran

Meeting Annette Grey (novella – ebook only)

Educating Kelly Payne

Calling Frank O'Hare

Loving Netta Wilde

Be the first to know about Hazel's latest news and the general goings on in her life. You can follow her in all the usual places or join her Readers' Club and get regular monthly newsletters, a free novella and the occasional free story.

https://hazelwardauthor.com

Printed in Great Britain
by Amazon